Acclaim for

A STRANGER'S HOUSE

"Bret Lott is a writer with a gift for evoking the small sadnesses of life and for describing action . . . with the luminous precision of a Dutch painter."

— *The New York Times Book Review*

"I deeply admire *A Stranger's House*. Bret Lott has the rare ability to slip inside the heart and mind of a woman. Claire Templeton is a complex, flawed, sympathetic character, and her frustrations and passions are our own."

— Meg Wolitzer

"Lott excels at characters in crisis . . . evoking their moments of truth with wit and passion. . . . CLAIRE IS . . . A MEMORABLE, MOVING CHARACTER."

— *Chicago Tribune*

"Coupling the small details of time and place with the grand scale of human emotion, Lott has created a moving second novel. . . . He probes, in understated prose, the subtleties of marriage and the parent-child bond. . . . MEMORABLE."

— *Library Journal*

"In the largest sense, *A Stranger's House* is about sheltering and taking care. . . . A SUSPENSEFUL AND POIGNANT BOOK."

— Charles Baxter

Grateful acknowledgment is made for permission to reprint an excerpt
from "For the Year of the Insane: A Prayer" from *Live or Die* by Anne
Sexton. Copyright © 1966 by Anne Sexton. Reprinted by permission of
Houghton Mifflin Company.

WSP

A Washington Square Press publication of
POCKET BOOKS, a division of Simon & Schuster Inc.
1230 Avenue of the Americas, New York, NY 10020

Published by arrangement with Viking Penguin, Inc.

ISBN: 0-671-68328-4

First Washington Square Press trade paperback printing January 1990

10 9 8 7 6 5 4 3 2 1

WASHINGTON SQUARE PRESS and WSP/colophon are trademarks of
Simon & Schuster Inc.

Printed in the U.S.A.

FOR MY PARENTS,
Bill and Barbara,

AND FOR MY CHILDREN,
Zeb and Jake

The author would like to thank the Ohio Arts Council, the South Carolina Arts Commission, and the College of Charleston for their assistance in the completion of this book, as well as John Moore, Ph.D., and Marcy Rosenfield for their technical advice. Thanks, too, to Mindy Werner and Marian Young for their continuing support, insight, and encouragement.

*Our inheritance has been turned over
to strangers, our homes to aliens.*

—Lamentations 5

*O mother of the womb,
did I come for blood alone?*

—Anne Sexton
"For the Year of the Insane: A Prayer"

A
STRANGER'S
HOUSE

SEPTEMBER

"Remote," I said. I was at the window, the glass dirty with rain-spattered dust. Just outside the window the forest began, thick with pine and birch and oak and maple. The first trees began not five feet away.

The realtor, behind me, said, "Remote is what you and your husband asked for." She giggled, and I pictured her: gold sport coat, brown polyester skirt, black pumps. Her hands would be folded together in front of her, head cocked to one side, a smile across her face that would show as many teeth as possible. I pictured her in the empty room, the room, house, entire barn and parcel empty, she had told us, for fifteen years.

Still I didn't turn to her, but only looked out the window, the trees heavy with shadow now, the sun already down behind them.

"But not too remote," she went on. "Not too. Twenty-five minutes from Northampton. That's not *that* bad, considering what you'll be getting: this lovely place with twelve acres and that beautiful barn out there. It's just what the doctor ordered." She laughed again. I heard her step back, heard the soft click of her shoes across the linoleum.

Sounds came from upstairs, footsteps cracking across the floors up there, then slow steps on the stairs behind me. I turned to the sound.

Tom said, "The floors up there seem sturdy enough." He had one hand on the banister and was moving down at an angle, almost sideways. "These stairs'll take some getting used to, though."

3

He came to a small landing where another set led to the other upstairs room; below the landing were no banisters, and I watched as my husband took each step carefully, his hands out to either side to keep his balance.

The realtor had turned to Tom, too. "A good-morning staircase," she said, her hands clasped at her chest. "The original. The less space a staircase took up, the more living space there was. That shows what intelligent builders they were."

She turned to me, her smile just as I had imagined it would be: all teeth, cinnamon lipstick to match her outfit.

I said, "But remote, I guess, is what we want." I looked from the realtor to Tom. "I guess it's not that far out."

He shrugged, went to the fireplace, squatted to look up the chimney.

"And it's a Cape, a three-quarter Cape," she said. "Just what you wanted, and it needs plenty of work." She moved across the room to the staircase. "You know, we like to call these a Handyman's Dream. That's what we call them." She looked around the room, that smile still there.

I looked around then, too. Cheap plastic paneling had been nailed to the walls, pieces of it cracked and broken back at the corners to show pale, flowered wallpaper. The linoleum, light peach, was dull and worn, gouged down to the black resin where furniture had been scraped along the floor. Banister ribs were missing here and there on the upper half of the staircase.

"And it's a clean place," she said, now moving toward Tom still squatting, still peering up into the flue. "The owner has made sure of that. He's had somebody come up here three times a year since 1973 just to clean the place, clear leaves and what-have-you from the gutters, sweep the place out, clean the windows." She laughed again. "Stuff I probably only do once or twice a year in my own home, if I'm lucky." She stopped in the middle of the room, her hands still clasped, and looked out the window as if she had just seen the world outside. "And the *country*," she said, and went to the window. "This is the real thing. A Cape. Everyone wants one. There's a waiting list for good ones, not that this isn't a good one. It's just that this is a Handyman's Dream, and it's out here away from everything. And I've been working with you so long. It's just what you wanted."

She was right. It was what we wanted: a three-quarter Cape. There was this room, the largest; on the other side of the staircase was another, smaller room that would be Tom's office if we took the place; leading off that room and in the opposite corner of the house was a small, windowless pantry leading into the kitchen and dining area, which led back into this room. One room led into the next and the next, a circle of rooms, a chain.

Tom had smiled when the realtor had shown us the room that might be his. It was a smile I had not seen before, one that showed nothing beyond simple pleasure, I imagined, at his own room, with a fireplace and windows looking out into trees.

He said, "But why are they selling now? After that many years?"

The realtor was quiet a moment, still looking out the window. She looked down, her face hidden from us. Then she quickly turned, and here was the smile again. "I'm not sure, actually, but I can talk to someone back at the office. I'm sure it's not anything structural. *That* I can practically guarantee you. This place isn't going to fall down tomorrow."

"Tom," I said. "What's upstairs?"

The room was turning dark now, the brown paneling giving over to black, the worn floor soaking up, it seemed, any failing light that came in through western windows.

He stood up and opened his mouth, and in the premature twilight caused by trees outside and the walls around us, his face began to disappear. I saw his lips move, saw his eyes, his hair, but slowly, slowly I began to lose him.

"A big bedroom," he had said, "with a fireplace. And another room a little smaller. Your room, for whatever you want."

"Unfortunately," the realtor said, "I'm afraid it's getting a little dark now. I'm not sure I want any of us going up and down those stairs. Not now."

I said, "I want to take a look, though. To see what condition it's in."

"Claire," Tom said from somewhere across the room, "it's the same as down here. Needs plenty of work, but nothing we can't handle." He paused. "We can come back Saturday. Just you and me." He stopped, and I thought I could see his head turn, maybe the faint reflection in his glasses of whatever light made it into the room. He said, "If that's all right with you."

"Me?" the realtor said, and she, too, had begun to disappear, disintegrate. "That's fine, so long as I'm positive you're interested. Why, the three of us, we've been looking for the right place for you for so long I feel as if we're family." She laughed again, a hollow, tin laugh that quickly echoed through the empty house. Then the sound disappeared, and there were no voices here, none that would stay. Ours were only dead air in this house.

I woke up, cold. I glanced at the clock on the nightstand. Two twenty-seven.

The cold air had thrown me off, and for a moment I did not know where I was. I thought that perhaps we had already moved into the house, the three-quarter Cape, that there had been some long period of time I had missed between our having seen the place for the first time in that spreading darkness and now—maybe months later—waking up already settled in the old house.

I sat up and turned to Tom. He had the sheet and blanket pulled up to his chin. He was snoring lightly, then stopped and rolled away from me.

I closed my eyes, swallowed, turned to put my feet on the floor.

I knew where I was. In the apartment, where we had lived for eight years. I stood, the floor cold beneath me. I held myself against the cold, and went around the foot of the bed and out into the hall.

I turned on the hall light, shaded my eyes from the fixture above me, and looked at the thermostat. I turned on the heat, set the dial for 72, and turned off the light.

I thought of going back to bed, but I couldn't. For some reason I felt as if I didn't live here anymore, as if that weren't my bed in there, my dresser, my armoire, my closet full of clothes, and so I went into the kitchen.

The apartment was the second floor of a Victorian some 100 years old. One bedroom, a living room, kitchen, and bathroom. The kitchen, I imagined, had been someone's master bedroom at one time, before houses here had been broken into apartments. It was a story a realtor had told us once when we had first begun looking for a house: how during the Depression people needed places to live, and homeowners needed money. Now most all the houses in this part of town had separate entrances for each floor, had stoves and sinks and toilets and tubs rigged up in what had otherwise been bedrooms. Our bathroom, in fact, was the same size as the bedroom, the toilet and clawfoot tub off to one side, the rest of the room only linoleum and paneling.

Realtors, I thought. I leaned against the counter, listened for the radiators to start up. Realtors had shown us homes for over a year now, Tom and I having started looking some nine months after my mother died, when finally the problems accompanying her death seemed almost over—her house near being sold, the outstanding mortgage ready to be paid off. The cost of the burial itself took a large piece of that home with her, but we saw we would be getting some money, and knew, somehow, that buying a home would be best. By this time we knew we would not have children, or at least had effectively buried our hopes deep enough to where we no longer spoke of children. We needed to move away from town, to start our own lives away from here.

And so, though we thought we made ourselves clear, realtors showed us places that in no way resembled what we wanted and had asked to be shown. Realtors had brought us to ramshackle buildings with ell upon ell, roofs falling in, floors broken out, chimneys crumbling, the realtors always saying all these homes needed was a little TLC. Tom had worked his way through college as a carpenter, putting up barns, taking them down, refurbishing some homes here and there, but nothing as large and detailed as what we were shown. Or we were brought to immaculate homes far beyond what we could afford, homes that needed maybe only a paint job, some wallpaper.

We had been shown Saltboxes, Greek Revivals, log homes, even a tri-level ranch. But we had wanted a Cape. There was something both Tom and I had seen in the design that had satisfied us. We had talked about the shape, the size, and then decided it was the simplicity, the easy symmetry of the house that we liked so much: the central chimney, that heart from which all rooms emanated. Heat from the chimney gave each room enough warmth for sleep through winter nights; each room had its own window to let through spring breezes, fragrant air.

Our apartment had none of that simplicity. It was just a jumble of rooms never meant to house a family other than the one that had built both floors a century ago. The only door into and out of the apartment was in the back, at the far end of the kitchen. One had to go through the kitchen to get to the living room, through the bathroom to get to the bedroom, a chaos of rooms we had wandered through long enough, saving money, believing for eight years that we knew where we were going, but never really knowing. Only waiting.

And I thought then of my mother's house, the house that had been mine when I was growing up, and how it had remained what realtors liked to call a "single family unit," when it was only a house, one that had survived, somehow miraculously, being divided into apartments, and for a moment I wondered if she wouldn't have been less lonely, less turned in to herself if perhaps that old house *had* been split up, as though her dying as coldly and silently as she had might have been changed somehow by the layout of a house. Of *our* house, and I thought of how she had lived there for so long— my father dead these twenty-one years, me, her only child, as good as dead to her, visiting her only twice a week, Sunday afternoons for cookies and coffee, Thursday nights for grocery shopping, our time together each visit more forced, more trying.

I swallowed, and I bowed my head and closed my eyes, and made myself think of something else, move somewhere else, away from my mother's house.

The radiators started up, first the slow whistle of air, then the building rattle of water through pipes for the first time since late April. It was September already, and the weather had finally broken: last night the temperature had been in the high seventies, the air so thick that even the sheet on the bed had felt like heavy wool.

I moved through the kitchen to the door, looked out the window. I still held myself.

The air out there was crystalline, and I could see everything: a tricycle in the yard two houses away, a plastic kiddie pool leaning against the garage of the house directly behind ours, other sets of stairs just like ours leading up the backs of other houses to other second-floor apartments. I looked at all these things, then saw something move in the next-door-neighbor's yard. It was a small movement, nothing measurable. I wasn't even sure I had seen anything, but still I looked at their yard, trying to find that movement, and I saw it again, a spark of light down near the foundation of the house.

I made out the neighbor's Christmas tree against the foundation, where it had been brought from inside last January, left there, forgotten. I had watched it over the months, seen it wither, turn brown, its needles fall. The light I had seen was from the few strands of tinsel someone had missed when taking down the decorations nine months ago, light reflected from somewhere, perhaps the half-moon overhead, as the pieces of silver moved in the small, cold wind outside.

I stood at the window, looked again at the kiddie pool, at the faint chrome arc of the tricycle's handlebars. I watched for the tentative light from the Christmas tree down there, and felt the emptiness again that finally made us want to leave the apartment.

I still watched the Christmas tree, and waited for some piece of light. We would take the place, I knew then. There was nothing more for us here. Only dead time, and the ghosts, perhaps, of children that never were, that would never be. Perhaps, too, the ghost of my mother.

I waited for the apartment to warm up before I would go back to bed, move in under covers, and again wait, this time for the light of morning.

 When light came, it fell into the bedroom at a different angle, the angle of September, and I could finally see that the sun was disappearing, moving across the sky in a different arc to form new shadows in the room so that what I saw—the same old pieces of furniture—were somehow new. Here was the footboard before me, new sunlight glancing off the dark oak grain to give it greater depth, sharper lines. Light fell on the hardwood floor to delineate each single strip of wood; dust motes on the air—the air warmer now that the radiators were going—ducked in and out of the light.

"So what do you say?" Tom said, and leaned in from the bathroom.

I looked at him, my eyes dry with no sleep and the warm air. His glasses were fogged over a bit from the steam of his shower, and I had to smile, my dry face wrinkling with the movement of muscles beneath my skin. It seemed almost too much work, but I smiled.

"I'm sorry," I said. I stretched and yawned. More dust motes floated up around me, some caught by the light and lifted even higher, others falling, disappearing. I said, "What were you talking about?"

"What else?" he said, and leaned against the doorjamb. He crossed one foot over the other. "The house up in Chesterfield. Weren't you listening?"

He stood before me naked, his hair wet, his deep-brown nipples clouded over with black hairs that spread across his chest.

10

I said, "Come back to bed and we can talk," and I sat up, pulled off my T-shirt and slipped off my underpants.

A smile seemed to twist from his mouth, as if it hadn't wanted to leave, as if he, too, could feel the muscles involved, the work of it almost but not quite more than he could bear. He came to me, and once inside me, my legs up above me and clasped around him, I could see his smile end, the muscles giving up. September sunlight cut through the air, through him, across his chest at an angle downward that gave his face and shoulders too much detail, each hair and pore and freckle too much attention, everything below the light falling to darkness, indiscriminate shadows of skin and flesh and bone.

The irony, of course, lay in all the precautions we had taken the first four years, the importance of *not* getting pregnant, the pills placed on my tongue like some sort of sacrament, my trips to refill prescriptions at the University Health Center pharmacy like pilgrimages each month, where I would wait amid runny-nosed undergrads for the small, gray-haired woman behind the Plexiglas window to hand me the oblong, pink package, pills that were only chemicals put into a body that had no use for them.

We had fights those four years, fights over when to begin, and it was always me who started them. I wanted to begin our lives.

I remember one Thursday morning, when, after making love, Tom had simply pulled away from me and had headed to the bathroom. All I had done was say, "Let's start now."

He hadn't spoken to me, hadn't said a word as I heard him take his shower, then towel himself dry. I climbed out of bed to take my own shower, all without a word between us, because we both knew what the other was thinking.

I'd dried myself off, then gone into the bedroom, put on my bra and underpants, when finally he'd said, "What do you think? Just what do you think?"

I went into the bathroom. He was standing at the sink, his razor poised at his throat, ready to swing up his chin, shave off the cream and stubble. He brought down the razor, and put both hands on the edge of the sink.

I reached across him and brought from inside the medicine cabinet the pills, and sat on the toilet seat. I hadn't dried my hair yet, and I could feel it wet on my shoulders, a single drop falling down my back.

I was looking at the pink plastic, at the foil center, half the pills already gone. Today was Thursday, and the Thursday pill sat there, ready for me to pop it out, swallow it. The days listed there on the package, I thought, were like some sort of strange calendar truer than anything you could hang on a wall. Twenty-one days on, seven days off. But I wanted off now. I wanted off.

He reached to the hot-water knob, turned it on, then rinsed the razor, though there was no shaving cream on it. He tapped it hard against the sink, and slowly brought the razor to his throat. He started shaving again.

He said, "You're not even thinking of the baby, it sounds like to me." He brought the razor down, rinsed it again. "It seems you're not even looking at the future. We don't have the money yet. Look at the schedule. We're not even halfway there. And you don't know if you'll be written into the next grant or not. At least that's what you told me. And my job"—he tapped the razor again, started in on his left cheek—"my job is still trash. You know I need a promotion. You know I want to be in town. I've had enough of this shit writing about house auctions in Williamsburg and car wrecks in Turners Falls. I want in town. That's where I'll be, too, in a couple of years. But I don't want a child until then. I just don't like the idea of me being outside of town is all. I want to be here. That, and the money."

He finished with his cheek, turned on the hot water again. He stopped, the razor just before the water, and looked at me.

He said, "Claire?"

"What?" I'd said, too loud, and I turned and stood, faced the bathtub, our old clawfoot bathtub, the shower ring and curtains rigged up with wires hung from the ceiling.

"Think of the baby," he said.

I still had the pills in my hand, my finger on Thursday, ready to postpone the future and what we both wanted, but I turned around to him. Tom, startled, dropped the razor in the sink.

He was wrong about my not thinking about the baby, because I was. I was thinking about him or her—it didn't matter which—and about the life, and I said, "I *am* thinking of the baby. You're wrong, goddammit," and I threw the pills at him, threw the package and Thursday and the other week-and-a-half's worth of drugs that damned whatever possible life was in me. "I'm thinking of it, and that's what's wrong," I said, and I cried, put one hand up to my eyes, covered them; with the other I leaned toward the toilet tank and put my hand on it, felt the cold porcelain. "I'm thinking of it, and I want it."

I wiped my eyes, tried to see. Through my tears I saw Tom kneeling, his face still not shaved completely. He was reaching under the sink, and then he stood. He held out his hand, the package in his palm.

I looked up at him. I said, "Goddamn you," and I took the package from him, and I pressed down on Thursday, and I put the pill in my mouth.

I stared at him, the pill on my tongue, and I decided to let it dissolve there in some act of vengeance. I wanted to taste it, to feel the dark magic that would fool my body into thinking it was pregnant, wanted to imagine each molecule of the potion there in my mouth, and imagine it washing away my hopes.

But Tom was right: we didn't have enough money saved, didn't have secure-enough jobs. There was just too much to wait for, and then, because the taste of the pill had become too bitter to bear, I pushed Tom away from the sink, filled the blue plastic cup with water, and I washed the pill down with huge gulps, afraid the taste would remain on my tongue forever.

Tom was standing against the wall next to the sink, his face still half-shaved. His eyes were down.

I stared at him and waited for him to look up, willed him to look at me. But he would not look, and I said, "Happy?" and went into the bedroom.

I heard him move in the bathroom, the hard tap of the razor on the sink, the water run. Then he turned it off. He said, "No, I am not happy. But we have no choice," and I remember seething then, my husband with this last word, when it was me, *me* who had ingested the drug, me whose body would someday be filled with life, neither of us knowing back then that that someday would not come. We would be waiting the rest of our lives.

I told Tom I wanted the place in Chesterfield, that it seemed the house needed what we could give it: repairs, restoration, care. He had nodded, tightened his tie to his throat as he stood before the armoire mirror. Next he took off his glasses and cleaned them with the tip of his tie. İt was a quick move, almost instinct, the left hand holding the frame, the right swirling the tie on the lenses, and I knew what it meant: he was thinking, measuring, deliberating. Every time he cleaned his glasses this way, so quick and business-like, it meant he was contemplating a decision. Right now, I knew, he was heading toward some move about the house, and I smiled.

He put the glasses back on, touched the tie at his throat again, and smiled at me.

"Well?" I said.

He shrugged. "We'll have to think. And go out there tomorrow." He paused. "We'll see."

I said, "We will," and then we were off to work, down the stairs and to the car as every day. The cold air outside was new, as new as the angle of the sun, crisp air that signaled there would be no return of the moist, green air of summer.

We drove over to the newspaper, where for the last three years he'd been an assistant editor, the five years before that a reporter. He still did stories a couple of days a week, just as most everyone else did on the paper. But Tom wanted it that way. He couldn't live at his desk, he'd found out only a month or two after he'd been pro-moted to assistant editor, sitting every day before the green screen of his terminal. Some days when he'd spent the whole day behind the desk, he would come home, take his glasses off and not put them back on until the next morning, though he was so nearsighted he had to wear his glasses while reading in bed. On those nights after the computer screen had killed his eyes we would sit in the living room, me watching television, him with his eyes closed, just listening.

The newspaper offices were in a low, ugly white building an architect some years ago had decided might make the paper seem more important, more in step. But to me the building had always resembled a ranch-style tract house, the roof moving up to a low peak of asphalt shingles, the walls of clean brick. All horizontal lines, all flat, all uninteresting, squatting here in the middle of a 350-year-old town.

I'd been inside the building only once, a few months after we were married. Tom had brought me in to show me his desk. The inside was just one huge room, partitions and cubicles here and there, all the rest simply rows on rows of computer terminals and men and women smoking, the click of keyboards like rattling bones.

He'd brought me to the middle of one row, the two of us weaving between people, all of them sunk into their chairs, eyes staring at the green screens. We finally stopped at a desk.

"This is it," Tom had said, his hands in his back pockets. People around us typed away, oblivious. The desk was covered with papers, the only sign the mess might have belonged to him the blue-green ceramic coffee mug I'd bought for him.

But even though Tom worked there every day, his desk no longer in the middle row but, now that he was an assistant editor, pushed up against one of the walls, that one time had been enough for me. I'd never been back inside, where a couple hundred people worked each day, typing, smoking, sweating over deadlines. There were too many people in there, too much sound, too much pressure. Let me work away quietly at the lab, I told Tom every time he asked me to come in. He could have that ugly place.

We were in the parking lot, and Tom climbed out of the car. "See you tonight," he said, and closed the door.

I said, "Think about Chesterfield," but I was too late, the door already closed, Tom on his way. But then, when he was at the door, one hand to the handle ready to pull it open, he turned back to me, gave a quick wave.

He was smiling, and seemed now to be a happy man, one looking forward to the future; looking forward, I imagined, to the house in Chesterfield.

 I leaned into the secretaries' office, said, "Hi," then moved on down the hall to the locker room. Paige and Wendy called out "Good morning," their voices echoing down the dark hall.

The locker room—only a converted men's bathroom—smelled like it always did: Lysol and urine. Bradford Hall, our laboratory, had for some twenty years been a men's dormitory on campus; that many years of undergraduate boys leaning over urinals and missing had chemically altered the tile and grout so that, no matter how much Lysol the janitorial crew used, the place still smelled the same.

Sandra stood at her locker, the door open. She shrugged off her backpack, hung it up inside, and turned to me.

"Good news," I said. "I think we found the house."

She pulled her lab coat from inside the locker, started putting it on. She smiled, and said, "You're kidding. You mean the happy couple's finally decided after a decade of searching that indeed a house exists for them somewhere in the universe?" She had on what she wore every day: a man's oxford shirt, white painter's pants and tennis shoes, uniform for most every psych grad student on campus. Today she wore her brunette hair in a French braid, her hair pulled taut away from her face. She had beautiful skin, healthy and tan from riding her bicycle from the married-student housing complex just north of campus to work and back every day.

"Finally," I said, and laughed. "At last count we'd seen three hundred and twelve houses. This, of course, spread out over twelve realtors, each of them feeling as if we were family." I hung my pocketbook on the hook inside the locker and pulled out my lab coat. "But this house is different. At least I think it is. The work we'll need to do isn't too difficult, at least from what we saw of it. It was pretty dark by the time we got out there to see it."

She had finished buttoning up the coat, and I saw the cuffs of her shirt sticking out from inside the coat sleeves. This would be her only concession to the cold outside: her shirtsleeves were rolled down.

"Where is it?" she said. She closed her locker door, leaned against it as I finished buttoning my coat. I looked into the mirror on the inside of my door.

"Chesterfield. Actually a little outside, just past the gorge. It's way out there."

"Chesterfield. I think Jim and I got out there once on our bikes. But when we got to the end of the main drag in town, we were at the top of this hill that led practically straight down. We figured we'd better stop there and head back. We didn't want to have to look in the face the ride back up the hill when we got to whatever was down at the bottom."

"That's where the gorge is," I said. "And the place is just past there, back in the woods. It's on a dirt road. And it's a three-quarter Cape." I touched my hair in a couple of places, but, as always, nothing happened. It was just there on my head, down to my shoulders. Just my hair, brunette like Sandra's, but too fine. I closed the locker door.

I turned and looked at her, just then taking in what she had said about riding bikes to Chesterfield. "You mean you rode all the way out there?" I said.

She shrugged. "Sure. It's not really all that far away, when you think about it. We've ridden to Boston before. Ninety miles. Try that out sometime, and *then* decide whether or not Chesterfield is way out there." She pushed herself off the locker door, spread her feet apart, and held her arms up. She started flexing them. "We're tough. We eat our Wheaties."

I shook my head and laughed, pushed open the heavy door, and we headed back up the hall to Wendy and Paige's office.

The hall was dark, a wiring problem that the Physical Plant had never ironed out, so that the hall, fifty yards long from one end to

the other, had only three lights, high-watt bulbs that whited out
your face whenever you walked beneath them. Past the light the
hall was nearly black again, the only light the reflection on the
linoleum of the next bulb down the hall.

We turned into Paige and Wendy's office, and I had to squint, the
sun from their window so bright. They were both at their desks,
mugs of coffee before them, the sunlight catching wisps of steam
rising from the mugs. Wendy had her elbows on her desktop; Paige
was leaning back in her chair, her hands on the chair arms. Both
stared at nothing.

"Wake up," Sandra said.

I said, "And smell the coffee."

They turned to us, their faces blank. Paige said, "This is how we
work best. In contemplation."

Wendy nodded. "We're simultaneously contemplating each other's navel." She picked up her mug and took a sip.

I said, "Group research?"

"No," Paige said, her face still blank. She leaned forward in her
chair and reached for her coffee cup. "Introspective wallowing. That
and the fact Will wants this grant done today, and we had hoped
to go home before eleven fifteen tonight."

I went to the coffee machine and filled my mug. All our mugs
hung on a rack beside the machine. Mine was the one with the
rabbits all over it; Sandra's had a nonsensical mathematic equation
with no ending and no beginning wrapped around it. Wendy's had
cartoon drawings of different animals—a turkey, a bear, a rabbit—
each saying *mug*. Paige's was painted to look like a can of RC Cola.

I pulled down Sandra's for her and filled it. The only one left on
the rack was Will's, an anonymous white mug.

"He's not in yet?" I said, and handed Sandra her mug.

"Nope," Wendy said.

I sat down in the chair next to Paige's desk, Sandra in the one
next to Wendy's. The chairs were aluminum-frame-and-black-
plastic things brought in from some classroom on campus. My chair
was positioned so that when I sat down the sun shone full in my
face. I closed my eyes to let the warmth go into me, both hands
around my mug. "How's Phillip?" I said.

"Perfect," Paige said, "except for day care. Not that there's anything wrong with the day-care center, but just the whole fact of it. The whole idea that in order to get along both Rick and I have to work so we can live, eat, wear clothes, and pay for Phillip's day care."

I heard her lean back in her chair, and I leaned my head against the wall behind me. My head just touched the bottom edge of Paige's bulletin board, and I imagined all the pictures of her boy, Phillip, she had tacked up on it. There was a picture of him in a bathtub, a yellow support ring around him that kept him from falling into the water. He was looking up at the camera, smiling, one hand reaching up as if to touch the lens. Another picture was of Phillip sitting on his father's shoulders. In the picture Rick has no shirt on, and Phillip is naked. They both look serious, as if the picture were some interruption of a private conversation. And there were other pictures.

I envied her, of course. I wanted that child, that beautiful boy. The day after he was born I'd been to the hospital to see him. A week later I held him, felt the small body in my hands, his eyes closed, his mouth moving in a sucking reflex, little lips in and out. Since then I had baby-sat for Paige and Rick most every time they asked me; it had become nothing for me to walk the ten minutes to their apartment and take care of the boy whenever they wanted to go out.

But they didn't go out that often, and I knew it was because they, too, hadn't had an easy time of having a child. Paige had had a miscarriage the first time. Not long after she had lost hers I went to her apartment, asked if she cared to talk, as if this passing on of misery might help her, help me. She had cried while trying to smile at me, as if she needed to hide her grief, and then she said, "It's pain. That's all it is. Two kinds of pain," and she had come to me and put her arms around my neck and sobbed into my shoulder.

There was nothing to say after that. I knew what she meant. Just two kinds of pain: that in your womb, and that in your heart.

So Rick and Paige weren't often willing to give up their baby for an evening; baby-sitting was seldom, and usually for no longer than two or three hours while the two of them had a quick dinner and saw a movie.

But on those nights I baby-sat I did nothing but watch the baby.

I watched while he ate, in awe of his small hand guiding a spoon into his mouth, in awe of his small legs carrying him across the hardwood floors of their apartment to the television where he would stand, two hands pressed up against the glass of the picture tube like small crafted templates, perfect toddler hands. Once the baby was asleep I would quietly go back into his room, sit in the rocking chair next to the crib, and watch him sleep, amazed at the simple act of rolling over in his sleep, at a small fist thrust into the air, at his third and fourth fingers making their way to his mouth to set him off sucking again.

I opened my eyes, the light shooting through me, and I was blinded a moment. I closed and rubbed them, then opened them to see Will standing in the doorway, his hands on his hips.

"You women ought to get working," he said. "The rabbits are waiting. They want you. I can hear them calling you. They're saying, 'We want women.' "

He didn't smile, didn't move, but stood there, waiting for us to say something. Wendy was the first. She said, "You be careful or these women will revolt."

Paige said, "We're the majority in this room. The only reason we allow you in here is to get your own coffee. That, and to pay us."

"We'll get the rabbits to revolt if they want us so much," Sandra said. "We'll train them to hook up electrodes to *your* nictitating membrane, then give you the shock treatment, see how *you* like it."

I said, "Then we'll train them to put you through perfusion. We'll have our own French Revolution here."

"*Vive les lapins!*" Paige said, and we all laughed.

Will just stood there, his face straight. He brought his hands from his hips and walked over to the machine, brought down his mug. He poured himself a cup, then turned and walked out of the room. Once in the hallway he said, "Let's go, girls."

Sandra mouthed, "Let's go, girls," her face all twisted, her chest out, and we all laughed again, loud enough, we knew, to antagonize Will.

Sandra and I got up from our chairs. "Good luck," I said to Paige and Wendy. "For whatever that's worth."

Wendy said, "It's worth more than 'Let's go, girls.' "

We stepped back into the dark hall and headed for Will's office three doors down.

He was already in his chair, the coffee cup set on top of dozens of loose papers spread across his desk. Inevitably he left coffee rings on important papers, whether reprints or originals, sometimes even grant proposals. Before the laboratory had enough money to hire Paige and Wendy, it had been me who had to take a bottle of Wite-Out and brush over brown spots, even retype pages and letters altogether. I'd bought him a ceramic coaster once, put his coffee on it one morning, but the next day I had come in to find half-a-dozen cigarette butts ground into it, the coffee mug back on a set of proposal guidelines, one more coffee ring to white out.

Sandra and I took our chairs, Sandra the overstuffed blue vinyl against the left wall, me the oak rocker against the right. We were facing each other.

As every morning, Will rummaged through the papers to find his memo pad, and started scribbling on it the list of the day's chores.

Sandra said, "Claire and Tom looked at another house last night." She was smiling at me, her mug balanced on her knees, her fingers just touching it to hold it there. "How many have you seen now?"

"Seven hundred fifty-three," I said.

Will finished his scribbling, and leaned back in his chair, the squeak of springs almost too high to hear, and I knew this leaning back would be followed by some great words of domestic wisdom from this professor who plugged electrodes into the brains of rabbits, and did it on government money. He loved these moments, I knew, when he put his hands behind his head, looked across the desk, and gave a smile.

He had done this same thing to me nine years ago when he'd interviewed me, a senior at the university. The lab hadn't even been in existence then, Will himself having been at the university only a year. He'd had more hair then, but wore the same oxford button-down and gray corduroys.

"Can you handle rabbits?" he had asked, and I remember I had looked past him to the window behind him, the shade up, heat shimmering in waves from the radiator beneath the window so that the snowflakes outside seemed to dance even more, hang an instant longer before falling to the ground. I remember thinking that rabbits were nothing to handle. Timid, stupid creatures.

"Handle rabbits," he had said again. "That's not as easy as it sounds, sweetheart. You don't go in every morning and sweep little rabbit turds out from beneath a cage. That's not what I mean. We've got flunky grad students to do that kind of shit. Hah." He had laughed, and then I had laughed, too, just to be polite, all this time ready for him to ask a single question of my training, my course work, my psych background, any one question that might undo me and expose me to be what I knew I was: only a girl with no real training other than her psych courses. A girl who knew nothing about neuroscience and behavior, but who needed a job. I waited for him to ask one single question that might make me fall apart, show me to know, really, nothing.

But no such question came. Instead Will had leaned forward in his chair, that same squeak in my ears. He had put his hands on the table, reached into the mass of papers, and pulled out a memo pad. He wrote on it, then handed it across to me. I held it in my hands, my hands trembling, and read it.

1. Running rabbits
2. Stereotaxic surgery and atlas
3. Perfusion
4. Staining, mounting

I could still remember that list now. It had been foreign to me then, merely procedures read about in textbooks. Now they were routine.

"When you're looking for a house," Will started in, and I looked at Sandra.

"Here we go," I said.

She said, "I asked for it."

Will ignored us. "You want to make sure you get a dry basement. Check out the basement first. That's the most important thing you can find in a house, a dry basement." I could tell by his eyes, and how they were beginning to crease closed, that soon he would be lapsing into the next state beyond words of wisdom, when he would begin to tell stories of either his first or second marriage. "It was our first house," he went on, leaning even farther back in his chair, his eyes closed to near slits, "that we lost hundreds of dollars in water damage. Books. Books, I remember."

"Will," I said. Someone had to stop him. "For one thing, I don't even know if the place has a basement. More than likely just a crawl space down below. But if it does have a basement, you can be sure we'll check to make sure it's dry."

Sandra said, "I'll vouch for her. She's responsible. Dry basements have always been tops on her list. I know it."

He opened his eyes, leaned forward in the chair, and brought his hands from behind his head without looking at us. He tore the sheet from the pad and handed it to me.

I took it from him, and he said, "I don't know why I put up with this. I don't."

"Because," Sandra said, and sat up in her chair, "we do good work. We do damn fine work, and that's why we're working for you."

The list in my hand, I looked across at her and could see she was serious. Because, I knew, she was right.

But Will only did what we expected him to do: he shrugged, still not looking at us, and simply waved us off. Slowly Sandra and I stood, still holding our coffee mugs. His mug sat on the middle of his table, there on a stack of papers, and I said on my way out, "You be careful with that coffee, not to spill it. Paige and Wendy have enough stuff out there to do, what with the grant and everything else. They don't want to be retyping manuscripts for spilled coffee."

He looked up at me, a piece of printout in his hand, his face without expression, but then he smiled and looked back at the paper. He said, "That coaster's around here someplace."

I said, "I think you broke it two years ago. The last time you tried to clear off the desk."

He only shook his head, smiling.

I pulled running rabbits to start out the day. It wasn't such a bad job, considering the option: sitting at the computer and punching up references for a paper Will would be delivering at a convention up in Montreal later this year. That was the chore Sandra had been

given, and when we left Will's office for the black of the hallway, I
had seen her look at me, her mouth all tight, her eyes wrinkled up
to give me a death look, one side of her face lost to shadow, the
other illuminated by the light from Will's office.

"Sorry," I said. "Life in the world of Neuroscience and Behavior."

"References," she said, and her face went back into the dark as
she looked down the hall and away from me. She looked down, and
her shoulders fell.

"See you at lunch?" I said.

She was silent, and turned to me. I could see her face again. This
time there was no expression, no look at all.

I placed my hand on her shoulder and gently rubbed it. "What's
wrong?" I said. I paused a second. I smiled. "You got your Wheaties
today, remember?"

She shrugged, though the movement, I knew, meant nothing. It
was only a sign to me that she could tell I was trying to make her
feel better.

She said, "There's nothing wrong, but then there's plenty. Sure,
we can have lunch." She looked at me. "In the computer room."
She paused. "But if I told you it was my period, would you believe
me?" She smiled. "If I told you I was part of that clinical study on
PMS they're doing over at Tobin, would you believe me?"

I laughed at her, at this woman I'd thought had been hired by
Will because she was pretty, because she was beautiful in her ath-
letic way. At first I'd been jealous, not for any secret love I held for
Will, but because, once I'd gotten to work with her in the laboratory,
I'd seen how professional she was, even though she was only a
senior back then; how meticulously she learned to block brains,
slice and set and mount and stain, all within a week and a half,
when it had taken me three. Since then Will had had her co-write
three papers, the latest with her name listed first, when the closest
I had come had been the second name on two papers, the third on
two more.

But that jealousy had disappeared over the last two years, when
I had seen in her that this was her career, that co-writing papers
and staining cresyl-violet thin slips of rabbit brain were what she
wanted to do for the rest of her life. She wanted to be here in the
laboratory, her white lab coat on, her eyes peering into a microscope

to trace lesions made in single cells of the Red Nucleus, all this to contribute to a larger canvas, that of Artificial Intelligence. She wanted to try to find exactly *where* in the brain reaction occurred, which particular neuron fired which particular neuron and on and on into the circuit that would inevitably make a rabbit blink.

There had been a time when I, too, had felt that way, when I couldn't wait to get here in the morning, to get things rolling, to go downstairs to the basement and run rabbits so that I might contribute to the whole of science, but that, like the jealousy I had felt toward Sandra, had been lost, too. Now I merely came to work— *work*—and assisted in research. I would stay here, I knew, as long as grants from the government held out, and, judging from the success of the research done in this former boys' dormitory, that money would keep coming in, and I would have a job. Nothing more: only a job. Sometimes I wept over this, over the realization that there might not be anything more for me to do than be here; but most times I just worked, collected my pay, accepted my benefits, comforted, somehow, by the knowledge that if indeed I ever had a baby, the insurance would have covered everything.

I looked at Sandra, and thought I had seen some sort of hope slipping away from her. I thought maybe she was losing something, or perhaps she had already lost it.

I said, "If you tell me you're having your period, I'll believe you. But if you tell me the truth at lunch, I'll believe you even more." I smiled at her, not sure whether or not she could see me in the darkness. "In the computer room."

"Okay," she said, and took hold of my hand on her shoulder. She squeezed it, let go, and turned toward the computer room at the far end of the hall. I watched her move toward the bare bulb at the hall's halfway point, and saw her burst into color as she passed beneath it, her white coat brilliant, her brunette hair shiny in the French braid, the pale blue of her shirt cuffs below her lab coat sleeves. Then she disappeared again into the dark.

 Rabbit running would be easy today. We were at the beginning of a new study, the rabbits fresh, delivered only last night by Mr. Gadsen, the animal supplier for most of the labs on campus. He was an old man, short and a little overweight, but you could tell by looking at him that he had been in shape at one time: his forearms were still thick and hard, his shoulders broad. He had a fringe of white hair just above his collar in back, and always had on his Boston Red Sox cap, the bill crumpled and soft. He always wore a red corduroy shirt and ancient, dirty Levi's and a Levi's jacket, the elbows worn through to show red shirt.

He was a good man, I knew; he treated the rabbits as best as anyone could, though none of us had ever been out to his farm in Leverett to find out what happened out there, how he was able to raise these animals so well. They were always healthy, bright, clean. Seldom did any of them come in sick.

But Mr. Gadsen—no one, except perhaps Will, knew him to have a first name—drank too much, his nose and face flushed no matter what time of day or year. A couple of times I'd stepped into Will's office, just after a new batch of rabbits had been delivered downstairs, only to find Mr. Gadsen leaning forward in the old rocking chair, Will in the blue chair, each with a Styrofoam cup in his hand, Mr. Gadsen with a fifth of some off-brand whiskey in his other hand.

"To new rabbits," Mr. Gadsen would laugh and look up at me each time. He always gave the same toast, holding the cup in the air as if it were fine crystal: "May your happiness multiply as quickly as do my rabbits," and he would laugh again, knock back the slug of whiskey, his BoSox cap never falling off no matter how quickly he snapped back his head.

I felt sorry for him, always smelling of booze and animals: rabbits, guinea pigs, blue jays, cats, everything else he handled. That smell made me want to cry for him sometimes, but most often I had to smile because he seemed happy, and he cared for the animals.

About a year ago, for no other reason than that he wanted to try someone new, Will decided to buy some animals from a different supplier, this one out near Worcester. When Mr. Gadsen had called to find out how many rabbits we would need for the next study, it had been left to me to explain that we had used somebody else, Will in London to visit a laboratory, everyone in our own lab busy with something else.

"Goddammit," he had said over the phone, though not to me. "I can't believe it, I can't believe it," he whispered again and again. I didn't know what to do, only held on the line while he whispered, and then he began to cry, a soft wheezing sound.

"Mr. Gadsen," I said. "Mr. Gadsen," but I could think of nothing else to say.

He caught a deep breath. "That's fine. That's just fine with me, little lady. You tell Will, Mr. Professor and rabbit professional nonesuch, that as soon as he's ready I'll be here. I'll be here with fine, healthy rabbits just waiting for His Royal Highness Will Flinter's mighty word, and then he'll have healthy, ready rabbits again." He hung up.

Of the twenty rabbits we took in from that new supplier, we lost twelve in two weeks to enteritis, the sickness passing from rabbit to rabbit to rabbit, though they were never in contact with one another, each kept in its own metal cage. When we called the supplier, told him all the rabbits were dying of diarrhea, he had blamed it all on us, told us we hadn't kept things clean enough in our lab. A lie. We kept our lab as clean as any on campus, as clean, according to an animal-use expert Will had called in to inspect our place before the university's biannual tour, as any lab in the state.

We'd had to call in Mr. Gadsen to help us save the last eight.

That Thursday morning Sandra, Paige, Wendy, and I watched from the secretaries' room window as he climbed down from the

cab of his rusted-out Chevy van, slammed the door closed, and
straightened out his collar. He tucked in his tails, though they hadn't
been out. He was smiling to himself, and took off his cap, ran his
hand back across his bald head as if there were still hair to keep in
place.

The four of us laughed a quiet laugh, and Paige said, "I love him.
He's perfect."

"He is," I said. Sandra and Wendy nodded.

He walked into the laboratory as if he owned the place; Sandra
and I had had to run from the office to the stairs down into the
basement to catch up with him.

As we went past Will's office Sandra called out, "He's here," but
Will didn't make a move, too proud, I knew, to admit to choosing
the wrong supplier.

We followed Mr. Gadsen into the rabbit room—the Green Room,
we called it—the walls painted a nauseating mint green some twenty
years ago. The Green Room, too, because it was the waiting room
for the rabbits, where they stayed before they went on to per-
form in the next room down, where those electrodes would be
clipped on.

He moved from cage to cage, saying nothing, merely looking,
peering in at frightened, white animals, each one jammed back into
the corner of its cage.

"God bless it," he whispered when he'd seen them all. He looked
at us for the first time. His eyes were full, not with the rheumy look
of old age, but with tears. He had his hands in his back pockets,
and stood there, just looking at us. Then he sniffed and looked down
at the cement floor, shiny with the thick coat of polyurethane that
helped the rabbit handlers keep the floors as clean and germ-free
as possible, the floors washed down two or three times a week.

"That bastard ought to be taken out and shot," he said. "The
bastard who sold you these animals." He moved one foot across the
floor, then gently kicked at nothing with his old Army boot. I looked
at his boots, noticed he'd shined them since the last time I'd seen
him. He looked back at the cages. "Not only are these godforsaken
things sick, but they're just not healthy. They're just not well-cared-
for in the first place. You can tell by their eyes, by the look, and
you can tell by the lay of the ears, whether they're up and hearty

or down and crushed, that's what you can tell. Whether they're sick or not, you can look at their eyes and ears and tell if they're taken care of or not."

I looked back at the animals, and saw that he was right, that their ears were a little different somehow, something so small I couldn't have seen it unless he'd pointed it out. Even then I wasn't sure whether I was actually seeing a difference, or if it had been merely the suggestion he had placed in me that made them look different.

It was in their eyes, too, just as he said, a cloudy look, a dead look you could only see if you stared at them long enough, let your breathing go slow while you just watched the rabbit back there in its cage, its front paws drawn up, its ears flat. That was death, I knew, death slow through the eyes, and I wondered if that was how it happened to everything: rabbits, blue jays, monkeys. People.

Sandra, too, was peering into a cage now, and I turned to tell Mr. Gadsen Yes, I could see it, but he was already gone.

When I got up to Will's office, Mr. Gadsen was leaning against the edge of Will's desk, knuckles of both hands resting on the desktop. He was shaking his head, and Will was back in his chair, his hands holding onto the edge of the desk as if to keep him from falling backward. He was looking up at Mr. Gadsen.

Mr. Gadsen said, "All's I can tell you is that they're sick. That's all. And that they came to you that way. I know about this place, know you and your people well enough so's I can tell you your people didn't make them sick." He stopped, looked straight down, his knuckles still resting on the desktop. "And I'll tell you," he said, "that there ain't no guarantee but I can save them." He quickly looked up. "You'll still lose another one or two irregardless, but you can try and save what you can." Then he straightened up, pulled from inside his jacket a ziplock Baggie filled with yellow powder. He held it up to his face and seemed to study it under the fluorescent lights. He squeezed it a little, then dropped it on the desk.

"Terramycin," he said. "Mix it with their water. Tablespoon per half-gallon. Just enough. And keep it in their water until I come back. And I'll come back, believe you me. I'll come back with a fresh batch, and you'll be goddamned if you ever buy from that idiot out in Worcester again." He had a hand in his back pocket again, his index finger pointed like a gun, each hard tap another shot through the desk and into the floor. "That's all I'll say. Just that if you want good rabbits, you'll come to me. That's all."

He turned, and if he saw me leaning against the doorjamb he pretended he didn't, and just brushed past me, out into the hall and through the heavy, steel double doors outside. The doors banged shut.

I said, "Well?" I had my arms crossed.

Will picked up the Baggie and looked at it a moment. Then he threw it at me, and I was quick enough to catch it.

He said, "Do it," and that was it.

We lost, just as Mr. Gadsen had figured, two more rabbits. The ones left were dull, dim-witted, and were never successfully conditioned. They'd been sacrificed without being of any use at all. And we'd bought every rabbit since from Mr. Gadsen.

I went downstairs to the rabbit room, to the green walls, to the shiny plastic and concrete floor. I went to the cages, six on each unit, two rows stacked three high on a metal frame with wheels so that we could move them around for cleaning. The cages were big—about two and a half feet deep—and as always the bedding was clean, the bottles full. There were eighteen new ones, I saw, and as I leaned toward the metal cage doors to look in at each rabbit I could have sworn I could still smell on them Mr. Gadsen's whiskey.

The rabbits had already been sorted, each cage labeled with an index card slipped into a small metal frame fixed to the door. On the card was written either LARGE or SMALL, and then a number. Large rabbits were anything from three to four kilos; small was anything under that.

"So," I said into the cages, "today's the day we start."

The rabbits looked at me, pink eyes open wide. They were watching me, waiting.

Because this was the first day for this new batch, all I would have to do would be to suture them, then put them through habituation. Easy enough, and so I took a breath, picked up the pair of canvas work gloves from on top of the cages and put them on, opened up the left top cage, and reached in for Small # 1. He made little movement to escape me, and I smiled at this, the end result of Mr. Gadsen's care. So what if they smelled a little of whiskey? The rabbits were healthy; this one was particularly happy, it seemed, as I held it in my arms, scratched behind its ears.

"A name," I said. "You're the first of the batch, so you'll get a name." It was something I did with each new batch, always the first rabbit, top left, that got a name. I knew it was a useless, silly thing to do, and I knew I put myself at risk each time I did it, letting in the possibility of getting a little too attached to a rabbit—a bunny—by giving it a name. Still, I did it. Just habit, part of my own habituation to a new group of rabbits. It was something no one knew about, this small secret of mine.

I carried the rabbit across the room to the row of four boxes mounted on a metal cart. The boxes, only plywood boards nailed together to form four cubbyholes on end, were each large enough to hold one rabbit snugly. The rabbits could see what was going on above them, could, if they wished, climb halfway out, rest their forepaws on the top edge of the box and watch the world, which is what Small #1 did as soon as I placed him inside. He seemed happy there, his ears straight up, his nose going nonstop as he took in all these new smells.

"A name," I said again, and it came to me. I said, "Chesterfield. Chesterfield," and I stood back from the cart to look at him.

He was fearless, content. I laughed, and he didn't even blink. I said, "Chesterfield it is, then," and I went to the cart and wheeled it over to the cages for the next three.

Small #2—he would get no name—seemed skittish, afraid; I reached into his cage and had to chase him with my hand back and forth a couple of times before I could get hold of him. Once I had him, though, he seemed to soften, his muscles relaxed as I placed him in his bin, Chesterfield still standing there in his, watching intently. He leaned toward #2's box, sniffed, then looked back at me.

Large #1, the second row cage on the left, probably weighed about three and a half, and was a pushover: he merely lay there, not even crouched, his hind legs flat behind him as he waited for me to reach in. It was as if Mr. Gadsen had already conditioned the rabbits for laboratory conditioning.

I opened the fourth door, Large #2. He was even bigger than #1, I could see; this one might be a little harder to handle than the others. He was backed into a corner, facing me, his ears laid back, his paws in front of him. His nose was moving fast, his whiskers shivering.

I said, "Come on, bunny. Come on, big bunny," and started to reach in.

He jumped at me then, boxed at my hand with his paws, shooting them out at me. I could feel through the canvas gloves the force he had, too, my first two fingers throbbing just a little with that contact.

His sudden move made me jump back, the other three rabbits having lulled me into forgetting just what it was these animals could do: break bones, pierce flesh, jump ten feet. I moved closer to the gate, still standing open. He hadn't moved again.

I put my hand in the cage as slowly as I could. It had been a long time since I'd had to treat some dumb rabbit as if it were a lion, but I'd seen the blood out of Sandra's hand once, blood from a bite she'd gotten through canvas gloves just like the ones I wore. It had taken five stitches and too many shots to fix her up. So I was careful, and I went slowly.

As I imagined might happen, the thing began to growl, the same sort of growl a cat might make: low and loud, much deeper, more resonant than what you would assume a small animal like this could put out.

It growled, but still I reached for it. And then it jumped at me again, hit my hand again, but with my other hand I was able to grab it by the scruff of the neck, drag it from the cage. I held it at arm's length like some sort of magician, its hind legs thrashing the air, its forepaws splayed out to either side, yet it had gone silent. It was only a rabbit now, muscles, bone, and soft white fur. I brought it to the last box.

The other rabbits were flat in the bottom of their own boxes as I wrestled with Large #2, his legs still kicking, resounding now against the wood, claws scrabbling to dig into something. Finally he was in, and I held him down in the hole with one hand. With the other I reached to the bottom platform of the cart for one of the square wooden lids, pulled it up to the box, and let go of the rabbit. He jumped at the lid, and I could feel the backbone hit the wooden piece, but there was nothing I could do. I could only hope that he would settle down, get used to things here.

I pushed the cart out into the hallway. Large #2 had finally stopped jumping, but still I held the lid on. If I were to lift it now, chances are it would jump. It had happened before. Everything had happened before, rabbits jumping from carts so that you had to chase them down, squatting and trying to run after a mass of fur and claws, pink and white, colors you wouldn't think of as being vicious enough to make a fool of you.

I wheeled them into the next room down, the running room. One whole wall was filled with ancient hardware—banks of old circuit boards, scopes, wires, tubes, all designed just to register the blink of an eye. Only that. Though our laboratory was a good one, our equipment in this room was at best archaic; all these electronics when one computer, even a PC, could record digitally what we were still running out on a polygraph.

Against another wall was a countertop, on it the Plexiglas Gormezano boxes the rabbits would be placed in for habituation, the trays of .04 sutures, a couple of needle-nose pliers, and an assortment of wires, alligator clips, and tools used to staple the wound clips into the rabbit's fur. At the end of the counter stood the four-drawer filing cabinet in which the rabbits would be placed. Wires came from the back and ran to certain spots on the circuit wall. Other than that the cabinet seemed only a gray, university-issue filing cabinet. Ugly, big, practical.

I took Chesterfield out first. He was still crouched down in the box, still spooked by Large #2's growl. They fed off each other that way, knew what each other was up to, knew the fear that another had, and they could pass it on to one another so that one growl stirred up the whole bunch, made them all cower.

I held him for a moment, stroked his ears and scratched down between his eyes and behind the ears, and then I gently placed him in one of the Gormezano boxes, a clear bin that held the rabbits down, wouldn't allow them to move, so that none of the equipment would be jostled, mismeasuring some sudden movement of the rabbit as a blink. Chesterfield slipped into the box easily, his head protruding through a hole in the piece that held it steady; he even made the claustrophobic box seem cozy as he sat there, head out one end, just waiting. And I wondered what might happen when I got to Large #2. I glanced over at the cart. The lid was still on the fourth box, and I heard no sounds. Perhaps he'd decided to cooperate.

Suturing came next, and I took from the tray at the end of the counter one of the green-and-white packages, no bigger than a small envelope, and pulled one end open to expose the sterilized needle and thread. I took off the gloves, and with a needle-nose pliers held the needle, the curved piece of sharpened steel like a miniature scythe. Gently I placed my index and middle fingers over Chester-field's left eye, then spread my fingers so that his eyelids were pulled open to expose the nictitating membrane, the thin sheet of pink skin that protected the eye, the second lid that allowed its red albino eyes to keep intact and safe. The membrane exposed, I took the needle and sank it just a breath's depth into the skin, turned the pliers so that the tip of the suture popped out an eighth of an inch away from where it entered, and nowhere near, I knew, the eyeball itself. Chesterfield had done nothing, only winced a moment when the needle had entered.

I pulled the needle through and tied the thread off in a small knot, a minuscule loop on the membrane to which we would connect the lead from the potentiometer after habituation. Then I snipped off the ends of the thread with a pair of scissors from the counter, and Chesterfield was ready. I pulled open the top drawer of the filing cabinet, and placed Chesterfield in his box inside, his head facing me and the front of the drawer, where a small speaker was mounted. Once they had been habituated—one half-hour session in the filing cabinet would be enough—we would put the electrodes in place, hook up the potentiometer like some small mechanical saddle perched on the rabbit's neck, and a quiet tone would come through the speaker for a moment every fifteen seconds. An instant after the tone would come the tiny shock so small—one milli-amp —that it couldn't be felt. A shock so small that only a few nerves would react to it, only enough to signal the eye to blink. Not enough to cause pain.

At least that was what we had always been told. Of course there was no way to know, but that was what I told myself so I wouldn't feel any more guilty than I already did.

It was then that what always happens happened: I began to regret my having given Chesterfield a name. There he sat, a rectangle of fur crammed into Plexiglas. He was still waiting, but only I knew what would happen. I slowly pushed the drawer closed, Chesterfield watching me, his nose going slower and slower as he disappeared into the black of the cabinet.

I knew what would happen at the end of all this, knew that he would have to be sacrificed. *Sacrificed,* I thought, and thought of the quality of that word, that joy of science resonating from it: sacrificed for research, when what it meant was that he would be killed.

The second and third rabbits went in easily, and I had them both in the cabinet within ten minutes. What was left, of course, was Large #2. I looked at the box, the lid still on. The scratching had stopped a long time ago. There were no sounds, but I knew it meant nothing at all.

I put my gloves on and as gently, as quietly as I could I placed my hand on the lid, pulled it up.

There sat the rabbit, his eyes open wide, the pupils, bright crimson, disappearing as they shut out the new light.

First I touched his ears, and he did nothing. I could tell his body was stiff, ready for something to happen, but I wanted only to comfort him, to let him get used to me, to my touch, even though through thick canvas gloves. We would be seeing a lot of each other from this day on, and I wanted him used to me.

After a minute or so I decided to go ahead, to try and lift him out. I reached in and pulled him out, a hand on either side of his chest. Even through the gloves I could feel the fragile rib cage, the heart pounding inside.

I held him in front of me, his legs hanging down, his paws out as if he were floating across the room in some sort of dream, and I was amazed at his weight, at how Mr. Gadsen must have fed the thing.

Slowly I lowered him toward the box, but before its hind legs even touched the Plexiglas it began thrashing and squirming. The growling began again, growling so loud I knew it must have been heard by the other three, and for a moment I pictured a polygraph gone wild, rabbits blinking away at the loud, cold, sharp sound coming from this animal, and in that moment, my mind on something else for an instant, the rabbit craned his head straight back, then to one side and the other. Its mouth opened wide, gaping open to reveal pink gums, pink as raw flesh, its incisors sharpened yellow fangs. It shot its head at my left hand, those teeth sinking into the canvas glove, through it, and into my hand just below my index finger.

All this in a moment, this searing heat and growl, all without leaving me enough time even to react, for my eyes to signal my brain that some movement, some evasive measure needed to be taken to keep from happening what had already happened: its teeth into my flesh, the rabbit now shaking its head as if it were a dog with a bone, tugging at my hand.

Still its feet kicked, and for another moment I was calm, trying to figure how I could get this rabbit latched onto my own flesh into the Gormezano box and the bottom cabinet drawer.

But then the moment was gone, and I screamed at the pain, at the heat, at the suddenness of this, and with the scream I tried to throw the rabbit away from me. I took hold of its head and tried to squeeze open its jaws, the rest of its body hanging in the air, thrashing, kicking in free space, kicking so hard that, finally, with one fierce last kick, the rabbit broke its own back, the *snap* so crisp yet quiet it could have been a small branch broken outside a window. With that snap the rabbit stopped squirming and released its grip on my hand. It hung on my arm a moment longer, and then its squeals began, the opposite of the low growl, a sound like a baby's muffled, long screams. A sound more common than the growl, but it frightened me more, and I shook the dead weight off of me, watched it drop to the floor.

Anger began to well up in me, anger at an overweight and spoiled animal. I held my hand, felt the pulse shine through my wrist. There was no blood anywhere, and for a moment I thought that perhaps it hadn't broken my skin.

Things around me began to pop, waver, so that the edges of the room and things around me began to lose distinction, the gray filing cabinet becoming an ugly black coffin on end, the plywood boxes on the cart dancing, shaking, and just then, light and soft, someone brushed past me, went quickly to the rabbit. It took me a moment, but then I recognized Mr. Gadsen's corduroy shirt and scuffed Army boots, the smell of whiskey once again. I saw him kneeling over the rabbit, the rabbit still squealing, and he turned and looked up at me, his hat off, the shiny scalp covered with age spots, his eyes clear and wet, his mouth wrinkled up in pain as he said to me—it must have been to me—*Merciful God, Merciful God, it's my fault, mine. She slipped into the batch. The wrong cage. This girl's pregnant. She's about to give birth,* and then he turned from me back to the rabbit.

I looked at the rabbit as best I could, saw it lying there on the floor, huge, growing larger each second as things around me continued to shut down, to give over to gray rectangles and squares that grew and popped. The rabbit's belly was huge. It could have been nothing but pregnant, and I had let it kick itself to death.

I closed my eyes for a moment, and then thought better of it, the squares multiplying in the darkness my eyelids created. I opened them again, and this time looked at my hand, the one I held, the one with the holes pierced through the canvas of the glove. I held it, watching it, wondering what it would do if I let it go. Then a line of blood, thick and red, slipped from inside the glove and down my wrist to meet with the white of the lab coat. Once there the blood blossomed, seeping into the weave of the white cotton sleeve, and I watched as it spread, amazed at the intricacy of it all, at each single thread soaking up the blood to give it a strange and new pattern.

Another line of blood fell, and another, until I stood staring at this bouquet of blood, my own, on the sleeve of my lab coat, each moment the circling squares of moving gray closing down on me until there at the center was only a red-and-white sleeve, caused by a pregnant rabbit I had let kill itself, and then the gray took over, and I fell into darkness.

Though I could not sleep that night, I could not come awake, and so I spent those hours in the dark, in my bed, moving, moving, my eyes unable to open as I tried to force them. I could feel Tom in bed next to me, the warm curve of his body, his pulse, but I could do nothing. Only move, dreaming.

I had dreams of things that made no sense, dreams of deep forests, foliage so thick I could see in only a few feet, lush trees that let in no light from above, and in my dream I wondered how anything could grow in such darkness. Then I dreamed the forest was gone, and I stood on a high desert plateau, only scrub brush around me, a hot wind breaking across the mesa, my hair lifted by the wind so that I felt as if I might fly. Then I tried to open my eyes there in my sleep, and the wind died. The desert shook, broke into pieces, and I felt Tom still next to me. I had fallen back into my bed, still unable to awaken.

I had another dream, too, one not so much a dream as a recollection of what had happened that morning, the images so real before me that they were more frightening than anything I could imagine.

There was first darkness, and then light, light from the long fluorescent bulbs on the ceiling. Here was Mr. Gadsen's face above me, saying nothing, only moving back and forth as if dodging my eyes. His mouth was open, the corners drawn up, and I could see his teeth, rotten and gray and dead. I wanted him to move away from me, wanted him to stop blocking out the light I could have from the bulbs above, but he would not leave me. I smelled his whiskey, and watched as he wiped his mouth with the back of his hand.

Mr. Gadsen looked away from me a moment, and here was Will, his face even closer to mine. He spoke to me, let out my name, and it came to me as if from a great distance across water, my name drifting toward me on cold air and settling down into my ears. I started listening, thinking perhaps he could tell me something I needed to know, but all he did was speak my name. I heard the squeals of the rabbit again, the wail, and I began rocking my head, the ceiling and those two faces swaying above me.

I said, "The rabbit," though I couldn't hear myself, only knew that those were the words my brain was gathering, the words my tongue in my mouth and the air across my larynx meant to form. Will tried to give a smile, his eyebrows and forehead wrinkled. I did not believe him.

My left arm did not exist in the dream, I realized. I tried to move it, but nothing happened, and I thought that someone had already come along and had cut it off at the shoulder.

Finally Sandra's face was above me, her eyes nearly closed, her mouth pursed as she glanced at my face, down to my left, then back to my face, and here was Wendy, and Paige, faces all floating above me like leaves on water, floating and bobbing, some speaking, some not; at one point Sandra leaned close, said, *I guess this means no lunch date,* and gave a forced smile, and I remember trying to do the same myself, and remember nothing happening. This is what a newborn must feel like, I thought, faces above it, words falling down, unable to move itself from its back as it lay there, eyes still and unfocusing, simply looking, looking. This is how I felt in my dream: a newborn, helpless, and waiting for help.

I sat up in bed then, my back straight and stiff, my left arm limp at my side. The bedroom was dark, but someone was in there, someone other than Tom and me, and as my eyes took in the shadows around the room, I saw them.

There were three children next to my bed, a boy and two girls. The boy, the oldest, I knew, stood in the center, the girls at either side. He was five years old—of course he was, I knew—and had a pageboy haircut, the soft, moonlit silver hair falling in straight lines from his crown to his forehead and ears. The girls—the youngest farthest away, her head just above the edge of the bed—were wearing little white dresses that encircled them like tutus, the sleeves all puffy, the embroidery around the sleeves little flowers of thread even whiter, glowing there in the darkness.

Of course they were my children. Our children. What we had created.

I reached to touch them, first the girl closest to me, my middle child. She clasped her hands in front of her as if she were saying prayers. I reached for her, reached, and then she opened her mouth to speak, and what I saw terrified me: her mouth became an empty, black hole, nothing there but black and black, an endless hole off into space, and from that mouth came the sound of wind, dark and cold against my face.

The other two opened their mouths as well, even the smallest one, my little girl on tiptoe down near the footboard, her hands grasping the edge of the bedspread. Their mouths opened to abysses, black pits, and the wind increased.

I pulled my hand away, felt a scream form in my throat, but no sound came, my throat hard and taut, as if I'd never breathed before. I tried to scream, to do anything to replace the vast blackness I saw in my children's faces, but nothing happened, and I brought my hands to my face to cover it, to block out what I saw. But still I saw them, my hands transparent, I imagined, until I saw that my hands had been severed, were merely bandaged stumps. I could feel the sutures beneath the bandages, the black threads laced across my wrists to keep my blood inside.

Wind filled the room, edges of the sheets lifting up, flapping in the wind, and still my children's faces were black holes. Now their hair swirled around their heads, the white cotton dresses lifted by the wind, dancing around the girls, dancing on the wind in my room. Then they were in the air, my three children lifted by their own wind, tossed about the room, above my bed, swirling and moving, and they fell in on themselves, disappeared into their own abysses, and were gone, the wind suddenly dead, the room still, empty.

I screamed, finally, the sound cracking through my head and arms and body and into the room, and I awoke, shot open my eyes.

I was alone in bed, the room light now, morning.

I rolled onto my back, looked at the ceiling a moment. I listened, and heard the faint pop and hiss of the coffeemaker in the kitchen, heard Tom moving around in there.

I lifted my left hand, and looked at the bandage. My hand shook with the dream, the fear still in me. White gauze had been wrapped across the palm and back of my hand, the dressing itself on the back of my hand between thumb and forefinger. It had taken seventeen stitches to sew up the wound.

I remembered then the drive from the lab in Mr. Gadsen's van, Sandra in the passenger seat, Will and I in the back, a couple of cages next to us, the smell of animals inescapable. Will held my hand with both of his, applying the pressure as best as he could, and I, still dizzy, leaned against him. Sandra, Will, and I said nothing the entire trip, but Mr. Gadsen had gone on and on, apologizing for the mixup, for the mistake, his voice high-pitched and cracking. From where I sat I could not tell if he were crying or not, but twice he wiped his eyes with the palm of one hand, the other on the wheel, maneuvering us through the campus parking lots and past security gates to the University Health Center.

"I was awake all night," he said, "awake all night, and I couldn't sleep because I knew something was wrong. That I knew, I did." He sniffed. "I knew I'd done something wrong and now, Merciful God, this is what I did. I'm sorry. I'm sorry."

We made it to the emergency room. He jerked the van to a halt, jumped out and came around to the van door, had it pulled open and slammed in place before Sandra had gotten out of her seat.

He looked at me as I eased out of the van, scooting across the floor while Will, squatting next to me, still held my hand tight. Mr. Gadsen looked at me, started to reach out to help me, but drew back against the van, whispering, "I'm sorry," once more. My right arm around Sandra's shoulder, the other hand still held by Will, the three of us wobbled toward the building. The doors shot open, but I hesitated, looked over my shoulder back at Mr. Gadsen. He was still leaned up against his van, his head down. He rubbed his eyes, slowly shook his head.

Then came the stitches, and the shots.

Tom came into the bedroom. He was already dressed, and sat on the edge of the bed. He said, "How'd you sleep?"

"Did I scream?" I asked. "I mean, did you hear anything?"

He looked puzzled, said, "No." He moved his hand to my face, ran his fingers back through my hair. "Did you have bad dreams?"

I could still feel the hard knot in my stomach, could still feel my hands shaking, but I lied. "No," I said. "Not at all. Just sleep." I looked away from him. There was, I felt, nothing I could tell him. It was only a dream, my dream, drug- and anxiety-produced sleep laced with thoughts of children we'd never had.

"Good," he said. He put his fingers to my face, and I could feel the backs of them against my cheek, the wrinkled, bony joints, the nails just touching.

He said, "Are you up to going out? Getting out of the house and going up to Chesterfield?"

I whispered, "Sure." I closed my eyes, opened them. I looked out the window. The sky was the same brilliant blue as yesterday. Clear and cool. "I need to get out of here."

"Fine," he said, and leaned over and kissed the top of my head. He stood, and it seemed he had grown taller overnight, that he'd become a different, bigger man suddenly.

He moved to leave the room, but stopped. From the corner of my eye I saw a bird fly past the window, slice through the blue. I turned to the window, but the bird was long gone. I looked back at Tom. He hesitated, then smiled. He leaned against the doorjamb, and said, "I forgot to tell you. Yesterday, Janet over in copyediting was typing in some report about a wreck on Route 9 and 47, there at the bend in Hadley." He looked down, still smiling, and crossed his arms.

Here was Tom again, winding up with another of his stories from work. It was something he'd started when we were dating, his telling me weird but true stories from the newspaper. He would bring me stories from his excursions around the Pioneer Valley, gossip from the office. He still did it, too, every time he thought I was down about something.

"Janet got this little story about a wreck," he went on, "and it turns out to have been her ex-husband who was in it. He'd been driving his Cavalier along 47 and hadn't even slowed down to pull onto 9, and just slammed into some Smith girl on her way to the mall. Janet hadn't heard anything about it."

I looked at him, said nothing.

Still he smiled. "Janet's ex only twisted his knee in the wreck, and the Smithy wasn't hurt at all. But Janet went ahead and changed the story. She punched right into the machine that her ex had broken his neck, that the Smithy was dead, and that he'd been arrested on manslaughter charges."

The adrenalin was fading in me, and I couldn't help but give a smile. Janet, whom I'd met at a Christmas party a couple of years ago, was small and nervous and talked a lot and, I knew, was still in love with her ex-husband; at the party she'd shown me his picture in her wallet, a Sears portrait that made the man look too happy, too clean to be the louse she made him out to be. Still, she kept the picture with her, even though they'd been divorced for three years by that time.

I smiled, too, for my husband, for his attempt to cheer me, though I didn't want it this morning. But I felt obliged in a way to speak to him, to acknowledge his attempt. I said, "You didn't let her print it—"

"No, no," he cut in, smiling and shaking his head again. "We just circulated her copy around the office. Everyone down there knows about her and her ex. She just let it float around the office."

I nodded, still smiling, and then he lowered his head again, a hand to his mouth, his fingers in a fist.

I said, "What?"

He glanced up at me.

"Go ahead," I said, waiting for this obvious change in topic.

"Oh," he said, and gave a little wave with his hand. "Nothing. Just nothing." He started to move through the doorway, but stopped again.

"It's just that . . ." he started, and paused. He looked at me, then at the bedspread bunched around me. "Just that, well, Mr. Gadsen's called. He's called three times so far this morning." He took in a deep breath and smiled at the bedspread. "I'm surprised the phone ringing didn't wake you up."

He sat on the bed again and ran his hand across the mound of bedspread. He still wasn't looking at me. "He says he's sorry, and that he wants to talk to you. Mainly that he wants to talk to you."

Finally he looked at me. His hand was resting on my knee now, my knee buried beneath bedspread, blanket, sheet.

He was looking at me, waiting, but I turned away. I said, "I know he's sorry. But he'll have to wait. I'm not ready to talk to him. Not now." I paused. "Maybe not ever." The words left me in barely a whisper, and I wished I hadn't let them out. For a moment I thought of taking them back, of apologizing right then for having those feelings, and I thought of calling Mr. Gadsen and just listening to him fall all over himself to apologize. But the image of the rabbit came back, that pregnant animal hanging from my arm, and the snap and squeals, and I thought, No; even if it was an accident, it was his fault. Accidents happened, certainly, but I hated that word. Accident was a fake word, an excuse, I felt: things were traceable to a source, whether it be rain on an oil-slicked road or a gun left loaded in a hall closet. Or too much whiskey and dozens of rabbits to keep track of.

I said, "Let's just go. Let's get out of here. I don't want to talk to him."

The room was silent a moment, and I could hear the two of us breathing. Then Tom took a short, quick breath, said, "Okay." He patted my knee, and stood. He looked at me. "But he's sorry. That's what he wanted you to know." He turned and headed through the bathroom. A moment later I heard him in the kitchen, plates being pulled down from the cupboard.

I lay there, unable to move. I thought of my dream, of three children that never were, that might never be. I thought of my hands gone, those stumps, and of Mr. Gadsen.

With everything I had I pushed back the covers, swung my feet around, and sat up. I felt dizzy for a moment, the blood falling from my brain down to my heart. It took a moment before the room became steady, the floor a place where I could put my feet and trust it would not move beneath me.

 We drove through town, the mid-morning September sunlight brilliant and cutting. For some reason the streets seemed filled with mainstreamers from the state hospital, men and women with nervous twitches and shambling feet and layers and layers of clothing. People who, when walking through town, might bump into you, call you by someone else's name and look at you as if there were something wrong with you. There was, of course, the short, stocky Suntan Man in front of the bank at King and Main, his shirt already off, his bald head and chest and arms greased up for the light. In front of the county courthouse strolled the black man with the carved wooden cane and high boots and wool cap, the man I'd accidentally brushed up against one summer morning when I was heading out the door of the Laundromat on Market, both arms hugging a basketful of fresh, clean clothes. His odor had stayed on the hand that had touched him longer than any formaldehyde ever had, though I scrubbed and scrubbed that hand when I got home, scrubbed it in hot water until the hand was nearly scalded, the skin nearly raw.

We moved through town toward Smith, perched at the top of the hill, that gray stone tower looking down at us all, and it seemed that the streets were suddenly taken over by Smith girls in long pre-winter coats belted or loose, some with colorful earmuffs, some with scarves, all with leather gloves or mittens. They traveled in packs, three or four or five at a time, stopping to read the menu outside the French restaurant, pushing open the glass door into the bank, looking through the tables full of used books in front of another shop. All adult, their cheeks flushed with the cold, their eyes bright, alive.

Of course I was bitter. I had always wanted to be one of them. I'd seen them all my life, watched them as I grew up, hoping that some day I'd end up there somehow, in one of those dorm-palace dining rooms you could see from the street, rooms filled with golden light at night, only the corners and top edges of oil paintings hung on the walls visible from the sidewalk. On spring and autumn nights the sound of crystal and silver and laughter resounded through open windows onto the street, where I walked when I was a girl for just that purpose: for sound and company and beautiful lights, my mother at home, closed up in the house the death of my father had left even more empty.

On those spring and autumn nights I walked around Smith, my hands deep in my coat pockets, my shoulders up in the cold. I always stopped and looked in those windows, watched for the faces of students, but from the street it was nearly impossible, the old dorm houses so high atop their basements that I could only see the lights of chandeliers, those pieces of portraits. I longed to go inside, to see those paintings in full, to stand back from them and take in the portraits of people long dead, and to know who they were and why their likenesses hung there. I wanted to touch the linen, the service, to eat dinner with those girls. To be there.

But inevitably I had to leave, to head down the hill and through the main street and beyond the bend in Route 9 to where my mother and I lived in a small old home, two stories with only two bedrooms. The house I'd grown up in, the house my mother had holed up in, afraid of the world.

Unlike every other friend I had when I was a child, it had been my father who had taken me to my first day of school. It had been my father who carried me from the car to the administration office of the elementary school, carrying me because, I insisted, my legs wouldn't work, Mother back at home, afraid already of what might happen to her only child. It had been my father who, me sitting on his hip, had said in his granite voice *This is Claire Shaw, my daughter, who will be starting school here today,* my name at once important and forever.

It had been my father, too, who had signed my grade reports after that, who'd helped me with my homework, who'd taken me for walks down to the river or to the playground, protecting me from cars racing past on Route 9 as we crossed, his judgment impeccable, always knowing precisely when to cross and when not. And it had been my father who'd taught me to tie my shoes, his big arms around me as I sat on his lap, his slender, rough fingers nimble with those clumsy shoelaces, and I was convinced he was some sort of magician.

So that, when the officer arrived on our front porch one November afternoon, my mother and I were irreconcilable strangers, not knowing one another: me, a sixth-grader, a grown-up, I believed; my mother, a child in my eyes, only someone to keep house, prepare meals, and wait with me for my father's return from work.

A freak accident, the officer said. He stood before us in our front room, the room decorated as it would be until my mother died: my father's chocolate Naugahyde recliner facing the trees and sky out the front window; the sofa covered with a wedding-ring quilt; thick, brown drapes; framed photos of the three of us on the walls. In any one of those pictures—from the pale, tinted colors of their engagement picture, my mother's head tilted to the right just enough, her chin held high, my father's face just above her shoulder, his cheek nearly touching hers, to the last picture before his death, a picture in which we three stand stark against bare, black trees, coats on, all of us smiling, my mother's hand up to block the setting sun—it is easy to see her fear, the wariness that signaled some hiding on her part, the startled shine in her eyes. It was easy to see.

The officer stood before us, snow that had collected on his shoulders and boots melting away, dripping off the parka and down his sleeves as he turned his hat in his hands, snow melting off the brim and crown, dripping to the rug beneath him. A freak accident, he said again, and told us of how my father had apparently taken his eyes off the road for a moment and, of course, off the truck in front of him, that truck loaded with soft, white pine two-by-fours and weaving its way along old Route 2. Perhaps my father had turned to light a cigarette; perhaps he flipped through some of his tally sheets on the seat next to him, rechecking how many cases of what food supplies he would send to the last restaurant he'd visited on his route; or perhaps he just looked at his watch, wondering how long it might be before he would pull into the driveway at home. But the look away gave him just enough time to miss seeing the red brake lights of the truck rear up at him, those boards sliding back at him, the road dusted with a fine, new snow as the boards slid backward across the hood of his car and through the windshield, the glass exploding into small green jewels splashed across my father, the boards sinking into him.

The officer, of course, did not use this language to describe what happened. Green jewels and soft, white pine and the look at the watch were only images I played in my head again and again while growing up here in the Pioneer Valley, my mother from that day on staying indoors even more, turning down invitations from neighbors to dinner or lunch, PTA meetings; those invitations growing fewer and fewer until they disappeared entirely. Not long after his death my mother moved his recliner away from the window, turned its back to that view, and pulled closed the drapes.

No, the officer's words had been only a report as he stood before us while a young woman, my mother, sobbed into her hands, me with one arm around her waist, the waist of a stranger, my other hand covering my own face as he said, *Failed to negotiate* and *Hazardous road conditions* and *Sincere regrets*. Those words.

A week later I was out on the blacktop at school, playing dodgeball, when suddenly one of us looked up to the sharp blue sky, and pointed. Most of us turned to the sight, a lone B-52 bomber banking across the sky as if it were some huge black bird drifting on currents of air. I heard some of the children talk of how bomb shelters honeycombed the hills between South Hadley and Amherst, a fortress where the military would hide when war broke out. *When* was the word they used, uttered without fear by children. Play resumed, but I still watched the sky, watched the big airplane until it disappeared behind hills to the south, and I began to know then the fear my mother felt, the world closing down around us, my father gone with the simple act of glancing at a watch and the gift from God of a light blanket of snow.

Though I was only eleven—only, I saw that day, a little girl—my mother began to make sense to me, her fear sinking into my chest like so many pine boards. Her fear was clear to me, suddenly, like the change in weather from the day of the funeral to that day with the plane. The day of the funeral the snow was still coming down, and the handful of flowers I tossed onto the casket sent the snow-flakes that had gathered there up and away like white ash in a light breeze. Now all that snow had melted, the sky open and clean.

She was right to fear, I thought, and I moved from the circle of kids still playing dodgeball to the chain-link fence encircling the playground. Her life came to me then, and pieces of it seemed to fit somehow: her own father had died, I knew, when she was only four. It had been in the spring, I remembered my mother telling me one time, and he and some friends had gone up to Sunderland for the first swim of the year in the Connecticut. He'd climbed a low-hanging tree just north of the bridge up there, and dived in head first, breaking his neck on a submerged log that hadn't been there the year before. So there was that loss, that vacancy with which to begin her life. When she had been a senior in high school— two weeks, in fact, before she was to graduate—her mother had been found to have cancer. Before summer was over she had died in a hospital room in Springfield, having lost fifty-six pounds—that number important enough to my mother to have been passed on to me—and leaving my mother to the care of an aunt and uncle in Newton. She moved to a town she'd been to only once before, a town at the other end of the state, where she knew no one, loved no one.

This was my mother's history, the only facts I knew that day, only a sketch, but one that made fear fill up in me. Accidents, I thought, are real and will happen. That was why the word had been created, a label for this unforseeable yet inevitable factor of life. And my life, I had seen, would be filled with them; my father had disappeared, and there was no one to protect me from them. My stomach seemed to tumble, and I was dizzy a moment, closed my eyes, leaned on the chain-link fence at my face. My father was gone, and I had been playing a child's game when I ought to have been waiting for yet another accident to occur. He was gone, and the sounds he made— the crack of the stairs as he went down them and to work each morning, the engine turning over in the garage and the crunch of tire against gravel as he backed out of the driveway, him stomping snow off his shoes on the porch outside the door at the end of a

day—would never come back, sounds simply gone from the face of
the earth.

I opened my eyes then, and the world was made of ugly colors
and shook in my tears. I put the back of one hand to my face, tried
to block tears from leaving my eyes while my stomach still twisted,
and I remembered his voice. But it was more than that, more than
memory: I *heard* him, as if he were just behind me to my left. I
heard him say *This is Claire Shaw,* and was astounded at how solid
his voice became inside me. I took in a breath and quickly turned,
expecting, *knowing* he was there. But he was not. There were only
kids, like me, playing a game that involved moving, moving from a
hurled object that, if you weren't quick enough or weren't paying
attention, might harm you. Only kids, and their own sounds in the
world: laughter, yells, running. Sounds I made. Things I did.

This is Claire Shaw I heard again, this time a whisper, warm in
my ear, my father there with me; and I decided then, only a little
girl, that I would not let fear consume me, not let it kill me as it
had all but done to my mother. Though he hadn't spoken to me
since that time, I listened, listened to this day. And I had lived.

 Tom and I said nothing on the way out to Chesterfield, through Haydenville and on past the lumbermill, Route 9 now narrow and twisting along the bank of the Mill River, water this time of year only deep enough to glaze the rocks across the bed. In Williamsburg we passed the General Store, the parking lot packed with cars. I wanted to tell Tom to pull into the gravel lot behind the place and let us go in, have a look around, but I said nothing. We were moving, driving somewhere, the earth turning beneath us, and for that I was thankful. We were going to what could be our house, I thought. A home, our own, and I settled back in the seat.

Outside Williamsburg we turned onto 43 and headed south, the road bordered now with trees, and for the first time I saw the changes in colors that had already come about, the hardwood trees giving up the green for autumn. The color usually started at the tops of trees, off to one side in a certain spot, where a single branch would be filled with yellow- and orange-edged leaves, a sprinkle of color that made you see the shape of the tree, shape you'd taken for granted since the trees had filled out with new leaves last spring. The farther out we got, too, the more trees had already begun the change until it seemed color was all around, not yet the cascades of red and orange and russet and yellow, but the hints, the edges, that let you know things were about to move into fall.

Chesterfield itself sat up on a hill, one of the first at the edge of the Berkshires; houses, some old, some not so old, sat along both sides of the highway. There was a church, and a gas station, a

market and post office, all the lawns neatly trimmed, some clapboard
sidings brown and weatherbeaten, others in clean, white lines and
angles, still others shingled over.

It was a beautiful, small town, and as we passed through it I could
see us stopping for gas and talking to the owner of the station, going
to the post office for Christmas stamps, stopping in the market for
milk on the way home. I could live here.

The road fell down toward the gorge, and from the crest, just
beyond the main strip of town, I could see the Berkshires before
us, and the colors etched into the green, here and there a stark
bush already gone red, the whole upper half of a maple given over
to orange.

I looked at Tom. He looked at me. He smiled.

"What do you think?" he said. He looked back at the road. He
was still smiling.

I said, "I can see us here."

He said nothing, put the car into low gear, and we moved down
into the valley, fields below us to the left, to the right those trees.
On both sides of the road ran old stone fences, rocks fallen over
here and there, but for the most part neat and sturdy. I wondered
how many days those walls had seen, how many sunsets and snow-
falls and thunderstorms and summer afternoons, and how many
anonymous cars just like ours had driven past them day after day
while they just waited for a shift in the stones, the giving way of
earth from rains and melting ice to make those breaks in the line
where stones had fallen back to the ground, back to where they
came from in the first place.

I could feel the engine running hard, feel the pull of the brakes
as we headed to the bottom of the valley, and then we crossed the
bridge, the stream only boulders and rocks outlined with slow-
moving water. On the other side of the stream two hills shot up,
the road going between them, following another stream, this one
to the right, on my side. Three or four houses were on this side,
some kept up, others a little shabby, but houses all the same.

I said, "Our future neighbors."

Tom said, "Don't jump the gun. We're just up here to look."

We were almost there; the drive up didn't seem half as long as
it had Thursday night, but then things had been different: the end

of a workday, the setting sun shining in our eyes as we headed down here, other cars of other commuters to contend with.

The houses stopped. We went another quarter mile or so along that stream, and took the dirt road off to the left. Slowly we drove another hundred yards back in, and we were there.

He turned off the ignition, and we sat in the car, just looking.

It was a different house now, here in daylight, the sun straight above us, no shadows to hide things, give darkness to detail.

A porch sat in front of the house, a makeshift thing, just two-by-fours and planks nailed together, two wooden steps leading up to it, no railing. Just a platform under which could live any number of small animals. The roof was covered with asphalt shingles, and looked strong enough. At least the roofline seemed straight. The chimney, though, needed some reworking, and I wondered how much that might cost, a few of the bricks at the rim looking as if they might fall off any second now.

"The porch will have to go right off," Tom said. "And we'll put up a new one. Probably in the spring. But I'd tear that thing off right now, if I thought we could get away with it."

I said, "But that would be jumping the gun."

Tom turned to me, and smiled. We kissed.

He pulled the keys out of the ignition, popped open his door. I was still sitting, looking; the cool gust of air from outside filled the car. He closed the door.

I climbed out. My left arm was still useless, and gingerly, steadily, I held it next to my abdomen, pushed shut the door with my hip.

The house had been painted an ugly sky blue years ago, the paint on the clapboard bubbled, chipped, in some places nonexistent; you could see the gray wood in patches across the front of the house.

I said, "The house has age spots. Those unsightly liver spots."

He laughed, and we moved to the front of the car. He put his arm up and I came to him, leaned against him with his arm around my shoulders. We took a couple of steps toward the house, but Tom stopped. He stood still, and I felt his body stiffen.

"Shit," he said.

I looked up at him. His arm was still around me. "What?"

"The keys," he whispered. "I forgot the keys. I forgot to go to the realtor's and pick up the stupid keys. Shit."

We were quiet, the two of us staring at the house, the engine ticking, a breeze high in the trees behind the house.

"Well," I said, and broke the quiet.

Tom looked down at his feet, then back to the house. He took his arm from around me, put both hands in his pockets. His shoulders sank as he moved toward the porch. He went up the two steps, those boards, it seemed, ready to break under his weight.

I followed him. Our footsteps on the planks of the porch were hollow, loud.

Tom had his hand at the door. The door, too, was scarred with bubbled and broken paint, and had nail holes in the wood where, I imagined, someone had once put a knocker or hung bunches of Indian corn. The exposed wood of the door was just as gray as anywhere else, and I was already starting to picture what we would do: how the front door would be scraped of its paint; the exposed wood stained; this porch, if I could talk Tom into it, kept, reinforced and replanked, a railing put on, maybe a roof put up over it so that we could sit out here on days like this and eat lunch or dinner, watch fireflies come out in the summer. There was so much I wanted to do, and I even envisioned a dried grapevine wreath from the General Store on the front door, some final, simple touch that would turn this Handyman's Dream into our home, regardless of the fact we would have no children to fill it, bring it alive with hope and care.

I wanted to go inside, too, to see what the place looked like in daylight, to see exactly where things would start, with exactly which room we would begin to rebuild. I wanted to see my room, that room upstairs.

Tom tried the doorknob. Nothing happened, and I walked to the left down the porch to one of the windows off the large front room.

Again my footsteps were hollow and heavy on the planks, and as I leaned toward the window, thinking of how loud my steps were, I thought I caught a glimpse of a shadow, movement out of the front room and into the kitchen.

I swallowed quickly, then looked again. Both the front room and kitchen were filled with light, but nothing was in there, only the floors, the doorway into the kitchen, that same dark, cheap paneling on the walls. It had been only my imagination, I knew, remnants of the dream last night still playing through my head. I took a deep breath, cupped my hands to the window, and peered in.

And then there was a face, right there, not an inch from mine, its eyes bloodshot, open wide, the mouth open, chin drawn back, and I screamed, staggered back and away from the window, still looking at that face, one I hadn't imagined. It was there.

It was a man, I could see now, gray hair thinning at the top and slicked back, his teeth white and horribly perfect, his mouth wide open. He was staring at me, his eyebrows up, his forehead wrinkled, but for all his expression his face was still blank somehow, and in that instant, I knew it was in his eyes, somehow dead, gray-green and dull, and this emptiness, I knew, was what frightened me most, what would stay with me.

Tom turned to me as soon as I screamed, but seemed frozen where he stood. I could not see his face—my eyes were still fixed upon the face in the window—but then the front door swung open, Tom, too, startled and flinching as if the open door were a fist coming at him.

Another man stepped out of the open door. My adrenalin was flying, the pulse banging in my bandaged hand, feeling as if the blood would spurt up through the threads, fill the dressing.

I looked to the man, saw that he was only a teenager, could have, in fact, been one of the undergrads I saw everyday: his hair was black and flat, and he had thick, black eyebrows, his skin pale and acne-scarred. He had on a white T-shirt and jeans, and stood dusting off his hands. He was grinning at us.

I looked at the window, but the older man was gone.

The teenager finished dusting off his hands, then put them on his hips. He was still grinning. He said, "What can I do you for?" He shook his head to get the hair out of his eyes, the sharpness and quickness of the move showing me he'd done it a million times. He reached up and tucked a lock of that black hair behind one ear.

Tom looked at me. I was still breathing hard. "Uhmm," he said as he looked to the teenager, then to me. He reached up and put his hand to the back of his neck. He said, "We, uh," and paused. He took a breath. "We're looking at the place, actually. Rita Longford sent us up here. The realtor?"

Tom looked at the boy, waited for some show of recognition, but nothing changed about him. He only grinned. I brought my hand down, took in two shallow breaths. I looked back in the window. There in the glass I could see only my reflection, and the trees behind me, so that it looked as if I were inside that empty house looking out at me, here on the porch, looking in.

I closed my eyes, took in one more breath, then opened them.

The boy had crossed his arms, and had stopped smiling. Finally he said, "Oh. In town." He looked at his feet. His hair fell from behind his ear and down into his face again. "You going to buy the place?"

By this time Tom had gotten himself together. He had his hands in his pockets, his feet spread. "Who are you?" he said.

The boy looked up. "Why? I should be asking you. You're the one who was jimmying the door." His arms were still crossed.

"Look," I said, and took a step toward Tom. I heard my footsteps again across the wood. "We're up here looking at the place. That's all. We might buy it. You scared us. Who are you?"

He looked at me as if he hadn't seen me before that moment, as if I hadn't existed before I spoke. His jaw was set, hands in fists beneath his crossed arms, his eyes taking me in. Then he smiled. He dusted off his hands once more, put out a hand to Tom.

"I'm Grady," he said. "My grandfather owns the place. He's the one who's selling it."

Tom, hesitant, paused a moment before he brought a hand from his pocket and shook with him. Grady put out his hand to me, and I took it in mine. He placed his other hand over the two of ours, said, "So pleased to meet you," and I could see his affected air, the forced adulthood. He was acting.

Tom said, "We got all the way out here from town to find out we'd forgotten to get the key from the realtor, from Rita." He put his hands on his hips. He'd never used that name before, never called her Rita. It had always been That Realtor. Tom, I saw then, was acting, too.

I wondered about the older man, that face. I said, "Is there some-one else in there? I saw someone in the window." I tried to smile. "That was why I screamed in the first place, actually."

Grady took one small step backward. "Oh," he said, and put his hands in his back pockets. He was a child suddenly, having lost his adulthood in just that moment. He kicked at nothing with the toe of his tennis shoe. "That," he said. "That was Martin. He's a friend of mine, Martin." He turned around, called into the house, "Martin, come on out."

There was silence then. Even insects in the trees seemed to shut down. The door stood open a foot or so, behind it darkness, and a head appeared, that same head, that same hair and eyes and chin. Martin moved from inside onto the porch.

He was tall, over six feet, and wore an old, long-sleeved khaki shirt, brown slacks with blue suspenders, the pants hitched up above his waist. He must have been in his fifties, the skin beneath his chin beginning to crease and wrinkle. He stood just past the threshold, and held in his hands a rag, what looked like a piece of old bedsheet. He twisted the rag, let it go, twisted it again. It was a practiced motion, something, I could see, that had evolved into a nervous habit over years. His feet were close together, the toes pointed out too far, and his shoulders were rounded, his neck and head that much more prominent. He didn't look at us, but at some invisible point a few feet before him on the wooden deck.

Grady cleared his throat, and smiled. He said, "This here's Martin. An old family friend." He went the few feet to Martin, put his hand to Martin's shoulder, clapped him a couple of times. Martin smiled, and I could see his white, white teeth, his smile wandering into a grin, and still there was no emotion behind his eyes, nothing that might invest in his face some life.

"He comes up here with me," Grady went on, and now he was the adult again, "the three times a year we're here to clean. This is that weekend, too. Quite a coincidence, you two heading down here today of all days." He was still holding Martin's shoulder. He looked at Tom, then me, then Tom again. "The perfect weekend, too. Tonight we'll get a fire going in the fireplace here, make us some dinner." He turned to Martin. "Ol' Martin here makes a mean roast beef hash and eggs, don't you, Martin?"

Martin hadn't stopped twisting the rag, hadn't lost the smile. He said, "Hash out of the can, yep," and gave a little laugh and a quick nod, still looking at the ground. He shrugged.

It was no surprise when Grady said, "Martin here's been out of the hospital now for six years. He's been up here with me to help

clean up the place three times a year for as long as he's been out.
Except, of course, when I was out in sunny California. He's a damn
fine worker, too. Does the windows so's you'll think he's gone and
taken the panes out, they'll be so clean."

Martin shrugged twice, nodded.

"So," Tom said. He looked at me. He, too, was smiling. "Can we
take a look around?"

Upstairs the rooms were filled with light, more light than I could
have imagined in a house with only two windows on the whole
second floor, one window at either end of the house. But still there
was light, and the view was tremendous: from our bedroom I could
see far back into the trees, the land rising up into the hill behind
the house; to the right was the road leading up to the place. From
the other upstairs room, the room that would be mine, I could
see the barn a hundred yards away, black wood shrouded by trees
and bushes.

Grady had led us through the house in a sort of tour, stopping to
show us precisely how sturdy the floors were by stomping them
with his shoe, and by stooping and reaching far back into a cupboard
in the kitchen to knock hard on the wood at the very back to show
us how solid that was, too. He also pointed out things that needed
extra work: the loose bricks of the hearth, six or seven of them just
set in place with no mortar; the hinges on the door from the kitchen
into the pantry and how they were pulled out of the door frame;
the soggy wood beneath the pipes under the bathroom sink. Things
only he would know about, only he would point out. Not what a
realtor would do.

All the while Martin was behind us, following us from room to
room. I'd positioned myself between Grady and Tom, though I knew
there wasn't anything to be afraid of. At least that was what I let
myself think, but still there I was between the two men, still afraid.

He kept back a few feet, too, every time we stopped, sometimes
not even coming into the room, instead standing back in the windowless pantry as we examined the linoleum in the kitchen, or
staying on the last step up before my room upstairs.

It was in my room that I'd begun to feel most at home here, and

I knew then some of the joy Tom must have felt the other night when he had smiled at his own room downstairs. This was my room, only half as big as the bedroom, the slanted ceiling cutting into the space, but still mine. There was work to be done, certainly, and I knew precisely where I would start: the walls, like the front room downstairs, had been covered over in cheap plastic paneling, here a dull gray instead of the brown downstairs. The paneling would go down first, and I would be able to see what I had to work with, see what was beneath, if it were more of that faded wallpaper downstairs, or just walls ready to be painted. White, I decided then, was the color I wanted.

Tom and Grady were talking, but I heard nothing, only looked out the window, at the trees, the barn. I could have taken a picture, the view seemed so perfect, and I decided I would do that next time we were up here: take pictures to show to Sandra and Paige and Wendy and Will.

I turned from the window, and my eyes fixed on Martin. He stood just outside the door. He was looking at me, not at my eyes, but at my bandaged hand. He held his own hand, gently rubbed the same spot on his left hand where the dressing was on mine. His mouth was drawn up, his eyes squinted as if he, too, felt the pain.

Then he saw me, quickly brought his hands down, put them behind him. He turned and moved down the stairs.

I touched my hand, felt the dressing. I turned to Tom and Grady.

"I don't know why," Grady was saying. "I didn't even know the place was up for sale myself until two weeks ago. That was when I heard. He's in town, you know, my grandfather. Over at the Maplewood Home."

"Whatever the reason it's for sale," Tom said, "we like it. But I want to know why he wants to get rid of it."

Grady frowned, gave a shrug. "But my offer still stands," he said. "Martin and me'll be glad to help you out with whatever you need. You just let us know." He turned and looked around the room, and for a moment he looked startled. He swallowed, called out, "Martin?"

"He's downstairs," I said, and moved to Tom. I looped my arm through his, and leaned on him.

Grady looked out the doorway, again called, "Martin?"

"Yes," came his voice, deep and stilted and hollow through the house, his throat, it seemed, constricted with the strain of just one word.

"You okay?"

"Okay," he called back.

Grady smiled at us. "Just have to let him know he's not alone. That's what he hates. Sometimes we'll be in here at opposite ends of the house, and, well, I'll—" He stopped and sniffed, rubbed his nose. Just a boy. "I'll think I'm hearing things or something, and I'll listen, and it'll be him in the room he's working in. I'll go in there, and he'll be sitting in the middle of the room and facing the wall, and he'll be crying." He gave a tentative smile, a quick shrug. "So, I got to check on him."

The room was silent a few moments, and I said, "So the place is your grandfather's. Are your parents in town?"

"Oh," he said, and he was turning, heading for the door. "They're out in California. They moved out there three years ago. I stayed with them a year and a half, then came back here. Too much sand and surf. Too many good-looking girls." He was at the threshold, and looked back at us, smiling. He gave a wink, another practiced adult move, and he was moving down the stairs.

I went next, down the stairs that met with the ones from the bedroom, then, with no banisters, down into the entryway. Tom was right: until they were fixed, the stairs would take practice.

Grady was already standing behind Martin when we got to the bottom. Martin had the rag and a bottle of vinegar, and was rubbing hard on the glass of the window. Grady had been right: the window, unlike the last time I had stood there looking out at the woods, was spotless, as if there really wasn't any glass.

"Look at that," Grady said, turning to us. "Work of art."

Tom said, "It looks great in here, Martin." He'd said it too loud, as if Martin were hard of hearing or spoke a foreign language.

"Beautiful," I said, and I too had spoken too loud, the sound of my voice ringing through the room.

Without stopping with the rag, he looked at us, his face all smiles, his eyebrows up, his eyes open wide. "Thank you," he said, his voice this time higher-pitched, the throat even tighter, perhaps, with the job at hand, and how much he enjoyed it, and how well he did it.

He turned back to the window, dipped the bottle onto the rag, went at the glass.

Tom nudged me, and said, "Let's check out the barn."

For an instant I was sorry he'd said that out loud, had hoped he would have whispered it to me, because now I knew Grady would accompany us out there. I wanted to be with Tom, to walk with him, consider alone for a few moments this place and the prospect of our buying it.

But as soon as Tom had spoken, Grady looked down at his feet, sniffed, and went to the bottle of vinegar next to Martin. He pulled from his back pocket a rag just like Martin's, an old piece of white sheet, and then picked up the bottle, tipped it into the rag. He was all movement, all action, all business as he took three big steps to the window nearest him. He started rubbing a pane.

Martin had stopped his rubbing. He sat still, the rag at the glass in midswirl, frozen. He was looking at the window, his back to us, and Grady said, "Martin, let's pick it up." Grady paused. "They're just going out to the barn," he said.

Martin was still for a few moments more, and then slowly he started rubbing, the circle he made growing in size as his hand moved faster until, finally, he was at full speed, just as he had been before Tom had made mention of the barn.

We left them there. I was puzzled at first, wondered why so abruptly Grady had decided to get back to work, but I was relieved, glad he wouldn't be back in that dark barn pointing out to us broken beams and rusted hinges.

The trail back to the barn was only wide enough for Tom and me to walk it side by side, my arm in his. The grass along the path was still green, the leaves of trees bordering it dull and crisp, about to change over. The barn itself was just large enough to fit two cars and perhaps some sort of workbench for Tom, and was built of black boards, a few shingles broken out, the sun filtering down and in, leaving traces, small slips of light filled with the shadows of leaves here and there on the ground.

It was cold in the middle of the barn, my arm still in Tom's, and I was looking up into the rafters, just looking, imagining in that cold someone here with a hammer and saw building this thing maybe a hundred years ago. I imagined it being put together, the

sweet smell of new wood in the air, the ringing through these woods
of hammer against nail, the roof not yet up so that the inside was
filled with September light.

Tom said, "Maybe next summer we'll get to this. After the house
is done and spring comes around."

I looked from the rafters, from that empty space up there, to him.
His eyes were looking up to where mine had been.

I said nothing, only pulled his arm a little closer to me, and as if
that were a prearranged signal between us, we both turned and
headed out of the dark into shadows thrown by the sun through
trees.

We stood with both car doors open, looking at the house one final
time. Grady, up on the porch, his hands still on his hips, said, "We'll
have this place spotless. Tomorrow we'll leave this place and it'll be
cleaner than it even needs to be."

Tom waved, said, "So how do I get in touch with you if you want
to give us a hand fixing up the place?"

Grady shrugged again, and for a moment, a flash, I saw in his
movement Martin's shrug, the hint of it somehow: the quickness,
the tilt of the head, and I wondered precisely how long he'd known
Martin. I wondered if that gesture were something Grady had given
Martin, or if it had been the other way around.

"I work at the Friendly's in Florence most nights. Come on down
there and we'll talk something out." He had a hand up and was
waving now.

"Fine," Tom said, and climbed in.

"Good-bye," I said, and waved with my good hand. I started to
get into the car, but saw Martin in the window behind Grady. He
was waving the rag at me, smiling.

"So long, Martin," I said, and the rag bobbed even more furiously
in the window.

Just before the bridge back to Chesterfield was a small brown-and-white sign that read CHESTER-FIELD GORGE with an arrow pointing to the right, and Tom pulled off, headed back on the old paved road. It was something he did often enough on days when we had nothing to do: just pull off, wander down any road to find what was at the end. In the early days—those days when we'd thought we were making a child, those days that seemed so long ago and so charged with anticipation, with expectation, when any sign of nausea on my part would signal some silent jubilation within both of us, until the next week or so when the blood would show up in my underpants like some sign of cancer—in those days Tom always asked if I wanted to turn down this road or that, and I always told him Yes, go ahead. It was a small ritual between us, merely something to do: ask, answer, go.

The things we found back then, too, amazed us. Once, up on the Mohawk Trail, we'd turned off and found Shelburne Falls, a town with magnificent waterfalls and the Bridge of Flowers, a bridge of concrete arches over the water and set about with flowering plants. The bridge was something both of us had heard about all our lives, but which we had never seen, and that particular day, a bright day in April, we felt as if the bridge and waterfalls had never existed before the moment we rolled down into town, drove along the main street, stopped and looked at the arches over the water.

Another turn another day had taken us to an old covered bridge, the road we'd turned onto dead-ending there. Huge boulders had been rolled onto the roadway at both ends of the bridge, signs posted warning that the bridge was unsafe for cars. We parked, walked across it, stopping to watch through gaps between planks the water pass beneath us and weave its way around the rocks down there.

These were our discoveries, places and things we felt were our own, and what had made these findings more our own had been that asking by Tom, his never assuming we could turn off, and my never saying no, an unspoken agreement between us.

Then the first time we had gone out for a drive after the doctor had told us we would have no children, Tom had simply turned off without asking. We were out beyond the Quabbin Reservoir, and he had slowed down, turned right onto an unnamed asphalt road, and driven on. I said nothing.

The Wednesday before, Tom and I had gone to the doctor's for what the doctor had called "an important consultation." We had sat in his office in Northampton, the office plush and warm, a lighted globe in one corner, the walls covered with dark oak paneling, book-shelves crammed with impressive books, everything from Plato to Dickens to Plath.

This was long after insurance had stopped paying for our trying to have children, long after we had had to pay for Tom's semen analyses, for the fertility drugs, for the laparoscopy I'd had and the hysterosalpingogram we'd had done at the same time, the dye in-jected into my uterus leading up through blind alleys and into dead ends. This Important Consultation, too, was after eight consecutive months of artificial insemination there in the doctor's office, my feet in cold metal stirrups, Tom's semen applied by the doctor. On those days when my temperature crept up almost imperceptibly I could not have felt farther away from my husband, his semen on the end of a surgical tool, Tom in another room, waiting. The last three times I had cried while in the chair, my legs spread for the doctor, for conception; cried while looking up at the acoustic ceiling, at the cold room, at fluorescent lights. I had cried, but we wanted a child, wanted to make our own so badly that we'd nearly finished off the money we'd saved waiting those four years. Our money was nearly gone, money we'd saved in order to have a start.

The doctor positioned himself in his leather chair, placed his hands on top of the desk, the same hands, I remember thinking, with which he tried to force my body to conceive. He laced the fingers together, smiled, and explained how there was no reason he could pinpoint, that we might as well stop trying, that adoption was always an option.

Adoption. Adoption was something we'd talked about long enough, not seriously at first, but as we neared this endpoint in our lives, a point we both pretended would not come, the idea figured larger and larger in our minds. But at the same time our money was disappearing. Who knew how much money adoption would take? Who knew how many years of our lives the process would eat up?

And the child would not have been created by us. I knew how small this made us seem; enough children needed parents who would give them the love we had to give. But our own child was what we wanted, a child in whose body coursed blood part mine, part Tom's. If we could not have that, we wanted nothing. My parents were dead, and I had no brothers or sisters. My family would end with me. Tom had only one brother, a man seventeen years older than himself, a lawyer living in Lowell and working for Wang, a man from whom we received Christmas cards, and nothing else. Tom's parents, too, were dead, ancient, he had told me enough times, even when he was born, parents too old and too tired of their own lives to give him much more than an allowance and a place to eat and sleep, his brother already out of college and married by the time Tom could begin to remember things. At stake for both of us were our lives. There was no one left beyond the two of us.

The doctor, seeing no reaction from us to what I knew he thought were kindly words, smiled again, unlaced his fingers, and put his hands out to his sides. He shrugged, smiling.

Tom, seated next to me on the leather couch, slowly took off his glasses and brought from his back pocket a handkerchief. He started to clean his glasses, this time his movement, the swirling of the cloth on the lenses, unsure and slow. If his hand with the handkerchief had paused a moment, I felt certain I would have seen the fingers shake with some fear, something dying in him right there in the doctor's office.

He hadn't looked at me or the doctor, his eyes instead on something outside the window, though I knew he saw nothing out there, only blurred shapes. Then he stood, walked around the sofa, and left the room. He hadn't put his glasses back on.

I could feel my tears already coming as the doctor and I both stood. He'd put his hand out to me, said he was sorry, but I did nothing, only walked out, the door closing silently behind me.

The next Saturday was the first day he pulled off without asking me, and after a few minutes of following the nameless road through trees, I could see off in the distance a huge abandoned barn, boards broken out, bushes waist high all around. Unlike the barn in Chesterfield, this one sat next to the road, behind it a huge field of nothing, only more brush. The barn looked as if it would fall down right then, tumble with the small push of wind created by any passing car.

But the roof, you could see, was still strong, still sturdy. It was made of slate, and as we approached the barn I could make out a design in the shingles. In the center of the field of gray was a large diamond of tan slate; inside that diamond was another of red slate, and finally, in the red diamond was an even smaller one, this one of the same dark gray. The three diamonds seemed to float on the gray slate roof, each one perfectly shaped, no shingles missing anywhere. Someone had built that roof right, I remember thinking. Someone had worked hard enough and meticulously enough to make a roof that would stand forever, if only the foundation—the barn itself—didn't fall.

Tom slowed down as we neared the barn, stopped the car when we were next to it. He got out.

I stayed in the car and watched as he made his way through the brush to the barn entrance. Once there he looked up into the rafters, into the darkness, the black wood. Above the doorway was an old hex sign, the round painting only faded reds and yellows and blues.

He was looking up, his back to me. He had on a red sport shirt, and his khakis, and a brown belt. I watched him, and then his shoulders began to heave, to shake with crying, his lifeless hands quivering at his sides, his head back.

I opened my door, and went to him. I pushed back bushes and

weeds, felt them scratch against my bare legs, but I made it to him, and I put my arms around his waist from behind, locked my hands together in front of him. He lifted his hands to mine, and we both cried, my face pressed to his back.

A few minutes later I looked up over his shoulder to see what it was he had looked at. Of course there was nothing up there, only the darkened peaks of a dead barn. More than enough.

Since then he had never asked if he could pull out onto an unknown road, but only did it. We still drove, still made discoveries, but the air was no longer filled with the joy of waiting. We drove, but I knew that that ritual having died was not any sort of deterioration of our love, of our marriage. It was only a settling in, a shifting of earth to more stable circumstances, the inexorable progress of love.

We drove along the road toward Chesterfield Gorge and past the dirt parking lot for the recreation area. We kept moving, the road becoming rougher and rougher, passing homes here and there, more old stone fences, the road shrouded with trees, open to a meadow to the right or left, shrouded again. Then we came out on another meadow, and Tom stopped the car, left the engine running.

He turned to me, the keys dangling from the ignition, the sun slanting down into the car and catching the metal pieces so that they reflected light into my eyes. I put my hand up to block the light, moved my head an inch or so, and the light was gone.

He said, "We really need to talk. Because I think I want that place."

I put my hands in my lap. The bandaged one seemed paler, and I thought of Martin watching me, me watching him.

I said, "Will it come furnished with Grady and Martin?"

"Optional equipment," he said. "But I wouldn't mind their help, if they really want to give it. We'll pay them a little money, have them help clear the lot around the house, maybe help with some painting or something." He was looking at my hands now, too, just staring.

"I love the extra room up there," I said. "It's perfect. It'll be my room for whatever it is I want." I paused a moment, and for no reason at all, just because it was what I was thinking of and because I wanted to hear my voice in the car, I said, "You know, that would have been the room for one of—"

"Don't," Tom cut in, and reached up a hand, not to strike me, but, I imagined, to fend off words. He held his hand in midair, then let it drop, let it hit the hard, blue plastic of the console between our seats. "Don't," he said again. "Why did you say that? Why did you have to say that?" He was quiet, and slowly he moved both hands to the steering wheel, held on. "You only know," he said, "that that's what I'm thinking. What we're both thinking of. Don't you go around thinking you're the only one of us who thinks about that."

"I was just talking out loud," I said. I tried to move the fingers of the bad hand, the very tips barely waving in slow motion. "Just words."

He looked up at me quickly, ready to say something to me. I knew it would be about words, about their nature, their ability to do more than any single act a man or woman could think of. He had given me that talk before; words were what he worked with, what he knew. He knew they lied, too, more than anything else, and for me to say *Just words* was a lie, because they were not only words, but something else. A life we would not know, human beings we would not create. Our house, that one behind us at the base of the hill where at this moment worked a boy and a retarded man, would, in the end, only have the two of us, and would only be filled with the words between us. Just us two.

He closed his eyes, took a long breath.

He looked at me. He said, "But the house?" and we were, I hoped, beyond the moment, beyond the lie of my words.

I leaned over to him. I put my arms around his neck, and said, "I already told you." I closed my eyes, remembered the view from my room. I lay my head on his chest, felt his chin touch the top of my head. I said, "I can see us there."

OCTOBER

We sat in the no-smoking section, but in a restaurant this small, the Friendly's Grady told us he
worked at, that distinction didn't really matter: there were only three
banks of booths running lengthwise, the room only some fifty feet
deep. Smoke from other tables would find us.

Tom leaned toward me, said, "He told me when we were out there
that he didn't know why. But all I'm doing is asking. That's all. And
I'm just trying to find out if he really wants to work out there with
us." He paused. "I just don't know if I trust him or not."

I said nothing. We'd had this conversation too many times, Tom
wondering out loud exactly *why* the owner, Mr. Clark, was getting
rid of the place. We could get no straight answer. Clark, just as
Grady had said, was living in Maplewood Home, a rest home just
outside of town on Route 9. It was a big old place, ugly yellow with
turrets and spires and dormers and screened porches, a place that
had at one time, we were told, been the home of the onion baron
of the Pioneer Valley back in the 1890s. But now it housed only old
folks, and was a private place, as private as you could get and still be
minutes from town. Though the house was set only a few yards back
from the street, it was surrounded with black wrought-iron fences
and had a security guardhouse at the base of the driveway. The
guardhouse, merely a shack painted the same color as the house,
was manned day and night. So far, we hadn't been able to speak with
Clark; all communications had been through Rita and the owner's
lawyer, a Mr. Blaisdell. The lawyer had virtually guaranteed, there
was no structural damage. We were buying the house as is.

I looked around, wondering if Grady were even working tonight. We'd come right over from work, Tom still in his tie, me still smelling of rabbit. But then I always did.

"Who are we going to trust?" I said. "We can't get a word out of Clark. Or Blaisdell. Grady's the only one who knows anything about the place. I trust him."

He leaned even closer. Still I wasn't looking at him, but at the cook station, at the metal door back into the dishwashing room, at the cash register. He said, "You don't even know him. You don't."

The metal door swung open, and there stood Martin, his hair still slicked back, his eyebrows straining high above his eyes. He had on the blue-checked polyester shirt the men here wore, the little name plate with the red Dymo sticker on it pinned to his chest. He was carrying a plastic bin filled with plates, his lips parted, teeth clenched. Quickly he walked from the doorway to behind the wood panels that hid the cook station and ice cream freezers, his head above the panels. All I could see was his profile, his high forehead, the sweat that glistened there. He made it to the end of the freezers, disappeared below the panels, and I heard the bin of plates slide into a cupboard of some sort back there, heard the bin hit the back wall with a metallic thud. His head popped up above the panels, and he weaved his way back between waiters and waitresses, pushed the metal door open, and disappeared back into the steam and bright lights and kitchen sounds.

I turned to Tom. His eyes were still on the door. I said, "Did you—"

"Yes," he said without letting me finish. He turned to me. "I guess I shouldn't be surprised, really." He put one hand on the tabletop, drew an imaginary circle, tapped the center of it.

I looked back to the door, and remembered once more him staring at my hand. Without looking I touched the spot where the dressing had been a month before, felt the little raised slits of flesh, felt, I imagined, the red color of that scar. Touching the skin made it almost tickle, and I stopped, flexed the fingers. Though they were still tight, the flesh between thumb and forefinger a little tender, they were limber enough to begin surgery the next day, and I thought of putting Chesterfield, soft, white Chesterfield, into the Gormezano box, placing him on the surgery table, lining up the stereotaxic frame, and the work that would begin. I swallowed, caught a breath, because it was just as it had always been: a mistake to have named the first rabbit.

Rabbit running had been canceled until I came back the Tuesday after I'd been bitten. I'd needed the extra day, that Monday, just to sit in the empty apartment, Tom at work. I needed to sit and watch television and read magazines and sleep.

Tuesday morning, though, I had gotten right back to business. I wanted to go in there and do what I had to do, not let any fear settle in me. But Will and Sandra and Paige and Wendy insisted on asking me again and again how I was. I only smiled as best I could, afraid to tell them I just wanted to be left alone, to do my work. To get these rabbits run.

Finally I went down to the basement, closed my eyes a moment, and pushed open the heavy door into the Green Room.

There sat Chesterfield at his cage door, his nose going again, ears straight up.

My eyes next went to Large #2's former cage, where a new rabbit sat. Mr. Gadsen had already been in to cover himself.

I crossed the room, and saw atop the cages a brand new pair of canvas gloves. I picked them up, the material stiff and white and coarse. Pinned to the left glove was a scrap of old notebook paper torn from a three-ring binder. On the piece of paper was written:

> Dear Miss Claire —
>
> These are for you. I am sorry.
> You will have to forgive me.
>
> yours with deepest sorry —
>
> Mr. Gadsen

I crumpled up the note in my good hand, threw it in the trash bin next to the cages.

I habituated them that day, the same work I'd intended to have

done the week before, and by Thursday I had them used to the dark
and to the tone, ready to be hooked up to the potentiometer. All the
rabbits had come through fine: a little irritation in a couple of the
rabbits' eyes, but no major problems. Only yesterday, Wednesday,
had Jack finally given the go-ahead for surgery, the rabbits' conditioned inhibitions at high enough of a percentage to warrant our
going into their brains.

I still hadn't called Mr. Gadsen, hadn't seen him, and didn't
intend to.

Someone placed two glasses of water before us on the table, and I
looked up.

It was Grady.

He was smiling, the order pad in one hand, the other holding his
pen, ready to write. "You ready to—" he said, and stopped. He got
a puzzled look on his face, his smile faltering a moment. I glanced
at Tom. He was looking at Grady, too.

"Wait a minute," Grady said, all smiles again. He put the pen
behind his ear, plugged back into that shiny black hair. "Now wait
a minute. I know you," he said. "I know you two." He put his hands
on his hips.

"Chesterfield," Tom said. "Your grandfather's place?"

"You shouldn't have told me," he said, and shook his head as if
he were going to scold him. He even pointed a finger at Tom, then
at me. "I would have guessed. I would have."

Tom and I smiled, looked at each other. "I don't doubt it," I said,
and Grady's smile grew until I could see most of his teeth: clean,
white. Not what I would have thought, for some reason.

He said, "So, what brings you out here?"

"Would you believe a Fribble?" Tom said, and gave a small laugh.
I smiled.

"I know better than that," he said. "You told me you two live in
town. You could get that at the Friendly's on King instead of coming
all the way out here." He was still grinning. "You two are up to
something else."

I said, "The jig is up."

He lost the smile for a moment, and I saw the kid in him again, the puzzled boy. He was practiced at the adult, but not proficient. He said, "Excuse me?"

"The jig is up," I said again. "That means the game is over. That you figured us out. You figured out we were lying to you." I folded my hands together in front of me on the table. I was looking up at him. Cigarette smoke from somewhere drifted into my lungs.

"Oh, oh," he said, and laughed. "It's Claire, right? That's your name."

"Right," I said. "Good memory."

"Not really." He shrugged. "It's Martin, actually. He's the one with the memory. He's the one who remembers everyone we've ever met. Seriously. He does." He turned to Tom. "And you're Tom, right?"

"Right again."

"We wanted to know if we could talk to you," I said. "About the house."

"You guys really buying it?" he said. He had quit smiling.

I looked at Tom. He said, "We put in the bid, your grandfather took it. Or at least his lawyer took it. We're just waiting for escrow to clear now." He paused and smiled at me. "I guess we are."

"So," he said, "sure we can talk, but—" With one hand he pulled the pen out of his hair, and half turned from us to point to the rear of the room. He turned back to us. "If you'll look back here to my right and behind me, ladies and gentlemen," he went on, "you'll see my manager. She's back there, as always, with Leo, one of Northampton's finest. If she sees us talking too much over here, she'll ride my butt the rest of the night and on into tomorrow, too."

I looked past him to the last booth. There sat the manager, a plump girl with a perfect tan, her golden hair up and in curls atop her head. She wore the white blouse female managers wore, hers too tight, straining against her breasts so that the seams in her bra were visible beneath the material of the blouse. Leo was sitting next to her in his dark blue uniform and black nylon jacket. He, too, was overweight, his neck thick, face puffy. He had a sundae in front of him, and was looking at it, laughing. The manager said something to him and took a drag off her cigarette.

"Real executive material," I said.

"Can't argue with that," Grady laughed. "Tell you what," he said. "We get off in twenty minutes. You want to, we can talk after that. We can shoot the breeze then."

I looked at Tom.

He said, "I don't mind, if you don't."

We ordered, and when Grady was gone to get us our coffees I looked back at the manager to see if she'd even noticed Grady at our table. She was still whispering things to Leo, her cigarette sucked down almost to the filter, the stub in her pouty mouth, and I knew she hadn't even seen him over here. He just wanted to get away from us, and I wondered what he would be able to tell us.

Then for some reason I glanced back at the metal door, and saw Martin there in the small, square window.

All I could see was his face, nothing else, filling the glass, looking at me. He turned and was gone, and I realized then that that was the reason I had looked to the window, what I had expected to see: a man who remembered names, remembered people. I wondered, too, if while he looked at me he were again touching his own hand, imagining on his own flesh a scar like mine. The same scar I was touching now, the adhesions mountains at my fingertips.

I took my hand away. I took a sip of water, let an ice chip slip into my mouth, and felt it melt, my tongue cold against the roof of my mouth once it was gone.

"What we wanted to know," Tom said, and I could see his breath out there in the parking lot, the small clouds illuminated by the little lamps on the side of Friendly's, "is why the heck now. I mean, why are they selling it now? After so many years. Sure, we're buying the thing, but this lawyer just won't tell us anything. We just want to know."

We were leaning against the trunk of our car, the metal cold on my bottom. Tom and I stood as close to each other as we could.

Grady stood a few feet off, his back to the restaurant and the lamps. I could barely make out his face, his shoulders up in the cold, one hand jammed deep into his pants pocket, the other holding a cigarette. He held it with his thumb and first three fingers, as if it were some little peashooter. I knew he imagined that was how adults did it. He looked away from us, took a deep drag off the cigarette, and held it. He didn't say anything.

I took in a breath, the air sharp and clear in my lungs. I said, "Is it something structural? Because we've had some people out to look at it, some experts, and—"

"What experts?" he said. He turned his head to me. "What did experts have to say about the place? What do they know about the place?" I couldn't see his face, but on his voice was an edge, not an assumed toughness, but real emotion: hate, I thought, or maybe fear.

He looked at his feet, shot out a breath. The cigarette hand was down at his side.

"I'm sorry," Grady said to the ground. Tom looked at me, and back to Grady, cleared his throat. I could feel my hands in my coat pockets begin to sweat.

"It's just that," Grady said, and looked straight up into the night. He shifted his weight from one foot to the other, just barely lifting one foot off the ground, placing it gently back on the pavement, lifting the other. "Just that, Jesus. That that's the house where my daddy grew up. The house where he was born. In that old house Martin and I go out to three times a year. And my grandfather, my grandfather never asked me about selling the house. He never even asked. That's what's wrong."

I could see now that his eyes were closed, and I lost him. I had no idea who he was, I saw, no idea of his age, where he lived, anything. Maybe Tom was right; maybe he was not to be trusted. For a moment I was frightened, felt the cold burn into my eyes, then remembered this boy, remembered he was only a person, that he had a father and a mother, must have had someplace to live.

I said, "Where do you live?" and my voice sounded small and fragile in the air. "What do your parents, your daddy, think of this? Selling the house. Have you heard anything from them?"

"Hah," Grady said, a loud, violent burst of air, a cloud shooting from inside him. He looked at the ground again, then at us. He took another drag. "My daddy. My daddy. He's dead, so he doesn't think much of this arrangement at all. He doesn't think anything of it, I imagine. He's dead. He died seven or eight years ago." He paused a moment, leaned his head a little to one side. He was still shifting his weight, gently rocking from side to side. "Nine years. That's it. Nine years ago. One tends to forget these things, you know. I was ten years old."

"Oh," I said. "I'm sorry."

Tom pulled his hand from his coat pocket, put it around me, and I leaned into him.

"Yeah, me too," Grady said. He was quiet a few moments, and said, "And my mother. There's a case. She's living out in California someplace. Some place named something Spanish. Mission del Mar or something. Jesus, she left about two months after my daddy died." He stopped, slowly shook his head. He let the cigarette drop in front of him. It hit the ground, and a few sparks floated up, disappeared. He stepped on the butt, moved his foot away, and the three of us stood looking at where the amber piece of light had been only a moment ago.

He took a deep breath, and put his free hand into his pocket. He shrugged. "That left me reared by my grandparents. My grandmother, well. My grandmother, she's dead, too. She was beautiful. She was a beautiful lady, and she loved me. She took care of me. But my grandfather. What an old fart." He paused. "We lived in town here, in this big old thing a few doors down from the coffin factory. You've seen that, right?"

He looked up at us a moment, and I nodded, though I'd only heard of the place, never actually seen it. Kids used to talk about it when I was in school, and would dare one another to ride bikes out here to Florence and past the place at midnight, but I'd never been one to take the dare.

"I was with them until about four years ago. That was when my grandma died. And that was when I figured to go it on my own." He was looking straight at us, waiting, I knew, for us to say something about that, about his moving out when he was only fifteen.

I went along with him. I said, "But you were only fifteen. You were too young." I took my hands from my coat pockets, crossed my arms, holding myself in this cold.

"Yeah," he said, and nodded his head, and I could just make out in the dark the faintest smile on his face. "But I got a job. This job right here. Been here for four years. Believe it? Four years at a rinky-dink Friendly's." He laughed. "I think it's some kind of record. For somebody my age, at least. To be here for that long, I mean."

I was starting to get cold now, my feet beginning to feel like stones, my cheeks beginning to tingle. He still hadn't answered our question. I said, "But the house. Is there something wrong with it?"

He stood still a moment, quit shifting his feet. He was looking at me, and seemed to have stopped breathing.

Just then the door at the rear of the restaurant shoved open, and light spilled out onto the cement and pavement.

Someone leaned out to look at us, and though he was about twenty yards away I could see it was Martin. His head hung there out the door, looking at us.

Grady quickly turned to the scrape of the door across the ground, to kitchen sounds escaping the building, and I felt warmer. Just that sound, the comfortable sound of glasses and silverware and people talking, warmed me up.

"Hey hey," Grady said, almost shouting. "The man of the hour. Come on out and say hi to the—" He turned to us. His eyes were half in light, and were shiny, some moistness caught by the lights of the building. He was smiling. "What was your last name?" he said.

"Templeton," Tom said, and took his arm from around me.

"Templeton," Martin said from the door, and his voice, taut and high-pitched, seemed to echo with some sort of strength across the lot and through the cold air. He came out wearing only the blue-checked shirt and pants and workboots, and started toward the three of us, his steps heavy, his arms swinging forward and back in an exaggerated gait. He said, "Templeton. That's a good name," the word *good* accented, his voice tightened even more on that word, the pitch a notch higher; and I imagined for a moment someone's hands around his throat, squeezing out puffs of air, words, ideas from this man's head and heart, as if forcing them were the only way to get them out.

"Whoa whoa whoa," Grady said, and quickly took a few steps toward Martin. Martin stopped, halfway across the lot. He let his hands fall to his sides. Grady stopped, too, said, "Now wait a minute. You're forgetting something, right? What are you forgetting?"

Martin stood there, crossed his arms, put his hand up to his chin, a pose you could tell was instinct for him, the move so quick and smooth. He said, "I'm thinking."

"Good," Grady said. "But I hope you don't freeze to death while you're at it."

Martin looked up and snapped his fingers, a loud, hard pop in the air. "Ah," he said, and wheeled around, taking the same heavy steps back toward the restaurant, where the door still stood open. He disappeared inside.

Grady hadn't moved, still stood a few feet out in the lane, half-turned to the door.

A moment later here was Martin again, now wearing a thick, heavy CPO jacket, green buffalo plaid. He already had it buttoned up to his neck, the collar turned up. He was putting on a knit cap, too, and was walking right toward us. "My coat," he said, his hands at his head, adjusting the cap, making certain his ears were covered, the cap far enough down on his neck. "And cap."

"Precisely," Grady said, in his voice not condescension, not fun, but congratulations. The sound of encouragement. Martin made it to Grady, who put his hand on Martin's shoulder, shook it. "Exactly. Great, Martin, great." They turned and started back toward us.

Finally Martin stopped adjusting the cap. He said, "Templeton is a good name. It's a good name." He put out his hand to Tom. "Tom Templeton," he said, "my name is Martin Hosmer."

Slowly Tom took his hand from his pocket and shook. This, too, was an exaggerated movement, Martin working his hand up and down five or six times, then stopping suddenly.

He turned to me. He said, "Claire Templeton is a good name, too."

He held out his hand, and I took it. We shook just as he and Tom had: up and down, up and down, up and down, the sudden stop. His hand had been warm in mine, and I thought of him washing dishes back in the Friendly's, the hot water and clouds of steam.

He said, "Is your hand okay?"

"I'm fine," I said, "just fine. No problems anymore." I heard my voice. It was still too loud.

"Good." He nodded several times and sort of bowed at the same time, his eyes on my hand, then me, then my hand again.

"Well," Grady said, and took his hand off Martin's shoulder. He put his hands together in front of him, and started the rocking movement again. "I don't know what it is your experts told you, but there's not anything wrong with the place. I showed you around. I showed you some of the basic troubles of the place, but none of that's of any matter, really. And that's all the problems I know of, actually. But I'll tell you what." He paused a moment and glanced at Martin, who now stood with his hands clasped in front of himself, too. "I'll tell you what. Martin, here, well. Martin here is good with wood. He's good with fixing things, with telling what's good wood or what's bad, weak places in the wood and stuff." He put his hand to Martin's shoulder again.

Martin gave a quick shrug, almost too fast to catch. He was looking at the ground, grinning.

"We'll meet you on Saturday morning," Grady went on, looking now at Tom. "And we'll look the place up and down to see what really needs to be done. What do you think?"

Tom said nothing for a few moments. We stood there, the four of us, our breaths turning the circle of air before us into thin veils of white in the dark.

Tom said, "Okay." He seemed to straighten his shoulders, set his jaw, and I knew that to be a look of resolve. He pushed himself from off the trunk. His feet were spread. He said, "This Saturday. Around 11:00."

"Great," Grady said, and he turned, an instant later Martin turning, too, and they headed back toward the rear of the restaurant.

I said, "Where are you guys going? Aren't you off work now?"

Grady turned and, walking backward, called out, "Oh yeah. We're heading home. Got to get the bikes."

Martin disappeared behind the large, black dumpster pushed up against the back wall of the restaurant, then Grady went behind it, too. Tom and I looked at each other again.

From behind the dumpster came first Grady, then Martin, both pushing bicycles, three-speeds, I could see, Martin's with wire side baskets, Grady's with a wire basket fixed to the handlebars. They came toward us and into the lane; Grady put one foot on a pedal, took two quick steps with the other foot, and climbed onto the bike.

Martin, only a few feet behind him, did the same, and the two were riding through the lot.

"Grady," Tom called out. "What about a phone number?"

Grady was almost at the entrance to the lot, but wheeled sharply back toward us, Martin, again, doing the same, and as they came toward us I could see their generator headlights, the dull yellow light given off because they were moving so slowly through the lot. They reached us, and Grady said, "No phone. That's a luxury. I'm a runaway, remember?" Slowly he passed by us, and then came Martin, his hands gripping the handlebars, his eyes on the rear tire of Grady's bike. He had a huge grin on his face, sheer joy, I imagined, at follow-the-leader through the Friendly's parking lot.

"I've got to get Martin over to his place," Grady said, and turned back toward the entrance. "Then I'm on my way." He was quiet a moment, and said, "You two ought to get bikes, too. Keeps a human being healthy." He took his hands from the handlebars, and clapped them to his chest a couple of times. "Just breathe that night air," he shouted.

I laughed; Tom only smiled. I watched to see if Martin would try riding with no hands, but he was still looking at Grady's tire, still leaning forward. He closed his mouth, though, and took in a deep breath. He was only doing what Grady had told him: taking in this night air. He was still smiling.

They moved past us to the entrance, Grady now with his hands on the handlebars. He slowed, looked both ways, and then, so quiet I wouldn't have heard it had there been another sound in the air, he said, "Okay, Martin, let's head on home. It's a good night," and they turned left onto the street, Route 9, leaving behind them only the soft tick of gears in the cold air.

 "I'm going to find out about this guy," Tom said as we drove home. I looked at him. Headlights from oncoming cars played across his face, turned his features into strange, contorted shadows, changed his skin, clothes, hair from the gray of night into white, ignoring any real colors there. His eyes were on the road.

I said, "What? What about him?"

He turned to me, his face gray again. "What do you mean? Weren't you listening to him back there?"

"To what?" I looked back at the road, then at Cooley-Dickinson to my right, that hospital where Paige had had her baby. As I did every time we passed here, I thought for a moment of when I'd visited her there, of the row of babies in the nursery, all of them crying except for Phillip, little Phillip lying there in his crib, his body wrapped tightly in pure white, the lights bright, keeping the room warm.

I turned my head as we passed the hospital, trying to see back behind the addition to the old wing and the window on Paige's room, just an old window with a frame and twelve panes; an ordinary window, but one from which I wanted to gaze and see cars passing on Route 9, and I wondered who was in that room now, and what the child's birth had been like, whether vaginal or C-section, if there'd been any fetal distress, if the father had been there to coach the mother on, to hold her hand, to feed her ice chips and to yell *Push.*

"Claire?" Tom said.

I turned back to the windshield. "What?" I took a deep breath, smoothed out my skirt.

"Didn't you hear what he said back there?"

"Yes," I said, and I touched my hair, put my hand to my forehead. "But what?"

"He said his dad died nine years ago. But that day when we were out at the house the first time he said both his parents were in California."

We'd already passed the Smith dorms, those rooms still full of light, as if nothing in this world had changed since I was a girl standing before them, except that now the windows were closed against the October air. We slowed to a stop at the light just before the drop into downtown.

I said nothing.

"I take it you also didn't hear what he said a month ago about living with his parents out in California for a year or so, then moving back here a year and a half ago. Of course, that doesn't jibe with his world-record four years at the Friendly's in Florence." He was quiet a while, the light still red. "He's lying," he went on, "about something or another. About his parents. Who knows what else."

I said, "What are you so worried about? Maybe the kid's parents are out in California, maybe they're *both* dead. What difference does it make?" but as the words came out of me I knew what was the difference. We really didn't know who this kid was. All we knew was what we saw: he was with Martin, cleaning the place up; he worked at the same Friendly's he told us he did; and, it was plain, he cared for Martin.

The light changed, and he pulled ahead. "Just that, maybe," he said, and stopped. "Just that maybe this Grady isn't any relation at all." He was quiet, his jaw tight. He stopped at the crosswalk outside Thorne's to let an old couple pass in front of us. The woman, in a down stadium jacket and crocheted beret, leaned forward with each step, and held onto her husband's arm. He stood erect, tall, and had on a tweed hat and blue parka. He looked at us, gave a quick wave and nod.

I put up my hand and gave a little wave, though I was certain he couldn't see me for our headlights shining in his face. They made it to the curb, and we moved on, under the railroad overpass, and turned left onto Market Street. I didn't say anything.

I didn't say anything because I didn't know what to think. I hadn't caught it, hadn't heard the fault in his story, and for a moment listened again to Grady telling us his father didn't think anything of the grandfather selling the house because he was long dead. I saw Grady again, his head back, him looking at stars. I looked and listened and tried to remember, but heard, finally, nowhere in the words he'd given us a lie. He hadn't been lying. I felt I *knew* that.

We turned right onto our street, the same street we drove every-day: I knew the potholes, anticipated them by putting my hand to the dashboard to steady myself through ones that had existed for years; the only repairs made were when the road crews came out every spring and shoveled cold, loose asphalt into the holes, and backed the truck over the spot, as if that might cure this terminally pitted road.

Then we were at the house, and Tom turned onto the driveway alongside our place, followed it to behind the house where it widened into a patch big enough for two cars. The people who lived below us, a man and two women whom we'd met only once, all three of them grad students in the hotel-and-restaurant-administration pro-gram at the university, weren't home, and we sat in the driveway, the engine running. Still there were no words.

Tom cut the motor, and the car was silent only a moment before the ticking of the engine took over, filled in the empty air between us. The cold started seeping in, too: first through the windows, my shoulders and face going cold, next into my toes again.

Tom said, "I just think it's strange. That someone would lie right off the bat. He's just a kid."

"So why did you agree to meeting him out there in the first place? If you don't trust him, you don't want him, right? So why ask him out there in the first place?"

My words had come out in a rush, in one breath, and I took in a new one, the air cold in my lungs. A moment ago the car was warm. That warmth was gone now.

We both stared out the windshield, the glass quickly fogging over.

"Because," Tom said, his voice breaking the silence. "I think he's okay. I think he's basically a good kid. I like him. And Martin, too. I kind of want to see what he means with Martin and the wood."

"Then why?" I said, and I put my left hand up to the back of his neck, gently rubbed it, though I could feel the adhesions in my hand drawing up in the cold, the tight pull of skin and muscle. He let his head drop.

"Why," I said, "are you so worried? It's obvious they're the ones who clean the place up. How else would they know someone was supposed to take care of the place three times a year?"

"But the lie," Tom said, and suddenly his head was up, his hands on the steering wheel as if he were going to drive across the small patch of grass before us and right through the gray picket fence that separated our backyard from next door, where, I knew, that Christmas tree still leaned. "The lie," he said again. "Why lie? Why?"

"Don't be stupid," I said, and took my hand down. "You're being stupid now. Everyone lies. I lie, you lie. Just because you work for a newspaper doesn't mean you don't lie. It doesn't mean you've got some sort of monopoly on the truth." I put my hands in my pockets again, turned toward the windshield. "It's his life, not yours. It's a lie. So what?"

"You can't even put two and two together, can you?" he said, and things had changed, our conversation taking the step into argument. Into fight. His voice had made the subtle twist from quiet and resolved to edged and clenched. He said, "It's like I said already, if you were listening. If he's lying about this, he may be lying about the house. There may be something wrong. And we're buying the thing, remember? We're buying the goddamned thing." He was in full swing now, his hands gripping the wheel, letting go, gripping again.

"But he wasn't lying," I said, quiet.

He turned to me. "How do you know?"

I shrugged, knowing full well that my answer would not suit him, would never be enough of an answer for him. I said, "I just know," and decided I would say nothing more. It was a move I knew would work. We had fought often enough for me to know which tactics served me best, and silence was among them. When he went off onto his own course of reasoning in a fight, I would go quiet, letting him ask question after question, letting him dig his own grave. He couldn't stand it, I knew, but with that cut in his voice he had already decided: Grady was a liar.

"That's a good answer," he said. "That's one of your beautiful stock answers. 'I just know it.' That's a good one."

I was through then. I opened my door, climbed out, slammed it shut. He didn't say a word, I could see through the glass, and I turned, headed back alongside the house and down the driveway. When I got to the foot of the driveway I heard his car door open, close.

I was at the street now. I looked both ways. To my right the street ended about a quarter-mile away at the town cemetery, circled by a chain-link fence. The moon was out, and I could see down there the black masses that would be trees. In daylight I could make out tombstones, but now I could only see black shapes.

I looked to the left. The street ended fifty yards away, forming a T with Market, and I could see behind the houses the raised platform of dirt where the train tracks ran through town.

I stood at the foot of the driveway a moment, listening. I waited to hear Tom's footsteps behind me, wanted him to come up and put his hands around my waist and hold me to him. I didn't want an apology; I didn't want any explanation or reasoning. I only wanted him with me, to feel him, just to feel him behind me, the two of us out in the cold.

But I heard the faint scratch of his steps up the outside stairs, the opening and closing of the kitchen door, then silence again.

I shuddered, not from the cold, but from, down deep, some fear, the kind, I knew, I had unwillingly inherited from my mother. I tried to shake it off, tried to understand what it was that I was afraid of, but could come up with nothing. Only the dark, an empty street, and the kernel of fear I knew had been there since birth.

When I was thirteen I brought home to my mother a new word, one I wasn't exactly sure how to pronounce, but one that worked well. It was a good, sound word, one that was real, that had meaning, and when I stumbled through it the first time in my Health Science textbook, a word that would have slipped through unnoticed among so much assigned reading, I had to stop, reread its definition, then the word again. I read it out loud, the sound clumsy in my throat, and I read it again and again. I had found a word, a name for something that had been in my home, my world, for as long as I could remember.

I ran home that day, repeating the word to myself, the textbook held tight against my chest, against my new breasts just beginning to show, and the world, everything, seemed ready to start, ready to begin to grow.

When I got home, I held the book out to my mother, showed her the paragraph, and said the word: *agoraphobia.*

She was at the stove, stirring something in a pot, the other hand at her side. I held the book while she read the paragraph about how some people were afraid of open places, afraid of crossing fields or streets. Some people were afraid of their own backyards, some even of their front porches, while others couldn't even bring themselves to look out windows.

She finished reading the paragraph, and looked back at the stove.

"Agoraphobia," I said again, knowing of course I would end up a doctor someday, get my degree at Smith, move on to Harvard Medical School. "That's you," I said, and reread the passage again to myself, though I must have known it by heart.

"I know that," she said.

I looked up from the page. She turned to me and gave a feeble smile.

"You know that word?"

"No," she said, now looking at the pot again. "Not the word. But the feeling. Always I've known it." She pulled the spoon from the pot and set it in the ceramic spoonrest between the burners, the same spoonrest my father had brought home one evening as a freebie from the company, his distributorship's name printed in the hollow of the rest.

She put her hands on my shoulders, me only an inch or so shorter than her. She looked in my eyes, and I could see just how much work it was for her to do that, even to me, her only child: her eyes blinked again and again, darted down and down and down before settling into mine. She said, "I've lived this long this way. I've lived this long. Now your daddy is gone, and there's no one, just you. So let me go on. Let me."

She held onto my shoulders, her grip tightening a moment, and slowly she let her hands slip down my arms. Her eyes started going again, tearing away from mine in quick glances down, until the moment was over, and she turned to the stove, the book still open in my arms to that page, and to that word.

An insignificant one, useless. Just a name given to something unknown, I knew, to make someone more comfortable with that unknown. Mine was the same old world. There was nothing new here; only the knowledge that, though I had heard my father speak to me, kept his words in me, her own fear still existed, always ready to edge into me, willing to take me over. I saw that day, my mother's back to me, the spoonrest empty as she stirred the spoon in the pot, that I would have to work to avoid her fear, fight to keep myself from being like her. I closed the book, and backed away from her without another word. She was comfortable in her fear, I saw. She wanted it no other way.

And nothing was ever new while I grew up. Nothing was new, even when, some three months later in a bathroom stall after school, the sheet metal walls around me a cold army-green, nicked and scarred with graffiti about girls and boys I never knew, I found the small spot of blood in my underpants, that spot the shape and size of an oblong quarter. Though the blood itself *was* new—I had been waiting for this moment for so long, all of my other friends having had their first periods months and even years before, that the thought of my first period actually happening had receded from my mind, buried itself somewhere in my brain—the *idea* behind it, what having a period really meant, was ancient in me. I knew from the films we'd been shown and all the lectures we'd had, some of the boys looking bewildered when we filed out of the class for the nurse's office, other boys snickering and jabbing each other with elbows, that this meant my body was now ready to reproduce.

I had gone home that day nearly running, afraid of soaking through and ruining my underwear, not knowing how very small that period would be, and that the next would not show up for another eighty-one days; I ran home to my mother to give her this news, to let her know of my growing up, of my becoming a woman, even though I knew there would be little reaction from her, if any.

She did not let me down: when I told her, blurting out on my way through the living room for the bathroom, "It's finally here. My period," she slowly looked up from a magazine she had across her lap, and stared at me. By the time I was in the bathroom, sitting on the toilet with my underpants down to examine that stain—it had grown no larger, though I was certain it should have at least doubled or tripled in size—I heard her slowly stand from her chair, place the magazine on the coffee table, and start down the hall toward the bathroom.

She stood in the doorway, her eyes not on me, but on the cupboard below the sink. Slowly she knelt, as if the knowledge I had given her were already weighing her down, already burdening her. She opened the cupboard, reached in, and pulled at her own box of fat pads. She opened the top of the box, reached in.

Finally she looked at me, and she did her best, I knew, to smile at me, in her smile and eyes some sort of tentative investment, some sort of quiet care.

But this time it was me who had scared her away: as she stood, pulling from the box one of her awkward, ugly pads, I said, "Mother, I'm okay. Look in there again," and she lost the look, on her face now a puzzled expression, with that puzzlement always the accompanying fear in her eyes. She knelt again, leaving the pad in the box, and looked, reached in, and brought out the box of tampons I had bought for myself over a year before, convinced way back then that this day was only a week or, at worst, a month away.

She brought out the tampons, looked at the box a long moment, and then held it out to me.

I smiled, trying to give back to her that feeling of help she had had only a moment before, and she, too, smiled at me, though behind it I could see nothing, in her eyes only the remote fear of me that had been growing and growing since my father's death.

I said, "I'm sorry, Mother. It's just that—" and I stopped, because I did not know what I could say to her. In that moment the air suddenly changed: I realized what I was doing, my underwear down and stained, my mother there in the doorway, and I felt embarrassed, as if she had known me too well before all this. As if she had known me too well. But before I could do anything—pull up my underwear, pull my dress down over my knees, either of these movements a signal to her that I wanted to be alone here—she said, "Excuse me," as though she had come upon a boarder in her house, and not her daughter. She turned from me and went into the hall, pulling the door closed behind her.

I stood at the foot of the driveway, and I knew I had to do something, had to move from here, from our driveway, our apartment, still honoring my father and his voice in me, still listening for him and my name, and though it took more effort, more strength than it had in years to do it, more courage than I could have imagined, I took a step. Then I took another, saw that I was heading toward Market and those train tracks, beyond them King Street and lights and people and downtown.

I took more steps, wondering why it had taken so much for that first one, and I wondered if, as I grew older, I weren't becoming my mother, more like her each day, more turned into myself. My dreams of the ghosts of imagined children, for one thing, came back to me most every night since I'd been bitten, those children continuing to surround me, to gawk at me and swirl and disappear.

I stopped a moment, only a couple of doors down from the house. I turned around, looked up to the second floor of our house, to our apartment, and as I did a light went on, and a hand was inside the curtains. Tom's hand, pulling down the shade, and suddenly I felt as though I might be a boarder in this house, too, a stranger; Tom up there alone, self-sufficient, not caring what I was doing out here in the cold, not climbing out of the car and walking down the driveway to me to talk things over, to urge me upstairs.

Slowly I took a few steps backward, suddenly not caring what lay behind me, if anything, on the sidewalk.

Moving was what counted. I would walk. I would move my legs, have them carry me where I wanted, and I turned, headed off down the street. I would walk for a while, come home later. We could talk then. I would tell him what I thought of Grady, and what I thought of Martin. I would plan with him to go out to Maplewood to try and talk to the grandfather, that man we hadn't yet met, without going through the lawyer, and for a moment I wondered whether or not this grandfather, this Mr. Clark, even existed, or if he were merely someone's sad joke, the lawyer's, perhaps. Or Grady's.

*   *   *

I got to the end of the street and passed between two houses, one, on my left, dark and empty, the other dark, too, except for a single light in an upstairs window on the back of the house, and for a moment I felt the adrenalin a burglar might feel, a stranger intruding upon someone else's home, someone's familiar objects alien to me: in the moonlight I could see a hibachi atop a picnic table with X-legs in the yard of the dark house, in the other yard a lawn chair and a busted, abandoned washing machine, its door torn off to reveal the large, black hole like an unblinking eye, watching me.

I shuddered, then moved as quietly as I could to the rear of the yard, afraid I would make a sound, break a twig beneath my feet or suddenly cough, my presence known, and a face would be at that window, I knew, and I would be found out down here.

I made it to the row of trees at the rear of the yard, behind them the dirt and rock embankment up to the train tracks, and I stopped. I turned, put my hand on the trunk of the tree next to me, a small maple, and looked up through the leaves gently moving with the cold breeze at that lit window, someone inside waiting for me to make a sound, I knew, waiting.

I had no gloves on, and the trunk of the tree was cold, rough. It felt good. It felt real, and with my eyes on that window, the light— there was no curtain inside the window, only a shade pulled down— I reached up and touched a branch, felt the leaves trace themselves around my hand. I took hold of one of the leaves, gently pulled it, tough and green, a leaf that had made it through spring and summer and now to fall, when soon it would drain itself of its green, leaving only its bones, red and orange and brown.

I took that leaf, my eye still on the window, and pulled on it, pulled harder than I could have believed I needed, as though there were no strength in my arm, no pull of muscle against muscle, and the branch came toward me, the leaves coming down to hide the window. Then the leaf snapped off, the branch popping up into the tree with the certain strength of life, and I heard the quick, loud whisper of those leaves banging against other leaves as the branch swayed slower and slower until once again it barely moved with the cold breeze.

I could see the window again, waited, held my breath for a shadow to appear, for the shade to fly up, for someone's face to find me out.

And nothing happened. I only stood with the leaf in my hand, its cold green waxy and tough, and for a moment, an instant, something new came into me: I *wanted* someone there at the window, someone to look out and see that it was me here in his backyard, that it had been me to have pulled that branch, let it pop back up. Me.

The breeze picked up, shook the highest branches, the sound coming down to me, a sound in the dark so much louder than my small branch jumping back up into place had been. I looked at the window a moment more, knowing then that nothing, nothing would happen, as if I had never been here, and, the dark green and resilient leaf clenched in my left hand, I turned, started up the embankment, my right hand out, touching the ground before me a couple of times to keep my balance.

Once at the top and on the train tracks, the cold wind moving down from Canada and through me and on south to the rest of the world, twisting the branches of countless trees, the air around me filled with the static hum of leaves against leaves, I held the leaf out to that wind, held it by the stem so that it whipped and whipped, a frantic dance in the air. I wanted to let go of it, to invest in this act some sort of significance, as if the leaf had only existed until this moment for me to come and tear it off its branch, let it fly away. I held it in the wind, held it, my fingers ready to let go, but then I stopped. I brought my hands together, felt the leaf between my palms, a thing so useless now but so real. Gently, slowly, I rolled it up, held the small piece of green with my left hand, and I put it into my coat pocket.

I started moving.

 I walked from one end of town to the other, from the train tracks, where I'd walked the rail as if it were a balance beam, then down the other side of the embankment behind the Calvin and out onto King, past the shops and boutiques and restaurants on Main Street.

I walked and walked, sometimes thinking, sometimes not. When I thought, it was about Tom, and it was about different feelings I had for him; at any given moment I was loving him or hating him or not caring one way or the other.

I finally got to the end of downtown after crossing and recrossing Main, staring in windows at books or jewelry or clothing. Inside a bookstore was a display of children's books, one book opened to beautiful pictures of unicorns and faeries and trolls, another one a pop-up *Goodnight Moon,* the white moon through the window, and the old lady whispering "*Hush*" there in three dimensions.

I stood looking at the books, and heard from behind me loud laughter, the deep, rolling laughter of a man I imagined was drunk. Then came a woman's high-pitched laughter, laughter somehow broken, disjointed, as if she thought she shouldn't have been laughing, but couldn't help it. The laughter of lost control.

I turned around. Across the street was Pulaski Park, a small lot where benches had been set up and sidewalks poured and a plaque erected to the Polish hero of the Revolutionary War. Though it was dark I'd expected to see someone, the sound seeming so close, but there was no one. Only the darkness, and the bushes and trees.

I looked down and turned, headed up Main to State Street and the base of the hill, that beginning into Smith territory, and I thought for a moment of going on up there and looking in dorm windows once again, but decided not to. That part of me was over, I thought. I'd gone to college, gotten a good enough job, and was now about to buy a house, and I'd done all that without this venerable institution. That was what I told myself, though a part of me still wanted up there, and, I knew, always would.

I paused a moment, and went north on State.

A few yards down I came to a hobby shop, huge windows across the front of the building, shelves inside the window filled with everything from toy train sets to rows of basketballs and soccer balls and footballs to bicycles hung from the ceiling.

But on the far-left side of the window were dollhouses, and I crossed the small parking lot and went to them, put my hands up to the glass. Ten or twelve dollhouses were in the window: three Victorians, a saltbox, a Queen Anne with its turrets and gingerbread, a split-level, two log cabins. And there was a Cape, this one a full. Some were painted, others left unfinished, the wood soft and pink. One of the Victorians, too, had been furnished, each room in the house filled with miniatures: in the kitchen sat an iron stove and a rocking chair, on the floor a round braided rug; in the living room was a fireplace with wood in it, an overstuffed chair and divan, even a minuscule newspaper lying flat on a dark-wood end table, its legs carved into claws. Upstairs was a girl's bedroom, the wallpaper pink with rows of bouquets of roses separated by thick stripes of white from floor to ceiling. There was a white-lace canopy over the bed, and a small, white rocking horse. In the other room, the boy's, was a bunkbed and football, postage-stamp-sized circus posters on the walls. On one wall hung a dart board with six darts pushed into it.

I stood there for what seemed an hour, taking it all in, forgetting about moving. I just looked, examining the details, trying to imagine how I would have decorated a girl's or boy's room. I tried to imagine this, but nothing came to me, and I wondered whether that was a good sign or bad, whether my inability to imagine what might never be was a sign I had accepted our not having children, or if it meant my imagination had died, if that part of my brain used to muster images of what I wanted had been obliterated somehow. I could see nothing but what lay before me, all miniature, all toy. Not real.

I took my hands from the glass because the cold had started working on me again. I put my hands in my pockets, felt the leaf in the left side. It was still warm from my having held it all the while I had been walking.

I saw where my hands had been on the glass, the faint dusting of heat and moisture on the window, my ten fingers and two palms, and I watched as they disappeared, as if I'd never been here, had never gazed in on a dollhouse filled with evidence of imagined life.

I turned and headed back to the street, continuing on up State. I had to get my feet moving again, but now things were different, and that small fear I'd had before was coming up again, and I became conscious again of putting one step down and then the next, of one breath in and one breath out, of muscles and ligaments and bones all working to move me, and as I passed the State Street Fruit Store with its outside bins empty, waiting for the next day and the fresh fruit and vegetables that would fill them, I thought of Tom, and his face, and the fight.

His face had been in the dark during the fight, but as I thought of him and his words, his face wasn't hidden. It was full and lit for me, because I knew that face. I had seen it every day for years, and there was nothing to conjuring it up, even in the dark. It was his face, *his*, and in the set of the jaw, the straight eyebrows unmoving even in the midst of the fight, his eyes clear and glistening, I saw that I loved him.

I saw again the one I'd accidentally sat next to at a basketball game when I was only a senior, back before I'd gotten the job in the laboratory. Our knees had touched again and again and again during the first two quarters, but at the half he left with the boy he had come in with, and I was disappointed, hurt in some way, though we hadn't said a word to each other. Then he reappeared, carrying with him two hot dogs and two Cokes, and sat down. He turned to me and smiled. I could see him from the corner of my eye, looking at me.

He said, "Would you turn me down if I asked you to dinner?" and held out to me one of the hot dogs and a Coke.

I turned to him, acted surprised but cool. I looked into his eyes for a moment, and I could not help but smile, say, "Such a sumptuous meal, too," and we laughed.

When the game resumed, our knees touched even more, and we filled in the slow places in the game with the obligatory small talk, talk of roommates and classes, futures. He told me he was a year out of college and a stringer for the *Hampshire Gazette;* within a year he planned to be a full-time reporter. I told him about the possibility of a position as a research assistant in Neuroscience and Behavior.

The game over—we had thrashed Holy Cross, I remember—we had filed out of the bleachers and into the night air, air at once cutting and welcome after the hot, smelly air of the old gym.

We stood outside, light from inside the gym falling down on us, and his face was half in light, half in darkness. I hadn't known his face then, I thought as I kept walking on State, the leaf still tight in my hand, my steps still heavy. I remembered I had been afraid of him that night. Not afraid in the sense I wanted to flee or to hide—not the fear that gnawed at me now, a car passing as I walked, its brights on and blinding me until the driver flicked them off only a few yards before passing me—but fear of departure, of taking off. The fear, expectant fear, welcome fear, of the prospect of love.

We'd gone from the gym to a loud bar in town, the place packed but all the more joyous to me for that. I wanted to be around people, wanted to hear laughter, wanted to feel my throat and lungs fill with warm air again after the cold walk, the two of us with our hands in our pockets, watching the sidewalk and our steps instead of looking at each other.

We stood just inside the front door, and Tom, taller than me, surveyed the room. He looked back at me, said something that was lost in the noise of the place, but I nodded, smiled. Then he took my hand, just reached for it and held it, his hand big but tender, and led me through the crowd, past the waitress station and bathrooms to a smaller room in the back where he was able to round up two chairs for us, but no table. We held beers in our laps, and talked.

I pictured him as he had been that night, his hair longer, parted in the middle and with no gray hairs, no small creases beside his eyes. He was younger, of course, but much younger than I could ever know because I, too, was young, and had thought we were both such adults. Now I knew enough to be confused about that word, still not knowing exactly what the term meant, what being an adult entailed.

And then I pictured him at different times in our lives, different places, different events: I saw his face our wedding night, a night at an inn in Yarmouth Port, the room filled with dark wood furniture and the sound of wind in trees outside, saw in his face his delight in me when I let the straps of the white chemise I wore slip from my shoulders, let the silk fall about me; I saw his face looking off at a sunset as we sat on the terrace of the Plantation House up in Charlemont, where we were celebrating our second anniversary, saw that he was looking forward to something, his eyes to the west, looking beyond the long, green lawn before us, beyond the stone fence that bordered it, beyond the forest and the Berkshires and the horizon to something else.

Looking toward children, I knew, because we had started planning then, started scheduling amounts of money we would have to save, promotions and raises we would need to have secured, all for the sake of our children.

I saw his face on any one of the thousand days we had talked of those kids, saw the shine of dreams in his eyes as he talked of trips to sugarhouses to show our children exactly how maple syrup was made, the roaring fire, the long, shallow pans filled with boiling, steaming sap; talked of picnics to the Quabbin and Mount Tom, and tours of the museums in Boston, and playing catch and making up nonsense words.

I saw his face the moment we finally decided we would begin to try, saw his face after an evening's calculations, sheets of yellow legal paper spread out on the kitchen table, pages littered with numbers, account balances, goals, years, our lives mapped out before us: if the baby were born within the next year, we figured, he or she would graduate high school in 2002, college in 2006.

We looked at each other then, both of us smiling. He reached his hand across the table, and I took it.

He said, "Now the real work begins," and I felt as though I were blushing as my eyes fell from his to the tabletop, and I nodded.

We had stood, still holding hands, and went through the living room, the apartment dark, and through the bathroom into the bedroom, where Tom let go my hand, went to the nightstand and turned on the light.

I was already at my dresser, pulling open the top drawer. I brought out a small tissue-wrapped bundle, tied off with a white ribbon.

He'd stood there, his hands on his hips. He tilted his head, and said, "What's that?"

I said, "A surprise," and I turned, went back to the bathroom.

Inside the tissue paper was a sleeveless white cotton nightgown, the low neck and shoulders done about with lace and pink ribbons. It was something I'd bought a few weeks before at the lingerie shop downtown, when I'd sensed that this night would be coming soon, our savings recently having reached the level we'd decided four years ago would be adequate.

I put on the cool, white gown, felt it soft against my skin, saw in the mirror the lace and ribbons and the pale skin of my shoulders and my chest and neck, and I brushed out my hair, touched up my makeup rather than take it off as I did every other night. I smiled at how I felt: perhaps even more nervous than the first night in Yarmouth Port, though this evening, this making love, would be no more than a symbolic gesture of our beginning; tomorrow would be my first morning off the pill, next week I would get my diaphragm, and we would wait three more months, we had agreed, before I stopped using it, three months to wash from my system all the drug that had for years given me periods like clockwork, the blood coming just after noon of the second day the last pill of the month had been taken. Now would come the waiting for that period, the surprise of it, my periods before the pill never having been regular occurrences, some coming three weeks apart, some five. A constant surprise. But if all went well, I thought as I brushed my hair again, we would see only a couple of more periods, and they would be gone, and I would be pregnant.

All that waiting would begin the next day, I knew, but there before the mirror, my hand bringing the brush through my hair one last time, I felt in me some quiet adrenalin, the brink of beginning, of bringing into the world what we had waited so very long to bring, and then I placed the brush on the counter, and I turned out the light.

Tom lay in bed on his side, propped up on his elbow, his shirt
off, the sheets at his waist. The light was off, too, but he had lit the
candle in the small hurricane lamp I kept on the dresser. He still
had his glasses on, his face lit with pale orange light, the reflection
dancing in his glasses. I stopped at the footboard, put my hands to
my sides, and took hold of the gown, brought my arms up so that
the gown was out to either side, and I turned in a circle.

"For you," I said when I had made it around to face him again.
He said, "My," and smiled. He put out his hand to me, drew me
to him. I lay next to him, and I reached up, took off his glasses. I
said, "We don't need these now, do we?" and I turned and placed
them on the nightstand.

I turned back to him, and there was his face, his fine nose and
soft brunette hair, his cheeks and chin rough with a day's growth.
He was nearsighted, and wore his glasses all day long, so that
whenever I looked at him without them I was astonished, surprised
at the face familiar yet new, eyes warm and deep brown, pupils
nearly lost in that dark color. I looked at him, and he smiled, said,
"Now I can see you," and he kissed me, his lips warm and soft on
mine. He pulled back. He said, "Shall we begin?"

I said, "Let's."

Finally, me walking on a cold street at night, my steps hard, my
toes growing colder, my feet heavier, I saw his face again the day
we had stopped at the barn, saw his twisted and quivering mouth,
saw the pain in the color of his cheeks, and I ended with seeing
his face that night, just a couple of hours before, the engine ticking,
the windows fogged over.

I reached Sunset, turned and headed down the hill to the intersection. The cold wind I'd felt up on the railroad tracks had begun to
pick up now, my hands burrowed deep into my coat pockets, the
leaf still there. Home wasn't far away anymore, just across the
intersection and under the railroad overpass, then right and then
left. I would be on our street, and I would be home.

And suddenly it didn't matter that we had fought, that we had
had fights before, that we would fight again. It didn't matter, either,
that I had left, had walked these streets to think about things for a
while. None of that mattered, because there were years behind us,

I saw, and years ahead of us, and tomorrow I would wake up, and there would be his face, I hoped, that same face. The only constant I knew.

Then I knew the fear I'd felt at the foot of the driveway, knew that it was a fear he would be gone with his steps up the stairs, the kitchen door being pulled closed, the hand descending inside the curtain, and I nearly ran under the overpass, a train now passing overhead, tearing across the metal, screaming above me; before the train was gone I was on our street, then mounting the stairs, the wind suddenly hard, a strong autumn wind that shook through limbs already bare, and I shuddered, opened the kitchen door, closed it behind me, my breathing hard and loud.

Tom was at the kitchen table, all the lights in the house off except for the fixture above him.

Library books were spread out over the table. They were how-to books, do-it-yourself books, each opened to specific details about rebuilding a house that we would have to face once we started in on ours. One book lay open to a chapter on sanding and staining hardwood floors, another to chimney repairs, another to clapboards.

I pulled my hands from my pockets, took deep breaths, and leaned back against the door. I closed my eyes a moment, opened them and let my head fall. My hands were in fists, my knuckles and fingers white, the scar still there on my left hand. I turned the hand over, and opened it. The leaf, an even duller green than I'd thought it would be, lay crumpled in my palm, stiff.

Tom looked up at me, then back at the book he was reading. One elbow was on the table, his forehead in his hand, the other arm flat on the tabletop. His glasses were off, lay on one of the other books. He leaned closer to the page, peering into it.

I said, "You're here," and started to the table, my steps slow and deliberate, though my breath hadn't yet come back.

He looked up at me again, squinting, trying to see me. "Where else would I be?" he said. "Where would I go?"

I stood at the table, pulled one of the books over to me and started looking at it. It was the chapter on chimneys. I hadn't yet taken off my coat, didn't, in fact, know if I had the strength.

I said, "Nowhere. You wouldn't go anywhere." I looked in the book at different chimneys in differing stages of decay. One picture was of a chimney top, the little lip of bricks around the top edge—what the book called "corbeling"—falling apart, the mortar between them all gone, two or three bricks missing; another picture was of a hearth, the bricks before the fireplace itself sunken an inch or so below the wood floor. I turned the page, wondering precisely how much work would have to be done on our own fireplace, but there were no pictures on this new page, only words. I looked at the words, studied them, but I could not put them together into any real sentences I understood. I turned back to the pictures of the chimney top, the fireplace. Pictures I could just look at, not think about.

Tom closed his book, and brought his hand to his face, rubbed his eyes, the bridge of his nose. He squinted, looked across the table for his glasses. My blind husband.

He found the glasses, put them on, and leaned back in the chair, his hands behind his head. The apartment was still, and I looked through the doorway into the living room. It was dark in there, black. I could see nothing beyond what was in this room: the brown-and-white gingham curtains on the kitchen door and windows, the gray radiator, the shelf and the plants above it, the old white enamel gas stove, the table, the books. Books that showed us how much work it was going to be.

Later, the house completely dark, we lay in bed side by side. As every other night, there was with us the moment of silence once the sheets had been pulled up, the light turned out, our bodies settled. We lay there, and I heard the wind lift and fall, the windows give with the sudden push against frame, the wash of sound from leafless trees.

"Oh," Tom whispered, breaking the moment of no talk between us, bringing us into that time when we would whisper until all the small things we'd forgotten to say, little incidents we'd wanted to relate, were through; whispering, as if there were guests in the house who might overhear us. Whispering, I thought, as if we had a baby in a crib at the foot of the bed.

"Oh?" I whispered.

"Nothing," he whispered. "Something I wanted to tell you about, but I don't need to. It can wait."

My eyes were closed, and I could feel him move his arm, could hear the shift of sheets.

I opened my eyes, and in the darkness I could see his profile, his hands clasped on his chest.

"Just say it," I whispered. I closed my eyes again.

"Okay," he whispered, and he took a deep breath. "This press release comes across my desk today. From some group called the Women's Union for Self-Reliance and Perpetuation. I'm not joking. That was the name. You ever heard of it?"

Another of his stories. "Nope," I said. My eyes were still closed.

"Well," he went on, "neither has anybody else at the office. But this press release comes to my desk. Judy hands it to me and tells me she'd gotten it in the mail. It was on good quality bond letterhead, with a printed envelope, too. They even had their own logo, this double-edged ax, behind it, this stylized flame, and beneath it was printed 'Founded 1979.' "

"And?" I whispered.

"No," he said, "it's nothing." He rolled over away from me. "I shouldn't have even started. Good night."

"Now, wait a minute," I said, my words even louder than his had been. I sat up in bed. "You can't do that to me. You tell me. You started this. Now I want to know."

He lay still for a moment, then moved onto his back. He let out a breath.

"Okay," he whispered. "Okay." He paused. "So we get this press release. And it's on this impressive paper, this nice letterhead. Across the top it reads in caps FOR IMMEDIATE RELEASE, and beneath it is this headline, VALLEY COUPLE'S TRIUMPH COMPLETE. And then I go on and read it, and it reads something like, 'Amherst—Linda Schulbred and Sky Winter found they were victorious last week when they were told they were indeed pregnant, this after months of emotionally debilitating efforts—"

"I gather this is two women," I cut in.

"Wait, wait, wait," he said, "there's more. And it is. Two women." In the dark I couldn't see his mouth move, only felt his words rise from somewhere next to me. "This release goes on and on, the first paragraph using all these words like 'strife' and 'glorious' and 'suc-

cess.' Then the second paragraph, and the rest of them—this thing
went on for four pages—went on to tell about exactly what happened. Turns out that one of them got her brother up here from
New York and got him to hand over some semen. Then she took
the semen and used a turkey baster to get the other one pregnant.
And they got pregnant."

I said, "A turkey baster? Are you serious?"

He said, "I am." He paused. "But it's okay. Their having a baby
is kosher, I guess."

"Why?"

"Well," he whispered, "for one thing this Schulbred and Winter
are married. And because this press release quoted the happy
mother and mother as saying they would, quote, 'assure this child,
whether female or otherwise, of a strong familial home-structure.'
Unquote."

Whether female or otherwise, I thought, and I wondered who
these people were that they could become pregnant in this plastic
way and then discount the possible results, a boy merely referred
to as "otherwise." Whether a boy or a girl, it would be a life. A life.

Tom sat up next to me, put his arms around me. He whispered,
"I wonder what kind of press release we'll receive if they get an
otherwise child," and I smiled, and then I laughed, something, some
pressure in me broken, a laughter that was deep in me and that
was caught up by Tom, so that the two of us were laughing in the
darkness, holding each other, the sound of our laughter like some
foreign language in our room.

 With the scalpel I gently cut into Chesterfield's head, the scalpel so sharp it was as if I'd only let it touch the pink skin, barely pulled it across to find a line of red chasing after the blade. Once the cut was finished, a four-inch incision across the top of the skull from just above and between the eyes to immediately behind the ears, I drew back the skin with three hemostats so that the bleeding would stop, and to expose the skull.

Here was the next step in running the rabbits, this surgery. Chesterfield hadn't suspected anything, only settled right into the Gormezano box as if it were a second home, ready for the black of the filing cabinet. Instead, I'd taken him upstairs to the operating room, just another ex-dorm room, and given him the injection of Thorazine to mellow him out, a few minutes after that the Nembutal. Twenty minutes later I pinched his hind foot, got no reaction, then gently tapped his eyeball. Nothing happened, no jerk, not even a groggy flinch. He was out.

I'd slipped the box into place on the surgery table, and moved into place the stereotaxic frame, the system of bars and joints and clamps that would hold the drill and, later, the electrode in perfect, measured place, allowing three-dimensional coordinates that would ensure I entered the brain at precisely the right point.

I'd done this enough times now so that I figured I'd feel nothing, but today was different somehow. I thought about it as I bent over the exposed skull, the bone covered with the thin fascia, the tissue that was to protect the skull but which was useless now. I scraped away the tissue with my scalpel.

Perhaps this odd feeling was because of Chesterfield, my pet now, a rabbit who had taken to eating out of my hand; sometimes I carried him around in my arms like a big cat. But it wasn't him, I knew. A particular sadness came over me whenever I operated on the rabbit I'd named, a childlike sadness, a sadness I indeed felt just then, the scalpel in hand, the tissue pushed back to the hemostats. But there was another feeling in me, a different, darker, more penetrating one.

Finally before me lay the scraped and clean pink of the skull itself, the midline fissure like a thin fault, the anterior bregma and posterior lambda fissures crossing over the midline like thin, red wires meandering across and perpendicular to the midline. These crossings were my landmarks, simple lines on a skull that signaled where to begin measurements: 8 mm posterior the bregma along the midline, 1 to 1½ mm left lateral the midline, that point marked with the tip of a pencil. That feeling, the scratch of graphite across hard, dull bone to leave a small gray x, was at once awful and exciting to me, entry into the brain only moments away now.

I moved into place the drill and small-bore bit, the whining piece of machinery that reminded me always of visits to the dentist, of buffing and polishing, of grit in the mouth and friction against bone, my bones, my teeth; a sound that sent chills into me in a moment. I brought the bit down into place, the tip poised a fraction of an inch above the skull, and I switched on the power, heard the high-pitched whirr. With the calibrated dial at the base of the frame, I lowered the bit even farther, touched bone, sent small grains of it into the air. Here came the grinding sound again, and those same chills went right into me. I gave the dial a moment's more pressure, and I was through the bone. I retracted the bit.

For a moment the dark feeling in me had left, gone with the whine of the drill, the disintegration of bone. I took the drill from the clamp on the frame and replaced it with the electrode carrier assembly, its needle insulated with Epoxylite everywhere but at the tip; the exposed metal, that portion that in a few moments would be in the midst of the Red Nucleus, would burn only the brain cells immediately around it. Burn them into extinction, we hoped, so that the conditioned response, the blink before shock, back inside the file cabinet, would disappear.

The feeling was gone, but as I fixed the alligator clip first to Chesterfield's right ear, then attached the opposite end to the lesion maker, and as I attached the second clip to the top of the electrode carrier and the appropriate end to its own post on the lesion maker, that strange feeling came back, with it a notion as to *why* I had the feeling, this feeling of dread. That was it, I knew: dread, a dread deeper than that caused by what I knew I was doing to Chesterfield, my pet: destroying brain cells, wiping them out in the Red Nucleus in the hopes that what little he'd been taught would be forgotten, that pieces of whatever small thought the animal could muster would be exterminated.

It was my dream that was causing the feeling, I thought, the dream I'd had again last night: children and wind and black holes. The dream had changed, I realized. In some minute way a detail had been added, something that might mean nothing. But my dream was different now.

I sat with the needle suspended over the hole I'd just drilled, but I did nothing. I did nothing, except try to remember the dream.

And then there it was, the small thing, the insignificant: the boy, my oldest, the child who stood in the middle of my three, had lifted his hand up from the edge of the bed. He'd lifted it up, and had started moving it toward me as if, I saw, he'd wanted me to take it. His hand had been milk-white in the moonlight, a young boy's hand, soft and unwrinkled and dimpled at the wrist. He'd held it out to me, but in my dream my hands were stumps, useless. I could not have taken his hand even if I had tried.

The dream had gone on as usual after that, the wind picking up, the children swirling round the room, disappearing, me waking up with my eyes wide open to the alarm clock, to my husband snoring quietly next to me. To this day, and my job entering brains.

I felt a touch on my shoulder, and I realized I'd heard my name. I turned. It was Sandra.

She said, "Who were you talking to in here?"

"What?" I said, and I tried to smile, to look as if I hadn't blinked out in the middle of surgery.

"Who were you talking to in here?" she said again, the same puzzled look on her face as the first time she had asked. "I was in the staining room blocking brains, and I could even hear you over the radio in there. It sounded like you were saying the same word again and again." She paused, waiting for me to say something. "Come on," she said, "you know what I'm talking about."

I didn't. I said, "You're kidding me. Jack put you up to this, or Paige or Wendy. I'm in here working, and you guys are trying to give me a hard time."

She was quiet, her mouth open, and for a moment I didn't recognize her, didn't know the woman before me. Her skin had gone pale somehow, the color lost, and her hair, usually up in a clean bun or perfect braids, had been only clipped back with barrettes, the ends shaggy, wisps of hair down over her forehead. Her eyes, too, seemed smaller, the skin around them a little darker than the rest of her face, a pale blue I hadn't seen before.

"Claire," she said. "What's wrong?"

I said, "Nothing," and adjusted myself on the stool, shook my head. "Nothing. If I was talking in here, I didn't know it." I smiled, put my hands together in front of me. "Maybe I was just goofing around in here, singing or something, and didn't even know it." I paused, and looked in her eyes, trying to turn this conversation away from me and back to her, because the idea of me talking in here by myself frightened me. I couldn't remember anything. Just the dream.

I said, "You're asking me if I'm okay, when it should be the other way around. You don't look very well. Are you okay?"

Suddenly she changed, became animated, took her hand from where she'd had it on the door frame and touched it to her hair, looked down, smiled. She stood straighter, put her other hand in her lab coat pocket and fished around for something.

She said, "My hair. It's just my hair. I got tired of wearing it back and tight and worrying about a hair being out of place." She stopped, seemed to have found what it was she was looking for in her pocket. She pulled out a pencil, examined it and, without looking at me, said, "You're in the middle of things, though. You've got surgery going on, so I'm getting out of here." She looked up at me, gave a faint smile. "You just keep on frying brains in here."

She turned, started out the door, but stopped and leaned back in. She said, "Who's Martin, anyway?"

I swallowed too fast, and coughed hard, felt my face going over into the heat of red, the blood rushing there as I coughed. She came to me and patted my back. "Settle down," she said, "settle down."

When I got my breath, I said, "How do you know Martin?"

Again she gave that puzzled look, her eyes focused on me as if I were some stranger. She said, "That's what you were saying in here. At least that's what it sounded like to me. That name over and over."

I took a few more breaths, my hands on my knees. I turned from her and looked at the floor.

I said, "I can't remember. I just can't."

She gave me one last pat, said, "You take it easy," and left.

I turned back to the surgery table, the needle ready to slip down into the burr hole, then pierce the dura mater, that sheet of tough, thin tissue keeping things whole inside the skull, and plunge into the brain itself, sink into the Red Nucleus, where, indeed, it would fry brain cells.

I pictured the electrode down inside the brain, saw the tip of it send out sparks I knew I could never actually see, saw brain cells fold and implode one after another, unable now to regenerate, dead for all time.

Then I saw the electrode, the current off, lift from inside the brain, track up along its own path, up through the dura mater sealing itself off once the needle had been pulled up through it, the electrode emerging from the burr hole, the needle clean and harmless and gleaming. Next I pictured the Gelfoam being packed into the hole, that toothpastelike synthetic material we pretended was as good as bone, tamped down and sealing off the skull as if it were a tomb we had entered only to steal small items, nothing significant. Then came the removal of the hemostats, the skin pulled back into place, and the black thread—always black, a horrible, stark black against pink skin and white fur—that would lace things back together, Chesterfield as good as new, but never as good as new.

I looked at the table, at Chesterfield's skull still exposed, the electrode waiting. I had all that work to do; had to finish this surgery, then do Small #2, then the next rabbit and the next, on and on, and I saw that today would be filled with rabbits, each moving a few brain cells on to their deaths, and that it wouldn't be over when I operated on the last rabbit. It would go on forever, go on, my life here with this table, these skulls, these fissures. That was who I was. This was my living.

I was crying, the tears welling up, blurring my vision, the white and the red and clamps and pipes fusing into bizarre permutations of their original shapes, and I put both hands to my eyes to try to stop myself.

Martin, I thought. Martin. He was who had come to me. Martin. But why?

I'd been thinking of children in a dream, and the dread in me they had somehow caused.

But why Martin?

I swallowed, took my hands from my eyes. I caught a breath, glad for it, though it stank of formaldahyde and blood and bone.

Martin.

I focused on the electrode. I had things to do. A job. Things that had nothing to do with Martin, with my dream, with crying over the future of dumb animals, and so I put my hand to the dial again, and began lowering the electrode, lowering it, until its tip disappeared into the skull, and it sliced down toward its destination, clean and easy.

By lunch I had finished four rabbits, each one placed back into its cage to sleep things off.

I went up to Paige and Wendy's office, got my sack lunch from the small, dorm-sized refrigerator beneath the table the coffee machine sat on, the refrigerator door covered with wood-grain Contact paper, someone's idea, I imagined, of making the refrigerator look more natural, less a metal box pouring out warm air.

Wendy was gone, Paige working at her typewriter. She was facing the wall, her head turned toward a handwritten manuscript on the paper stand, a yellow plastic magnetic bar clamped onto the page to hold it in place.

On the bulletin board above her were those pictures of her boy and her husband. But now there was a new one, put up, I imagined, just this morning; otherwise, I would have noticed it before. I looked at the bulletin board and the pictures every day.

The paper sack in my hand, I moved closer to Paige and the

board. The new photo, like all the others of her son, was one I
wished were mine.

Phillip, his back to the camera, stood at a low windowsill, his feet
spread apart farther than necessary, his head turned to his left just
enough to show the soft curve of cheek and chin, the outside corner
of his left eye and the thick, almost girlish eyelashes. He had on a
navy blue jumpsuit, the wrists and neck ringed with blue and white
stripes, and he wore thick, red socks. One hand, the right, was
grasping the edge of the sill for balance, the other hand holding a
baby-blue hairbrush up to his mouth. Light fell through the white
curtains of the window before him, diffused light that seemed to
illuminate the outline of his body without blocking out the details
of him: the fine, brown hair down over the neck of the jumpsuit,
the tiny fingernails of the hand holding the edge of the sill.

I stood directly behind Paige now, nearly touching her, my eyes
still on the photo.

Without moving, without missing a beat of the rhythm she had
created at the typewriter, she said, "Tom called. You were in surgery,
so I didn't want to bother you." She paused a moment, leaned toward
the page, and went at the typing again. "He said you guys are
meeting with the lawyer tonight."

I was still looking at the photo, taking in as much as I could,
trying to be there with soft light on the hardwood floor, there with
the pale, pale skin of his hands and ears, skin almost as pale as the
boy's in my dream. I said, "What lawyer?"

She stopped typing, and I glanced down at her. She was looking
at the photo now, too, her hands in her lap. "I don't know," she
said. "I thought you would."

We were quiet then, looking at the picture, our eyes, I knew,
roving, searching, recording this small life before us, Paige knowing
more than I would ever know: the tear and seizure of birth, the fire
and fear, the joy at hearing cries, new sound in the world where
once had been nothing. She knew what I would not; knew the love
of creation, of giving life.

She knew the fear, too, the well-founded kind, anchored in the
black knowledge of death. There was a word for children who lost
their parents, but none had yet been formed for the parent who

loses a child. I envied her for that willingness to bring in life in the face of the possibility of loss. One had to accept death, I saw, if one wanted to have a child.

Paige looked at me now, her head leaning back so that her face was upside down below me. She smiled, moved her head forward, and looked at the manuscript a moment. She started typing.

Outside, the sky was clear, the air cold and windy, dead leaves from trees around the lab scraping across the sidewalk. Everywhere, too, were students, now the mad rush at lunchtime. Cloistered in the lab, I seemed to forget more and more often that this was a campus of over 20,000 students, every one of them, it seemed, crossing back and forth in front of me, the sidewalk that ran alongside the lab the main thoroughfare between campus and the Tower Dorms.

The wind was cold, but it hadn't yet deterred any students. It was still only October, and they hadn't given in yet to the firm truth of winter. Boys and girls still wore walking shorts and Bermuda shorts and gym shorts, or wore sweatpants with the legs pushed up to just below the knee. Some girls had on short, tight denim or sailcloth skirts with flats or sandals. Every boy had on either a pair of deck shoes and no socks or a pair of unlaced Reeboks, tongues of the shoes cockeyed and flapping as they walked.

They were working-class kids, you could tell, just normal kids, kids who'd probably hoped for a better school than this—who in Massachusetts didn't think they might go to Harvard or Smith or Amherst or Mount Holyoke?—but hadn't the money or the grades or both. Kids, I knew, who were a lot like me. I'd gone here. I'd graduated. I'd never left.

The kids continued moving past. I knew I had to cut through them and the parking lot beyond to get to Whitmore and the snack bar. There was no way I was going to have lunch in the lab, not after that morning.

And here was the feeling again, that fear creeping into me. I didn't want to have to pass between people, cross the parking lot, walk into the ugly white concrete building with narrow black windows. All this space, all this air and movement around me.

But I did it, took the step into the crowd and maneuvered my way between kids, and then I was in the lot, walking along the rows of parked cars. A moment later I had my hand on the door of the administration building, and I was inside.

It wasn't quite noon, the snack bar not yet full. The snack bar was a small room, one wall all glass with a door that let out onto a patio, Whitmore actually a square building with the center a sort of atrium furnished with metal outdoor tables and chairs.

Around the room were small, square tables of white Formica, chairs with seats and backs of hard plastic. The wall opposite the windows was where the food was kept: a stainless-steel-and-glass counter ran the width of the room, on it two trays of donuts; a refrigerator case lit with fluorescent bulbs to display tuna, ham and cheese, and roast beef sandwiches, all wrapped too tightly in cellophane; the stainless steel tank of a coffee machine. Behind the counter was the grill and deep-fat fryers and the larger refrigerator case and, of course, the old women, short and squat and dressed in white uniforms, their hair always up in hair nets; occasionally there was some poor work-study student back there, given the job of changing the oil in the fryer or of scrubbing down the grill.

Though I'd worked here on campus all these years, had gone over to the snack bar at least two or three times a week, still the women acted as if they did not recognize me, as if each time I ordered what I did—always an onion bagel, always with cream cheese—I was someone they had never seen before, the order something alien to them. They always placed the bagel on the counter before me, always gave a quick smile without our eyes ever meeting; always I smiled back, hoping that they might see I was somebody. But nothing ever changed, and every time my smile faded, I wondered why I had put it there in the first place. And every time I realized that they were only working, only doing their jobs. They would be paid no more if they were to smile. They gave students and faculty and staff alike the food they ordered, and went on to the next person, thinking, I imagined, only about when the last person would come through, the last burger cooked, the last bagel served. They would go home then to cook even more, I imagined, this time for a husband who maybe worked over in Physical Plant or somewhere else on campus, their kids already grown, gone from the house. I could not blame them for not having given a smile that meant anything.

I went to the end of the counter to the cash register, where yet another short woman sat perched on a stool. She rang up my order, I paid, and I began looking for a place to sit.

There in the corner of the room, her table pushed up against the glass, sat Sandra, alone, bent over a sandwich on a paper plate, a wad of cellophane on the table. Next to the plate sat a Diet Coke and an open bag of Doritos.

I'd never seen her here before, never known her to come over except for coffee runs whenever the office ran out. But here she was, about to bite into a sandwich from the refrigerator case, sandwiches that seemed so flat, squashed, and older than we could know. The only food I'd ever seen her eat was what she brought from home: juices in small, clear bottles, fresh fruit, yogurt and carrots and celery sticks.

I made my way to her table and set down my bagel and sack lunch. She had the sandwich up to her mouth, then lifted her eyes to me.

She stopped, put the sandwich down, dusted off her hands and put them in her lap. She gave an embarrassed half smile as I hung my pocketbook on the back of my chair. I sat down.

I said, "What are you doing over here? And with that food? What is it?"

She picked it up again, smelled it. "I think it's egg salad. That, or tuna fish. Either one would probably smell this bad."

We both laughed, but stopped at the same moment, the air suddenly gone dead between us.

I opened my lunch bag, peered inside as if there might be something other than what I had put in there this morning. I said, "So you think I was talking to myself in there, huh?"

She was looking at her sandwich, and for a moment I thought she hadn't heard me. "Sandra?" I said.

She looked up at me, startled, her eyes quick with alarm, open wide. "What?"

"You said I was talking to myself in there. In surgery."

"Oh," she said. "Yeah. That's right." Again she put the sandwich down. "I could have sworn. I could swear you were saying that name again and again. Like it was some sort of mantra for you. It was crazy."

Her mind was off what she'd just been thinking about, I could see. She put her arms up on the table and crossed them in front of her, leaned toward me. "So who is this guy?" she said. She was smiling now.

"Stress," I said, and I popped off the top of my yogurt container. I didn't know what I was going to say, how to get beyond the topic of Martin and my dream, didn't know how to get around the fact that I'd been talking and had no recollection of ever having spoken. "Stress," I said again, "is probably who it is. The truth is there's this guy who's involved with the house whose name is Martin. He's one of the two guys who goes out and cleans up the place during the year. He's—"

"Is he cute?" Sandra cut in, still smiling. Though her face was pale, her hair out of place, a plate of nonfood in front of her, this was more the real Sandra, the one I'd grown to love, the one I'd talked with enough times to say anything I wanted.

During the last three years we'd spent enough lunches in the computer room, the lights out so that Will wouldn't think to look for us there, sitting in the dark and talking of things, things that would have been enormous or irrelevant in the light of day. In that dark, things seemed small enough to handle; we could talk of death, of life, of women and men and love, all without inhibition because we could see nothing except the crack of light beneath the door, that crack our focal point, the only thing we needed to see while we ate our lunches.

Now, I wanted that Sandra. I wanted her back, wished we were in the computer room again instead of here, the words *Martin's retarded* poised on my tongue and ready for release. It was because of the look on her face—the conspiratorial grin about a man she thought could be cute, though she, too, was married—that I wanted her back. She was, right then, the happiest I'd seen her in weeks. But I could only imagine what would happen if I were to tell her what I wanted to say about Martin.

I lied. I said, "Yes, I guess so," and I looked into my yogurt. With my spoon I pulled up through the white a burst of dark, red fruit. I was smiling.

"So?" she said, and leaned even closer.

"So nothing, okay? So he's cute. That's all."

Though I hadn't intended anything, any maliciousness, any anger, she seemed to shrink away, moved her arms off the table and back to her lap. Her eyes fell to the plate before her again.

I stopped stirring the yogurt. I said, "I'm sorry if I said anything."

"It's me," she said. She crossed her arms, looked out the window. She squinted at the light, the sun as high in the sky as it would be this late in the year.

It *was* her, I saw. She had changed, changed in ways I'd thought unimaginable for her. Slow changes that, I realized, had been at work for weeks, changes nearly imperceptible until now, right now, when they hit me full on: she really didn't care anymore. There was her hair, her skin, the food. It had been three weeks since I had seen her bike in the locker room, Sandra taking the bus now. Last week Will had had her completely rewrite a short article she'd written, calling it sloppy and inarticulate. I had gotten hold of a copy, ready to defend Sandra against what I imagined must have been yet another of Will's needless tirades. But he was right; the paper was poorly written, hardly publishable.

Just the week before, I'd gone down to the running room to find her sitting next to the filing cabinet, the fan going, the potentiometer ticking away. She sat with her knees together, her arms crossed, her head down. She was asleep, while her own batch of rabbits were running. Asleep, instead of monitoring them for any skipped stimuli or malfunctions.

I'd said her name once, and she had awoken, startled, her hands quickly moving to the edge of her seat and holding on tight, her head darting around as if she were expecting something to hit her any moment. It had taken her a full minute to come around, to see where she was, what she was doing. To recognize me.

And finally, there in the snack bar, her face turned from me, things fell into some order: I remembered the morning the rabbit had bitten me, remembered our conversation in the hallway, remembered losing her face in the dark of the hall. I remembered she'd wanted to talk to me about something.

I'd forgotten. Forgotten it completely, caught up in my own preoccupations, my own life: that bite, the house, my dreams, my job, and Grady and Martin and lawyers and realtors. Caught up in just living.

A month ago. It had been a month ago when her hair had been beautifully braided, her skin tan.

I said, "My God. I'm sorry. I'm sorry. You wanted to talk to me. I'm sorry." I put the yogurt down, placed my hand on the table, showed her I wanted to touch her.

She did not move.

"Sandra," I said, and moved my hand closer to her.

Slowly she looked down at the table. She said, "That was a while ago. A month ago. A whole month. I wanted—" she said, and stopped. She bit her upper lip, her chin quivering now. She put a hand to her forehead, closed tight her eyes.

"I'm sorry," she whispered, and took in quick, short breaths. "It's me. It's nothing you did. Nothing."

Before I could move she blinked several times, rubbed her nose, and stood. She placed the open bag of chips and the cellophane on her plate. Still not looking at me, she picked up the plate and the can of soda, dumped them in the black-plastic garbage barrel next to the door, and left.

I sat there a few moments, stunned, not moving. Then I looked outside, where within the last few moments shadows had begun to fall over the furniture out there, the air already going colder, the sun already descending.

I found her where I knew she would be, the first place I looked. No light came from beneath the computer room door, and I pushed it open. The door was near one of the few lights in the hall, and when I opened it, there sat Sandra, one hand up to block out the light. She was off to the right, her feet up on a chair.

She said, "Just close the door."

I looked for a chair, the light from the hall giving me only a view of half the room, and when I thought I saw the outline of an old straight-back I closed the door behind me, sealed us off. I headed to where I'd seen the chair, a hand low in front of me, the other still holding my lunch bag. My hand wasn't low enough, though, and my knees hit the chair, sending out into the dark the cold scrape of old wood on linoleum.

I turned, sat down. I put my lunch on the floor beside me.

I said, "Talk." I paused, the silence inside all the more loud for

the dark. My eyes were on the thin line of white beneath the door.
I said, "I'm sorry that I didn't listen before. I'm sorry. That's all I
can say. But talk now."

"Please," Sandra said, too loud and too quick. "Please, just shut
up. Will you please just shut up?"

She went quiet. A moment later I heard her take in quick breaths
and then breathe out in a silent cry, one long hiss of air.

We sat for a long time. There was only the dark, and the crack of
light on the floor, light that crept only a foot or so out onto the
linoleum, no farther. I stared at it, and as I did, the light seemed to
make the rest of the room disappear, the blackness around me
nothing, just space, the slice of light some strange sun, me hovering
just far enough away to keep from being pulled into the center of
it, just close enough to keep from hurtling away and into whatever
black was behind me.

"Okay," Sandra finally said. She hadn't moved; there was no creak
of chair, no sound of material against material as she moved an arm
or crossed her legs. Just that single word.

I said nothing.

"Then," she said, and nothing more. I could feel in the air her
waiting for me, but still I said nothing. She took in another breath,
and said, "So what do you want to know?"

I said nothing.

"Claire?" she said. She paused, then said, "Oh, you're going to
play quiet." She paused. "Fine."

I said, "I'm here." I was quiet a moment, and I said, "The last I
heard you were with the PMS study. Is that your problem? You kill
your husband because of cramps?"

At last she laughed, and I could hear in her the pain involved: it
was more a cry than anything else, her throat tight, her laughter
escaping in quick, desperate bursts. She laughed and laughed, but
suddenly stopped.

"If only," she started. "If only that were it. Cramps. If it were only
that easy." I heard her weight shift in the chair, the twist and grate
of a spring.

"Ohh," she breathed. "To laugh. Jesus. What a thing."

"Just talk," I said.

"PMS," she said. "PMS. I wish it were that. But to start it. Okay." She took in one more deep breath, and on the sound of air going in I could hear the faint hiccups from her crying, the little spasms of breathing. "It starts," she said, "with me being pregnant."

"What?" I almost shouted. I sat up in the chair and turned to her voice. I could see nothing, only the luminous purple shadows inside my eyes from staring too long at the light beneath the door. "Sandra," I said, my eyes trying to locate her, if only some vague outline. "Sandra," I said again, moving to stand up. I wanted to go to her, to hug her. "That's fantas—"

"No it's not," she said, her voice loud, cutting me off, and I froze, half-standing, half-sitting. I held that stance for what seemed a full minute, then slowly I sat back down. I was leaning forward now, my elbows on my knees. I made out her silhouette: her head in profile, her legs, it appeared, pulled up in front of her, her feet on the edge of the seat.

"It's not fantastic," she said, her voice now solemn. "It's not fantastic at all. It's not anything. And so you see, I hope, why I haven't said anything to you at all. Because I knew what you would say. I knew how you'd react. Just like this." She paused. "Like the whole world wants precisely what you want."

I looked away from her, looked at the floor. I clasped my hands between my knees.

"I found out about seven weeks ago. Eight weeks on Tuesday. So that morning, that morning you got bit, I think things were just starting to sink in. It hadn't really started to hit me until that morning. That was the first morning I threw up."

I said, "So throwing up's going to make you not want to have a baby. Is that it?" and I heard my words in the dark, too harsh, too cutting.

"Just shut up," she said. "Just shut up and listen," and I saw then that the darkness of the computer room could work both ways: it could free us up to wonder at the universe, but it could also force us to see how ugly and small we really were, how little we knew of each other, of ourselves.

"A diaphragm baby," she said. "Hah. A diaphragm baby. So much for diaphragms. So much for taking and plugging something up into yourself in the hopes that some little sperm won't get past a

vulcanized rubber wall. So much for that. I didn't take the pill—I
know that's what you're thinking right now, thinking, Why didn't
she use the pill? I didn't take it because I didn't, don't like the idea
of all that progesterone and estrogen and the warnings and symp-
toms and everything else you read on those slick little pamphlets
they try and give you. All that shit. I didn't want any of that in my
system. I'll tell you. So this is what I do: I put in the diaphragm, I
use the spermicide, and there I was a month ago. And I'd wanted
to talk to you."

I let the silence after her go for a while, and said, "It wasn't my
fault I got bit. That much should be obvious." My eyes were still
on the floor, and I thought I could see the outlines of each individual
square of tile, though I knew, really, I could not.

"Obviously," she said. "But you. You're so filled with yourself,
that's it. You and your hubby looking for your Dream House. And
you moping around after that bite, just moping and moping, drag-
ging ass around here. But here's the sad thing: you've been doing
that for years, and you don't even know it. You don't even *know*
how much you drag ass around here, mourning yourself. And now
it's only gotten worse. You haven't given me the time of day since
that day, and now the only reason you're over here right now is
because I practically had to drag you over here. Had to stand up in
that crappy cafeteria and drag you over here."

My face and hands and neck had gone hot, and I wondered what
color my face was, how hot a red I'd become. Still, I did nothing.

She said, "And you and Mr. Gadsen. You don't give a good goddamn for him. That old guy. You won't even talk to him. You've
seen his truck here before and sneaked back into Paige and Wendy's,
or back to the locker room. I've seen you. I've seen that, seen you
move somewhere just to stay away from him, just to avoid having
him apologize to you."

I looked from the floor to the line of light. A shadow passed outside,
making the light waver, thin out, return: Will or Paige or Wendy
moving down the hall. Or Mr. Gadsen, a ghost moving around in
this building.

"So what?" I said. "What does he have to do with your being
pregnant? Is this why you got me in here? Just so you could bitch
at me? Just so you could sit there and bitch and moan because

you're pregnant and don't want to be? Just because you got pregnant and things weren't quite right enough for you right now? Just—"

"Just shut up!" She cried, sobbing fully now, echoing in the room so that it sounded as if there were three women in here, crying, crying. "Just shut up," she said again, this time quieter. "Shut up, because I *want* it. I want the baby."

"Oh God," I whispered, and I stood, making my way through the dark to her, both hands in front of me. Finally I touched her, gently placing my hands on her to find she was sitting as I'd thought, her hands clasped and holding her legs to her chest, her feet up on the seat. Her head was down, and she was crying into her knees.

I knelt next to her, gently patted her shoulder.

"Don't touch me," she said. "Just don't even touch me."

"Sorry," I said, "but I am," and I kept patting her, kept touching her. I said, "What's wrong? What's wrong with keeping it?"

She tried to stop crying, going silent for a moment and holding her breath, but then she seemed to burst, and her sobs came out even louder. She took one hand and rubbed her eyes—I could only feel the movement in the dark, the shift of an arm from in front of her legs to her head and back—and she tried to whisper. "Because of Jim. Because he doesn't want it." The words came out broken, some whispered, some on the loud voice of her crying.

Suddenly her head was up, and she leaned it back until it rested against the chair. My hand was on her neck now, but I didn't move it; instead I gently rubbed the muscles there.

She sniffed, swallowed. She said, "Because Jim doesn't want it right now. He thinks we've got a lot more to do first. He thinks we have to climb the Himalayas first, and then sail the Atlantic, then walk across America." Her voice had toughened up now, some of the sounds of tears disappearing.

Though she spoke of her husband often enough—of their bike rides to Boston and to Hartford and, once, all the way to Buffalo, I had met the man only twice. The first time was during the worst snowstorm I could remember. It was only a couple of weeks after Sandra had started, a day when I was training her on staining and mounting. We were in the staining room, both of us leaning over the microtome, the fixed and frozen rabbit brain ready to be sliced into thin sheets and placed on slides, when I heard a sound from behind us. I turned, a slide in my hand, and dropped it, startled at what was there.

It was a man, no one I recognized. He was short, but I couldn't tell how he might have been built for all the clothing he wore: he had on a huge, green parka, the hood tied tight around his face. All I could see of him were his sunglasses and nose and mustache, all ringed by the brown fur of the parka hood. He had on thick nylon-shell mittens, blue ski pants and knee-high snowboots. He was dusted with snow.

Sandra turned only after the slide had hit the ground, and shattered. "Jim," she said. "What are you doing here?" She came around me and moved toward him.

"Help," he said. "I don't think I can move in all this." Sandra was at him then, loosening the parka hood. He pulled off a mitten, and Sandra pulled back the hood.

He had blond hair and a full, red beard that had been hidden inside the parka, and he was smiling. They kissed quickly, and Sandra turned to me.

"This is my husband, Jim," she said. With one hand she started brushing snow off his shoulders.

"Pleased to meet you," he said, and took off the sunglasses. He had brown eyes, bright, and with that smile he looked like a kid, all set to play in the snow.

"I hate to be the bearer of bad news," he said, "but the campus is closing down. That's why I walked over here, to get Sandra." He turned to her. "The place is going to shut down, and so I thought we could walk home through this. I thought it would be fun. But we have to go now. It's going to get too deep to make it through."

Once Sandra had gotten her coat and hat and mittens and boots on, they left, and I went to the staining room window to look outside, see just how heavy things were out there.

Snow was already halfway up the tires of cars in the parking lot, the sidewalks nonexistent, only drifts of snow, and here came Jim and Sandra, Jim ahead of her, running, Sandra behind him, stooped in the snow. She pulled up a handful, made a snowball, and threw it at him. She nailed him square in the back, and I could hear above the bubbling of the radiators their laughter.

The second time I met him—the only other time—had been in midsummer. Jack had given me a draft of a paper he and Sandra had written for *Brain Research,* asked me to take it up to Sandra's apartment in North Village, where she was home sick.

I walked, the trees bright green and new, the students all gone, the campus like some small city evacuated for whatever reason. It was beautiful, quiet.

North Village, one of the married-student housing centers for the university, was about a half-mile north of campus, and by the time I got to the place, I had worked up a good sweat, the air heavy with humidity.

The complex was made up of one-story duplexes. Big Wheels littered the place, in yards, on porches, on the street. Each unit had a small patch of ground before it, mostly bald dirt where kids had played. The duplexes themselves were covered with gray, wooden siding, the trim all gray, the roofs gray and flat. Huge blue dumpsters sat here and there around the complex, some overflowing with trash, others empty.

I found their apartment halfway back into the complex, in the G section. Their lawn seemed to have a little more grass than most of the others, and I figured it must have been because they had no children.

I knocked on the door, a cheap, hollow gray door, and heard Jim shout from inside, "It's not locked."

I pushed too hard to get the door open, slamming it into the wall inside. I nearly fell into the room, but then I got my balance. I looked up.

Jim stood in the front room in red nylon running shorts and black running shoes. He was pulling on a T-shirt, his chest bare and hairless, his stomach flat. The shirt was covering his head, and when he pulled it down, he was looking at me from the corner of his eyes, his head turned a little away. His mouth was shut tight.

I didn't recognize him. He was hurrying to dress, I could see, as he straightened out the shirt, knelt to tie first one shoe and then the other. He didn't have the beard or mustache now, and his hair was short. He was thin, terribly thin, and he was shorter than me, too, something I hadn't noticed during the winter, and for a moment

I thought that I had busted in on something illicit: a stranger hurrying to dress, Sandra somewhere, perhaps dressing in the bedroom,
me arriving here unannounced.

He started in on a couple of stretches, spread his legs and leaned
first toward one foot, then the other.

I said, "I'm Claire Templeton. From the lab? Jack sent me over
to give something to Sandra." I was still leaning against the open
door.

He didn't look up at me, but merely stopped one stretch and went
into another, twisting from side to side, his hands on his hips. "She's
in the bedroom," he seemed to grunt out. "Says she's sick."

He stopped and, still without looking at me, came toward the door
and jogged out. When he got onto the grass he called, "Close the
door. Air conditioner's on."

"Claire?" I heard from farther back in the apartment. It was Sandra, her voice faint, weak.

I closed the door, saw in the wall the hole where the doorknob
had hit probably a thousand times before. I went for the doorway
at the far end of the room, looking at everything. An old brown
couch sat against one wall, the cushions nearly flat and sunken into
the frame. Above it hung a poster of El Capitan, thumbtacked into
the wall. Beneath the front window, the window that looked out
onto the lawn and parking lot, were brick and plywood bookshelves
crammed with textbooks and Stephen King novels; atop that sat a
small portable television. Various sports equipment had been tossed
or stacked around in the room: two sleeping bags, two backpacks,
a Coleman stove, a canoe paddle, baseball bats and gloves. For a
coffee table they had a telephone wire spool, one of those huge,
round wooden things. On it lay issues of *Consumer Reports, Mother
Earth News, Outside,* a dog-eared copy of the *Whole Earth Catalog.*

I made it to the doorway, to my right the kitchenette, only a recess
far enough into the wall to allow a sink, stove, and small refrigerator,
above them miniscule cabinets maybe eight inches deep.

"Claire?" Sandra called out again, and I went through the
doorway.

The room was nearly dark, the curtains drawn, the shades down.
The room, too, was ice-cold, the air conditioner in the window on
full blast.

I sat on the edge of the bed, Sandra lying in the middle, just a sheet over her. More posters hung on the walls; in the dark I thought I could see an Ansel Adams and a Harvey Edwards. Still more sports stuff was in here, against the wall and below the air conditioner their two bicycles, in another corner a soccer ball and some tennis racquets.

"Sandra," I said, "what's wrong?"

"A cold. That's all," she whispered, her nose stuffed up, I could hear. "A goddamned cold is all. I thought I could whip it myself, but I couldn't. Here I am."

I said, "What's with Jim?"

She let out a deep sigh. "Oh, Jesus. He thinks it's my fault. He's up there with Linus Pauling, holding that the cold can be prevented with Vitamin C. So now it's all my fault."

I handed the manuscript to her. "Will's get-well gift. The *Brain Research* paper. Final revisions."

"What a guy," she whispered, and reached for the manuscript. Our hands touched, and her fingers were hot.

I stood, leaned over her, and put my wrist on her forehead. She was burning up.

That was when I took her to the Health Center, where they'd had to put her on antibiotics to get rid of the sinusitis she'd contracted.

So that now, in the dark of the computer room, these were the images of Jim I had in me: a kid ready to play in the snow, and some bastard who held her personally responsible for getting a cold.

"So," she said. "You tell me. You tell me what to do. My husband gets me pregnant. I want it. He doesn't. So you tell me."

My hand was still on her neck. I said, "I know what I would do." I paused. "But I'm not you."

"Easy answer," she said.

I waited a moment, and said, "Will he leave you if you have it?"

"That's the thing," she said, and leaned her head forward again, let it rest on her knees. "He's just pissing around with his course work. He is. He's not interested in the Ag stuff anymore. He doesn't study. He's not attending classes. He's got his job with the Ag department, handling animals and cleaning sheep shit, and that's it. Otherwise he's out playing fast-pitch softball, or over at Boyden playing basketball, or ice-climbing or running cross-country or God knows what else." She sniffed, then whispered, "Stuff I used to do." She was quiet. "But he hasn't said one way or the other. No ultimatum. Not yet."

She started to cry again, her breaths almost silent, silver sounds in the dark. She cried, and said, "But here's the problem. The problem is that I love him. And what I keep wondering is, Why should that be the problem? Why should the fact that I love my husband be the problem?" She tried to come up from her sobbing, to take a deep breath, but nothing happened. She cried, saying, "And I look at you. And I hate you, because you have what I want. You love your husband, he loves you. And you want to get pregnant. And here I am, just the opposite. I don't have any idea whether or not he loves me, and here I am pregnant. He tells me to get rid of it, that it's in the way. He tells me to go get—"

"Stop," I whispered. "Now stop."

"Why?" she said, and her head was up again, her back stiff. Though I couldn't see her face in the dark, I knew she was looking at me. "Don't you want me to say the word?" She'd stopped crying, too. She sniffed again, took in a breath. "Don't you want to hear it? Here: *Abortion*. That's what he tells me to go do. To get an abortion."

It was me who was crying now, whatever shapes I could see in the darkness disappearing as my eyes filled, as I bit my lip to hold in my breath.

"That's the word," she went on, "that's what he told me. 'Why don't you just go on in and get an abortion?' he says to me, him standing there in the living room in shorts and a T-shirt, holding a basketball. He's just back from the courts, where he and some buddies have had a good, refreshing, brisk workout. 'Abortion,' he says. That's the word."

I closed my eyes.

"So," she said. "What to do?"

"Leave him," I whispered.

"Not that easy," she said. "That's Claire talking as Claire. That's not Claire trying to think what Sandra should do."

"Why?" I cried finally, letting out my sob, my chest collapsing. "Why ask me? Why ask me if you know I can't help?"

"Because," she said quickly. She paused, took a deep breath, again on that air in the faint hiccups. "Because now I've told you. Now you know."

I leaned into her, and cried, trying to whisper *I see,* but unable to form the words, any words, that might comfort her, and that might comfort me.

I said nothing.

 I began to feel as if my life were happening in dark rooms, that that was where I lived, where I talked, where I slept and ate. Here we were now, too, in the office of Mr. Clark's lawyer, only two lights on: the green banker's lamp on his desk, and the ginger jar lamp at the end of the sofa. The rest of the room was dark oak paneling and books.

Mr. Blaisdell stood looking out the curtainless window of the office down onto Main Street, his office on the second floor of one of the older buildings. His back was to us, his hands jammed into his pockets, his suit coat flared out at either side.

He was an old man, what I figured was apropos: he and the as yet unseen Mr. Clark could see eye to eye, know what each other thought, regard people like us the same. They understood each other.

He was short and round, his thick, white hair in something of a pompadour, only enhancing the roundness of things. His arms were short, the fingers fat and stubby so that whenever I shook hands with him—this was the third time we had met—his fingers only came to about the middle of my palm.

He gave out a heavy sigh, let his shoulders drop, all with his back to us. He looked down, and his head disappeared, before us only the back of a round body clad in a brown pinstripe suit.

He turned from the window, came around the edge of his desk, and did the best he could to sit on the front corner. When he finally situated himself, he was blocking out the light from the banker's lamp, and suddenly I wanted away from this flush-faced old lawyer gearing himself up to tell us something we didn't want to hear.

I wanted out. I wanted to be outside on the street, the streetlamps just coming on, the sun now down, the sky, what I could see of it from where I sat, deep violet, the first evening stars glimmering in. I wanted on that street.

But then I thought of something better: I wanted to be in Chesterfield right now. I wanted to be settled in front of the fireplace in the front room, wanted some hot food going on the ancient stove in the kitchen, wanted our furniture in.

And then too many things crowded in on me. First was Sandra; after we talked that afternoon, we sat there in the dark for an hour without saying anything. To hell with Will, I was thinking, and with the rabbits and brains and sutures and running. To hell with it all. But as if on cue we had both stood up, left the room, still without having spoken. She went to the left and down the hall to whatever project she had been working on, and I went to the right, and down to the basement and to the next rabbit.

And then those thoughts were shoved out, because I started thinking of Mr. Gadsen, of this part of me left undone by my holding against him that accident, because what she had said was true: I had avoided him. Only last week I had seen him in the hall, saw him facing the wall and leaning against it, his right arm from palm to elbow pressed against the cinderblock, his head down. He was hacking, coughing something up into an old, yellowed handkerchief there at his mouth. He'd glanced up, and I knew he saw me coming out of the staining room. I had meant to go down the hall and to the basement, a path that would have led me right to him, fifteen yards away, but instead I gave him a quick smile, looked away, and turned toward the women's room across the hall, pushing into that door. From the corner of my eye I had seen him turn toward me, seen him raise an arm as if to wave at me, saw him already moving toward me. Then, just as the door closed behind me, I heard him call out "Missy," and I went to a stall, sat on the toilet seat, and waited until I heard his footsteps recede down the hallway.

The old lawyer put a fist to his mouth, cleared his throat into it. "You know," he started, his solemn lawyer's voice full and booming in the small room. "You know that there are always reasons why someone sells a house. Reasons that, oftentimes, defy any sort of rational orientation."

I put my hand to my forehead, my elbow resting on the soft leather arm of the sofa. I closed my eyes.

"And I think what you'll find here is that this is indeed the case," he went on, and I opened my eyes. The fist had become some sort of visual aid, the index and pinky fingers pointed, the two middle fingers folded down. He seemed to be aiming at something across the room. His eyes hadn't yet met ours. "The point being that Mr. Clark is selling the house to you for a fit price, one mutually conducive to both parties—"

I brought my hand from my forehead and placed it in my lap, took a deep breath in the middle of all this talk.

"—and since that is what has been agreed upon," he continued without losing a moment of his old lawyer's pace, the tone of righteousness, "there seems no further reason to delve any deeper into any particular personal, idiosyncratic reasons behind his selling you the house."

He stopped, and I looked up at him. He was looking at Tom now.

Tom took in a deep breath. He was warming up. He was ready to fight, and I wasn't sure whether I wished him well, or if I wanted him, too, to be quiet, to get us out of here.

"So," he began, "what you're saying is that there's no reason that you're willing to talk about. From what I'm hearing, I think there *is* a reason, a specific one, but you're not talking. Is that right?" He crossed one leg over the other, folded his hands in his lap, and I knew then which way we were going.

Mr. Blaisdell looked down. He, too, folded his hands together, tried to place them comfortably on his belly. He ended up looking as if he were keeping his stomach from tumbling out over his belt.

"Well," he said, and gave a quick nod. "What we're doing right now, our talking about it, is something we don't have to do to begin with, young man. You called me on the telephone to ask why we're selling the house, and I could have given you the cold shoulder, son. But I didn't, and I think this gesture of goodwill shows my sincerity, as well as Mr. Clark's. So here we are."

"And you've said nothing."

I reached over to Tom, put a hand to his arm to signal him to ease up. We didn't need this, but Tom only looked at me a moment, and back at the lawyer.

With something of a grunt the lawyer climbed off the edge of the table, went back to the window. He struck the same pose as before: hands in pockets, back to us, head down.

"Look," he said. "What you don't understand is what this place is to this man." He paused, brought his head up. "The house has been in his family since before the Civil War. That's something you should know. And you should know that he's about dead now, and he knows it. His wife died four years ago." He looked down, his head disappearing again. "He's got no heirs either, so—"

"Now wait," Tom said. "Hold on. What about this kid Grady?"

Mr. Blaisdell turned around too quickly, nearly knocking into his chair. His eyebrows were up, his mouth open. "How do you know him?"

Tom gave a small smile, delighted in this change, the reversal of who was in charge. "Suffice it to say," he said, "that we've run into him a couple of times, and he's told us some things about the house."

"That boy," he said, and shook his head. "You probably know he's the grandson. If you didn't, there isn't any harm as I can see in your knowing it now." He looked around as if to search for the chair next to him. He looked at it, turned and sat. He was still shaking his head. "He's no heir, though. I drew up the papers myself as soon as he turned eighteen, just last year." He looked up at us. "He's disowned."

I closed my eyes, took my arm away from Tom. I heard my voice say, "Why?"

"Miss," he began, and though I could not see him, though I had heard only that one single word, I could feel the condescension there. "He was a juvenile delinquent. He was apprehended for shoplifting twice in grocery stores. Picking up *food,* when he had his grandparents, especially his grandmother, taking care of him quite well back at home. Apprehended twice, and he was a runaway time and again, disappearing for days at a time, giving his grandmother, and, of course, Mr. Clark, no end of grief. Some days I'd see him myself from this very office, from this very window." My eyes still closed, I heard the creak of his chair, the give of leather as, I imagined, he pointed to the window behind him. "Just tooling around town, riding his bicycle and daring his grandfather to do something. All the while he was in school, managing just to squeak by, while his grandmother's heart was dying for him. And, too, Mr. Clark's." He stopped, and I heard the leather again, imagined him leaning even farther back. "Finally moved out when he was sixteen, a year after his grandmother died. Mr. Clark decided that he had had enough of him, and he let the boy live on his own. When he turned eighteen, Mr. Clark rid himself of him. I can't say as I blame him, either."

Tom said, "But his parents. He's told us about them, too. What happened to them?"

I'd heard enough already, heard enough grief about this family. Tom, though, still wanted to know more, dig deeper. He wasn't through yet. He was still trying to prove his point to me, I knew, about Grady's being a liar.

I said, "Let's go." I opened my eyes.

The lawyer leaned forward. He put both hands on the desk, his red face and white hair and old, spotted hands bright from the light of the banker's lamp. "The father," he said, and looked at those hands.

I said, "Let's go now, please," and I touched Tom's arm. He didn't move. I moved up to the edge of the sofa.

"The father was killed in Vietnam. So they assume. MIA since 1969." He paused, laying his hands flat on the green-felt blotter, still looking at them. "The mother—the Clarks' daughter—committed suicide."

Though I was on the edge of the sofa, every muscle in me tensed for standing, suddenly I could not move. My hand fell from Tom's arm.

"So I hope that now you have what you came for," Mr. Blaisdell almost whispered. "There's a lot to the house he just doesn't want to carry with him what little time he has left. He wanted just to get rid of it, get rid of the house he was born in, the house their daughter was born in, the house his juvenile delinquent grandchild was born in. It's better out of his hands. That's why he's selling."

Tom breathed out. He said, "Oh."

I stood. I turned and left, went for the glass-and-oak door, pulled it open to the second floor landing.

I heard Tom stand, heard him say a quiet thank you, heard the crack of the lawyer's chair as he stood. Then Tom was behind me, his hand at the small of my back. For some reason he seemed to believe he needed to push me gently before him, but I moved forward quickly, moved down the stairs to another glass-and-oak door, this one letting out onto the street.

It was dark, and I could smell food cooking at any one of the restaurants in town. People walking on the sidewalk had to weave around me as I stood facing the street. I heard the door behind me close.

I said, "Are you happy?"

"I'm sorry," he said. "I am. It's closed. I want him helping us. I want Martin, too. They can use the money, both of them. We can use the help."

I said, "Wasn't that always the case?"

"Yes," he said.

I turned. Tom next to me, we headed east, toward King and the courthouse, lit up now, the fountain out in the grass going. Soon that will be turned off, I thought, for the winter.

I said, "Sandra's pregnant. Jim wants her to abort it."

I waited for him to say something, waited and waited: first to the end of the stone and wrought-iron fence encircling the courthouse, then while waiting for the four-way stop light at King and Main, then until we were under the awning of one of those restaurants, people in the windows sitting at their tables, steaming plates of food before them, colorful drinks in hand, everyone laughing and talking. They were happy.

He said nothing, made no comment on Sandra and Jim, and that was what I wanted to hear: nothing. Any comment, even any single word would have trivialized it all, as if the problem could be analyzed and solved with the utterance of some phrase such as *Too bad* or *I'm sorry* or even the single word *God*.

I stopped at the steps up to the door of the restaurant, looked in the window at lights inside. I turned to Tom for the first time since inside the office. A man and woman moved past us and up the steps, and I heard quiet laughter as the door fell closed.

I said, "Let's eat here."

"But we ate out last night," he said. "Friendly's?" He had his hands in his pockets.

I turned to the window. "But the people in there seem so happy," I said. I looked back at him, his face again in darkness. "And it's light in there."

He was quiet a moment, and I thought I could see on his face a smile, though I could not be certain for the dark out there.

"Okay," he said, and we went up the steps.

 "What the hell?" Tom whispered as we pulled up to the house.

Martin stood on the top step of an old wooden ladder leaned up against the side of the house, the side that had Tom's room upstairs, mine above. Martin's cheek was pressed to the wood, and he had what looked like an oblong rock in his hand. Grady, smiling and waving at us, stood at the bottom of the ladder, one hand holding it to keep it steady.

Even before Tom had the engine off and his door open I could see that Martin, oblivious to our having arrived, was tapping the house, the rock in his hand gently knocking against the clapboards, his ear pressed to the wood, listening, I imagined. But for what, I could not say.

"What's going on here?" Tom said as he strode toward them, his hands already in his back pockets. I was a few steps behind him.

"Shh," Grady said, and put a finger to his lips. He pointed to the side of the house. Both Tom and I turned and looked.

From just above the stone foundation, right where those clapboards began, on up to where Martin was perched atop the ladder were rough Xs marked in the wood, unsteady lines intersecting one another. Not every board had an X on it, only about every fourth or fifth one, but there were Xs all the same, scratched right into the blue paint or right into the gray, naked wood. There was only one X per board, too, but together, all those markings spread across the side of the house, they looked frightening, as if some strange form

135

of meticulous graffiti, each mark exactly alike, each hesitant X precisely the same.

Martin started down the ladder, and for some reason I took a step back. When he got to the bottom, he seemed not to see us; instead, he only picked up the ladder, moved it a few feet farther down the side of the house, mounted the ladder again. At the top step he leaned against the house again, slowly started tapping again. Then he stopped, moved his hand from the clapboard, and drew an X on the piece of wood. It seemed to take him an hour to do it, to take that stone and press against the wood, make two lines, his hand shaking with purpose. He pressed his ear to the next clapboard up, started tapping it.

Grady whispered, "Those are clapboards that'll have to go. They're ones that'll need to be taken off and replaced."

"What?" Tom said, and took a step closer to the house. He squatted, his hand just touching one of the marked boards near the foundation.

"You don't believe me," Grady whispered, "so you just have a look-see for yourself. You just take a screwdriver and give that board you're touching there a good gouge and see what you come up with." Grady pulled an old, rusted screwdriver from his back pocket, its clear yellow handle spattered with dried red paint. He held it out to Tom. "The way I see it, if you're serious about taking us on, you damn well better make sure we're doing the job the right way."

Tom hesitated a moment before reaching up and taking the screwdriver, then turned back to the clapboard and took a tentative poke at the wood, the screwdriver doing nothing, leaving no mark.

"You'll have to give it a little more spunk than that," Grady whispered, then laughed.

Tom pushed hard at the wood, the sky blue giving in a little before the shaft punctured the wood, sinking into the clapboard.

"Now twist it," Grady said. I looked at him. He wasn't smiling anymore, his forehead wrinkled with worry, as if he were not quite sure himself the wood would be rotten.

Tom twisted the screwdriver, turned it to one side and the other, and then the shaft broke out of the wood, the clapboard nearly bursting, sending a small shower of dead, gray splinters to the ground at Tom's feet.

Grady's face broke out in a smile. "What did I tell you?" he said. "What did I tell you?"

"Shh," Martin said from above us. I looked up at him. He hadn't moved, his head still against the clapboard.

Tom was poking at the hole in the wood, and I watched as rotten timber flaked away at the touch of his fingers.

"Now try the one above it, the one he didn't mark," Grady whispered.

Tom poked at it with the screwdriver, trying to break through the wood. Nothing happened. He pushed harder, and harder.

"Hard as granite," Grady whispered, and looked back up at Martin. He squinted into the light, held his hand above his eyes. "Old Martin here is, as you can see, marking up ones you might want to replace, either for dry rot, like what you've got down there with that piece you poked at, or for cracks or warped wood or what-have-you." He paused, let his eyes fall to Tom. "And he's a lot cheaper than any of your experts. We're a lot cheaper."

Tom stood, and the three of us watched Martin, who was still feeling the wood, his eyes half-closed, his mouth slack.

He looked as if he were in some sort of trance, his concentration so intense, and there, blinking at the autumn light and a man perched on a ladder, I thought again of Sandra, of the day before, Friday, and how she, too, had been in a trance all day, her hair only clipped back again, her bike nowhere, her face pallid.

Yesterday, the day after our time in the computer room, she had not spoken to me at all, had not even looked at me. She had come in late, spent her lunch hidden away in the building somewhere, the rest of the workday spent down in the basement running her own batch of rabbits. She had left early.

And still I had not called Mr. Gadsen. Maybe she knew I'd backed off at the thought of confronting that old man, of seeing him, of breathing him in, having the thought of that rabbit's dead, pregnant body hanging from my hand, and the stitches and the scar, and the dreams that had begun that night.

I wanted to talk to him, knew I needed to. But now was the weekend. I could call him on Monday. I could do that, and I could let Sandra know, and then we could talk even more.

Suddenly Martin was down the ladder, stood back from it with both hands on his hips. He looked up at the side of the house, and we three did the same, as if Martin's lead would bring us to the same sort of wisdom of wood he had.

He said, "What I will need is a bigger ladder. I will need that to get up to the roof, because the roof is the next part of the house that we need to check."

Grady turned to Tom. "What say we get one? We can rent one in town."

"I'll think about that," Tom said, looking up at the house. "Maybe tomorrow. I don't really feel like driving all the way back in right now. We just got here."

Grady shrugged, rubbed his nose. He turned to Martin. "Martin," he said, "what say we go check on the rest of the house, give the Templetons here a taste of your expertise?"

"Okay," Martin said loudly, giving a hard nod of his head. But he was still looking up at the house, at, I imagined, the roofline. Then he pointed at the roof, his arm stiff and straight, cutting right through the air. It was a quick move, and startled me. He said, "But one thing is for sure. For sure the fascia is going to need to have to be replaced. The fascia."

Fascia, I thought, and immediately my hands were together in front of me, holding, gripping one another. I looked down at them, saw how pale they were, the skin around the knuckles the yellow-white of no blood. There, too, was the scar, two ugly, bolt-red streaks.

I looked at Martin. His arm was still out in front of him, his finger still pointed. "What?" I managed to say, thinking of that word from his mouth, *fascia*, his taut throat forming the sound, and I thought of the thin membrane surrounding the skull, the membrane I scraped back to expose rabbit skull after rabbit skull all day the past two days.

"For sure," Martin said, still looking up, "the fascia is going to need to have to be replaced." He turned to me, his mouth still slack, eyes half-closed. He was still in his trance.

"The fascia," Tom said, "is that board up there at the edge of the roof." He, too, pointed, but his movement was casual, his finger moving up at an angle to trace the roofline for me. "That board up there that sort of seals off the rooftop so that there's a good place to nail down the shingles at the edge."

"The fascia," I said. "That's the word?"

"Sure," Tom said.

I looked at Martin. I said, "Where did you learn that word?"

He didn't move, didn't blink, but only stared at me. He gave a quick shrug, his arm still out and pointing at the roof. Wisps of his gray hair lifted and fell with the brittle morning breeze.

He let his arm drop, slapping it to his side. "Foundation next," he said. He turned and headed off into the woods behind him, his eyes on the ground as he walked.

The three of us watched as he kicked through dead leaves, taking small steps, the sound of broken leaves beneath his feet like fire. Then he stopped, leaned down and pulled from the leaves a thick, sturdy-looking branch about two feet long. He headed back to us, turning the piece of wood over and over in his hands, feeling it, looking at it as if it were some expensive tool he'd just invested in, or as if the thing were alive.

He said nothing, and went right to the foundation, where he began pushing at the mortar between the stones. He did it quickly, methodically, each touch at the gray between those stones in a pattern that started from the first visible line of mortar above ground on up each successive layer of stone, about two feet. When he reached the bottom clapboard, he moved down a few feet, did the pattern again. Occasionally the mortar would break away at the push of the stick, and Tom would stoop, run a finger along the soft patch.

"Fieldstones," Martin said. "A good foundation."

Tom, stopping, said, "You're right, Martin."

They reached the corner of the house, Martin leading, Tom close behind, Grady behind Tom a few feet, his hands on his hips, the three of them just prodding, touching, looking at the foundation of the old house.

Then they disappeared around the corner of the house, working their way along the back, and I was left standing alone, my hands still together in front of me. I watched where they had been, that corner; watched for nothing, simply looking at the wood siding, those clapboards marked with Xs, and at the fieldstones of the foundation.

I let go my hands, and held one above my eyes to block out the sun. I looked up at the roof, at that board there, the fascia, and suddenly I realized how alone I was, though I could hear the voices of my husband and Grady just around the corner of the house. I looked away from the fascia, but would not look to the woods, would not look out there to a place that went off for who knew how far. ·

I was alone, and as quickly as I could I moved around that corner to where the three still jabbed and poked and fondled the foundation, some form of rough diagnosis of the ills of a house that would soon be ours.

There had been only three sore spots in the foundation, places where the mortar disintegrated into sand when Martin poked it, and both he and Tom seemed unconcerned at that, though on one side of the house, the west side, Tom had even managed to pull out five separate fieldstones, leaving a hole right into the crawl space.

He had turned and looked up at me, almost proud, it seemed, like some little boy who'd broken a window at which he'd intentionally aimed. "Just so long as they're not loose at the corners," he tried to assure me.

He knew what he was doing, and I had faith in him that, yes, so long as the corners of this foundation were secure, the house would go on standing.

"Yep," Martin said, as though Tom had been talking to him. "Just so long as they are not loose at the corners." Already he had been moving forward, still tapping.

When they had finished the foundation, we had gone from room to room downstairs, checking the lay of the floor. In the front room, Martin had pulled from his pocket a marble, a large yellow cat's eye. None of us said anything as he crossed the room to the hearth, and squatted on the bricks. He gently placed the marble before him on the floor, then took away his hand as though he'd burned his fingers on that piece of glass. We watched as slowly it rolled away from him, and, in a smooth arc, toward the wall opposite him, where it bounced once, rolled back from the baseboard, and settled against the wall.

Martin had stood then, his eyes on the floor, and I could see in the unblinking severity of his gaze that he was recording the path of that marble, storing it away somewhere in his brain.

He went to the marble, picked it up, and positioned himself on the hearth a foot or so away from where he had been before. We watched as he squatted, let the marble go.

The marble was much slower to start its movement this time. But once it was three or four feet from Martin and heading for the wall, the marble took a strange turn, rolling almost perpendicularly to the path it had been following.

"Bubble!" Martin shouted, and he gave a quick smile, though his eyes were still half-closed, staring as the marble regained its momentum, starting back on its inevitable trek toward the wall.

Once the marble had stopped, Martin moved to where it had rolled out. He placed one foot on the linoleum, put his weight down, and almost imperceptibly the linoleum gave way, went flat.

He looked up at Tom. He said, "Are you going to take out this floor?"

"The linoleum?" Tom said.

"Yep."

"Yes, we are," Tom said.

"No worry about this bubble, then," Martin said, and moved back to the hearth where he positioned himself at the end of the bricks, facing the front wall.

He'd done all the rooms downstairs—Tom's, the pantry, the kitchen—just that way, his eyes demarking the path of the marble each time, remembering those curves and bumps and rises and valleys in the floor.

Now Tom and Martin were in the crawl space, having gone down through a trapdoor in the pantry. I was standing in the kitchen, leaning against the cabinets, the counter with that ugly yellow Formica scarred and pitted.

Grady was in the living room, and I could hear his footsteps as he walked back and forth, the floor creaking beneath the linoleum. I wanted the linoleum out first, I thought, and the paneling in there and in Tom's room and in our bedroom and in my room upstairs. I could hear just beneath me their movement, the dull, muffled scrapes and taps, occasionally some comment from Tom, a one-word answer from Martin, their words veiled by the wood between us. I wondered what they saw down there, how cobwebbed and filthy and cramped it must be.

Grady stood in the doorway into the kitchen, his arms crossed. He shook back a lock of hair from his forehead.

He said, "I can bet I know what you're thinking about." He grinned, and I wondered what was behind him, inside that same, practiced grin, and it finally came to me how it *would* be practiced, how hard it must be for him even to give that much: his father killed, mother having committed suicide, grandfather disowning him. His only friend a dishwasher at the Friendly's he worked at, from every indication his job waiting tables his job for life.

So I smiled, smiled as hard and as best as I could, because it was about all I could give to him right then. I smiled, and crossed my arms. I said, "All right, you tell me what I'm thinking about."

He said, "What do you bet?" He was rocking back and forth on his heels now.

"Lunch at Burger King in town. Or Wendy's."

He looked down and shook his head, still grinning. "Don't you think I get enough burgers at work already?" He looked up, hair down in his face again. He shook it back.

"Chinese, then. Tom and I will take you and Martin to that take-out Chinese place on King."

"Deal," he said. He closed his eyes and put his fingertips to his forehead as if he were some sort of medium. "I see," he said, his voice a monotone, "I see, I see . . . a woman who is wondering how these two men who will be helping work on her house got all the way from Florence out to Chesterfield. This is what I see."

It was not what I was thinking, but now that he'd said it I wanted to know. I hadn't thought of them getting here before; for some reason their being here seemed a given, something that came with the house.

I gave him a puzzled look, tilted my head a little to one side, and said, "That's it exactly. Really. How did you know that? And how *do* you get out here?"

His fingers were still at his forehead, and he shot open his eyes. For an instant his face gave up his surprise at my answer, his eyes opened wide, his mouth drawn closed. He let his hands drop, and he smiled, this time a genuine one, the corners of his mouth much higher, his teeth there, that perfect white. He looked down again.

"You're patronizing me," he said.

"No," I said. Then I said, "Maybe," and I smiled, too. "But how do you get up here? Really?" I paused a moment. He was still smiling. I said, "You don't ride your bikes, do you?"

"You said it," he said. He looked up, and his face was different now. He was younger, much younger, that adult demeanor now seemingly lost altogether. He was standing with his hands in his pockets, and shrugged. "We stash them back in the woods a few yards so's nobody will get to them." There was no trace of the grin anywhere, just the real smile, the authentic one that made his eyes softer somehow, his build seem even more slight.

I said, "Why don't you just put them back in the barn? That seems like a good place for bikes."

"No," he said too quickly, "no. That's not a good place. The woods are a lot better." He tried to laugh, but couldn't. "Not the barn."

He leaned against the doorjamb, brought one hand from his pocket and reached over to the other arm, held his own elbow. Hair was down in his face again, but now he made no moves to shake it back. That hair was always there, always would be. It was just a part of who he was: a scared boy, frightened, I imagined, at becoming a man. This house, I knew, was most likely his last connection to who he had been, to his childhood, to any love that had existed in his life outside of the companion-love of Martin. Now the house was disappearing before him, slowly changing over into our hands, ownership shifting from his family to ours, sealing off for good his childhood. This was what I imagined as we stood there in the kitchen, the subtle, almost inaudible scuttling of two men below us.

Quietly he said, "But I think I know what you're thinking about. Or at least were."

I said, "What?"

"Martin and me. Probably how we met. How we know each other."

I said, "You're right," and I made no smile, no move, only stood leaning against the counter. I was not patronizing him. I wanted to know, but at the same time I wondered how much truth he might give. So far he'd told us two different stories of his parents, neither one of which was true, according to Mr. Clark's lawyer. But what made me think that Mr. Blaisdell, that fat old man with the deep leather chair, was telling the truth himself? I did not know what to believe. I only knew that I wanted to hear whatever Grady had to say. "Tell me," I said.

He paused, let his shoulders fall, all the while his hand still clutching his elbow. "It has to do with this house, I guess," he started, and then he looked up, out one of the windows to my right. He wasn't looking at me.

I looked to the window, too, not so much to see what was out there, though what I saw was beautiful: a cut-glass sky, the hill behind the house rising up into it, some trees bare, some with the dull russets and coppers and cadmiums of the last few leaves yet to fall, green pines mixed through.

A cloud passed overhead, and those trees and leaves and the room went dark, the air almost imperceptibly gone cooler, yet the sky out there above the hill still so blue I thought I might have been able to see stars if I stared at it long and hard enough.

No, I looked out the window just as he had so that he wouldn't feel my eyes on him, wouldn't feel embarrassed at having a thirty-year-old woman watch him here in this kitchen, *his* kitchen, while he told of his retarded friend. I wanted, too, to see what he saw out that window, wanted him to know I wasn't sorry for him, there clutching his elbow.

The cloud passed, the room and forest and hill bathed in light again, and I ran my hands up and down my arms. I had goose-bumps now.

"Keep going," I said. Wind from somewhere swayed the branches of the pines. From beneath us I heard a soft tapping on wood.

"He was a friend of my daddy's," he said. "They always knew each other. Martin, he was born over in Worthington, just another mile or so on down the road. You know where that sugar house is over there? Bourne's Sugar House? The one down at the bottom of the ravine."

I said, "No," and closed my eyes. Something in his voice made me *want* to know where he was talking about, made me want to see that sugar house, but I could not, and so I stood with my face toward that window, my eyes closed. I listened.

"Well," he said. He paused. "Well, there's this house over there, just a cabin, beat out now. That's where he was born. And my daddy was born in this house."

He stopped, and it was then I caught the lie, if it was that: Mr. Blaisdell had said it was Grady's *mother* who was born here, the child of Mr. and Mrs. Clark. He'd said that, I remembered, but still I didn't know whether to believe him, the lawyer, or not. I didn't know what to think. And so, for now, it was Grady's *father* who was born here. My worrying over this detail would not stop anything, and the best I could do would be to let him go on, make my judgments, if any, later.

"They both grew up together," he went on, "and they played a lot together, all the time. Mainly over here, too, because Martin's family didn't care at all for my daddy's family. My grandfather, the man you're buying this place from, had a feud going on forever. It had to do with my grandfather accidentally killing one of Martin's uncles or something by running him over. My grandfather was the first man this far back from Northampton to have a car, and he was the first one in this county to kill somebody with a car." He breathed out what might have been a small laugh. "That same car. His claim to fame."

I said nothing.

"So my daddy and Martin grew up together, and like I said, most of the time was spent over here, and most of the time was spent without my grandfather knowing any of it, him working at a bank in Northampton. In town. Gone all day. Gone all day every day, killing himself with his job. A job worrying about money, so that my daddy and Martin were always around my grandmother. My Grandma Clark."

He stopped and swallowed hard. "She was," he said, his voice a little quieter now, "she was a good woman. She loved my daddy. And she loved Martin, too. I think she loved Martin more than his own daddy or mother did. Because of how much time Martin spent over here. He ate over here. He played over here. Sometimes he even slept over here, slept up in that room, the smaller one upstairs, with my daddy, my grandma knowing about it all along, even helping Martin sneak upstairs after my grandfather had already gone to bed. Martin slept over a lot in the summer. Here, or they camped out up in those woods. They were friends."

My eyes were on the woods right then, and for a moment I thought of two young boys taking off up into them, up to the top of the hill.

I thought of them rolling out sleeping bags, a small campfire before them, sparks circling up into the night air, and I wondered what stars must look like, the millions of them, on a cool summer night in the Berkshires.

"But that's why he hates Martin to this day. Because Martin was of that family in Worthington. A trashy, poor family over in Worthington. My grandfather, of course, had to keep that in mind, being as how he was a banker. To have it known that my daddy, his son, was associating with that family—and with its retard son to boot—just didn't work. It just didn't work right for my grandfather. So, the hate. His hate for Martin, especially."

There was more tapping now, this time right beneath me; I could feel the hard taps in my feet, the vibrations more noticeable than the sound. I opened my eyes, and the blue sky seemed even deeper, darker.

I said, "So you've known Martin all along?"

"Yep," he said, his voice from behind me, both of us still looking out that window. "Just like I told you. An old family friend. He was in the hospital for quite a few years until, like I told you before, six years ago when they let him out."

I turned to him. His arm was still across his chest, guarding him somehow, his hand still gripping the crook of his arm. He was looking down, and it looked as though his eyes were closed.

I said, "You don't have to answer me if you don't want to, but—"

"So we've known each other all our lives. Or at least all *my* life," he nearly whispered, going on as though I hadn't started to say anything, on as though he were trying to avoid giving an answer to the question I was about to ask. His head remained bowed. "Nineteen years. Longer than my daddy ever knew me. Longer than my mother ever knew me. And he needs me, that's what's fine about him. My grandfather doesn't give a good goddamn for me, but Martin does. I have to see to it that he gets to work on time, that his clothes get washed, that he eats right. That his rent and utilities get paid at the right time."

At that moment my question, the one I'd wanted to ask, paled and shriveled before me: all I'd wanted to know was what exactly was wrong with Martin, whether he'd been born as he was or if his brain functions had been dimmed by a childhood disease or trauma, damaged in a car accident or something. A trivial, petty question, I saw, as this boy told me of the responsibilities he had, responsibilities for a life other than his own; and I knew that that concern of mine, my physiological, Neuroscience and Behavior Laboratory attitude had been conditioned into me, transforming me into some odd strain of heartless human, I thought, whose preoccupation was with how it happened instead of *how to live with it*. And I wondered how I'd ever thought I could raise a child, how I could nurture a child from birth on, when here before me was an example of what real care was, real love. A nineteen-year-old boy caring unconditionally, it seemed, for a fifty-year-old man, loving him. I felt tears well up in me, felt them brim, break, fall down my cheeks, tears that were for me, I realized, as much as they were for him. I knew truths about him he would not tell: his mother's suicide; his father missing in action, and the unresolved hope for his father's return he must have hidden away in him somewhere. Unresolved hope, hopeless hope, much like my own hope to conceive someday, to bear children, to love them.

"Hey," I heard him say, and I opened my eyes. He was moving toward me, wavering through my tears, across this kitchen. Then he was before me, and placed a hand on each of my shoulders. I brought a hand to my eyes, blinked back those tears that still came, and gave him a feeble smile, the best I could muster. "Hey," he said, "don't cry. You don't have to cry," and that was all he said, in his boy's voice a certain confidence emerging, letting me know that yes, I didn't have to cry. I didn't, and he patted my left shoulder once, twice, and brought both hands down, put them at his sides, and smiled at me.

I took in a deep breath and quickly nodded, my eyes still wet, the edges of the room still shivering. "I'm okay," I said. "I am."

He went back to the counter, leaned against it, his palms on the edge of the Formica top. He looked out the window again, and cleared his throat. "So Martin knows this house from top to bottom, knows it better than anybody. He knows it even better than my grandfather." He was talking now as though nothing had happened, as though I hadn't cried, as though he hadn't comforted me.

"That's how he knows this place, knows its weaknesses," he said, and stopped, the expression on his face changing to one of deep thought, his eyebrows knit, mouth pursed. He said, "But the thing of it is, is that he knows how to fix things, too. House things. That's how come he can look at all these things in the house and sort of troubleshoot it. I figured it out, too. I've read some things."

He was changing again, not back into that pseudo-adult, but into an excited, animated teenager, the opposite of the sullen boy a few moments before. He was charged now, and his fingers on the edge of the Formica began tapping.

I said, "What have you read?"

"Oh," he said, "some books, and I've read about these people, these retarded people like Martin. I saw them on TV a couple of times, too. There's this one guy, he's blind and retarded, much worse off than Martin, and he can hear a song once and then sit down at a piano and make this beautiful music, play that piano and sing that song just like the record. I've heard him sing, on '60 Minutes.' "

I nodded. I knew what he was leading up to: Martin's being an idiot savant. He was probably right, though I'd only read case histories in textbooks, stories of mentally disturbed and retarded men and women with prodigious talents in only one certain area, whether it be sculpting or music or mathematics. Martin's outward signs seemed true enough, too: when he was working he was doing nothing else, staring at the marble as it jogged right or left of its true path across the floor; pressing his ear to wood and tapping it, his eyes half-closed; that trancelike state.

"It's what's called an idiot savant," Grady said, "but that name they give it I hate. It's a stupid name. I mean the idiot part. Martin's no idiot. Not by a long shot he isn't. You can give him a piece of wood and some nails and a hammer and saw, show him a mahogany dresser, and I'll be damned if he won't sit down and do his best to make one out of what you gave him." He was looking off now, not at the window or floor, but just off into the space of the kitchen. "So he knows this house, and he knows how to fix things. I think this place is going to be fixed up fine. If you use him. Us."

I took a deep breath, nodded. "I've read about them, too, savants. But what I've read is that they have to have some sort of example, something they can imitate—"

"Yeah, yeah," he said, and slowly shook his head. "Martin learned all this stuff he knows from the first job he got when he was mainstreamed. He got a job as a gofer for this contractor, a guy who specialized in refurbishing. Martin starts out by just handing up pieces of lumber to these guys, and by making sure they've got plenty of nails at hand, while all this time he's watching these guys, until one day, when the contractor and his crew are working on a house over on Massasoit in town, one day Martin stops the boss and shows him that there's two or three rotten clapboards that he's missed picking out, and things just go straight to hell from there. Martin ends up losing his job because in a month or so after that little incident on Massasoit, Martin's now laying in parquet floors better than the guys who're doing it professionally. So Martin gets the boot, and he gets on at Friendly's."

He paused a moment, laughing a little to himself. "So," he said. "I guess I lied to you."

I took a quick breath. I said, "What?"

"About Friendly's. Martin's got the world's record for that Friendly's. He's been on there for longer than I have. I'm not the record holder there. He is." He shrugged. "So I guess I lied to you."

I breathed out, and smiled. I said, "That's nothing."

"I'll bet, too, you're wondering how I know all this. I mean all about Martin and that job, right?" He looked at me. His fingertips on the Formica had stopped drumming.

"I imagine he told you. That, or you asked."

"I watched," he said, staring at me, waiting, I knew, for some reaction from me.

I said nothing, and only gave him my same smile.

He turned and got that thoughtful look on his face again, staring off. "I watched it all. Nobody knew about it. Not even Martin. My grandfather, he found out Martin was getting out of the hospital, and he forbid me to see him. He forbid me outright to see Martin. Like he could do that. But there was no way that old bastard could stop me from seeing. No way. So that's when I started cutting school, to go see him work for these guys. I'd ride my bike, ride it all over hell and back, just riding. There was no way I wasn't going to watch Martin, see who he was. I wanted to see him. I could only remember a little about him, from when I was a kid, before my grandfather had him put—"

He stopped, startled at himself, it seemed. He pushed himself off the counter, and he was the adult again, shaking back that hair, tucking a lock behind one ear. He blinked several times, coughed into his hand, and I wondered what was going on, what had caused this, and then I realized that, of course, he'd told me something he didn't want known, some small piece of story that had slipped away from him when he was only the boy he was, that teenager.

His grandfather had had Martin put away.

"Keep going," I said.

He kneeled and tied his shoe. He coughed again.

"Your grandfather had Martin—" I said, but Tom and Martin came into the kitchen.

"Speak of the devil, here he is," Grady said, turning and standing as they came into the room.

They were filthy, their faces and arms and hands streaked with dirt, mud ground into the knees of their pants. Cobwebs dusted Tom's shoulders and hair, and the first thing I did was to brush them away, the delicate threads disintegrating at my touch.

Tom said, "You should have seen us before we brushed off in the pantry," and laughed. He kissed my cheek, and I could smell the cold, musty crawl space on him, a smell like old, abandoned furniture. I quickly leaned back from his kiss, made a face.

"Yep," Martin said, smiling.

"So," Grady said, and put his hands in his back pockets. He started moving up and down on the balls of his feet. "What did you see?"

Tom said, "A few floor joists are cracked where the foundation, those fieldstones, are loose. No big deal, at least nothing, I don't think, we can't repair. A couple of bad ones, dry rot, that we'll have to replace, too."

Martin, behind him, was rubbing his hair now, trying to get rid of those cobwebs.

"It's beautiful down there," Tom went on. "Rough-cut oak. The support beam's in great shape, too. The mortar on the fireplace base needs a little work, though. That's not stuff I know much about, and so I'm not too sure I'll want us on that. We may just want to hire that out." He was looking at me. "That's money we'll have to put out."

I said, "We knew that going into this."

Martin, still behind him, grinned at me, and then at Grady.

Grady said, "You'd be surprised at what this guy can do with a trowel and a sack of cement," and nodded at Martin. Grady laughed.

Tom and I turned to Martin, who, still grinning, only shrugged. He said, "Upstairs is next," and gave Tom's shoulder a hard pat. He moved past us and into the front room. A moment later I could hear the moan of the stairs beneath his weight.

Tom said, "We could hear you two talking up here. Martin, I think, kept hearing his name, because he'd stop and listen a second every once in a while, then start hammering a floor joist again." He dusted off his hands, looking first at me, then Grady.

"We were just talking about him, about his fixing things," Grady said. He stopped bobbing, and glanced at me.

I said, "He's a savant. With wood. With building and repairing things." I reached up and dusted off Tom's shoulder again, though all the cobwebs were gone.

He said, "I can believe it." He started through the kitchen, but paused just before the doorway into the front room. "He's a good man," Tom said, and disappeared into the room.

I looked at Grady. His mouth was open, but he smiled, closed his eyes for a moment before heading after them.

Martin was squatting on the hearth in our bedroom, the marble already coursing along the linoleum toward the far corner of the room, once again rolling around bubbles before it made it to the baseboards. But this time, once the marble had stopped rolling and was sitting there at the wall, Martin went to it, picked it up, and walked over to Tom. He held it out to him.

Tom, who stood next to me just inside the doorway, looked at Martin, almost bewildered, his eyebrows high. Slowly he reached out and took the marble from Martin's hand. He held it up to the light for a moment, the sun falling in from the one window to fill the glass ball.

Martin, his movement as stilted and awkward as ever, let his hand drop to his side. He turned and walked back to the hearth, where he squatted again. He looked up at Tom, then pointed at the bricks next to him.

Tom smiled. He walked across the room to the hearth, and kneeled. Slowly, gently, he placed the marble on the floor, let it roll. A few feet out it hit a rise and rolled away.

Martin nudged Tom with his elbow, and Tom looked at him. Martin nodded toward where the marble had rolled out, and then Tom said, "Oh. Bubble."

Martin burst out with laughter, slapped his thigh hard so that the clap of his palm shot through the room. He laughed, his eyes nearly closed, his shoulders heaving.

Grady was laughing, too, his arms crossed in front of him. And I laughed, too, Tom smiling and shaking his head, looking at the floor.

"That's funny," Grady said. "*He's* teaching *you*. That's what's so funny."

"That's what's so funny," Martin managed to choke out, his eyes wet and full with laughter.

When we were done in that room—Martin had tapped out the paneling, cracked back a corner to show bare green wall, opened and closed the window several times and touched and poked and prodded the mortar of the fireplace—I went down the stairs to the landing and up the other set to my room.

I was first in. We were all having fun by that time, Martin and Tom laughing and making jokes about bubbles, Grady with his arms crossed, saying "That's funny" every once in a while, and so I entered the room, the others behind me, and I raised up my arms as if to touch the ceiling. I said, "This room is *mine!*" and then let my arms fall around me so that I was holding myself in the room. I turned in a circle, my eyes up to the ceiling, and I stopped.

Tom was behind me, and put his arms around my waist. We were facing the window now, the barn outside in shadows that had shifted as the day moved on, shadows lighter now that the sun was directly overhead, shadows more buoyant, moving with the breeze that had picked up, the branches nearly empty of leaves, but still filled with color this autumn.

Tom said, "All yours."

"Excuse me," I heard from behind us, and Tom let go of me. We turned to see Grady standing just inside the doorway.

"Excuse me," he said again, and moved to one side. Down on the landing stood Martin, his hands clasped in front of him. His eyes moved up to us and down, up and down, and the sunlight from the window cast a white sheen over his skin as he stood in the near-dark of the staircase. His skin looked gray and shiny, and I knew he didn't want us to see him.

Tom said, "What's wrong?"

"It's just," Grady said, and stopped. He held out a hand palm up as though to explain, but let the hand drop. "It's just that he won't go into this room. That's all." He shrugged, blinked. "He just won't. He never has, either, as far as I can tell. Just look at that window. It's not nearly half as clean as old Martin gets them. That's because I'm the one who does this room." He smiled, shrugged again, and moved back into the doorway so that we could no longer see Martin. "So I guess you're on your own with this room. You got the marble?" He put his chin out, squinted and nodded toward Tom.

He put his hands in his pockets, brought from the left one that marble. "Right here."

"Okay," Grady said, and the two of them went down the stairs.

I turned to Tom. "What's going on?"

"You know as much as I do," he said, his attention on the floor, sizing things up, I imagined, trying to guess where a bubble might be. He went to the hearth, and squatted once again. He held the marble an inch or so above the floor, the linoleum battleship gray with brown flecks scattered here and there. "Except," Tom said, still looking at the floor before him, "that when we were down in the crawl space and I mentioned his helping work on the barn next summer, Martin froze. He nearly died. He dropped his hammer as though someone had stuck a gun to his head. All he said was 'No' one time, nice and loud so he knew I wouldn't ask again. And I didn't. So it's no surprise, really, that he doesn't want to work up here. Or there." He placed the marble on the floor. "He's got his idiosyncrasies, maybe superstitions. I don't know. It's his choice. He can do what he likes."

He let it go, and for some reason I held my breath, listening to the surprising quiet in the house, the only sound the calm, sonorous roll of the marble coursing toward the wall.

NOVEMBER

 The appointment for signing the papers was set for eleven at Mr. Blaisdell's office, and so both Tom and I had had to take off from work. We took, in fact, the whole morning.

It was about to happen. We were about to own the place.

To celebrate we decided to have breakfast out. Tom went down the stairs to start the engine and scrape the windows of frost while I finished putting on my makeup, and then I went to the door, and paused a moment.

I looked back at the kitchen, at what I could see of the living room through the doorway. Though the rooms were filled with our furniture, with us, suddenly things looked different, changed: the table, chairs, those gingham curtains and potholders on magnets on the refrigerator and the coffee machine seemed out of place, alien in this room from which we would soon be removing ourselves. The walls, pale yellow, seemed strangely barren, though there were pictures hung and a shelf with antique plates we'd collected and a counted cross-stitch of a lighthouse I had gotten when we'd gone down to Mystic one time. But the walls still seemed lonesome, all these furnishings, signs of life, ready to go, to move out to Chesterfield.

I opened the door. The cold air outside broke into the room, and sent a shiver through the bottom edge of the tablecloth, minutely moved the stack of papers—bills, flyers, coupons—piled on the counter.

Though we would be back later today, wouldn't be moving from here until the house was nearly finished sometime early next year, we had figured, I said, "Good-bye, good-bye," and pulled the door closed behind me.

We went from the apartment first to the newspaper, where Tom had to stop in and look over his desk, more a symbolic gesture to his editor than any real devotion to the job. Then we went for breakfast at the Miss Florence Diner, a brick-and-oak Deco place left over from the forties or fifties, we could never decide which. Above the restaurant was a neon sign, the name spelled out in orange and set against a large green chevron of sorts.

Inside, construction workers sat at stools along the counter, buffalo-plaid shirts and down vests and scuffed workboots on, cups of coffee in front of them. Most of the booths were full, men and women heading to work, tabletops covered with plates of food: eggs, sausage, waffles, bagels. Where each table met the wall was a miniature jukebox, above each a glass case with a knob on the side. Inside the cases were pages and pages of song titles; when you turned the knob the pages fell forward or back to reveal more songs: tunes by Elvis and Linda Ronstadt and Bob Seger and the Beatles and most anyone else.

We walked to the left along the booths, moving toward the back where we liked to sit. At one booth sat two Smith girls, black turtlenecks on, pale faces and chopped hair, cigarettes out. At another booth sat a businessman in a three-piece charcoal gray wool suit, *The Wall Street Journal* in one hand, a coffee cup in the other. At one other booth sat two old men, both wearing flannel shirts, one bald, the other with a full head of white hair. Both had their hands wrapped around their cups, and were staring out the green-tinted window onto Route 9 and the cars heading into town.

We slid into our booth, and the waitress was there with two cups and a pot of black, black coffee.

She didn't even ask, but went ahead and poured us each a cup; then pulled from her apron a handful of half-and-half containers and dropped them on the table. We'd had her before, and she always looked like this, always had the same hairpiece on, a coffee pot in hand. The only thing that ever changed about her was the addition or subtraction of her sweater, depending upon what time of year it was.

"It's a nice frost today," she said, and smiled, nodding as if in agreement with her own observation.

"Not long before snow," Tom said, and broke open a container, dumped it into his coffee.

She said, "But then that's when winter really comes on, and I can wait for that. These frosts don't do anything other than make you drape your bushes at night and scrape your car in the morning. That's fine by me. That snow, though," she said, and scowled, shook her head. She hadn't yet looked at us, but held the glass coffee pot and stared at the cups as though they might move. She was waiting for us.

I said, "I'll have pancakes and sausage. Short stack."

"Same here," Tom said. "And o.j."

"Me too."

She gave a short, hard nod, turned and stopped to fill three more customers' coffee cups before she made it back to the cook station.

He was looking at the jukebox, and reached up, started flipping back the little laminated pages of selections. I reached across the table to him and pinched his forearm.

"Ouch," he said, and looked at me. He said, "How about Johnny Cash? 'I Walk the Line'?"

I leaned back and looked at everything, took in the smell of coffee and food, looked at the people and our waitress, now filling the cups of the construction workers. "I love this place," I said.

Tom reached into his pocket, his shoulders going up to get at, I imagined, the change buried in the corner of his pocket. "I'm glad you're so enamored of Miss Flo's, sweetheart," he said, his smile more of a grimace now that he was digging in the pocket. He pulled out a quarter, relief on his face, his smile easy now. "Because," he went on, "this is the caliber of the kinds of places we'll be able to afford from now on. This and Friendly's."

He reached over and dropped in the quarter, punched a letter and a number on the machine. Johnny Cash came booming out, his voice black gravel. Two of the construction workers looked over at us, men with flushed faces and small eyes and big hands. The businessman glanced at us over the top edge of his paper.

"Turn it down," I whispered loudly, and Tom laughed. He leaned back in the booth and put his hands behind his head.

"Come on," he said. "Enjoy this music. It's a luxury now."

I turned it down myself, fiddling with the little knob on the front of the machine. I didn't turn it down as low as I should have, and I sat back, too. Let them watch, I thought. Let anybody watch. We're buying a house today.

By the time we'd finished breakfast, most of the frost had melted, the street outside now merely darker in spots where the moisture had not yet evaporated, lighter in spots where it had. Some of the puddles of water in the parking lot beside Miss Flo's were covered with the thinnest, most delicate sheets of clear ice, traces of cracks patterned across them, bubbles like clear, round drops of silver trapped here and there beneath. I was careful not to step on any of them for fear of some bad luck.

Tom held open my door for me, and before I climbed in I kissed him, putting my arms around him. He let go my door and held me, and we kissed there in the light and in the cold.

Tom pulled up to the parking lot exit, waiting for traffic to clear up.

He said, "You want to go this way?" and nodded to the right, toward Williamsburg, toward, of course, Chesterfield.

I said, "Go on ahead," and thought nothing of it for a moment until, when we were out on Route 9 and moving past the old homes in Florence, I realized that he had asked me if we could go this way. His question had seemed only natural, my answer just the next logical thing to say, and here we were, heading down Route 9, in the car once again, and it felt filled with that expectation, that shared apprehension and excitement at the prospect of the future; and for a moment hope, that ancient seed of hope I'd kept smothered as best I could, crept back into me. I let myself hope, as we passed now the glistening frost of the fairways in Leeds; let myself hope that somehow I still might get pregnant, have a child, keep hold of it and love it and nurture it, its soft, white face there at my breast, drinking from me milk to keep it alive, to keep it growing.

That hope in me felt like some lost friend, an old and loved relative come home at last, launching into my heart a host of other images:

the room I called my own in the house now turned into a nursery, that gray paneling torn down, the walls covered with pastel wallpaper of teddy bears and balloons, an oaken cradle filled with soft flannel blankets, a changing table and a crib and curtains and a wide oval braided rug, and a rocking chair for me, stuffed animals scattered across the room. The trappings of my dreams, dreams I hoped Tom hadn't let go of quite yet; his asking me if we could go down this road, beginning again our lost ritual, seemed a sign to me, a sign he hadn't lost it. Hope still lived in him somewhere, I knew.

I reached over and held his hand the rest of the way out.

We pulled into Chesterfield proper, and the cluster of homes and lawns seemed more beautiful, more our home than it had any day we had driven through it so far. The frost was thicker out here, the lawns glazed, it seemed, with shimmering ice as we drove past them.

Tom said, "We need gas," and pulled into the service station at the main intersection in town, though there was no signal, not even a blinking amber light.

The gas station was an old one; gas station mini-marts hadn't yet made it out here, and for that I was thankful. Two gas pumps stood under a high metal awning, the station itself only a one-bay garage and an office. Inside the window of the office were colorful cans of oil stacked in a pyramid; around the side of the building was a Coke machine.

From inside the office came an attendant, a man in his mid-thirties with a thick, black beard and black hair that hung out from beneath the baseball cap he wore. He had on a blue shirt with the station's insignia above the shirt pocket, the shirt crisp and clean. Under the shirt he had on white long underwear, the sleeves showing at his neck and wrists, the forearms of the shirt rolled up to his elbow. He had on Levi's, black and shiny with old engine oil, I imagined, and he had on black rubber boots.

He was handsome, but everyone I saw that morning appeared that way: I was taking in faces in a new world, remembering details, trying to take in the day as deeply as I could. We were buying a house today.

He came around to Tom's window, and leaned toward it as Tom rolled it down. "Fill it up, please," Tom said, and the attendant nodded, first at Tom, then at me.

"Tom," I said. "This is the day. *This is the day.*"

He simply smiled. He pulled his wallet out of his pocket, found the right credit card. He said, "This is the day the real stuff starts." He was examining the credit card as though it weren't his own, the name there someone else's. "This is the day the real worries start up." He paused a moment, and looked out the windshield. "Get ready for the postpartum blues," he said, a faint smile on his face.

It was a joke we could both let go on this day.

The house had seemed somehow brighter, sharper, the November air thin and cold, much colder than back in town. As every time we came here, we sat in the car a few moments before getting out, just staring at the house. Things *were* different: the foundation mortar to the right of the porch was a new gray, and stood out stark against the near-black fieldstones, that work already done, Tom and Martin and Grady having repaired it three weeks ago now. Mr. Blaisdell had given us the okay, this down from Mr. Clark over in Maplewood, to go ahead and start working on the place.

Tom had had two weeks of vacation coming, and so arranged with his boss, an old woman with blue hair coiffed high on her head and thick glasses that magnified her dull eyes, to let him take a series of three-day weekends to get as much of the structural repairs finished as he and Martin and Grady could.

That first Friday Tom had borrowed a truck from one of the paper's stringers, an old, beat-up green Dodge, and then had met Grady and Martin at the Friendly's parking lot, and headed out for the house. He'd already had lumber—four floor joists—delivered, had rented a Sawzall and hydraulic jacks and everything else he knew he'd need. The money from the sale of my mother's house was already going, but that was fine. This was what we'd saved it for.

When I'd gotten off work, I picked up a bucket of chicken at Jim Dandy's and headed straight out to Chesterfield. The drive seemed strange and long, but once I'd cleared town and had headed down into the gorge, the twilit sky before me orange and blue and violet all at once, above the deepest violet crystalline sparks of stars, I felt for the first time I was indeed heading home.

When I pulled up, the three of them, filthy and sweaty and smiling, were on the floor in the front room, a fire going in the fireplace. The electricity hadn't been turned on yet.

"Two joists in just today," Tom said to me. He was lying on the floor, propped up on an elbow. He was grinning, his face, it seemed, moving with the shadows of firelight.

Martin, who sat Indian-style before the fire, smiled up at me. "Shimmed in ship-shape, also," he said. Grady and Tom both laughed, Martin still looking at me.

I said, "C rations for the troops," and held up the bucket of chicken.

So that now, this new mortar meant more to me than just a new color, more than just the fact the floors had been leveled out over the past month, more than the fact the fieldstones had been mortared in, scraped and chinked clean of that old, dusty mortar and replaced, all of which we'd done over the second long weekend. As we sat before the house, the new mortar meant more than I had let myself imagine about buying this house: it let me begin to swell with hope, with the act of repairing and revising and restoring. That hope had multiplied in me. *This was the day.*

We sat there, and sat, still no words. Finally Tom popped open his door. I knew what his mind was on, what he was thinking about. Though his crack about postpartum blues was meant to be a joke, he was not kidding. Each time he looked at the house now he saw all that still needed to be done, what portion of the house would be repaired next, what timber and supplies we would need, which tools to ready for the next weekend. Even now, as he climbed out of the car, his eyes were on the house, focused on the next tack he would take, the next place he and Martin and Grady would tear apart only to put back together again.

"The roof," he said, almost shouting, as though to the house itself, some sort of fair warning to the structure of what would happen next, or some sort of soothing words to let it know which ailment, which wound, would be taken care of next.

He went to the front of the car, and leaned against the hood, his arms crossed.

I got out and went to him. I looked up at the roof.

"We'll get up there on Friday morning, if it's not raining. We've been blessed with good weather this far. I just hope it'll hold out." Again, though I was his audience, the only one listening, I knew that if I hadn't been here, if he'd been standing here alone, his words would have been the same, spoken with the same inflection.

I could not blame him. Already he had worked three long weekends, fourteen- and sixteen-hour days; Monday mornings it took me an extra half hour just to get him out of bed.

He pointed at the roof, and drew an imaginary line across the length of it. "It bows there at that one point, then next to the chimney. And it looks like there's a few depressions off to the left." He paused, brought his arm back to his chest. "We'll have to rent the ladder again."

Slowly I started toward the house, and then I stepped up onto the porch.

"This porch," he said, this time to me, I could tell, his voice different, softer. He pushed off the hood and started toward me. "That porch we can take off this weekend, too. You and Grady, if you feel like it. I think you can do it."

Until now the only jobs I'd been given were, on that first weekend, inventorying precisely what sort of interior nonstructural repairs needed to be made: the paneling taken out everywhere, the kitchen cupboards and that leak beneath the sink, the bathroom and the cracked sink and the broken tile. The second weekend I'd spent cleaning those fieldstones, which had been a community affair, all four of us camped out next to the foundation, the pile of fieldstones before us, each of us with a different tool in hand: me with a small hammer, Tom with a heavy screwdriver, Grady with a chisel, Martin with a mallet.

Martin worked like an automaton, his hands quick and steady as he held a fieldstone in one hand, the mallet in the other. He would hit the stone with the mallet just hard enough to free up the mortar, give the stone a quick flip and catch it, then hammer that side and any edges where the mortar remained. He put the stone on the pile next to him, his growing more rapidly than anyone else's, those stones cleaner, too.

Each Sunday afternoon Tom paid them both. He paid them flat fees, each getting seventy-five apiece, and when Martin had that money in his hand, he fell back from the automaton, that robot, into the slow old man I'd first seen here, the grin with those teeth, his hair messed up. He held the money in his hand as if it were a bar of gold, just looking at it, his shoulders going up and down in excitement. Then Grady would gently take the money from him, fold it over and tuck it into his left front pocket. He took his own money and put it in his right front, and we would leave, the four of us talking about nothing the entire ride back, Martin as always simply reiterating whatever it was Grady said, whether about the progress on the foundation or floor joists, or the prices at Friendly's going up again, or the coming cold and how both their heating bills would take giant jumps next month. And then we were at Friendly's, and they were wheeling their bikes out from behind the dumpster, Grady waving us off as they mounted them.

They would never let us take them home, and this puzzled me. The third weekend I'd done the best I could to insist we give them rides to wherever they lived. Martin and Grady and Tom were still working at the foundation, this time the weak spot at the middle of the back wall, where the fieldstones had fallen into the crawl space. The piece of wood that supported the house—"That's a floor joist," Tom had informed me—was snug and secured to the bottom of the house; all we needed to do was rebuild the wall, make it tight.

"This joist has been like it is for a long time," Martin had said while examining it, his voice clear, his enunciation precise. His trance brought along with it, I realized, an utter clarity to his world, reflected even in his speech. "There is no reason," he'd gone on, "that we should worry about repairing it. No need. Just rebuild the wall is all we need to do." They had been the most words I'd heard him string together since I had met him.

Tom had looked at the beam, hit it a few times with his hammer, pushed on it. He said, "Sounds right to me. Let's rebuild the wall."

That was when I started in on them to let us give them a ride home. Grady and Tom were picking up the stones already on the ground and piling them a few feet away, where we would soon be scraping them. Martin was examining the foundation, gently pulling the loose stones from the wall, and placing them on the ground.

I said, "Why don't we drive you home tonight? It's getting colder, you know."

Grady hesitated only a moment, a move hardly noticeable if I hadn't been watching him. He kept right on moving after that. Martin did not even blink, but went on eyeing, touching, feeling the stones and mortar.

Grady said, "You know already. You know we like riding our bikes. It's our exercise."

"This isn't?" I said, and Tom laughed a moment, still moving, still piling.

Grady glanced at Tom, and gave a small, nervous laugh. He stood and wiped his forehead with the back of his arm. The canvas work gloves he wore seemed huge, just hanging on the end of his thin arms.

He gave me his adult smile. "Well, you know how much we appreciate the offer, of course, but the bikes, you know. They're already at Friendly's. We can't leave them there overnight."

"They'll fit in the trunk," I said. "At least I think they will. Tom?"

He shrugged, moving in rhythm now, leaning over, picking up a stone, moving it to the new pile. "Think so," he said.

"No," Grady said, and resumed picking up the stones.

"At least let us try," I said, and took a step toward him.

"*No*," he said, and stood up straight, his mouth closed tight. He wasn't looking at me, but at some point off in the distance, his eyes focused, concentrated on something.

Tom stopped in mid-movement, a stone in his hands. Even Martin paused, squinted up at us from where he was hunched at the foundation. Then he went on to the next stone.

"Listen," Tom said. "It's only a suggestion. Something to just help you guys. You don't want a ride, we're not going to give you one."

Grady broke into a smile again and looked down, embarrassed. He put his hands on his hips, made a small circle in the dirt with the toe of his boot.

"Sorry," he said. "I'm sorry. But we need the exercise. Even on top of what we get here." He looked up at me. "Even in this cold, too. Neither Martin or me have ever gotten a cold since we've been riding those bikes. And that's why. Riding those bikes has done that for us. When the snow gets too thick, that's when we walk. That's the way we live." He glanced down, and up at me again.

The pile of loose stones had been moved by this time, the last stone the one in Tom's hands. I hadn't moved any closer, only stood there, looking away from Grady to the stones, Martin still working away.

Tom came to the porch, and I walked across it, hollow, vacant sounds of footsteps across plywood again. I was still wondering, that morning of the signing, why Grady refused, why he was so adamant, and I wondered if it had to do with his overseeing Martin, his taking care of him.

I could not see Tom now, my back to him. My arms were crossed, and I was looking off to the east, the sun not yet past the trees, its light cutting through the branches, broken by crooked, black limbs. I said, "Did you know that Mr. Clark had Martin put into the state hospital? That he's the one who had Martin committed?"

I hadn't yet told him this; for some reason, perhaps because it had appeared that Grady's telling me had been an accident that day in the kitchen, I had kept this fact to myself, hidden it away in some loyalty to Grady, to his hands on my shoulders and his comforting words while Tom and Martin had been muscling around in the crawl space.

"What?" Tom said. I heard his footsteps up onto the porch. They stopped a few feet behind me. "How do you know that?"

Already I was sorry for having spoken, sorry I'd marred our day with a fact I'd only surmised from an uncompleted sentence Grady had not wanted me to hear. I closed my eyes, let my head drop.

"Well?" he said.

"He told me," I said. "I'm not sure why. I'm not sure, either, what it means."

"It means," Tom said, "that we're dealing with a real bastard. Which is, I imagine, what we've known all along."

"Yes," I said. I wanted to say no more of it, to get off the subject, and I realized then how long it had been with me, the image of Grady as a boy following Martin around from job to job, watching him, watching him. That was when he started cutting school. That was when, I imagined, he started stealing things, and I wondered if it hadn't been things he'd taken to give to Martin, food from grocery stores for this retarded man he wanted to know better.

And for some reason, perhaps because my thoughts on Martin and Grady and Mr. Clark had made things slip, brought the day down from the high I'd felt all morning, I thought of Sandra, and of how I'd seen her only two or three times since we'd spoken, her huddling in the basement or in the computer room, and how *I* was the bastard here, just as useless in Sandra's eyes as Mr. Clark was in mine.

But then I took a deep breath, tried to clear myself of what I ought to do, of talking to her. I had my own life here. She hadn't wanted any help from me. She'd wanted nothing.

I let out the breath, leaned my head back, my eyes closed.

I opened my eyes and turned to Tom.

I said, "So after the porch is down, does that mean there won't be another one?" I uncrossed my arms, and I was smiling now. I could see the faintest wisps of air before me, my warm breath in this cold air. "Tell me," I said.

Even Mr. Blaisdell seemed thinner, healthier, his office brighter and more comfortable. Rita Longford was there in her gold sport coat and polyester skirt and that lipstick; she'd brought with her the lawyer retained by her agency to represent clients like us, people who had no lawyers. He was young, overweight, and had on a brown corduroy suit, his belly poking out below the bottom edge of the vest. A future Mr. Blaisdell, I thought.

Ruth said, "Tom, Claire, this is Donald Finestra. Donald, Tom and Claire Templeton," and we all shook hands. His hand was soft, too fleshy.

Tom said, "Rita's told us you're the best at these sorts of things, at reading contracts." Tom smiled and crossed his arms.

"Well," Finestra said, and adjusted his horn-rimmed glasses. "It's my job, and I'm glad to be of service to you." His smile seemed genuine.

Rita, especially pleased at this exchange, gave an even bigger smile. "Well," she said, and patted me on the shoulder. "Can we get started?"

"Why certainly," Mr. Blaisdell boomed, taking charge of us all. He put out a hand toward the couch, and Tom and I sat. He sat in his leather chair, and read us several pages of the mortgage contract, Rita and Finestra standing off to his left and a little behind so that they could read along with him. Finestra had a brown attaché under one arm, Rita a black leather folder held tight against her chest.

Blaisdell finished, and Rita produced from her folder a gold fountain pen, held it out to Tom.

He stood up from the couch, the Naugahyde crackling with his movement, and he was at the desk, signing again and again, Mr. Blaisdell quickly flipping the pages for Tom, who hesitated before signing each time, then seemed to attack the predesignated slot with the pen, scribbling his name.

Rita nodded at me, her face still as solemn as ever, and I stood, signed on the lines just below every place Tom had signed.

I finished the last signature, and looked up, handed the pen back to Rita. She took the pen, handed it to Finestra. He smiled, gave a shallow, quick bow, and moved toward the desk. Mr. Blaisdell let the pages of the contract fall back to the first, where Finestra signed it. I watched his hand move with the pen, his signature huge and billowing at the bottom of the page. He handed the pen to Blaisdell, who scrawled his signature, only a series of odd angles, a long, smooth figure-eight flourish beneath it.

Mr. Blaisdell gave the pen back to Rita, who held it out to Tom.

"A memento," she said, "of this fine occasion. May your home be a happy and prosperous one, filled with love and peace." She smiled, and it looked as if tears were in her eyes.

Tom took the pen, and turned to me. He rolled his eyes a little at this display of emotion on Rita's part, and he smiled at me, and hugged me. Mr. Blaisdell put out his hand, and Tom and I shook it. Rita came around the desk to me and gave me a hug, our shoulders just touching. She kissed my cheek and said, "Congratulations."

"So," Mr. Blaisdell said, "Mr. Clark wanted me to let you know how pleased he is that such a fine young couple as yourselves has purchased his home."

Rita picked up her purse from the edge of Blaisdell's desk, and she and Finestra started toward the door. "Sorry," she said, "but we've got to be going. Another appointment!" She waved over her shoulder as she opened the door. Finestra moved the attaché to the other arm, smiled, and gave another quick bow. They disappeared into the hall, Finestra pulling the door closed behind him.

Mr. Blaisdell laughed. "She's too busy. Realtors are always too busy. Good ones, that is."

The room was quiet a moment, and Tom said, "So this is it?"

"Well," Mr. Blaisdell said, and looked down at his desk. "Just for you to get your copies of all this material for your own files, and I imagine that will be it." He started flipping pages of the mortgage contract back, peeling off sheets for us. "Other things will be following in the mail. More information and payment booklets from the bank and the like. Those things."

Finally he had a stack of papers together, bounced the bottom edges on his desk to straighten them out. Without looking at us, he said, "You haven't, by the way, had any more trouble with this Grady Clark, have you?" As nonchalantly as he could, I saw, he opened his desk drawer with one hand and fished through the clutter in there for a paper clip. He pulled one out.

"He's never been any trouble to begin with," Tom said. "He's—"

"We haven't even seen him since that first day," I cut in. Tom quickly turned to me, and I gave him a glance. Only that. A glance, my eyes meeting his for a moment. He looked at me an instant longer, I could see from the corner of my eye, and I hoped he was seeing what I wanted to do, and what I didn't want this direct line to Clark to know.

Mr. Blaisdell gave the papers one last bounce, then fixed the clip to the top edges.

"Good," he said. He hadn't looked at us, and lay the stack on the desk again, lifting up a few of the pages. He was stalling, the air too quiet, his movements too easy as he let first one page fall, paused a moment, let two more go.

He said, "I don't suppose you've seen . . ." and stopped. He let one more page fall, then picked them all up, handing them over to us. He was looking at us now, his face warm and friendly and open. A lawyer, I thought. "I don't suppose," he said again, "you've encountered his compatriot. Martin Hosmer is his name."

I did my best to battle him, giving him a puzzled, poignant face, my head tilted a little, my eyebrows with just a hint of thought as I tried to remember any acquaintance of Grady Clark's.

"Why no," I said after what I thought was a long-enough moment of reflection. I turned to Tom. "Tom?"

"Who?" Tom said, and it was everything I could do to keep from laughing.

"Oh." Mr. Blaisdell laughed, and put his hand out in front of him as if to wave off some nonsense he'd uttered. "Nothing, nothing at all. Just the crowd that boy runs with. I'm glad you haven't seen this Grady again. You won't, either. He's been told to steer clear. He will. He's just a punk."

We all shook hands again, and then, just to top off the lie, the small charade between us, I went around his desk and leaned over, kissed his cheek. "Thank you," I said to him, and did my best Sincere Rita Longford imitation.

"Oh." He blushed, and said, "You just go make your house a home."

We stepped onto the sidewalk just outside the door.

Tom said, "You."

I smiled, relieved I wouldn't have to explain to him why we'd lied. "I love you," I said.

He said, "This is the day," and I knew then that hope really *was* in Tom, that he was still ready for new life, ready to start.

I pulled him to me, held him close, my eyes closed, my chin on his shoulder, and I could feel my smile, no longer work, no longer anything but love for him.

Then I opened my eyes, wanting to take in the blue sky above these buildings on Main Street in a town from which we would soon be moving, but what I saw was the window of Mr. Blaisdell's office above me, and his face at the window, a face sagging with old flesh, his white pompadour. He pulled away from the glass the instant he saw me look, and disappeared.

That night we made love, sweet, hopeful love, Tom's lips warmer and softer than I could remember, and as I moved above him, felt him deep inside me, felt his warm tongue gently caress my nipple, felt his hands softly touching my back, I knew that if it were ever to be, if we were ever to bear children, to conceive, it would be on this night, the eve of our beginning, entry into a new world.

 I dreamt that night, the dream now rote, now dead, no longer something I feared. The children at my bedside were as familiar as a mother could imagine, children I loved and dreaded at once, predictable in their silence, their eyes on me. The only new feeling I had in me, if it was a feeling at all, lay in my waiting for my son's hand, to see if he would offer it again. That was what I waited to see.

Finally that part in the dream came, and he raised his hand, just as soft, just as pale and cool as every other night. Then his lips seemed to quiver, the corners of his mouth rise, to change, and I saw on his face what might have been the beginning of a smile, a child's tentative, apprehensive smile at some stranger: me.

Slowly he lifted his head up as if to take me in, and I could see the soft porcelain skin at his throat and chin, his smile growing wider, and I braced myself, ready for the abyss inside him once his smile broke open. Still he held out his hand.

I was suddenly frightened, my skin prickling, my mouth dry and hot, my neck sweating, and I realized all in a moment, all in my dream, that I did *not* want to touch him. What I'd waited for for so long, the touch of my child, of these children, was about to happen, and I saw that I did not want it, because the waiting would be over, that subtle progression from nothing to something, from despair to hope, would be over. The children would be here, and I would have to look in their eyes, and I would have to know them.

But then he smiled, a brittle smile, the edges of his mouth breaking with the movement of muscles, his thin lips almost disappearing.

Finally I could see his teeth, hard, white, and nearly glowing, whiter than his throat, his chin.

His smile held, and he reached even closer, until his hand was right before me, inches from me, and it seemed miraculous that he hadn't yet disappeared, that he wanted to touch me, wanted me to hold his hand, though I knew I had only sutured stumps.

Then the middle child, the girl closest to me, lifted her hand, too, and she smiled, and the smallest girl, my baby daughter at the foot of the bed, both hands clutching the edge of the bedspread, let one hand go. She reached for me, and I could see the light half-moons of her nails on the tips of her small fingers.

My two girls smiled, their smiles as light as my son's, the abysses, the black infinite space that had come each time before, gone, the three of them smiling at me and smiling, each with a hand held out, waiting for me, waiting.

I *saw* these children, knew them somehow: in their eyes, their sharp, obsidian eyes black and glistening, the whites brilliant against the gray of skin in moonlight, I could see Tom's eyes, his dark irises, the soft eyelashes; and in the curl of their mouths, the corners drawn up, the two girls still with baby teeth, I could see me, *me*. The boy and the younger daughter had Tom's high cheek bones, his near-black hair; the middle daughter's hair was lighter, the shade my own.

I looked at them, at my children, these three at once alien and familiar, known and unknown, and my fear ceased. It disappeared, and I sat up in bed, wanting to take their hands, to touch them, to let them lead me wherever it was they wanted me to go.

Suddenly the room was not the bedroom in our apartment, but was my own room out in Chesterfield, and I had in me the same feeling I'd had the first night after we'd seen the house, when I'd awakened to the new cold, and thought that perhaps we had already moved into the house. Now I was here, the fireplace to my left, a small fire burnt down to embers filling the room with a deep orange glow. To my right was the window; through it I could see the dull, leafless trees of late fall, and the barn, a dark silhouette, above it a lonely quarter moon, ashen and empty.

Even though this was my room in Chesterfield, it had our bedroom furniture in it: against the wall before me was the dresser; on Tom's side of the bed was the armoire, and here was our bed. The walls were clean and white and free of the ugly paneling, the room just as I had imagined it would be, just as I'd wanted it, except that this was now our bedroom. It was no longer my room, but ours, and I did not mind. I felt good in here, as if this were a better idea, the way things should have been all along.

The children still held their hands out to me, and the baby, my baby, nodded at me, her fingers closing over her palm and opening again, closing and opening.

I could move. I leaned toward her, and I hesitated a moment, swallowing at the thought of putting out to her one of my stumps, but I went ahead, and as I did I saw I had my own hands again. I put my left hand out to her, amazed that those black threads had disappeared, and that here, here was my hand again. I looked at it and saw, too, that there was no scar there, those two raised pieces of flesh like short, red worms gone, the hand perfect and unblemished, just as it had been before Mr. Gadsen's rabbit.

Fear was gone, and when our hands touched, hers warmer than mine, the three of them moved back from the bed a little to allow me room to climb down. This is what they wanted, I knew, though no one spoke, no one motioned. We were silent.

I stood, the hardwood floor glistening and warm, the linoleum long gone. I looked down at the floor, and saw that I was naked, remembered I hadn't put my nightgown on after having made love with Tom, that sweet love in which we'd conceived our first child. This I knew, still holding my baby's hand, the three of them standing around me, smiling up at me. Then the boy took my other hand, my right, and started across the room, slowly leading me, half-turned toward the fire, his face toward me so that he was silhouetted by the orange embers. I felt my daughter's hands on my legs, too, gently prodding me to follow.

For some reason I felt full, almost bloated, and I felt strange walking across the room in our finished home, felt as though my center of gravity had been altered somehow, that if I had leaned forward only a little I might fall, and still I followed her.

We were headed for the armoire, I realized as we passed the hearth, the fire's warmth on me, led by a boy who seemed familiar and seemed a stranger, though I knew he was my own. He brought me to the armoire, and the three of them moved behind me, and I could feel on the backs of my legs three sets of small hands, on my body the warmth of the embers.

I looked in the mirror on the armoire door, and I caught my breath.

I stood naked before the mirror, my abdomen swelled with a child. I was pregnant, before me my image, bathed in the sweet glow of that fire, illuminated. Immediately I put my hands to my abdomen to touch myself, to make sure this wasn't some trick, some distortion of glass. To make sure that at least in my dream I was pregnant. And it was true: the skin was swelled out and hard, taut, a child inside me. The skin, too, was smooth, and as I caressed it with my fingertips, swirled my hands over it again and again, I felt the silent flutter of a kick, my baby's kick, inside me.

I looked back to the mirror, looked at myself. I wanted to see, *see* what I would look like nine months from then, this dream a prophecy, I knew, a promise.

My breasts were now round and full, my nipples and aureoles large, soft with the warmth of the fire, the light moving across me. I touched them, touched the nipples to try to raise them, to see if perhaps the first traces of warm liquid were there, to see if I were ready yet to nurse, though I knew milk came in only after birth. Yet it happened: my left breast, the nipple now aroused, erect, gave out a single drop of liquid, and I put the tips of my first two fingers in my mouth, tasted precisely what I had hoped for: the sweet, sweet milk that would charge my child with life.

The children, still behind me, leaned their faces toward the armoire, and we looked at one another in the mirror. With one hand I touched the crown of each child's head, and they smiled up at my reflection.

Then I brought up my hands and let them fall slowly down my abdomen, lingering as long as I wished, registering in my brain the feel, touch, tightness of skin. In the light from the embers it seemed I could see a shine in places where the skin had been pulled too taut: stretchmarks, I knew, small vertical shiny lines beside my abdomen that signaled my baby was ready to be born. Stretchmarks, something I'd not thought about before, but which now, as I took myself in, I did not mind. They were signs of life.

I touched my navel, too, felt and saw how it protruded, a hard, tiny knot at the apex of this swelling, and for a moment I imagined the umbilical cord of the child inside me, and my blood passing through that cord and into that baby, me inside it, it inside me, a miracle.

I let my hands go even farther down, and looked at myself in the mirror, in the light. My pubic hair was thicker now, had grown broader below my abdomen, a confluence of vague lines that met at my pubic bone, and I felt the softness of that hair, wondered at why the body decided growing more hair would accompany a woman's bearing children.

I looked at myself. I looked and looked, not daring to close my eyes, not daring even to blink, for then, I knew, the dream would be over, and I would have to begin the nine months of waiting before me. I wanted to savor this vision as long as I could.

And I looked at the faces of my children, because I wanted to remember them, too; remember their clothes, their white, soft hands on my legs; remember each child's eyes and nose and mouth and cheeks and hair, because they were the ones who had brought me here, who had given me this vision. I looked at them: at the tallest, oldest, who came to my waist; at my first daughter, who stood to the left of me, the side of her face pressed to my thigh; and at the youngest, only a little taller than my knees, who held onto my leg the most ferociously of the three, the material of her white dress soft against my calf.

Then I felt it, the flutter again, and I looked at my abdomen. In the dim orange light I could see the movements of the baby, evidence of life inside me showing outside: high on the right side of my abdomen my flesh poked out momentarily, a shadow raised, a simultaneous kick inside me, like some gentle bird slowly spreading its wings, proof enough for me that I *had* conceived this night, had made life with Tom. The baby kicked again, and again the skin pushed up, a shadow formed. Lower and to the left was another movement, another push of skin, and I knew then how the baby lay in me: its feet tucked high and up, just beneath my ribcage, rows of bones spread and distended to allow for the great size in me. Its feet were up there, and down below, on my left, were its head and arms, and once again I ran my hands across myself. The lower left side felt fuller, rounder, and I knew this was its head. I knew.

Just as suddenly I felt a drop in me, a quick shift in my center of gravity, a falling, and I saw my abdomen move, too, all of it seeming to slip lower as I watched, and I knew that this was birth, and I could hold in me no longer the elation, the joy I felt at this fruition. I put one hand on my lower abdomen, and with the other moved to touch again the heads of my children.

I looked in the mirror as I brought my hand down to my son's head, my left hand, and saw on the flesh between thumb and forefinger those ribbons of scar tissue, the remnants of that bite back now, and I shuddered.

The boy had lost his smile, and I looked at his reflection, hoping for some show of emotion, some shine of happiness in his eyes, but there was nothing. Only his sharp, ebony irises and blank whites of his eyes, and as I watched in the mirror his face suddenly went deep gray, the cheeks sunken, the eyes drawing back into their sockets, his hair—that glossy, black hair—lifting and flying on some invisible, untouchable wind that shot through him.

I could do nothing. I needed to scream, to move away from him, but nothing happened: I only opened my mouth, trying to let out that scream, but felt cold, dead air shoot into me, fill my lungs. The shifting in my abdomen continued, weight moving lower and lower, and still I tried to scream.

I looked at the girls, hoping somehow that they might comfort me, but their faces, too, were going over to the gray and black of my son's, their hair flying, eyes sunken. Then they opened their mouths, and I was not surprised to see black holes again, the girls' dresses pick up and dance on the wind in the room. All three opened their mouths, and I could feel the cold wind on me, my skin scratching over with goose bumps, the back of my neck drawing tight, my eyes tearing with the cold.

They flew through the room, their faces gone to black, the embers in the fireplace dying and shooting up sparks and dying again, the warmth here and then gone. The children flew, and as always imploded, disappeared into themselves.

I put my hands to my face, and between my fingers I caught the last glimpse of me before the mirror, my pregnant body, my abdomen huge with the advent of birth, the dead room behind me, my own face ashen, my eyes lost in their sockets.

I screamed, finally, the strength given me from somewhere, and then I closed my eyes, shut them as tight as I could, my scream letting loose the terror I felt, and launching me into the pain of imminent labor I felt low in my abdomen. I shut my eyes tight, my hands still at my face, and screamed, before me now the same circling squares I'd seen when I'd passed out after having been bitten.

Then the wind stopped, and my scream tore into the black quiet around me. I stopped, and my ears filled with the rush of blood through my head, the pierce of that silent, high pitch.

"Claire?" Tom shouted from behind me. I heard him throw back sheets, turn in the bed, his feet on the floor. Then his hands were on my shoulders. "Claire?"

I opened my eyes, took my hands from my face.

In the mirror was my reflection. Me. I stood before the mirror, my body the gray of moonlight through a window, my skin covered with goose bumps. I was not pregnant, my abdomen flat and shallow, my navel a small black hole leading back into me. My pubic hair was the same small black triangle there between my legs. And my breasts were small again, insignificant, the nipples and aureoles the same size as always, the nipples erect, not from being ready to give milk, but from the cold of the room.

Our room, the same old room in the same old apartment, the same old walls around me.

Tom said, "Claire?" again, and I felt his warm body next to me, pressed into me. "What's wrong?"

I was shaking with the dead adrenalin in me, and I wanted to tell him it was a bad dream, a terrible dream, but I wanted to take those thoughts back, because I remembered the glimpse of the future, me there and pregnant, my body with our child, and I knew, *knew* that even though the children had disappeared I was still pregnant, that we had but nine months to wait: we would by that time have finished work on the house, my room in the home in Chesterfield changed magically into a nursery, waiting for this new baby.

I still felt pressure down below my abdomen, still had that bloated feel, and I felt in spite of this dream somehow happy, rewarded for having come through, and I turned around to Tom, and I held him, felt his warm hands on my back again.

But then there came a sudden, small movement deep inside me, and I felt the wet issue descending, and I felt the warmth between my legs.

I pulled away from Tom, still without having said a word. I put my hand down to my vagina, gently placed my first two fingers there—the same two fingers with which I had tasted my own milk—and brought them close to my face. The blood there on my fingers was thick and sticky, as black as blood ought to be in the dark of a cold bedroom. My period had begun.

"What is it?" Tom said. "Claire?"

I said nothing, merely turned from him and headed, still silent, still in darkness, to the bathroom.

I listened all that week, waiting for my father's voice, waiting, waiting. I listened for him when I stood in the shower, and when I climbed down the stairs to the car, and when I drove over the bridge into Hadley, headed for work, the fields dead, covered with ancient corn stubble like long rows of twisted and broken bones sticking up from the earth. I listened for his voice as I ran the rabbits, Chesterfield and all the rest now, as planned, successfully void of any remembrance whatsoever of that conditioned behavior. Now, when the tone came, they did nothing, only let the electric shock spark into them, rush through their bodies in some sort of tacit agreement that, yes, their brains had been tampered with; yes, they could not remember that they should wince at the coming pain; and, yes, the search for Artificial Intelligence moved on.

And I listened whenever I saw Sandra, paler now than ever, her face fatter, her hair greasy. I listened when I passed her in the hall, listened as I caught glimpses of her staining and mounting, listened as I saw her walk into the computer room at lunch now, alone.

I listened, and listened, ignoring everything and everyone around me. The rest of the week I spoke little to Tom who, I assumed, only imagined it was me having my period, that I ought to be feeling this way, that it was my right to say nothing, to do nothing, only come home at night to lie on the couch with the television going until after midnight, then coming to bed and sleeping as far away from him as I could possibly get. He said nothing to me.

*   *   *

The next day, Friday, was the day perfusion began.

Sacrifice was the word used, uttered by Will and Sandra and myself and in all the literature, a word that veiled what we did, hid the fact that we killed them next; a word that elevated things somewhat, and made us feel, perhaps, that indeed we were doing some sort of favor to these animals for whom we'd already destroyed some center of thinking, cells that made them blink in anticipation.

Sacrifice.

Still I was listening for my father, the image of my dream still with me four days later, seared into my own brain every time I went to the bathroom, each time I had to pull out the swelled and brown-red tampon and drop it between my legs into the toilet, where I would flush the thing down, those bits of possible life shed voluntarily by my own body, a traitor. Still I bled, and bled, and bled, as though this steady flush from my own system were one long re-iteration of the truth: I could not have a child, my pregnant body only a dream. Nothing more. Some accident of God, who'd given me this. An accident.

Sacrifice.

Chesterfield was the first to go, and I felt nothing. I wore no gloves, merely picked him up from the cage in the basement, walked with him upstairs, cradling him, his paws up in the air as I scratched his chest. I felt nothing for the animal, felt only its rapid heartbeat beneath my fingertips.

I started down the hall, and saw that Paige and Wendy's office door was open. From inside came a low voice, Will's, perhaps, speaking in a quiet monotone, and then it stopped. I was even with the door, and looked in.

There were all four of them: Paige and Wendy both leaning on the edges of their desks, heads down; Will leaning against the back wall, his arms crossed; Sandra in the oak rocker, her elbows on her knees, looking at the floor.

They all looked up at me, as if they had prearranged it, the four of them waiting for me to pass. Their faces, though, were blank, eyes dead. They didn't move, say anything.

I hesitated a moment, wanting to know what was going on, but

then I moved on down the hall. I had a rabbit in my arms. I had
my job to do. I was listening for my father.

I moved down the darkened hall, all the way to the far end, to
the perfusion room, a room whose walls were covered with green
tiles, what had once been the dorm showers. When I reached the
heavy wooden door, I leaned my back against it, and looked down
the hall, half hoping Sandra would be following me to fill me in,
and half hoping that no one would be there.

There was no one, and I pushed hard against the door, and
moved in.

The room was actually two rooms, the front room set up with
necessary equipment: water bottles, tubing, metal shelves laid out
with scalpels and Rongeurs shears, hemostats, boxes of syringes
and surgical masks and gloves, bottles of Nembutal. Everything
needed to sacrifice an animal.

In the room beyond was the stainless steel sink, over it the rack
with its four small pieces of nylon rope, one fixed to each corner,
upon which the rabbit—Chesterfield—would lie; above the sink was
a shelf holding two huge plastic bottles, one of saline solution, the
other of Formalin.

Chesterfield lay still in my arms, content, his nose slowing down,
his eyes nearly closed.

I took him to the table, where sat yet another Gormezano box,
and I placed him in it, closed off the two Plexiglas ends. I got a
syringe from one of the boxes, and drew from a bottle of Nembutal
a little over three milliliters. A lethal dose, one that would lull him
at first, then slow his heart rate down next to nothing.

I pulled up the scruff of his neck with my left hand. There, on
the back of my hand, was the scar. That God damned scar on my
hand, that pregnant rabbit never leaving me, and though I'd no
reason to, though Chesterfield had never been anything other than
the calmest, most cooperative, most peaceful rabbit I'd ever handled,
still I took the syringe with my right hand, held it up to pop off the
last small bubble at the tip of the reservoir, and I jammed the needle
into the rabbit, jammed it hard, so that Chesterfield, startled and
pained, let out the first scream I'd ever heard from him, a small
shattering of sound that broke through the room and boomed and

ricocheted across the tiles and stainless steel to settle into my ears, the sound magnified by the room, loud and shrill and cold.

I pulled out the syringe, and I started waiting.

Ten minutes later he was out. I took apart the Gormezano box, and laid Chesterfield on the table. I put my hand to the fur of his chest, felt his brittle ribcage. His heartbeat was almost nonexistent, just a small, muffled vibration every second. Almost nothing.

I picked him up, limp in my hands, so much dead weight, as though he had doubled in weight since just a few moments ago, when he had been in my arms and awake.

I took him into the second room, and put him on the metal rack over the sink. I touched a finger to his chest. The pulse was slowing down even more. I had to work fast, I knew, to start perfusion before the heart stopped completely. The heart had to be pumping in order for the fluid to be taken up. Perhaps I'd given it too large a dose; perhaps, with the jab of the syringe, I'd startled it too much, its adrenalin rushing its heart rate, the dose taken up too quickly. I had to move.

And I felt nothing, no remorse. I wondered at this; each first rabbit I'd ever named I'd felt sorry for, felt pained by this point at having to put the thing to sleep.

But now. Now I was cold, my hands smooth-moving and unhesitant as I flipped the rabbit onto its back, pulled its forelegs up and to either side and tied them to the rack with small pieces of nylon rope, pink now from so many sacrifices. I tied its forelegs down, and did the same with its hindlegs, pulled down and to the side and tied off so that the animal lay on its back, limbs pulled taut and away, ready for the next step.

I touched the chest. Slower still.

I went to the metal shelves in the other room, got a paper surgeon's mask from one of the boxes, put it on. Then I got a pair of surgeon's gloves, pulled them on, and picked up a pair of surgical shears, a scalpel, a clamp and two hemostats, and the Rongeurs shears.

I went back to the sink, turned on the water, let it run as I uncoiled first the tubing from the saline jug, next the tubing from the Formalin bottle. I connected the tubes to the juncture, a Y-shaped piece of tube that would allow me to feed through the same tube and into the animal first the saline, then the Formalin. I made sure the clips that held the tubes closed at the base of the jugs were tight so that no liquid would escape until I let it. I turned to the animal.

I took the scalpel and made a small cut just below the sternum, right into the pink skin and fur.

Still I felt nothing, only watched my hands move in their calculated, practiced manner. I watched as my hand put the scalpel on the stainless steel countertop next to the sink, and picked up the shears.

The shears were small, sharp, and I held them open, pushed the bottom tip deep into the incision, and I started cutting, moving up through the sternum, through that small, flat bone, and on up through the ribcage, each *snip* of the shears laying open the chest of that animal, more blood with each cut, the bones so fragile and thin I could have been cutting through thick paper.

Then I was finished, and rinsed the bloodied shears off in the water, the red only faint in the bottom of the sink. I placed the shears next to the scalpel, fixed the hemostats in place to clamp off the blood from the flesh, and with both hands I pried open the ribcage, pulled it open wide to reveal the chest cavity.

Before me lay first the lungs, wings of soft pink barely moving, surrounded by red, bloody tissue, the ribs blue and red. Below the lungs lay the diaphragm, the thick membrane wall that moved too slowly.

I peeled back the lungs to the heart, nearly buried beneath other organs—the liver, the stomach, the pancreas. It was still beating, a regular but weak jump of maroon muscle, blood still pumping through it, the animal still alive.

I wriggled a finger down below it, pushed back organs to expose the descending aorta like a red worm, and I got the clamp from the countertop, closed it on the aorta so that, now, all the blood was circulating up into the brain.

I picked up the scalpel, held it, poised above the heart.

I wanted to stop, to stare, to wonder at the moment of death and the act of deciding which moment it might be; and I thought of my own brain, wondering which neurons would fire into which synapses to start the chain of firings on down from inside my skull through my muscles until the endpoint, some particular muscle in my forearm, would contract, and the scalpel would sink into the tough muscle of this animal's heart. I felt something then, too, some sharp pain at the center of my head, some show of something going on there that made me want to cry, and I thought that this was emotion, that it was in me after all, my feelings for a rabbit, for Chesterfield, hidden and buried under all the dead tissue of my life, hidden under my dead womb, under my dream of being pregnant. I wanted to cry, to let the pain in me go, but suddenly, as if out of reflex or some unrecognized instinct, a muscle in my forearm contracted, and the blade, sharp and glistening and silver, sank into the heart, that thick red marble; sank into the left ventricle at precisely the correct spot, precisely the correct depth, precisely the correct length. And just as suddenly, just as precisely, my hand and the scalpel moved lower on the heart, made another incision in the vena cava, just a small slip of the blade, and the moment of wonder in me, of awe, of wanting to hold back from this task, was gone.

I let the scalpel go, watched it slip down between bars of the rack and heard it clatter at the bottom of the steel sink, then took the tube leading from the juncture and pulled back the clip from the saline jug to let the liquid go. I hesitated a moment, looking at the chaotic order of organs open before me, the animal splayed, limbs tied back, heart pierced, and I placed the loose end of the tube, saline solution flowing, directly into the ventricle, slipped the tip into the heart, let gravity and muscle bring fluid into the body, pump it through.

This was perfusion, flushing the animal's body with liquid while it was still alive, cleansing the system of blood, preparing it for the Formalin, a substance that would harden the veins and arteries and, of course, the brain of the rabbit, turn all that tissue to gelatin so slices of its brain could be examined microscopically.

My job.

The saline started flowing, coursing through the arteries and veins, and I stared at the animal, watched as the body cavity began to fill with blood, drowning those organs, its own heart.

"Happy?" Sandra said from behind me.

I was startled at her voice, the only other sound in there the running water, and I flinched, though I did not look at her. I would not look at her.

"Happy?" she said again, this time louder.

I stared at the body cavity, watched as the blood rose, now covering the lungs.

"About what?" I said. My teeth were clenched, the muscles in my face and neck tight. I did not want to talk to her, hadn't, I realized, since that day in the computer room, not since she had given her problem to me and yet asked for no help. She had let me know she wanted no help. I would give her none.

"Don't kid me," she said. I tried to imagine what gestures she might be making, whether she were standing with her arms crossed, or hands on her hips, or hands in pockets. But, again, I could picture nothing. I could only hear her voice, the familiar pitch and timbre, and recognize the meanings of her words.

I said nothing.

"You can't be that cold. You can't be that dead."

I said, "I must be." Still I watched the rabbit fill with its own blood.

"Let me tell you, then," she said, her voice gone flat, dead. "Let me fill you in." She paused a moment. "Let me tell you," she said, her voice almost lost, washed out by the running water, "that Mr. Gadsen's dead. He's dead."

Blood broke over the edge of the cavity, trickled through white fur in a thick red line down the left side of the animal and toward its back, and I watched as the blood first dripped, then evolved into a steady stream into the sink, where water washed it out, diluted it, made it seem less significant than what it really was: what kept the animal alive. And I thought how similar we were, this rabbit and myself. We were both having life washed out of us, me with the primitive trick of the moon and the shedding of the walls of my uterus, the animal with the trick of advanced science and technology. We were both alike, both of us nearly dead.

"What do you want me to do?" I said, my voice an imitation of hers, inflectionless and remote.

She said, "I wouldn't want you to do anything. Nothing at all. I'd expect only what you've done all along. All along since the rabbit

bit you. Just forget him. It'll be a lot easier for you, too, now that
he's dead." She paused. "And you can just keep on the same with
us, too. With me. Just keep going the same with me."

Now the blood was thinning out in the cavity, the saline working
its way through, flushing the body, clearing out arteries and veins
and capillaries, the whole system. The liquid pouring from the animal, leaching into its fur, was losing its bright-red hue, its thick-
ness, duller now, pink.

I looked up at the saline jug. I'd put through about a half gallon.
Still a half to go before the blood was gone.

"You're doing just fine," she said. "You're doing just as I'd expected you would."

"I didn't want to let you down," I said. I was looking at the rabbit
now, the cavity filled, the organs gone beneath the surface.

"Oh," she said, and she moved closer behind me. "Oh," she said
again, right behind my ear. "You didn't," she whispered. "You didn't
let me down at all. But you let someone else down. You let down
Mr. Gadsen, just an old man who was about to die anyway. Who'd
been waiting for it for years. Who'd been only passing time doing
what he knew best how to do. Just working." Her whispered words
were cold on my ear, and I shuddered suddenly, completely, my
spine, I felt, almost whipping through me.

Water in the bottom of the sink was only a pale, pale pink now.

"Yeah," she went on, speaking now, her face still just behind me.
"He'd been dying for a long time now. Will knew that. Nobody else.
That's what he was telling us just a few minutes ago in Wendy and
Paige's. You just pausing at the door as you go by." She stopped.
"Nobody else knew because there wasn't anybody else. He had no
kids. He had no wife. He had nobody. Just a bunch of academic
bastards he supplied animals to. That's it. So now, who knows what
will happen. There's a farm somewhere up in Leverett where there's
all these animals, and there's going to be no caretaker for them.
That's what Will was telling us, too. That there's no caretaker up
there, all these animals sitting in cages in rows, and they'll just get
put aside somewhere." She paused. "Probably get bought up by that
shithead in Worcester, and they'll all die of enteritis because he
doesn't know how to take care of them properly. That's what will
happen."

She stopped, and took a deep breath. I stared at the rabbit. Just a carcass. The wash in its cavity was now only a faint pink, the organs now visible beneath the surface. The white fur, drenched in pink now, clung to the body, the carcass thin, insignificant.

I reached up, pushed in the clip to the base of the saline jug, and then I reached over and pulled the clip from the jug of Formalin.

"And you, because you got bit, and because the rabbit was pregnant, and because you're so preoccupied with feeling sorry for yourself because you two can't have children, you wouldn't let him apologize to you like he wanted, do what he could for you."

"It's not that I didn't—" I said, but I stopped. The pain was there in my head again, a shard digging into my brain, but I held on. I watched the rabbit, watched as the Formalin took its path into and through this thing, watched as the effect took place: the rabbit, spread open as if to reveal itself to me, to show me how it worked, began to jitter, just barely shake, the paws moving, and then the head and neck shook, too. The rabbit quivered as though—after exposing itself to me, giving its heart and its brain over to me in all faith I would do it no harm—it realized I intended to kill it. As if it were afraid of me, quivering with the jolt of Formalin, its muscles constricting as the substance settled into veins and arteries, already hardening, already turning that all-important brain, that jewel, into gelatin.

My knees were shaking.

"And me," Sandra said, oblivious to the quivering. She'd seen rabbits die this way often enough. But, I realized, I'd seen even more. Maybe, I thought, I'd seen enough. "No," she went on, "you didn't let me down. You didn't let me down at all, because you know what?" She stopped. Her voice, those last few words, had taken on some different tone, some different pitch; her voice, I realized, was quivering too, as though she and I and this rabbit were all three dead, all three shot through with Formalin, all three of our bodies giving over to the constriction of muscles. Her voice shivered.

"You know why you didn't let me down?" she said. "Because you couldn't have. I'd already let myself down. I'd already let myself down long before the day in the computer room when I told you I was pregnant, and I told you I wanted to keep it. I lied to you. I lied to you, that's how I let myself down." She was almost crying now, and I heard her sniff, take in another deep breath.

The shivering of the carcass slowed down as the Formalin set up, the rabbit's limbs now stiff, the neck twisted back at an ugly angle. Still my knees shook, and the pain dug in.

"I lied to you," she said, "not about wanting that baby, because I do. I want it. I want it to love and to care for and to feed and to share the world with. The same things you feel. Those same things, I know. But I lied to you. I lied. By the time," she said. "By the time I talked to you that day, by that time—"

I reached up just then and shoved the clip back onto the Formalin jug tube, picked up the rack, and as roughly as I could, as violently as I could, I banged it once on the edge of the sink, and turned it sideways to let the Formalin and saline in the body cavity pour out into the sink, the liquid now clear, now clean, devoid of any life. Of anything.

The rabbit hung there on the rack, its head held in place at that angle by thick, dead tissue stiff with Formalin.

As quickly as I could, I lay the rack back over the sink, untied the cords, then removed the hemostats and the clamp, and dropped them on the countertop.

I wanted her out of here. I wanted her out, because I knew what she was going to say next.

The rabbit loosened, I turned around. Sandra was right there, and I did not acknowledge her, did not even look at her. My shoulder pushed into hers as I went for the far corner of the green-tiled room where, washed and shiny and ready, sat the guillotine.

The guillotine. It was precisely that, a guillotine, a small one built for exactly this moment, this job. For chopping off the heads of rabbits.

My job.

It stood about two feet tall, the blade-edge at the top of the carriage angled down, surgery sharp. The base had a small cutout half-circle in the steel, and a handle that, when pulled, brought the blade down and through the neck. It was, after all, the head we were after, the brain inside. Chopping off the animal's head was the next to last step before staining and mounting that brain.

I pulled the guillotine to the middle of the floor, positioned it next to the drain at the center of the room so that when I was finished I could rinse it off, wash down the drain any blood and saline and Formalin that might issue from the rabbit.

Guillotine, I thought. Not a word like sacrifice, but a word that hid nothing. It told precisely what happened, and for some reason I liked the fact nothing was veiled about this instant. The machine did what it had to do. It had a name that hid nothing. There were no secrets.

I glanced up from the guillotine as I centered it perfectly before the drain, and I saw Sandra there, her back to me. She hadn't yet moved, still faced the sink where I had been, but her head was down now, her hands in front of her.

This was when the heat started up in me, the shard in my head now several pieces of broken glass, something in me that wanted out, and I thought of the blood still coming from between my legs, blood for no reason, an empty symbol, and I thought, Isn't that enough from me? Isn't that enough for me to let go? This blood in me? But the pain grew, and the heat, and I had to blink back the pain in my eyes, because I knew she was about to say it, and I knew what would happen when I heard it.

I stood up, my knees wobbly, not from having squatted, but from pain creeping down into me, into the rest of me. There was sound now, too, a high rush of undefinable sound, and I made my way to the sink.

I picked up the carcass. It was stiff now and growing more so each second, its brain nearly ready to demystify the world with what it would tell us, and I turned, went back to the guillotine, my knees shaking more.

Then, as I knelt there, placing the rabbit into position, twisting its head around so that it faced forward, I heard her move, even through that increasing din in my ears, a sound that was no sound. I heard her move around, so that now my back was to her again.

I reached up to the lever on the guillotine with my left hand, and through the yellow-white, opaque surgeon's glove, I could see the ridges of that scar, the little mountains pressed into the latex glove.

And in that moment, the rabbit in place, my left hand on the lever, my right hand cupped beneath the head, ready to catch it as it fell, I wondered whether or not this was an empty symbol, my

left hand, my scarred hand bringing down the blade that would
decapitate Mr. Gadsen's best rabbit ever, Mr. Gadsen now dead.

The pain was seeping into my shoulders, seeking exit, but I would
not allow it. I pulled hard on the handle, watched as the blade moved
down through the tracks and into the pink, drenched fur of the
rabbit's neck. The lever gave just a moment's hesitation as the blade
severed the neck, and the head fell into my hand, tumbled forward,
the long, soft ears flipping over like thin, white fingers, and I held
it in my hand, the head upside down, its lips drawn back slightly
to show its incisors, those fangs.

It had weight. It seemed significant.

I picked up the carcass by the scruff of the neck, that same scruff
I had jabbed with a syringe only minutes ago. Its limbs were still
out to its sides, and from its body cavity poured more liquid as I
brought it once again back to the sink. I lay the head on the counter,
and pulled out the garbage can from beneath the sink. I took off
the lid, and dropped in the carcass, the body swallowed up in the
green plastic bag. I pushed the can back under the sink.

Now was the last step, and I knew I had only seconds before the
pain—now at my elbows, at my ankles—might envelope me, my
job demanding to be finished, to be completed with no emotion, no
caring. And I was doing that, the head in my hands nothing, only
the head of an anonymous animal from a dead handler.

"*Listen to me!*" Sandra shouted. Her eyes were closed, her hands
in fists at her temples, but I could not stop. There was nothing to
stop me. I had to finish my job.

I took from the counter the thick, stubby Rongeurs shears, shears
that looked more like pruning shears than a surgical instrument.

The pain, this cutting through me, was at my wrists now, and in
my eyes and mouth and tongue.

I put the tip of the shears to the skull where the ears met, and I
took the first snip, cut through bone. It had taken more effort, more
muscle than I could have known.

"I only wanted to know what to do," she said. She was crying
now. "I only wanted to know. Is there anything wrong with that?
Just to know the right thing to do? What the right thing to do was?"

I took the next snip up, and the next, clipping through the skull,
right along the bone, thick and ungiving.

"Because I wanted to hear from you what was right, because I trusted you and I loved you. Because I didn't know, I really didn't know, and because I'd already done it." She was sobbing now, her voice octaves higher, beyond quivering, beyond trembling.

I pushed the tip deep and toward the nose. I took the last snip, watched the bottom blade of the shears surface through bone, meet with the upper blade.

The pain was at my knuckles, a tingling, a sharpness.

"I had it aborted before I ever even talked to you," she said, her voice suddenly gone steady, quiet, stone cold, and I looked up at her, the pain solid now in my eyes, in the movement of muscles winding back into my brain.

She was looking at me now, our eyes finally meeting.

She said, "I went to the University Health Center. I climbed up on a bed. I spread my legs open for them, for a smiling woman, *a woman*," her teeth clenched, the word *woman* seething from her. "A smiling woman did it to me, brought it out of me, talking me through it while things inside me twisted and pulled, and all the time I listened to her I didn't hear anything. I only heard Jim's voice, saw him wearing that sweaty T-shirt and shorts and those basketball shoes, the basketball there at his hip. I just heard him saying 'Abort it,' and here I was. There I was. I'd already done it before I even talked to you. And so your not helping me, your never talking to me, your hating me since then wasn't a matter of you letting me down. Because I'd already done it. I just wanted to see if you were human enough to talk to Mr. Gadsen. That's all I wanted to know from you. And you weren't, and so anything you may have told me to do—abort it, keep it, or just comfort me, just talk to me—I knew I could ignore, because you ignored that old man." She stopped. She let her eyes leave me, and looked down. "So, no, you didn't let me down."

I turned to the skull, its fruit inside, ready to be displayed, ready for science. I was trying to let her words mean nothing to me, trying to keep them outside of my head, out of my ears, my attention here on this research, this head, this job.

I dropped the shears to the floor, the pain in my hands near my fingertips, and I thought that if I could get to the brain I would know something, know why we were here, all of us, and I thought that the pain in me would disappear, too, and so, the head cupped in my hands, I placed my thumbs on the edges of the skull along the cut, and I pried back the bone, pried and pulled, cartilage and thickened tissue giving way and tearing, and then the skull was open wide.

Inside it lay the brain. The brain. The center of the animal, the center of us all. It was gray, convoluted, a gnarled mass of cells like small thick worms nestled snug and safe inside the skull.

It showed nothing to me. There was nothing I could see, only the tissue now gray gelatin, the Formalin set. It was only a brain.

The pain in me broke, but, instead of the sharp cry of fire through me that I'd thought would happen, it was only a dull ache, the immense pressure of my blood through me, through my own hands and legs, through my own brain, and through my heart. It was only my own blood banging through me, seeking somehow release, the pressure simply too much to bear, and so I dropped the skull, the brain, watched it fall as if in slow motion to the floor, where the brain shattered, broken into a half-dozen pieces, useless now. Of no consequence.

Chesterfield, I thought, and I moved away from it lying there on the floor next to the guillotine, backed up until I touched the green-tiled wall. *Chesterfield,* the name of a rabbit, a pet, and the name of the town we would move to. The place where we would, I finally saw, forget about hoping for children.

Slowly, carefully, I peeled off the gloves. I gave no thought to the scars, gave no thought to the stink of Formalin-thick air as I pulled off the surgical mask. I put my hands to my temples, closed my eyes, my eyes, it seemed, swelling with the pressure, my tongue filling my mouth, choking me as it, too, swelled with the ache of blood in me.

Sandra said something to me, words I couldn't recognize, and I opened my eyes. She looked at the brain on the floor, then at me, her eyes open wide. She said something again, and started moving toward me.

I could not hear her, I knew, because I was listening for my father, listening for him one last time, waiting to hear my name because I knew that if I did hear him I could live through this, could live through anything. I'd lived this long on just the one time he'd spoken to me when I'd leaned against the chain-link fence and had watched the bomber slice through the sky. I'd lived this long. Now I needed him again.

I listened for him, and I heard nothing, just the growing momentum of white sound already there, the sound of blood through me, cleaving me with its silence, slicing through me. Only silence.

I watched as Sandra still came toward me, a hand out in front of her, reaching for me, her mouth moving, her eyes full, but I heard nothing. I knew hope was dead in me, dead and gone with the dead air in my ears, dead and gone with my father, my inheritance my mother's fear of the world, and now I had only to wait, I saw, until the world took over, and killed me. There was no hope.

Sandra's hand touched my arm, and I shook it free, twisted away from her. I looked at her one last time, her face without expression, her hand taken back, no longer reaching for me. I turned and left the room.

When I got to the house in Chesterfield, I immediately got out of the car rather than sit in the front seat and look at it, as Tom and I had done every time before. I was through with sitting in some sort of wonder, awe at a house. There was work to do, and I knew where I wanted to start.

I went around to the trunk, put the keys in, popped it open. I reached in to Tom's toolbox, fished through all the paraphernalia in the huge, red metal box, and pulled out a claw hammer. Next to it lay an old shovel, and I picked this up, too.

I went to the porch.

I stood there only a moment, looking at the old porch, at the gray plywood, the nailheads, and then I dropped the shovel, and started hammering, banging at the two-by-fours of the steps up, the hammer like ice in my hand as I banged away, busting rusted nails, splintering wood, the vibration through my hand, my arm, my body a welcome jolt, some hard, real thing in me.

It took me all day, but I dismantled the porch by myself. I'd torn off piece after piece, my mind on nothing but wood, nothing but the task at hand, nothing but the splintered, beat lumber and rusted nails I broke up and tossed aside. The porch supports had come out easily, those posts merely a foot or so into the ground, no concrete poured to anchor them down. When I'd finally gotten the platform of the porch off, gotten the planks twisted free of the frame, I found fieldstone steps up to the front door, steps hidden by an ugly porch.

The first thing I did was to find a strong piece of wood, one of those two-by-fours that hadn't been killed by dry rot, and start poking at the mortar between stones, checking just as Martin had to see if it had gone bad, if any stones were loose and needed to be re-mortared. None did, and I dropped the piece of wood, then kicked at the stone steps. They were sturdy, strong; the stones, I could see, carefully selected so that the steps themselves were flat, level. As soon as I cleared them of the lumber, saw how carefully they had been put together, I went to the trunk of the car and got a tapemeasure from the toolbox. I measured the height from each step to the next. They were each exactly eight inches high, eight inches deep. Exactly.

Then I stood, looked at the wreck of wood, at the dull ground that had been covered for who knew how many years. I looked at those beautiful steps, steps right up to the front door, and I decided I didn't want the porch Tom had promised. I wanted these steps, my discovery, some sort of triumph while working out here alone, Tom somewhere in Northampton right now, reporting on a case at the courthouse or a rezoning move in the City Council chambers. This is all I want, I thought. These steps.

I looked at my hands, saw the blisters, some popped, the skin white and dead, others bloated with fluid. I flexed my fingers, felt the pull of muscle and skin. I hadn't felt the blisters, had felt nothing all day, only the cold hammer, the rough wood of the handle on the shovel. I could see my own breath in front of me, the calm roll of steam with each breath out, and I saw that the sun was already down.

I went home.

 I went into the apartment, my hands finally aching, taking in the pain of destroying the porch all day. But, I reasoned, the pain was something I could take home with me from the house, and from my steps.

I walked into the kitchen. Through the doorway I could see Tom in the living room, a beer in his lap, a sack from McDonald's on the coffee table. He was staring at the set, "Jeopardy" playing on it. He'd been home for a while, and had put on an old flannel shirt and jeans.

Without looking from the set, he said, "Will called the paper today."

I said nothing, merely pulled off my coat. I felt my hands, the skin, tightening up. I hung the coat on the back of one of the chairs in the kitchen, and moved into the living room, past him on the couch. I went into the bathroom, and brought from the medicine chest a bottle of alcohol, the box of Band-Aids and a few cotton balls from the half-empty bag beneath the sink.

I sat down on the toilet seat, and said, "What did he have to say?" With one hand I gently twisted the cap on the bottle, broken blisters on my fingers. I got the cap off, and tipped the bottle onto a cotton ball, started swabbing the palm of my left hand. The alcohol was cold at first, but then it dug in, and the pain just went deeper. I tipped the bottle back again, soaked the cotton ball again, swabbed again.

Tom stood in the doorway, leaned against the doorjamb. He was chewing something. He swallowed, said, "So you quit."

I didn't look at him, but touched the blisters, dabbed at them. I was watching them, looking for some difference in them now that I'd applied first aid. But nothing happened. The blisters were only dark red, near-raw flesh beneath thin sheets of dead skin.

I said, "I guess so." The cotton ball in my hand was a soft pink now, and for an instant I thought of Chesterfield, thought of his white fur and his blood, but I pushed that thought away, replaced it with the stone steps I'd found, the clean lines of the cold stone, the sturdy feel of them beneath my feet. I looked up at Tom.

He had his arms crossed now. He looked somehow content, settled, ready to stay where he was until I gave him what he wanted, whether it was the words *I'm sorry I quit* or *I'll go back tomorrow and apologize for walking out.* For a moment, my husband waiting for me, waiting, I thought of giving the words to him, of just telling him what he wanted to hear so that he would leave me alone, let me tend to my raw hands by myself. I thought, too, of telling him of the stone steps, of the ice-cold feel of rock mortared into place, hidden for years by a poorly built porch, the steps hidden away like some secret the house didn't want to give up.

I opened my mouth, ready to speak. I wanted him out of here, and I knew speaking would do it for me. I took a shallow breath, readied myself to force words from me, but I stopped. I stopped, because I knew that if I spoke, told him of rock steps he would see himself soon enough, I would lose something of the peace I'd collected all day, and something of the accommodations to the loss of hope I'd gathered out there in the cold, my blisters growing with each hard bang of the hammer, each shovelful of cold ground.

Because, I knew then, that was what I had been doing all day long. I'd been trying to accommodate myself to a new world, one in which no hope for children existed, no hope for the sort of love only children can give, the love that looked upon you as though you could do no wrong, though you knew how wrong you could be, knew the lie in it, that you could, indeed, do everything wrong.

I'd been working through the day to accommodate myself to a loss that had never existed, a feeling that some part of me, a physical piece somewhere hidden in the contours of my heart, had been excised, removed as though through surgery. Now, though I'd felt hope *were* there, I knew in my brain it was not. I'd spent my day aligning myself with this new freedom, freedom from hope. The stone steps leading up to the house were my own, I saw. Not his.

I swallowed, and I looked down from him. Giving him the words he wanted would be too easy. It would be simple for me, and my world wasn't an easy one now, I saw. I would have to fight my way through it, even if it meant fighting with him. My words were my own. My discovery of those steps was my own. He could wait.

I dropped the cotton ball into the trash basket beneath the sink, pulled another from the bag on my lap. I tipped the bottle of alcohol again, started swabbing my right hand, the pain cool, welcome.

He took a deep breath, let it out, and said, "You were going to say something?"

"No," I said. "Nothing at all."

"What happened to your hands?" he said, and hidden in his voice I thought I could hear some concern for me, but concern cloaked in his wanting to know more about my quitting than the state of my fingers and palms.

"Work," I said. I was watching my fingers, still hoping to see some change in them, some beginning of healing, but nothing happened. I said, "At the house. I went out there today," and I stopped. I would tell him no more of my day than that. I could feel my muscles tense up, ready for his questions, for his probing, for his bringing into our apartment his reporter's skills to get at what happened today.

But he only pulled off his glasses, started cleaning them again, this time with the front tail of his shirt. He was quick about it, the same old movement, the same old husband.

"Here's a story," he said, and moved into the bathroom. He leaned his back against the wall across from me and slowly eased down the wall until he was sitting on the floor, his knees up in front of him. He closed his eyes, finished cleaning the glasses. "Saw it today, from Phyllis, one of my stringers." He slipped the glasses back on, opened his eyes. It wasn't getting the glasses clean that mattered, I finally saw, but doing something with his hands that mattered. He looked down to the linoleum floor, his arms crossed. "At seven twenty this morning," he went on, "one whole wall of an old house over in Belchertown collapsed. The owners, a retired couple who moved out from Boston last year, were in the house. The husband was in the kitchen downstairs, and managed to get out. He'd thought the whole place was coming down."

He wasn't smiling telling me this. It was, of course, another of his attempts to cheer me, but it wasn't a real attempt, only the recitation of a story, news for the paper, nowhere in his voice the spark of humor he'd always had before. His arms were still crossed, his eyes still on the floor.

He said, "But the wife was in the upstairs bathroom, brushing her teeth. It took a couple of minutes, too, for the wall to fall down. Phyllis said the husband watched most of it from outside on the lawn. The wall just disintegrated, bricks peeling off in rows starting from the top. The husband described the sound to Phyllis as a 'cascade of bricks.' 'Just a cascade of bricks,' the man said over and over."

He paused, and looked up at me. He said, "Do you want me to go on?"

I was still looking at my hands. After a few moments, I said, "Go on only if the wife is okay. If she's dead, don't."

"She's fine," he said, his eyes back on the floor. "She's not hurt at all. Once her bathroom wall started disappearing, she tried to get out and couldn't get the door open, though it turned out it wasn't even locked. The wall kept falling, the wife pressed up against the bathroom door, the bathroom wall just peeling away." He paused. "When the wall finally finished falling, there was the wife, standing in the bathroom upstairs with her robe on. Her husband was down on the lawn, looking up at her. One whole wall of the house was heaped on the ground, the bathroom, their bedroom, a study, and downstairs the kitchen and living room like some sort of dollhouse, the rooms all open to the outside."

He paused, waiting, I knew, for some word from me, but I gave him none.

"The wife went hysterical. She broke down, crying, scared to death. Neighbors had started coming out by then, the fire department showing up a few minutes later. By this time the husband was upstairs, trying to get her to open the door, but she wouldn't budge. She's sitting on the floor of the bathroom with her back to the door, more neighbors accumulating, looking up at her. Finally an EMS squad is all that's able to get her down, the husband back

downstairs and outside looking up at her. They get her to open the
door and take her downstairs, and her husband comes up to hold
her, but she breaks down all over again. Turns out she's gone crazy
because, in addition to the wall falling down, her husband didn't
try to save her. Phyllis was there by that time, and heard her crying
to her husband, 'Don't you touch me. You left me up there. I don't
know who you are.' " He paused. "That's a quote." He stopped again,
took a breath. "Finally the EMS truck takes her over to Cooley-
Dickinson, the husband following in his own car. They were married
for thirty-seven years, and the wife wouldn't even let her husband
ride in the truck."

He stopped, and let out a heavy breath, as if there were air he'd
held inside of him through the whole story, something he'd kept
back from me.

I said, "Point of story?"

"Point of story," he said, "is that you know me. We've been
through a lot, maybe even more than a wall falling down, and I've
been here. I haven't run out of a house on you yet, and I'm not
about to. And so I'll keep the volume on the TV down low for you,
and I'll fix breakfast for you, and I'll bandage your hands for you,
and you can quit your job, too. I'll even send flowers to Gadsen's
funeral, if you want me to."

I looked up at him, too quickly. He was still looking at me. "Will
told me," he said, and slowly I looked back at my hands.

He said, "But you're scaring me now, because I'm not sure I know
exactly who you are." He paused. "I just want to make certain I
know *you,* and that you won't run out of a house that I'm in. I want
to know you."

He waited a few more seconds, waited for me to say something,
anything, I imagined, and then he pushed himself away from the
wall, stood, and moved into the living room. A moment later I heard
the sound of the McDonald's bag being crumpled up, footsteps into
the kitchen, water running.

The second cotton ball I held in my hand was the same shade of
pink as the first, and I threw it in the garbage. I wanted it away
from me. Then I bowed my head, my elbows on my thighs, my
hands out in front of me, the palms up, and I cried, cried for dead
hope, for a husband who, I saw, had just surrendered in his own

way to no hope, to living the rest of our lives with just ourselves, and though I tried with each breath in to make my body relax, make my muscles ease up, they did not. I sat there, the cold air of the room like an ice fire in my hands, my body wound too tight, and I cried.

DECEMBER

 "Uhm," Grady said from behind me. "Uh, Miss Templeton." He stopped. "Claire," he said. "Martin says that he thinks you're working too hard. That you're doing too much."

I had the metal scraper in my hand, shoving it up along the wall of the front room, the wall with the two windows that looked out to where the porch had been. The wallpaper solvent was working well; as I pushed the scraper up, wads of old, wet wallpaper were falling, leaving exposed the bare plaster wall, yellow with age.

We'd finally torn off the ugly brown paneling just that morning, the three of us—Martin, Grady, and I—each with claw hammers in hand. It had taken us only an hour to get it all off, the plastic coming down in brittle shards, shapes that looked like large brown pieces of broken glass. We worked at different places in the room, me beginning at the front door and working my way across the front wall, the wall I was peeling wallpaper from right now; Grady at the other windowed wall, the wall that held the window from which I'd looked the very first afternoon we had been here; Martin had started at the fireplace wall and gone on to the staircase wall, tearing out all the little detail pieces of paneling above the mantel and on the low wall where the banisterless staircase came down into the room.

It had only taken us that hour to get it all down, rip it from the walls to expose the ugly, pale flowered wallpaper I was peeling down now. Grady had been the slowest of the three of us, though I knew he wasn't taking his time. Martin was in his trance, and worked as quickly and proficiently as ever. I, too, I'd realized in the past three weeks, had my own trancelike state, the mode I clicked into whenever I entered the house. Every day, now.

Fifteen minutes more and we had gathered up all the plastic shards littered through the room and moved them to the junk heap, each of us gathering as many pieces as possible into our arms and carting them outside and dumping them. Grady had at one point taken one piece and sailed it like a Frisbee back into the trees, letting out a crazy yelp, but the piece didn't go very far, only flipped and tumbled through the air. I'd heard Martin give a little chuckle, and Grady had turned to me and smiled. But I would not join them in their small break from all the work we were doing, and I looked down at the heap, picked up a couple of pieces of paneling here and there, and tossed them to the middle of all the junk. Grady stopped, went to find the piece back in the trees, his feet breaking dead leaves everywhere, making a rushing sound, a static of sorts, as he headed through them back to the heap, the piece he'd thrown in his hands. Without a word he dropped it onto the heap, headed past me and back inside for the next load.

I pushed the scraper up again, and more wet wallpaper fell, cold on my arms, slipping down them and to the floor.

"Miss Templeton," Grady said again, and only then did I realize I hadn't answered him, hadn't acknowledged him at all. I was in that mode.

I turned. Both he and Martin were standing there, Martin, as always, a few inches behind him. But he was looking at me now, the ability to look at me for several seconds without letting his eyes dart away new in him. Now that we had been working up here every day, the three of us had become closer, friends, and Martin's looking at me and telling Grady he was concerned for me almost made me want to stop, to put the scraper away. To take a break from here, this house that, if all went right, we would be able to move into some time early next year.

But I looked past the two of them, saw the wallpaper on the wall, on all the walls, wallpaper with a thick pattern of bouquets of brown and pink roses in rows up and down the walls, and I knew that they were wrong, that I could work harder, that I could keep going. I could.

"I'm fine," I said. "I'm just fine. You don't worry about me. I've told you guys before that I'm fine." I turned, placed the scraper on the windowsill, and went to the stove in the fireplace. I opened up the front, tossed in a couple of chunks of wood, and stood back from it, my hands out in front of me, soaking up the warmth.

Tom had bought the stove last week in a costly celebration of the roof having been completed and the rotten and broken clapboards all replaced, as well as the fine brickwork Martin had done with the chimney and hearths through the house. He had been as meticulous measuring and marking the lay of bricks as he had been with the tapping out of clapboards and rolling the marble to find bad spots in the floor, and as a result the fireplace here, after having a chimney sweep out from town to clean things up, was ready for use. The stove had been a surprise, Tom last Saturday morning leaving us here to work by ourselves while he went into town. "For supplies," he had told me, with no show of any emotion, no smile, no shine in his eyes for the surprise. Two hours later he had shown up with two men in a flatbed truck following him, the stove, huge and black and cold, tied down in back. The four of us had simply watched as the men, burly teenagers who seemed no older than Grady but who could have easily snapped him in two, muscled the stove in, set it up on the hearth, and drove away.

I was glad for it here in the front room, the stove bulky and warm, the sky outside cold and gray and threatening as it had been most days the last three weeks, folds of gray and darker gray here and there a regular occurrence now.

They didn't have to worry. I was okay.

"Still, uh, Miss Templeton," Grady said, and took a step closer.

"Will you please?" I said, and turned from the stove. "It's Claire. It's not Miss Templeton. It's Claire."

"Claire," Martin said, his voice strong and clear, and I had to pause, look at him there behind Grady.

He was smiling at me. I said, "Martin. That's the first time you've called me by my name."

"Claire," he said again, grinning even bigger, showing even more of those teeth, and he looked down, moved his feet in some small, self-conscious shuffle. He looked at me again, only this time as solemn, as grave, as I'd ever seen him. "Claire," he said, "you do not need to work so hard. Not as hard as this." He put his hand out in an awkward gesture toward the walls, brought his hand back just as quickly.

The Saturday after I'd quit at the lab, Tom, Grady, and Martin started in on the roof, but not before Grady and Martin had taken a look at my steps. Martin and Grady both turned first to Tom, who pointed at me.

Grady had said, "Did you find these?" and took a tentative kick at the bottom step.

Tom stood with his hands on his hips. His head was down, and he stirred the leaves at his feet with the tip of one boot. We hadn't yet spoken to each other beyond asking if the coffee had been made, what the weather for the day would be.

I said, "All by myself."

Martin, smiling, not yet into his trance, looked at the steps and took the same small kick as Grady had. He turned to me. He said, "Nice job," and grinned, and we all laughed.

Then they were up on the roof, Martin with Tom behind him, the two of them pulling up pieces of asphalt shingles to show patches of decayed and rotting shake shingles.

By the following Sunday night they had stripped the front half of the roof of all shingles; cut out and replaced rotten or broken rafters with new pieces nailed right in against the old, what Martin called "sister rafters"; and replaced roof boards that had been broken or mildewed with new pieces of plywood. Then tarpaper had been laid over it all.

I had watched most of it, not able to do much, but wanting to. Martin, as always, was doing most everything, from working the Sawzall quicker and more proficiently than Tom, to laying out the odd pieces of plywood, to nailing them onto the rafters, his hammering strong, two hits and the nails driven deep and solid into the wood. Tom seemed almost an assistant, Grady when on the ground only handing up pieces of wood, when on the roof only throwing down broken, replaced pieces.

In my frustration to start working, to start up again, I decided I would form the junk heap, the boards from the porch before then only strewn around the front of the house. The broken, stiff asphalt shingles and the rotted shake shingles beneath them seemed to have rained down before the house, Grady almost gleeful at times in throwing them from the roof in twos and threes.

The first thing I had to do, I knew, was to find where I wanted to put all the trash, all the junk, some of it salvageable—a lot of the wood would be good for use this winter—some of it, like the asphalt shingles, useless. And so I went around the house, the sky still gray, gray all weekend long, gray every day since I'd done perfusion, and for a moment, just a moment, I thought of Mr. Gadsen, and of Chesterfield, and I tried to imagine who would be at the old man's funeral. Will, Sandra, Paige, and Wendy. Those people. But not me. I was working.

I walked around the house, trying to find some cleared area that would hold all this trash until we had somebody come haul it away. To the right of the house was out; the trees were thick there, and as I looked back into them and away from the house, some dark feeling fell into me, and I thought for a moment that it was a cramp. But the darkness of that feeling—a low twist, not an ache—told me that that wasn't it.

I stared back into the woods, and felt at the base of my spine, the skin on my back tightening up, the beginning of a shudder, and I looked down, took in a deep breath, my skin prickling over.

I went around to the rear, and I could hear the men working up on the roof, Grady saying something about a custom skylight. "I'll just put my foot right through this roof board," I heard him say, "and presto, custom skylight." I heard him laugh, heard Tom give a small chuckle. I heard nothing from Martin.

The area behind the house was clear, just ground covered with leaves and gray, dead grass for about fifteen yards, then trees again. To the left was the narrow trail back to the barn.

I heard from the front of the house more shingles falling down, slapping onto those already lying on the ground.

The barn would be just as good a place as any, I thought, and I headed back, walked the hundred yards or so along the path overgrown with tall, dead weeds, trees on either side shoving into the trail, trying to take it over.

I had my arms crossed, holding myself, as I came up to the barn. Nothing was any different now than when I'd first been back here with Tom the day we were here alone, and my curiosity came back, the wonder at why Martin and Grady would not come out here, at why they seemed to freeze up when mention was made of the barn. They were glad to do anything else, eager to work, to be at this house, and yet they would not come out here.

I started looking at the barn, watching once again the rafters and the thick, black beams, and I thought for a moment of the barn with the patterned slate roof, the one Tom and I had stood at and cried. The barn that would never come down, I knew, ever, simply because the roof had been built right. Our own barn was nothing compared to the grandness of the other.

I went on inside, the world growing darker because of the clouds and the black wood around me, darker than any day here yet, and I looked back to the house, just to see it from here now that all the leaves were gone, now that the sky was gray. I wanted to see the house framed by the open barn door, a black frame that would surround the house, hold it down to size, make the work that needed to be done seem possible.

From where I stood, the open barn doors framing the house perfectly, I could see my window, the window on the room that would be my own, the room I had not long ago believed and hoped might someday be a nursery. But the window was black and empty, the room inside the same, I knew.

I looked at my window, at its emptiness, and suddenly I became aware of what was behind me as I stood staring: nothing, only the emptiness of the barn, beyond the broken planks of the back wall only woods on up the hill, beyond the hill more trees, and more nothing. I was afraid to look behind me, to *see* that nothing, and yet I looked.

I saw nothing, and I shuddered, this time all the way down and into my arms, and I ran, ran as fast as I could, the distance between me and the house seeming to grow as I ran, the trees all pushing toward me as I ran along that path.

Finally I made it to the front of the house, where shingles still came down, two, three, four at a time. Tom and Martin and Grady were out of view, from above me merely the sounds of hammers and the low screech of nails being pried up. They were no longer talking.

I picked up a piece of plywood, pulled it away from the house to where the trees were not so thick. I pulled the piece of plywood as far as I imagined was necessary, just far enough to get it away from the house, to keep it from making the place look like the town dump. I let the piece drop flat on the ground, the whoosh of air from beneath it sending up dead leaves that collected over the tops of my shoes. Quickly I knocked those leaves away, went to the pile of junk, and started moving things.

But I could not shake the fear I had had of almost losing myself in the barn, the feeling of the forest closing around me, just as the garbage bag in the perfusion room had swallowed up Chesterfield's carcass. That would have been me, I knew, if I'd waited in the barn any longer. And I thought I knew then why neither Grady nor, especially, Martin would go out there. It had been that feeling of being swallowed, I thought. Of being lost.

That night, after Tom and I had dropped them off at the Friendly's, I had asked Tom if Martin and Grady could work weekdays on the house. I told him I was going to be out there anyway, that I might as well have company, and company that would work.

He looked both ways down Route 9, waiting for traffic to clear, and pulled out of the Friendly's parking lot.

I said, "Tom?"

"I heard you," he said.

He was quiet awhile, and in the darkness I saw him shift in his seat. These were the most significant words that had passed between us since he had watched me cleaning the blisters on my hands. My hands were still bandaged, and I had worn canvas work gloves all weekend long, hauling those pieces of wood and shingles. My hands ached as I sat next to him, waiting for an answer. But I did not mind. The ache was for a good reason. We had gotten work done.

We were almost to Cooley-Dickinson Hospital by this time, but I did not look for the maternity wing, would not stare back at the window of the room Paige had stayed in when Phillip was born. I would not do that anymore, and as we passed the hospital I kept my eyes on the road, listening for an answer.

I said, "You guys are almost done with the outside. You just have the rest of the clapboards to go. And then. Then comes all the inside stuff, and you know I need the help. I can't be out there all day by myself and expect to get much—"

"The money," he interrupted.

"The quicker we get this work done, the better," I said, "and let's be honest, those two aren't nearly as expensive as what we'd be paying otherwise."

"We'd be doing it ourselves otherwise," he said quietly.

"That's the point," I said, surprised at how quickly and efficiently my words came from inside me, as if it weren't me doing the planning, the calculating. "We'd be taking forever to get all this stuff done, killing ourselves all our weekends. And I don't expect they'll turn us down, either, even though they're working week nights. I don't have to stay out there all day. We can cut off around three or so, and I can get them back here to town so that they won't miss work. I think they'll say yes. So the quicker we get the work done the better." I paused, took a breath. "The quicker we get it done, the sooner I'll be able to go back to work. At the lab, or wherever. Then the money will be coming in again. And the work will be done already. Except for, you know, things that we'll do next summer, like painting." I paused, took another breath, this one deeper, the air colder inside me. "And the money we have already," I said, "is from my mother. It's from her house, for our house. That's what it's for." I was looking at my hands, at how the plastic Band-Aids reflected light from streetlamps we passed under. My hands seemed plastic in places there in the dark, all gray and shiny. They seemed artificial.

He turned and looked at me a moment, and turned back to the road. He hadn't looked at me long enough to allow me to turn to him, so that when I did his face was away from me, looking out his side window.

He had said no more, and I took that to mean what I wanted it to mean. Two days later—a Tuesday—I dropped Tom off at the newspaper, then picked up both Grady and Martin in the cold early morning of the Friendly's parking lot.

They enjoyed working every day, too, as far as I could see, talking with one another as they tore out the cupboards and cabinets in the kitchen, me in other rooms breaking back baseboards. All the kitchen cupboards and cabinets, Tom and I had decided, needed to go. It would be easier just to buy new ones, the old ones scarred wood painted over blue, hinges bent and broken, shelves splintered and cracked. Next to go in the kitchen, once I'd gotten the baseboards pulled out, had been the linoleum floor, Grady starting at one corner, Martin the other, the two of them gently rolling back the edges, the linoleum breaking in places into huge scraped and beaten dull-yellow pieces, large, odd shapes like the maps of foreign countries. The two of them had contests to see who could get the biggest piece of linoleum up without breaking it, and, of course, Martin won each time, each time his face breaking into his old grin, Grady acting perturbed and incensed and disappointed, all to make Martin smile that much more.

Beneath the linoleum was the hardwood floor, the brown of wood murky and hidden beneath the remnants of black resin. Still, I had felt good that day a week or so ago, felt as though somehow, finally, things *had* begun. Starting again had finally shown me something tangible: a gutted kitchen, pipes naked and shiny, waiting, the walls empty now. Martin and Grady and I had been working hard, filling our lives with emptying this house.

"Okay," I said, and put my hands on my hips. The fire in the stove popped, that sound followed by a slow hiss inside. "Okay," I said again, "we'll take a break. All of us. In celebration of Martin's calling me by my first name." I rubbed my hands together, felt the warmth from the stove on my back. "I'll break out lunch, and we can all relax."

"Sounds great," Grady said.

Martin said, "Sounds great." He paused. "Claire."

I moved toward him, standing in the doorway to the kitchen. He backed up, let me pass by him, and I patted him on the shoulder. I said, "Thanks, Martin," and he smiled again, gave what I thought could have been a blush, his face going a little red all the way up to the top of his head and on into the gray, slicked-back hair.

 Every day now I brought with us a picnic basket full of food, a small cooler with a six-pack or so of soda, and a thermos of hot coffee. The soda wasn't for me; after a week solid of offering them coffee, and having them turn me down, I'd finally asked Grady what they would want to drink. "Nothing," he'd said, then he said, "Soda pop's fine." Since then I had brought the cooler, even though each day the highs had been hovering around forty degrees.

I was in the kitchen, and said, "Why so much concern for me now?" I knelt next to the picnic basket, opened it up. I brought out sandwiches I'd made that morning and paper plates. Grady and Martin were in the kitchen, and I handed each a plate and sandwich. Then I popped open a Tupperware container of carrot sticks, took a few out and set them on my plate next to my sandwich. I said, "I haven't changed my pace any since you guys started."

I stood with the thermos in one hand, my plate in the other, and I passed between them, went into the front room. I sat on the floor before the stove.

"That's just the point," Grady said, and I heard him open the cooler and reach in, knew what he was doing: reaching in for a can, giving it to Martin, than taking one for himself. Almost simultaneously came the wet bursts of sound, their cans opening. Grady came in, sat to my right. Martin sat a little behind Grady.

I said, "Come on, Martin," and looked back at him. He already had the sandwich halfway to his mouth. He stopped, and slowly set

down the sandwich. I patted the floor next to me, on my left. "Come
sit over here. It's warmer nearer the stove."

He looked at Grady, who looked first at me, then to Martin, then
to me again. He glanced down at his plate, and nodded. "Go ahead,
Martin," he said.

Immediately Martin stood, came over to my left, and sat down.
He didn't look at me, though; instead, he picked up the sandwich
and took a bite. Slowly he chewed, his eyes on the stove as if there
were something written on it he could decipher.

Grady said, "That's what Martin means. You haven't stopped. You
got all these baseboards pulled out yourself, the baseboards in all
the rooms. And you got all that paneling in the kitchen out, too,
and did your fair share of the paneling in here. When you're working,
too," he said, and his voice went a little quieter, "it seems like you're
not much, you know, different than Martin." He stopped, and I
looked at him. He was sitting Indian-style with the palms of his
hands on each knee, just looking at his food, at the soda can on the
floor.

"That came out wrong," Grady said, and I turned away from him.
I took a bite of my sandwich, swallowed hard to get the food into
me. I took a sip of coffee from the thermos lid.

I said, "How did you mean it to come out?"

"Different," he said quickly. "You're not like him, you know,
you're not—"

"Okay," I said. "I get it."

He glanced at me and gave me a quick smile.

I said, "Eat."

We sat that way for a while, Martin oblivious, merely eating the
food he needed to continue working, supplying his body with what
it needed, and I wondered what things he thought of, what sorts of
images came to his mind when he sat this way, and what sorts of
patterns or ideas came to him when he was in his savant mode,
every bit of him focused on the task at hand, whether it be the
mortaring of hearth bricks or measuring and cutting clapboards. I
wondered what he thought, what he knew, what words were in
him, and how they moved through his brain to do what it was he
knew to do.

And I wondered if Grady weren't closer to some truth than he'd thought, wondered if Martin and I weren't more alike than I could know.

I looked at Martin. He was still silently eating, now on his second sandwich, and before I knew what I was saying, before I realized what words had lined themselves up in my throat and mouth, but because I wanted to know, to *know* perhaps how his mind worked, to *know* how I was like him, I turned to Grady and said, "What can you tell me? About Martin, I mean. Was he born like this?"

I stopped, embarrassed at my own cruel curiosity. As though I might be able to bury my words, pretend I hadn't spoken them, I said, "I'm sorry. I don't mean to be asking anything that's—"

"Okay," he said. He looked at me. He said, "I get it," and we both smiled.

It had been a long time since the child in Grady had surfaced, not since the day we stood with Martin and Tom below us in the crawl space, the sky blue, the trees colors I couldn't imagine anymore now that winter was almost on us. Not since the day he had laid out that small piece of history about Martin and his daddy and Mr. Clark, and how he'd had Martin put in the state hospital. Since then he hadn't forgotten letting himself show, letting down his guard, the smile he had given me that day never returning, his hair always tucked back and away instead of ignored and fallen in his face.

But now, the food before us, the stove warm, the house gutted and less and less a home, he seemed to falter again. It was in his shoulders and how they seemed to sink, and I thought of pine boards sinking into my father, and of my mother sinking into herself, growing older and older.

His hair, too, was down in his face again. He didn't bother to push it back. Then he reached one hand out to his sandwich and picked it up. He took a bite, swallowed it.

"You really want to know," he said, not as a question, but as observation, some judgment made upon me.

I was silent.

He took a quick breath and smiled, one last stab at regaining his adult air. "You keep working like you are," he said, "and that info won't really matter. You'll be dead, or broken-backed. You keep up this pace." He went quiet again, and looked down. "I don't know that I should say—"

"Say," Martin said from beside me.

I turned to him. He was looking at Grady, not me. He, too, was sitting Indian-style, his elbows on his knees. He held his sandwich with both hands. He swallowed. "You tell her. She can know."

Slowly I turned to Grady, me sitting there between them. Something was going on here, something I couldn't understand; I saw on Grady's face, that boy's face, and felt in Martin's words some subtle shift in authority, in who was in charge. Something had changed here.

Grady said, "Do you think—"

"I think," Martin said quickly. "She can know."

Grady swallowed again, though there was no food in his mouth. He reached for his can of soda, tipped it back and took a sip. He set it down. He wasn't looking at me.

He said, "I don't think this is the wisest thing. But, hey. Martin said it's okay." He cleared his throat, put a finger to the rim of the can and slowly ran it around the edge in a gentle circle. "Martin's the way he is because he was born that way. He was born retarded. But it wasn't—" He paused, and I watched his finger stop before continuing on with its circle. "It wasn't, you know, in his genes that way. He's not retarded retarded. He was just born that way."

I heard the high screech of the stove door, and looked up. Martin was standing there, and tossed into the red and orange a large piece of wood. The piece landed with a dull thud, and I could see inside the shower of sparks sent up. With the stick he'd used to open it, he pushed closed the door. He sat down.

This time it was me who wouldn't look at him. I was ashamed at my question, at my wanting to know. It didn't matter, I saw. What happened to him, how he was born, didn't matter. He was just a man.

But Grady went on, obedient to Martin's wish. "The story starts with that family I told you about over there in Worthington. I've already told you about them, but there's other stuff you need to know. About that family." He took a breath, held it a moment. "But this story, this particular one, starts with a hobo." He paused. "A hobo, you know? Riding the rails."

I nodded, my eyes now on that flat, black stove and the heat waves shimmering up from it to make the air dance, waver.

"A rail-runner," he said, "and it's time for the sap to run, March, and he comes into Chesterfield looking for work, and finds out there's this job at the sugar house in Worthington, and he gets on there, gets a job just tending to the firewood. To keeping sure there's enough firewood to make sure the sap keeps boiling day and night. That's his job." He paused, and took in what seemed a huge breath of air, then slowly let it out. "So he meets this girl named Elaine out there in Worthington, the sister of the man my grandfather Clark hates so much. But this man, this brother of Elaine. This brother of Elaine is a son-of-a-bitch. He's terrible. He's evil. When he gets wind of these two, of this hobo who's only trying to make enough money just to eat and of his sister, he goes off the end. The brother does, and he forbids the two ever to see each other again. He forbids them ever to even look at each other on the road if they ever pass each other."

He stopped, and I glanced down. His hand was around his can now, the grip firm, his thumb pressing into the aluminum, making the smallest dimple. He released his thumb, and the dimple disappeared, giving off a sharp *pop*. I watched his hand around the can. He lifted it, and my eyes followed it to his face. He was smiling, and took another sip, his hair falling back as he did.

He put the can back on the floor and uncrossed his legs, bringing the knees up. He held his knees together, his feet flat on the floor, and looked at the stove. He said, "But the joke of it was on the brother. The last laugh was on this brother because she was already preggers by this time. By the time the brother found out about the two of them having some kind of love interest, she was already with child. That's the joke."

"But," Martin said, and before I could turn to him, Grady went on.

"But," he said, "it's not a joke. Because the brother found out about her being pregnant, and he came down to the sugar house. He came running down there through the snow, through the woods, and he busts into the sugar house, and here's the hobo leaned over the fire, facing the fire beneath the vats of sap, and the brother lays into the hobo's back with a piece of oak. A good piece, about yay long—" He put his hands out, spread apart about three feet to show me how long the piece of wood had been. Then he put his hands back around his knees. "He puts a good one right into the hobo's back, and then there's this fight going on, the brother up against the hobo, and the hobo wins. The hobo beats the hell, just beats the hell out of the brother, and just before he's about to kill him— he's got the same piece of oak raised up to bash in the skull of this son-of-a-bitch—he stops. The hobo stops, and he just tosses that piece of wood into that fire, and he's gone. He just goes, hops another train, one heading south to where the weather's already warm."

"My God," I whispered.

"Your god," he said, and he gave that same sort of laugh again.

"Yours," Martin said.

I looked at both of them. They were looking at the stove, and then I looked, too.

"It's not over yet," Grady said, and shifted his weight. He still held his knees, but now one foot was tapping to something inside him.

"It's not over because now she, the sister, this Elaine, has her whole nine months to live out, after that a baby to raise. And those whole nine months, every day that's left of them after the hobo's gone, she's got to live out under this brother of hers, this son-of-a-bitch."

He went quiet again, and slowed his foot, barely touching the toe of his boot to the floor. "But she was beautiful," he said, and only then did I wonder how he knew all this, all the detail: the piece of oak and how long it had been, the tossing aside of that piece instead of killing the brother, the beauty of Elaine. How could he know? And of course it came to me: Martin. Martin must know all these things, must have told Grady. But still I wondered, because Martin had never shown me anything that would make me believe he could tell a story, even string three sentences together outside of his savant trance. But, I realized, I didn't know them. I didn't know what they talked about when they were alone. This moment was the closest I'd come yet to seeing, perhaps, the truth of the two of them, Martin guiding the conversation, Grady following.

"She was beautiful," he went on. "She was beautiful, and she was quiet and she was real fragile. And she was small, and she was scared to death of her brother. For the rest of her nine months he wouldn't let her, his sister, out of their house. He wouldn't let her

out. He told her she was vile. *Vile* was the word he'd used. That
was it. So she stayed in the house out there in the woods for the
rest of her being pregnant. Then in November it was time for her
to have a baby."

Martin sniffed, and from the corner of my eye I could see him
rub his nose, gently touch his throat.

"By this time she's almost dead. Her mind, that is. The brother
hasn't let her ever feel good about anything for a single day, when
he should be glad he's alive, the son-of-a-bitch, glad the father of
this baby didn't bash in his head that day. Not a single minute can
she feel good, because all this time he's been killing her with his
words, his looks, his threats. So that day, that day she's going to
have—"

His voice broke to pieces, quiet pieces, a certain quivering in the
words, and I reached a hand over to his shoulder. I let it rest there,
tried to give to him the same sort of comfort he had given to me
when we had stood in the kitchen that day, but he shook my hand
off with one violent move, his shoulders twisting.

"Grady," Martin said, firm and quiet.

"Well," Grady said, and swallowed hard. His eyes hadn't left the
stove.

"Don't go on," I said.

"Tough," he said, his eyes full. "That's just tough." He was almost
whispering now. "Because I'm going. Because you asked." He
paused, and took a breath. "So this is the day. And she's going to
have the baby. And because he's killed her by that time, killed her
mind, she decides that, no, she's *not* going to have the baby. Here
it is pushing out, the brother's wife—the wife. God. The brother's
wife. She's the only good thing about this. She's the only good person
the brother was ever lucky enough to have love him, though I don't
know why she would ever marry him. But since she's a woman and
she's married to this brother, all along the wife can't do anything
to stop the brother killing his sister." He paused. "I forgot to tell
you about the wife."

"But go," Martin said, his voice with that same taut, deep tone.

"Go," Grady said. He was still looking down. "Go, he says. I'll go.
I'll go." His voice was darker now, harder, and I could hear from
outside the midday, mid-December wind hitting through trees, a

sound I'd taken for granted now after all these days I'd worked out here, but a sound that surfaced just then, made its way into my ears as though that clatter of branches were somehow important. I wondered, too, if this were the sound she heard that day.

"So the sister decides she's not going to let it out," Grady said. "She's just not going to let it out. She's not going to let her brother lay eyes on the baby. She doesn't want that curse, doesn't want that hate on her baby, and so she holds against the pushing. She puts her legs together, and she holds it, she holds it in. She holds it in until finally she passes out, and the baby finally comes, and this baby is born wrong. It's born retarded, and not because of anything that's the matter with its genes, but because it was put through that kind of birth. And there you have him. You have Martin. You have Martin from day one." He paused again, the only sound the slow hiss of the fire inside the stove, and the black strain of leafless branches against December wind. "Now you know," he said.

I closed my eyes, because there was nothing for me to do. I had asked. And it had been Martin who'd made him go on, Grady only a sort of interpreter, a speaker for Martin and his history.

Grady moved to stand up, and I opened my eyes. He picked up his plate with the half-eaten sandwich on it with one hand, the empty soda can with the other.

"Wait," Martin said. "Wait."

"No," Grady said, still looking at the stove. "No more." He looked down at me, his eyes wide open, his hair down in his face. "There's more, by the way. Tons more. But at least I hope you're happy with what you've got. I hope you're happy with the story thus far."

He looked at Martin. "Now. We have to go back now. I forgot to tell you. We're working an oddball shift tonight. This afternoon. So—"

"Wait," Martin said, and he was moving, uncrossing his legs, standing. He looked at Grady, then at me. "She can—"

"*No!*" Grady shouted, and startled even himself. He seemed to shake with that one word, almost tremble. He blinked twice, and brought his arm out to point at Martin. The soda can was still in his hand. "Now. We—have—to—go—home," he said, the finger jabbing the air with each word, and things shifted right back then, any authority, any influence Martin may have had just falling away,

Martin almost cowering as his eyes looked down and away from Grady to his own plate and soda can on the floor. He picked them up, and stepped right behind Grady now on his way into the kitchen.

Heat waves still shimmered up from the stove, the world and its physics moving right along as though nothing had happened here. And yet I didn't even know what *had* happened. I only knew now why Martin was as he was, that trauma at birth. I knew, too, that there was something else, some story I would not hear this day, a story I knew I did not want to know.

I looked at the waves of heat, followed them with my eyes, trying to see how far into the air they went, where their influence faltered and disappeared, and I saw the wallpaper above the mantelpiece, that ugly wallpaper, beat and tired and ugly, ready to be torn off. Ready for solvent, for dousing with the sponge, for my scraper. I stood, knowing what I had to do: work. I picked up my plate, and went into the kitchen.

Martin and Grady stood next to each other in there, Grady's arms crossed, Martin's hands at his sides. They were waiting for me.

I dropped my plate into the garbage can, and picked up my purse from next to the cooler. I opened it, peering into it for my car keys.

Grady said, "We can hitch a ride if it's a problem for you."

"None at all," I said, and I pulled out my keys and held them up as if they were some sort of trophy. I tried to smile.

 I knew that things would be changed from now on, that Grady and Martin would be different around me. I had known it from the ride home, Grady in the seat next to me, Martin in the back, huddled in the far right corner so that I could not see him in the rearview mirror. The air had been different, dead and flat somehow, as all three of us thought over the story, me thinking of the small fragment I had, the other two of the rest of it, the huge one, I imagined, of Martin and his life. But the air was dead; for the first time Grady said nothing, made no comments on anything. He was silent, and because of that silence Martin, too, was quiet. I did not know if he were looking out his window or straight ahead or at the backs of our heads or at his hands. I knew nothing. He was just somewhere behind me.

Then I had dropped them off. Grady was leaning out of his open door when I said, "Tomorrow morning?" just to make certain they would return.

"If that's okay with you," he said. He stood with his hand on the door, ready to close it, waiting for me.

I said, "Fine," and he pushed it closed. Martin had closed his door, too, and they had both gone in the back door of the Friendly's.

Now here I was, parked on a side street off Route 9, a street a hundred yards down from the Friendly's. I was parked across from a small commons, an area of grass and trees, all dead now, a small monument of some sort erected in the middle of the lot, the lot fronting on Route 9. I was parked, waiting to see what would happen. From where I sat I could see the front porch of the Friendly's;

Miss Flo's was up the street from me, next to it the rest of the small shops—the post office, the drug store, the pizza place—leading up to the corner. From here I had a clear view.

I was waiting for them to leave Friendly's, because I knew Grady had lied. They had no odd-ball shift. It was only his way of getting out, away from the story. I was only waiting, waiting to see what would happen. And I could not say why.

Not ten minutes later, here came Grady, bundled up on his bike, looking up Route 9, pausing, pulling out onto the road off and away from me. Then came Martin, his wool cap on over his ears. He quickly looked at the road and pulled out, now only a few feet behind Grady.

I started the engine, and felt at once idiotic, silly. I felt embarrassed following these two for a reason I did not know, when what I *did* know was that there was work I could do back at the house: wallpaper to be scraped away, more paneling to tear out, more linoleum to break up and remove. But here I was, and I realized I wanted to know more of them, of that story, and thought that if I followed them home this once, saw where Martin lived, and then where Grady lived, I would know something of them, as if views of their apartments would give to me some hint of what they hid.

I waited for one car to go by on Route 9, and another, and then I pulled out and turned left. They turned right at the intersection, there at the pizza place, the red-brick building that seemed the color of blood in the gray December morning. I paused at the light, letting them get as far ahead of me as possible.

Then I turned, and I slowly drove up the street, the two of them clipping along, Martin's legs pumping hard, his head down, Grady's head up, hair flying.

I glanced in the rearview mirror, saw a car behind me. I pulled to the curb, and let it pass.

I followed them, pausing, letting more cars pass, picking up again, all the way to Bridge Street, where they turned right again across from the elementary school. The homes back here were nice, more expensive than anything Tom and I could afford, and I wondered where Martin lived, wondered if, perhaps, he lived in a single room of one of these homes.

But once they'd ridden a mile or so back toward King Street, the road itself turning slightly, lifting here, falling there, beside us all the way these houses and beautiful yards and trees and patios and garages, we came to another stop light, and I knew then where Martin lived.

In the midst of comfortable, middle-class homes was a large complex of squat, ugly apartments, square, two-story buildings with square windows, siding on the top story, brown brick on the bottom. Lawns were nonexistent, rubbed bare to dirt much like the lawn before Sandra's married-student housing complex over in Amherst. But these apartments had nothing to do with a college.

These apartments were government-subsidized housing, and I watched as Grady and Martin sailed through the intersection, and pulled into the small, paved parking lot before one of the rows of apartments.

I turned right at the light, drove a few yards down, pulled onto the shoulder, and stopped. I left the engine running. They were a hundred yards or so away; I was partially hidden from them by the trunk of a dead tree across the street from me, a tree whose roots cracked the pavement of that parking lot, the broken asphalt heaved up, dead weeds protruding, shoved this way and that by the cold wind and passing cars.

Grady hopped off his bike, popped the front wheel over the curb of the lot, and wheeled it up to one of the black doors of the apartments, Martin behind him. Grady pushed the bike right up to the door; with one hand on the handlebar, he put the other into his pocket and pulled out a set of keys. He found the right one, put it into the knob, and opened the door. He pushed his bike inside, and Martin followed, his front tire bumping into Grady's back tire as they disappeared inside.

Then a light came on inside, and the front door closed. The curtains were open, and I could see inside two silhouettes from where I sat across the street. I saw the two of them in there, watched as two shadows took off coats, settled themselves into where they lived. Then the curtains closed.

They lived there together.

This was what I knew, what I had known longer than I could have said. They were living together, the two of them, here in subsidized housing, where in summer children played in the dirt, where men and women sat outside on hot evenings, tipped back in lawn chairs, beers in hand. This small enclave of poverty in the midst of prosperous Northampton, home of Smith College and two art theaters and Thorne's Marketplace and any number of other cultural centers. Right here was a place I'd forgotten about, a place I never thought of, only drove past sometimes as a quick way through town, a way to avoid the boutiques and restaurants and slow, rich pedestrians on the streets downtown. Here was where they lived.

Yet what I had just seen was no reason to believe that the two were living together. Perhaps Grady had only stopped in to help Martin get a meal together, or to help him pay his bills or turn the heat up just the notch it needed to make the apartment a home. Maybe that was the only reason Grady had stopped in.

But there was the ease with which he had pulled out the keys, one fluid motion into the pocket, locating the key, inserting it and pushing in the bike, Martin clunky behind him. And there was how I had seen him slip off the coat, simply and easily. Only small things, but they told me more than I could have imagined. They told me that they lived here together, and that I didn't need to stay any longer with the car running, their curtains closed, weeds between cracks in the pavement whipped now by a growing wind. I didn't need to see if, in a few minutes, Grady would be pushing his bike back out, peddling off to wherever he lived. Because he lived here.

I could go back to Chesterfield now, back to the house we were trying to make a home by tearing it apart. I could go back to the wallpaper.

I put the car in gear, and I drove. I made it in less than twenty minutes, had the stove stoked and solvent in my sponge and walls wet five minutes later. I was working.

That night, back at the apartment, the same ugly apartment that was not home, that would never *be* home, I cried myself to sleep, Tom next to me, his steady heartbeat there, his presence. I cried myself to sleep because so much was pounding up against me and on top of me. Too many things: Sandra still pounding away at me, at my heart, digging into me and how I had failed her, and how I had heard nothing from her since the day I left her in the perfusion room, left her with the shattered head of a rabbit I'd killed; Grady and Martin, the story of a woman mad with hate, and the grief I felt at a granite hate that killed Martin at birth, forced him into a world where he would, fifty years later, wash dishes and ride a bike home, following a boy who took care of him, who loved him for no other apparent reason than that the boy's father had befriended the man, and the boy's grandfather hated him; and the grief in me that cried at denying birth, when all I wanted to do—all I *had* wanted to do, before hope had died in me—was to give birth, feel in me the same pushing Elaine had felt, welcome the same force inside me, let it go. And, as usual now that I had quit my job, had filled my days with work on the house with Grady and Martin, I had told Tom none of this, kept the story to myself like some piece of bad news all through dinner, through an evening before the television, through listening to him fall asleep, through his moving toward that soft hush of breath.

While I'd scraped the walls of the front room, alone there in the house, the only sound the scratch of the putty knife in my hand and the pop and crack of wood burning in the stove, I'd had nothing to do but think. Think, and imagine, and try to place myself somewhere else, someplace other than this house we had bought in the hopes of making it our home. I scraped, and I thought, imagined, tried to feel what effacing might be like, tried to feel dilation, tried Kegels, tried all I knew to make me become Elaine, or Paige, or anyone I knew who'd borne a child. That was what I wanted to do that afternoon. Just to imagine.

But I could imagine nothing, could feel nothing, only the scrape of the knife against the wall, only the grate against plaster, a sensation much like that of a pencil marking Xs on the raw skull of a rabbit.

I thought of my dream, too, the one I'd had before I abandoned hope, but what I remembered—the center of gravity shifting, the breasts full—were only shadows of the feeling I'd had when in the dream; those sensations were gone. Even the children I'd dreamed were gone now, and any comfort I might have taken in them, in just my *imagined* children, had disappeared. I hadn't dreamt of them since that night. The night my period had come.

And then, the knife in my hand and pushing up hard, a thin sheet of ancient wallpaper, cold and wet, dropping over my hand so that the knife disappeared, I thought of my mother. I did not understand why she would have come to me except, perhaps, to haunt me with more of my inheritance, more fear of the world outside the door, of empty rooms upstairs, of a barn outside that would have devoured me had I stayed in it a moment longer. But she came to me, and the smell of solvent in my head, the heavy work of holding my arm and pushing it against and up a wall again and again, brought me to my mother's home—my home, the Single Family Unit—and into her kitchen, the room now with those old photos moved in from the front room, her cot, too, moved into the kitchen, the TV in there as well, perched on the counter and turned so that she could watch it and lie in the cot at night, this room the only one she inhabited anymore. The room I found her dead in one Thursday evening in January, me ready to take her on our weekly grocery-shopping trip. My mother lay on her back, her arms at her sides beneath a blanket pulled up to her chin, tucked snugly around her.

This was how she had died, alone, comfortable, ready. But alone.

As I pictured her there on the cot, her face the gray of the dead, I realized that she, too, had been one of these women, the fertile in our world, the ones who could bear children, and that I had been the one she had borne. It had been me who had passed from inside her; she had felt the push and pain, felt the dilation and effacement, felt the tear, the fire, the sweat. The putty knife in my hand, my muscles aching once again from too much work, I thought that I hated her even more, hated her for having had me when, I knew, she would have preferred not to, would have preferred to move through her world without the additional burden I was to her, the added fear each time I left the house, whether with my father or alone, whether for grade school or college, whether for a loaf of bread at the store or to marry my husband. I was only that for her: more fear, when all I had wanted in my life was to bear a child with

Tom, and to face that kind of fear, the fear of life. Face it, and live through it.

Finally, the sun near down and Tom, I imagined, probably home, my hand dropped the knife in mid-push; the knife clattered to the floor, the last piece of wallpaper I would work on that day hanging from the wall, the edges frayed, the pattern lost, the thick paper crumpled and limp and dead. I reached up to tear the loose piece from the wall, but I stopped. I left the piece there. It would be as good a place as any to start up the next day.

Tom was asleep next to me, and I wanted to wake him then. I wanted him up with me. I wanted to find a reason to wake him, convinced I needed an excuse to wake my husband, when all I wanted was for him to hold me through this night.

I sat up in bed, moved my hand over to his shoulder, held it above him a moment, but I stopped. I needed a reason to wake him, I thought, but I knew that if I woke him and told him of my dead mother and of what she'd given me, my fear, a fear that kept me from entering a barn, he would think me mad. He would think me insane if I were to wake him and tell him I'd known I would die if I'd stayed inside the barn a moment longer that day, and might still die if I were ever to enter there again. That would cinch things for him, and he would know I was mad. And I wondered if I hadn't already gone, if this weren't how it happened: the sudden paralysis, the inability to make a decision, the right choice; the hand poised, unable to move for fear it might betray me, but wanting to move because I wanted him awake with me, a wind strong and loud outside, the rattle of branches like bricks dropped from some great height one on another, one on another, outside our window.

I wondered if this weren't insanity, the awareness of all things passing in and out of you until you could do nothing, or if this awareness were simply the terrain of the hopeless, the territory I had claimed for my own, the world I had taken on with giving up. I could not decide, could not see clearly whether this were insanity or hopelessness, and so I drew my hand away, lay back down in the bed of our dark room, beneath the gray clouds and night, certain of only one thing: I did not want to decide.

 When the alarm clock went off the next morning, the room was darker, immensely darker; when I shot open my eyes at the piercing buzz of the clock, I thought that somehow it had been reset, or that it was broken. Something was wrong. I knew something was wrong, and as Tom fumbled with the clock, I sat up in bed.

By this time Tom was sitting up in bed, too, and then he stood, slowly made his way to the window. He let up the shade.

"Look at this," he said, stooping, peering outside.

I pulled back the sheet and blanket, but I had already seen: snow was falling outside.

I went to the window and looked out, our shoulders touching, and he put his arm, still warm with sleep, around me, the two of us leaning over and looking out the window. It seemed awkward somehow, his arm around me as we leaned, peered out at the white: his arm around me felt forced, as though he were obliged to try to touch me.

The gray clouds that had been threatening for the last month had finally broken, letting snow sift down to dust lightly the street, cars, lawns, rooftops. A small snow, the wind gone now so that nothing drifted. Just first snow.

He said, "We got the roof done. And the clapboards. This is fine."

I thought of Grady and Martin again, of their riding bikes in the snow all the way to Friendly's. For a moment I considered driving over to the subsidized housing, stopping to offer them rides, but I dismissed the idea. They could ride bikes in snow, in dark. A morning darker than any I could remember.

At breakfast Tom said, "You know, you need to slow down." He said it just like that, out of thin air.

I said, "I know. I'm aware of that," and then I put my coffee cup down, looked out the window. Snow still fell, and I could see outside bare branches of trees filling with snow, white-edged black limbs, and I knew that when we left this morning, went out the door off the kitchen and descended stairs clouded over with white, I would see the dead Christmas tree still leaning up against the foundation next door. There almost a year now.

I said, "Tonight, when we get home, I want to start packing. I want to start putting things in boxes and lining them up in here so that when we go, when we move, we can go as easily as possible."

He had his cup to his lips, and looked at me over the brim, the reflection of the lights above us caught in his glasses, and I pictured him at work before his computer terminal, clicking up stories all day long, the green monitor with its green letters reflecting up into his eyes headlines like VALLEY COUPLE'S TRIUMPH COMPLETE.

He put the cup down, looked at the magazine open on the table before him, and closed it. He said, "You're not even listening. You're not even hearing me." He paused. He hadn't looked at me.

He said, "Let's get going. I'll be late, with this snow. We need to go."

When he climbed out of the car in the parking lot of the newspaper, he gave a small wave, turned and headed for the door, where inside he would work away at that computer, do his own job, his own work, reading more press releases, I assumed, of more women impregnated by turkey basters or anything else, sperm handed over in plastic Baggies from some willing masturbator. He would read of more triumphs today, more glorious victories.

When he had waved at me, there had not been even that small automatic smile, the thoughtless one. Even that was gone, his face straight, still.

*   *   *

Martin and Grady stood stamping their feet in the snow, both of them blowing into hands in fists at their faces, Martin's stamping exaggerated, his feet lifted a little too high, the time between dropping one foot and lifting the other a little too long.

Grady opened the passenger door, Martin his backseat door, and they climbed in.

Still there were no words between us. Still Martin shoved himself into the far corner. Still there was something dead hanging in the air.

Once we were through Williamsburg and on 43, back almost in the Berkshires, the snow was thicker, heavier, the road before me covered with snow except for two thin black lines stretching out in front of us.

I said, "So how was that 'odd-ball' shift you guys worked yesterday afternoon?"

"Work," Grady gave out quickly. "Just work."

Past Chesterfield, the black strips on the highway grew narrower, traffic through here lighter, and the valley and road falling down toward the gorge were new again, different once more: snow was everywhere, still not too heavy, but enough to have veiled the meadow to the left. To the right the leafless black trees were stark and quiet, the dark-green pines cloaked in white, uppermost stones on the fences bordering the road impossibly white, a soft, continuous cushion of white.

I'd seen this drive in late summer, and in autumn, and now I'd seen it in winter. The only season left was spring, and already I longed for that, for the burst of new buds, bright green from iron gray branches.

I longed for that, and it seemed, as we glided down the road toward the stream at the bottom and the narrow bridge over snow-hidden stones, that even the gray sky and snowflakes were pressing in on me along with all else, those things I'd cried over last night. Suddenly the inside of the car seemed smaller, the three of us crammed inside a machine that crept through the world outside our windows toward a house that would shelter us, and I was afraid. I wanted to be in that house. I wanted the stove on. I wanted the scraper in my hand.

When I parked the car, I looked out the windshield only a moment at the house, different yet again, new: snow had collected on the roof, the windows black below white, the chimney poking up into the gray sky, the yard hidden by white. The junk heap, I could see from here, was sprinkled with color: broken yellow Formica from the counters, fake, plastic brown from the paneling, sky blue from the clapboards, all shrouded in white, the colors that much brighter for it.

I was first out of the car, Grady and Martin slower than usual, as though there were something they wanted to discuss between themselves before heading in. They stood at the car a moment, looking at each other, and then went up the stone steps, stomped their feet once inside. Grady closed the door behind Martin, Martin shrugging off his jacket, though the room was no warmer than the air outside. He lay the coat across one of the sawhorses he had built, a piece of awkward, temporary furniture inside a house torn apart.

It was dark inside, and the first thing I did was head for the stove. I bent over it, moved my hand for the latch on the stove door, but here was Martin's hand right next to mine, reaching the latch first, his hand big and calloused and red from the cold, the nails bitten down to the quick, and I turned, looked up.

Martin's face was right there next to mine, closer than it had been the first time I'd seen him through the glass of the window that first morning. The day I'd screamed out of fear at his face, and I saw that no matter how sorry I had felt for him when he had been moving dishes around in Friendly's, or how much in awe of him I had been when he was piecing together a foundation or shimming in a floor joist, there had always been a piece of me that had held onto that fear of him, a piece of me that had clutched my first impression of him: head at the window, dull eyes, teeth together. That fear was always buried down deep in me.

Until now. Now here he was, his face near mine, his hand at the stove, ready to do for me what I had intended: to start up the heat in the house, to warm it up, to make it more and more my home. He wanted to do this for me, and his face no longer gave me that fear. Fear melted in me, all in an instant, in just that flash of time, long enough for me to see in the creased lines beside his eyes the sorrow that had been a part of who he was, and in the lines of his forehead the years of work at just living, and in his eyes the practice of just being, the forced preoccupation with getting along that involved the awkward stomping of feet against the cold, the staring at the wheel of the bicycle in front of him, the echo of words Grady gave so that it would seem to everyone, anyone—me—that Martin was only a human. Not any different from me. Not at all.

"I'll do it," he said. He looked at the stove, opened the door.

I stood up, and I felt good again, here, inside my house. Let the snow come. Let it fill these woods, that canyon, cover that road. I was inside here, and the open space out there was not a part of me. I was inside, and soon it would be warm here.

Martin squatted before the stove, and wadded up a few sheets of newspaper from the stack at the end of the hearth. He put them in, and picked up some kindling from the box next to the paper. He glanced up, behind me. He nodded.

Grady, behind me, said, "Look, I'm sorry about yesterday. About blowing up at you like that." He paused. "That story," he said, "that story's just not something I like to talk about. So I'm sorry."

I half turned to him, and I could see from the corner of my eye Martin striking a wooden match on the side of the stove, then gently placing it inside, the quick flicker of flame into life, the crack and hiss.

I looked at Grady. He had his arm across his chest again, clutching his elbow, just holding on, the arm useless at his side. He was looking at the floor.

He shrugged. "Martin thinks you should know more. He thinks you ought to know the rest of the story." He got a strange smile on his mouth, his lips parted, teeth together. He was still looking down. "He thinks you ought to know more about this brother and his wife and the sister." He gave a cold laugh, jerked his head up, and looked at the ceiling, at the cracked plaster up there, laths showing through in places.

I looked up, too, for a moment thought of the work involved and what we would be doing: scraping and scraping and scraping away, and then I was aware of the conscious shift in my brain away from the matter at hand: what Martin wanted me to hear.

"He thinks," he said, and blinked something back. With his free hand he quickly reached up to his eyes and rubbed them, let the hand drop. "He thinks you need to know what the story is. For some reason."

"Say," Martin said. He was still at the stove, feeding it bigger pieces of wood, and I could feel the first faint traces of warmth on my hands and face.

"He says," Grady said, his voice loud now, forced, "that he wants you to know because he knows you'll take care of this house. And he just wants you to know. Because he trusts you to take care of it." He stopped, and his voice rang through the room, through the house.

But there was nothing I wanted to know. There was nothing. I wanted only to work, to make the shift from Grady's grandfather's house to our house; wanted to attack that ceiling, to scrape it clean of old plaster, and examine the laths, tear out old ones, put in new, plaster over the ceiling again, and get on with living, with moving here.

I wanted to know nothing, and I said, "Don't say anything. I don't want to hear anything. If this has to do with Mr. Clark and what you almost told me once, I don't want to know. And if this has to do with you two living together, I don't want to—"

"Hah!" Grady let out. He was looking at me, his arm still across him, still holding his elbow. Martin was peering into the stove, putting in another, bigger piece. "Yeah," Grady said, "you and your espionage. You and your following us home from Friendly's. Wow. That's impressive, you and your research and investigative skills. That's a joke. That, and your telling fat old Blaisdell about me, and then him coming over to our place and telling me to lay off you guys. Hah, that's a joke. What do you think? Do you think this world goes on and I don't know anything? There's more I know than you do. There's more I know about this goddamned fucking world than you'll ever know, that's for certain. Like you think I don't know the same car that we ride up to this trash pit everyday is following us home and parking on the street across from us. Like I don't know that."

Martin was standing, finally, and had both hands in fists at his sides. He was looking at Grady, his jaw set, his eyes narrowed to slits.

"Well?" Grady said to Martin. I was between them again, the two looking at each other as if I weren't there.

Grady said, "You want me to tell her more. The truth. But I'm not going to do it."

"I don't want to know," I said quietly. I looked at the wall before me, fixed my eyes on where I'd left off scraping wallpaper yesterday, the jagged edge of paper like broken glass, above it the ugly pattern of long-dead flowers, below, the yellowed plaster wall. "I've got to work," I said.

"Are you shamed?" Martin said to Grady, and I closed my eyes, bowed my head.

"Ashamed," Grady nearly shouted. "*Ashamed* is the word. Not 'shamed.' " He stopped. "And no, I'm not. I'm not ashamed."

I wanted to say something to stop this, wanted to say anything. I wanted to walk across the room, pick up the scraper from the windowsill, and work, but I was frozen there, my hands now at the sides of my head, a few inches from my ears, as though that might keep their words from me.

They were both quiet, and I listened, waited for words from either of them. I waited, dreading any sound, my eyes closed, only the black before me, the heat now fading into me, seeping into my clothing. I listened, dreading any words that might break the silence, but then they came.

Grady said, "Because that's between me and you," and his voice had a broken edge to it, as if he were ready to cry but hadn't yet made that fall. "Because Grandma Clark's dead and Grandpa Clark's as good as dead. This is all that's left. And because I love you and it's between you and me, and when I say it, it'll be gone, just like this house. When I say it, it'll be gone, and this house will be gone."

"No, it will not," Martin said, his voice lower now, even quieter. "You are ashamed," he said.

"*No I am not!*" Grady screamed, and I squeezed my eyes shut, grit my teeth, brought up my shoulders as though to guard myself against a coming blow. "Can't you see?" he said, sobbing now. "Can't you see? When I tell, when I say, she knows, and it's gone. You and me. Who we are. Can't you see that?"

My eyes were still closed, and the words came through me all tied together, leading into one another, hitting and falling around me, and then the room was filled with Grady's quick breaths, his sobbing.

"No," Martin said, his single word huge and awful in me. "I cannot see," he said.

Grady's breath stopped, held in, I knew, and I heard him turn, felt his hard footsteps across the floor. I opened my eyes to see the front door slam closed behind him, and felt the cold push of air from outside move in. Through the windows I could see him running off toward the road. His back was to the house, the snow falling steadily. He ran, and when he reached one of the trees, a leafless, black-limbed tree like every other one here in these woods, I saw him jump and reach up, pull down a limb and break off a good-sized branch. The bough shot back up, snow that had collected on the branches showering down. Grady, still running, disappeared from view, edged out of the window frame.

"I cannot see," Martin said, and I looked back at him. His head was down, his hands still in fists at his sides. Then he whispered, "Come with me," and he turned from the stove. Slowly he walked across the room to the bottom of the stairs, and started up, forcing, it seemed, his feet to move up each step.

When he got to the landing where the stairs broke into two sets, one to our bedroom, the other to the room that would be mine, he stopped, and looked back at me.

I hadn't moved.

He said, "Come on." He paused. "It will be okay."

I wanted to back away, to get out, because I did not know what was going on here. That was what frightened me most. I did not know. Yet the only thing I could do other than follow him was to go out the door and into the world out there, the world outside this house, a world that would crush me, I knew.

I moved toward him, slowly, carefully, and found myself at the bottom of the stairs and moving up, first one step, then the next, then the next.

He had already turned, and I saw him hesitate a moment, look up toward the room that I'd claimed for my own, the room that, in a life previous to this one, I had envisioned as belonging someday to a child of our own. But now it would only be my room.

And it was the room Martin would not enter, I remembered, the room he had never gone into, from the first day we were in here, Martin standing a few steps down and looking in at us, rubbing the place where my scar would have been on his hand, to the day he would not roll the marble across the floor, to a morning just last week, when I'd called him up to help me with the baseboard and a nail that I could not seem to loosen. Even then he'd stood a couple of steps down, out of the room, just looking in at me, at the baseboard.

Now he was mounting those stairs, me at the landing, looking up at him. He got to the last step before the bedroom, and he stopped. He stood there a moment, and seemed to tighten his fists even more, bringing them up to his waist, then near his chest. He held them there a few seconds, and let them fall again, loose there at his sides. He stepped into the room.

I started up, a moment later in the doorway.

His back was to me, and he stood square in the center of the room, facing the only window. He was looking at the wall, at the gray plastic paneling. His hands were flat against his thighs, his heels together, as though he were at attention. He was looking at the wall, examining it from where he stood, his head moving slowly back and forth, from top to bottom.

Then he took two huge strides toward the wall, and he attacked it. He put his fingers up to the paneling where it met the ceiling, the molding already gone, taken off by me the day he would not help me. His fingertips fixed in the small space between ceiling and paneling, he ripped a piece of paneling down, and I could hear the high, quick screech of nails pulled out, and the sudden crack of paneling breaking off from the rest of the wall into one of those shards. With that pull, that snap, Martin gave out a high-pitched, small cry, just a crack of sound from him, and he let fall that piece of paneling, reached up to the top of the wall again, wedged in his fingers again, snapped down again. I could see the strain in his back, the force of his arms, the sudden give of the paneling, and the next cry as another piece broke off.

I stepped into the room then, and said, "Martin," but he didn't respond, only broke off yet another piece. His eyes never left the wall, and my stomach started to twist up, to cramp, because I didn't know what was going on.

The wall behind the paneling was no different than any other wall in this house: old, yellowed wallpaper, the pattern only dark blue lines that ran from top to bottom, I imagined, though he'd only torn off the top foot or so of the paneling, all with his hands, piece after piece. He'd already gotten off the narrow strip above the window, and now he was on the left, pulling, tearing, breaking it off.

He hadn't slowed down yet, and with each piece off, more and more of the old wall exposed, it seemed he was giving out more small cries. He pulled at a bigger piece now, pulled and pulled, nails crying against his force, and then it broke off, the sound cutting through me, my adrenalin growing now as he staggered back with his own momentum. He let that piece fall from his hands, went at the wall again, his hair loose now, wisps of it caught in the gray light of the snow-filled window before him.

He was at the left of the window, almost halfway down the wall, when he shoved one arm down between the paneling and the wall, the other hand reaching forward, toward the corner of the room, gripping the broken edge of the paneling. He was bent at the waist, his feet spread apart to steady himself. His face was half-turned to me, and I could see something of that trance he fell into time and again. But it was different now, fierce, the eyes half-closed but focused, as if searing the wall with his line of sight, his mouth open and teeth clenched, his cheeks flushed with work. Then, with one great cry, one great shot of sound from him, he pulled at the paneling, and the rest of that side of the wall, from the window to the corner, broke free, the nails moaning, then giving and breaking free, and he fell on his side onto shards already there, the huge piece of paneling on top of him up to his waist. But he scrambled up, pushing aside that piece, moving toward the right side of the window, starting into the paneling there.

For a moment I didn't see what he had exposed by pulling down the paneling, watched for an instant as he started tearing at the right side, but then I looked back to the left, to the wallpaper, and I saw the shapes.

They began at the corner, the smallest one there, the outline of a figure not two feet tall, the line smooth and clean, traced around the body of a child. There was the head, the arms, the fat legs next to the corner of the wall. Next to it, even overlapping it at the elbows, was the outline of another child, this one bigger, taller, drawn with the same sure, smooth hand as the first, the lines thick and black, drawn right onto the wallpaper. This second outline, second figure, had its arms positioned differently, the left one up in the air and cocked as if in some salute, the right at its side, its legs together. There was no delineation of fingers or toes, simply the soft, easy line that knew when to dimple in for the wrists, the neck, the ankles. Next to the second figure and closer to the window was yet a third outline, and then a fourth. The third figure's arms were out-stretched, up in the air, and it, too, was taller than the second. The head of the fourth outline was in profile: small nose, lips and chin, the forehead a soft curve up; otherwise it was standing with its back to the wall, its hands at its sides, the feet slightly spread apart.

They were strange lined up there on the wall, somehow fright-ening, bodies in motion, moving against ugly wallpaper, the lines so fluid, so confident and smooth, the point where the figures over-lapped almost linking them all together. There was space for one or two more before the figures would have reached the window, and their heights—smallest to largest—made it seem that perhaps someone had planned long ago to have that fifth or sixth outline, the tallest, meet the window. But the four figures stopped abruptly, short of reaching it.

I swallowed, and I focused my eyes on the figures, and I wondered what it could mean, when suddenly Martin ripped from the right side of the window another, last huge piece of paneling, having positioned himself as before, one arm thrust deep between wall and panel, the other gripping the top and tearing, tearing. Again he fell down with his own momentum, that pull.

But this time he did not try to stand. Instead he quickly pushed off the paneling, moved onto his knees and faced the wall, all in an instant, a move quick and agile. He stopped, his back straight, his legs beneath him. Slowly, gently, he eased himself down until he was sitting on his legs, his face toward the wall. He looked first to the left and those easy lines, then to the right, and the shapes there.

These, too, were figures, lined up in the same manner, the small-est nearest the corner, then on up from there. But these bodies, these outlines, were different. Instead of the smooth lines of the other wall, the lines here were sharp, jagged, as though electrified, jangling, circling the figures, the heads too big, hands and arms and legs too thick at places, too thin at others. The poses of these children seemed to have been intended to imitate the ones on the left: the second child stood at attention, arm up in salute, that arm outlined in chaotic angles so that the wrist was almost nonexistent, the two lines nearly meeting; the third outline, like the third on the left, had its arms outstretched, too, but the pose was forced, dead, the rough line deliberate, it seemed, yet apprehensive, hesitant. The fourth outline, this one a little shorter than the fourth on the left, looked as though the drawer had attempted a profile, but any features, any characteristics that might have signaled a human face, were lost in the wavering lines. And though there was room for one or two more outlines, none touched, these cold, misshapen bodies standing singly, alone, and I felt in my chest and throat the welling fear, the lurch of blood up into my heart at what this could mean.

Martin was still looking, moving his head from one set of outlines to the other, and slowly, stiffly he put out one arm, and pointed to the left wall, to those dark, even lines. He pointed at them, pointed, and I saw how the gray light from the window a few feet in front of him illuminated him in gray, his hand pointing at the wall now shaking, giving way to some fear, I imagined, as he took in a deep breath.

He said, "This is Martin," his voice tight, strangled, choked harder than I had ever heard it. He let that shaking hand move across in front of him until it was pointed at the right, at those near-shapeless bodies. "And this," he said, his voice still caught, still hard in his throat, "is Grady."

Still there was that feeling in my heart, that adrenalin in me, and I was taking quick, shallow breaths, ready for something, for him to let me know more, to let me know. I hadn't yet figured it out, but only a moment before he brought his hand back to the left, to the outlines of himself as a child, did I feel it coming to me, feel the words he was about to utter.

"This," he said, his voice nearly cut off, shut down by its own constricted muscles, "is the father," and as slowly as before he moved the arm and pointed at the outlines of Grady as a child, those frightened, serrated lines drawn by his own hand, I knew then, years ago, lifetimes ago. He said, "And this is my son."

He broke, his head and hand snapping down, his shoulders and back and arms heaving with heavy sobs, and his words hit me, a fist in my chest knocking the wind from me, emptying my lungs, my body, and I cried, my hands at my sides, my eyes closed tight, tears warm and then suddenly, surprisingly cold on my face. I put one hand to my eyes, pushed tears away, and I opened them.

I opened them, and I took in the room, a strange room in what felt a stranger's house now, a different house altogether, and I realized I was not surprised by this at all. Anything could happen now, anything in the world. There was nothing more that could happen that would surprise me, ever. Martin and Grady were father and son, and this had been the house where they both lived, and Mr. Clark had had Martin committed while Grady watched, and the son waited for the father's return, had followed him once he'd been out, had gotten himself disowned simply for loving his father, because he wanted to be with his father all along.

Suddenly Martin stood and moved toward the window, putting his big hands up to the panes. He looked out the window, stared out at something to the right, then turned toward me, stepped over the pieces of paneling on the floor. He came toward me, and I wondered what it was he would do now.

But he only moved past me, his eyes never meeting mine. They were focused on the ground, his mind on something else, on moving out of his old room, and I heard his steps on the stairs, the groan under his weight. A moment later I heard the front door open and slam closed, felt the subtle, gentle air go cooler. I looked back to the window, where I saw the faintest traces of condensation in the shape of human hands, evidence of Martin's being alive, evidence like that I had left one night months ago on the window of the toy shop downtown, when I had stared at a dollhouse, at the bedrooms of children, at things I now knew I would never have.

Then those traces, outlines of hands, of life, disappeared, and there was left in the room only pieces of broken paneling, gray light filtered and sifted through snow outside, shapes on the wall, and me here, alone.

I do not know how much time passed. The light in the room did not change: there was no shifting of shadows to signal late morning or noon or early evening. There was only the passage of time, some length of it moving through me, aging me as I leaned against the wall, unable to move, my breaths growing more and more clouded as I waited. I was only standing there, the palms of my hands against the wall, as if I were holding on to keep myself from falling. My tears had long since given out.

Then I heard the door open downstairs, heard it close. Grady called out, "Hello?"

I opened my mouth, tried to speak, but could only feel cold air inside me.

"Hello?" he called again.

My hands, my arms, my legs could not move.

He moved around downstairs, from room to room, his steps slow and quiet, pausing, moving again. He was at the stairs. "Hey!" he shouted, and started up.

When he reached the top, he stopped. He looked at the room, at me, at the room again, his eyes moving quickly, taking everything in: the shards, the shapes, the dead light. He walked to the middle of the room, stood just where Martin had before he'd torn into that wall, and then I saw in Grady his father, saw his shoulders, saw his neck and the shape of Martin's head, though his, Grady's, was covered with that fine black hair, his ears hidden.

Only as I looked at him, watched him staring at the room, his back straight, his arms stiff at his sides, did I begin to wonder where his other features came from, who his eyes—brown, not gray green, like Martin's—had come from, his hair, how his narrow hips had come to be. And only then, my brain working on this new idea, no longer preoccupied with the sorrow of his and Martin's lives, but now filled with a cold wonder at the boy's physiology, his inherited traits, did I find the power to speak. I had to force the words out, but they came, came in a harsh, rough whisper loud enough to break windows.

I whispered, "Who was your mother?" and I was sorry and ashamed for the words just out of my mouth. New words already dying, already gone, but the idea in them betraying me, showing me to be nothing more than interested in the science here.

He laughed. He laughed loud, his head back, his shoulders—his father's shoulders—shaking. He laughed and laughed, and then he stopped. His back was still to me, and he shook his head, his hair wet with melted snow.

He said, "I wasn't lying about that part. That's one of the few places I wasn't lying to you about, because she's out there in California somewhere. Maybe. At least that's what I think. That's the place she was going when she left me here. When she left me here when I was about six months old. But then even that's a lie. That word 'about' is a lie, because to be truthful I was five months and twenty-one days old. Martin knows that. He knows that number. He was here. He remembers." He nodded toward the left wall. "No doubt he remembers being outlined by his own mother, his cracked and crazy mother, this wall here her crazy version of a growth chart. Most people just make a line on a doorjamb. She drew around the whole body, and then Martin"—he nodded toward the right, those crooked lines—"he takes it up until he's sent to the asylum." He stopped, looking back at the smooth lines on the left. He said, "But she, my Grandma Elaine, she was made crazy by her brother. By Grandpa Clark, old Grandpa Clark. That story is true, too, which I'm sure if you have half a brain you've figured out by now, so this is all old news to you." He shook his head again. "That story about the brother and the sister and the brother's wife is true. That story about holding a baby between your legs until you wreck it for the rest of its life. That story is true, and that sister going nuts due to the brother is true, and so I guess I gave out to you a lot more truth than I figured." He paused. "Martin's being like he is is due to the brother of the story. Old Grandpa Clark."

He stopped, turned to me. He was smiling, but did not move toward me. "But my mother? So. All is clear to you except for that little nugget of truth, huh? You know who my daddy is, who my grandparents are, that hobo and Crazy Elaine. But what good would that truth be to you? What would it mean for me to give you words, tell you some story about who my mother is? It's only a bunch of words, when you won't ever know, because it's a *life* you're asking after. Don't you see that? I can tell you she left me here when I was five months and twenty-one days old and I can tell you she was headed for California, but you can't know who my mother is, because it's a life, and you can't *know* who Martin is, or who Grandpa Clark is or who Grandma Elaine is, or who I am. *Who I am*, because you haven't lived this life. You haven't been here."

He stopped, his mouth closed tight, his eyes squeezed shut, and I pushed against the wall behind me, my hands scrabbling for some hold, something to keep me from falling.

He took in a huge breath, and said, "Anything I say, anything, would be nothing. Nothing." His hand was in a fist now, his elbow bent, the fist out in front of him. "But I'll tell you who my mother is, just to please you. So you'll know, and so you'll know about this house. What you've bought." He paused, shook the fist once, twice, and said, "The brother. That brother. He and his wife," and he paused. He shook the fist again, as if to wring out of it his words. "Grandpa Clark and his wife had a kid of their own. And it was a girl. And it was raised by that brother, the same brother who killed his sister, killed his nephew. Killed Martin. The brother. My Grandpa Clark."

His eyes were still closed. "Can you imagine that?" he said. "Being raised by him?"

Then he opened his eyes and looked at me, and I wanted to disappear, just as the outlines of Martin's hands had; I wanted to fade away because I had asked my question, and now here was my answer, all of this from him, the answer to my one question.

He whispered, "No, you can't imagine that. Because this is just a story, and these are words, and you can't *know* Grandpa Clark. You can't."

His eyes snapped shut again, my hands still clawing at the wall behind me. He said, "And he and his wife raised the daughter, while all the time in this house"—he pointed at the floor, jabbed at it— "was Grandma Elaine and Martin. My daddy. These two here, in this room, until Grandpa Clark killed Elaine, killed her for good—"

I stopped moving my hands, stood still, and he stopped. My breaths had become even shallower, weight pushing down on my chest, my breaths thin wisps of white in the cold room, my eyes huge and dry in their sockets.

"You know why he won't go out into the barn?" Grady said, a cold smile on his face now, his breaths great clouds before him, turning him into a shadow at times, his face disappearing in mist. "It's because that's where he found her. When Martin's mother hung herself from one of the big, black beams up in the rafters. He found her there."

He turned and pointed at the wall then, at the outlines of his father, those clean lines. "He found her when he was this big. That's when," he said, and banged his fist at the fourth and final figure there, the boy in profile. "That's why they don't go any farther, why these outlines stop here. That's why. This is when she just gave up. When she just gave up to her brother. That's why they stop here."

He inched back to the right, to those outlines of himself. Finally he looked away from me, and gently touched his own outlines, himself at different ages, lines drawn by his own father, a poor imitation of the mother's, but real, lines his father had done his best to draw, and for a moment I pictured Martin, younger, bent over a black-haired toddler leaned up against the wall, his arm in a salute, while Martin, black marker in hand, drew that outline.

"The reason these shapes of me stop here," Grady said, still looking at the wall, one finger now tracing the jagged outline, "is because this is when Grandpa Clark sent him away." Then the hand stopped dead, and the finger folded in on itself, and Grady began to cry.

"And my mother is Grandpa Clark's daughter," he cried. "Martin's cousin. He got her pregnant. She was nothing. A cocktease. She was worthless. Because of her father." He tried to stop crying, sniffed and caught his breath. He said, "That's what's funny, because all of this is his fault. Everything. And there's nothing I can tell you about him, because he's evil, and there's nothing to say beyond that." He paused, took in a breath. "What can you say to that? What makes a man evil? That man? I don't know, and I *lived* with him, I *knew* him. So what can you expect to know about him? Just that he did all this, and now he's sold this house to you, and now it's yours and he's washed his hands of it, and that I'm glad he's as good as dead up there in Maplewood right now. As good as dead, and that makes me happy."

He paused, his face near the wall, his eyes now closed. "We used to come up here all the time, Daddy and me, not just three times a year. Not just that. But plenty of times we came here. Now that's gone. That's over."

He gave out a huge breath, his shoulders falling, his head falling, but then he stood up again, and I pushed even harder against the wall, wanted to vanish into it.

"*I am not ashamed!*" he shouted. "*I am not!*" and he was at the window, looking out.

He turned to me, and I looked away as soon as our eyes met. He said, "Where is he? Where did he go?"

I whispered, "I don't know," thankful, thankful that he had heard, that I would not have to repeat my words, because I did not want to speak again, ever. He rushed past me, cold air following after him as he banged down the stairs, opened the door, and left. I listened, waited, tensed up even more for the slam of that door, but it did not come. The door stood open downstairs.

I did not know what to do. I did not, and thought then, finally, undeniably, that I had followed my mother, aware of all things now, and unable to do anything. I had fallen, entered her deserted and lonely domain, what I had fought against all my life finally here, the fear, that paralysis all in a moment, hope dead in me, my brain finally acclimated to that thought, and I fell to my knees, slipped down the wall, my hands to my face, covering it, hiding it from space around me, the gray of snowfall, the dead-white sheen of air. I could do nothing for Sandra, having already lost her, I'd chosen to ignore Mr. Gadsen, when all he'd wanted was to apologize; I could do nothing for Martin or Grady, both of them lost to some ghost of dead love and the remembrance of hate; and I could do nothing for Tom, could bear no children, could no longer love him without thinking of the loss that was no loss, the children that were not to be children. There was nothing, and I lay on my side, curled myself into a ball on the cold linoleum floor, pulled myself into myself as tightly as I could, and I cried.

"Martin!" Grady shouted outside, out in the snow, his voice muffled, cloaked by that white.

I opened my eyes, the ceiling above me slowly spinning.

"Martin!" I heard again, faintly, farther away, but with that distant word, that name, a son's call for his father, I heard somehow my own father; I heard in the pitch and timbre my father's call to me the day I had stood at the chain-link fence, heard in Grady's voice desperation and hope and love all at once, and I knew for a moment, an instant, the hope and fear in him, a boy outside in the snow, searching for his lost father.

I saw that Grady was me, a child of lost parents, stuck here and floundering, the color of his voice, that last call to his father, the hue of looking and loss, just as I'd listened for my father for so long.

"Martin?" Grady called out, this time even fainter, quieter, his father's name now made into a question, the inflection a fear, and I felt again my mother's fear, and saw her the day she had moved the cot into the kitchen, a day only two weeks before she died, as though settling herself into the innermost corner of her house and surrounding herself with the photos, she would somehow make working her way down to dying easier: the house was empty save for this one small room. That day I had asked her why, why she would not leave the house, hoping finally for some small answer from her, though I'd given up on waiting to hear any truth from her other than the one I'd been given the day I'd come home with my new word. The truth that she was comfortable in her fear.

She had taken my hand in hers, brought it to her cheek, let the back of my hand gently touch her skin, skin as soft as a mother's face can be. But she said nothing. There were only her eyes, and in them the same old fear, the certainty of loss too much to bear.

And finally I knew her, my bones grown cold now, the floor against my face frozen and dirty. I understood her for the only moment I had in my life, though now she was dead. I *knew* her, knew in the sound of Grady's voice my mother's fear, the death of hope in her, because Grady had turned his father's name into a question.

Then, for what I knew somehow was the last time, I heard "Martin!" and with that one, small, insignificant word, the ceiling still spinning above me, the snow still falling outside, the shapes against the wall still dead but still in motion, I finally saw what it was my father had tried to show me all along, what my father's words meant coming to me after his death: it was *my name* I'd heard. Claire Shaw. That was me. Who I was. The name I'd been given by my parents when I was born. It was *my name*. All he'd ever wanted me to do, I knew then, was to know by my name that I was alive: tying my shoes, he'd only wanted me to learn to do it myself; walking me across Route 9, he'd only wanted me to learn to judge when to cross it myself; speaking my name that day when the bomber crossed the sky, and now, here against a cold floor, my hands clenched in fists of fear, he'd only wanted me to live. That was all.

I took in a deep breath, and I tried to hold onto my mother, to my father, tried to keep my understanding of them, the glimpse of them and who they were and what they'd tried to teach me, the opposite tacks they'd taken—my father's courage, my mother's fear—but then their images, their voices in Grady's voice, disappeared, and I was once again alone in the room.

But now it was a different room. It was a different room, though nothing had changed: the paneling was heaped on the floor, the air cold, the outlines of Grady and Martin still there on the wall. But it was different. Only that.

Slowly, carefully, I brought up my left hand, the hand with the scar, from where it had been in a fist in my lap, and I looked at it. I looked first at the palm, then at the top, and the red adhesions. I looked at my fingers, at my long, slender fingers. My father's fingers, I saw, fingers much like those with which he'd tied my shoes, and with that hand I touched my hair, felt how fine it was, and I pulled a strand away from my head and down in front of my eyes, where I could see my father's hair, the same brunette color, the same texture. And I thought of my mouth and my cheeks and my eyes, those features my mother's, but *my* mouth and cheeks and eyes. These were what they'd given me at conception, I saw, pieces of themselves, pieces of them already here with me, here all along.

I blinked. I took in another breath, felt the cold ache of it inside me, and then, with whatever small strength I had in me, whatever synapses and neurons and axons and dendrites, each cell snapping to the next and on and on until my muscles took hold of bone, pulled one against another, I got to my knees, my hands on the floor, and I was sitting on my legs, and then I was standing, and I, too, was moving toward that window as if it were some source of comfort, some way out.

When I got there, I put my hands to it, my face near it. Here, here was evidence of my own life, of me living: my breath, pearl-white fog condensed on glass. My breaths were real. I was alive.

I looked out the window, saw what Grady and Martin had seen: the world outside, dusted with the simple gift from God of a light blanket of snow.

"Martin!" I heard again, way off somewhere, and I saw Grady. He was at the barn. He stood before it, back in those woods, back where I'd known I would be swallowed up, but now I knew nothing could happen. They were only woods, and the barn was only a broken-down structure where, many years ago, a woman had succumbed to hate. It was only a place now, snow on its roof, black holes here and there in the roof where boards were broken out, and through which snow fell.

I turned from the window and went through the room and down the stairs. I opened the stove door and put in paper, pine needles, kindling, and I struck a match, lit the paper inside. I watched the fire build for a few moments, and then put into it the biggest pieces of wood I thought the small flame might be able to stand until I got back. Until we got back.

Martin's coat still lay on the sawhorse, and I picked it up, held it under my arm. I turned to the open door, where snow had blown in, making its way out onto the floor like spilled flour, and I thought of an officer in the living room of my mother's house, thought of those images of my father's death I had created—the glass like green jewels, my father glancing at his watch—so that I could see my father's death, be there; and I realized that Grady's story of Martin's birth, and those details he had chosen—the brother tearing through woods to the sugar house, the hobo stoking the fire, then him, with that piece of oak raised above his head, ready to crush Clark's skull—were only the same sorts of creations I'd made: embellishments, embroidering upon simple facts until the story lived in us, breathed, and kept us remembering, fiction becoming more real than any truth of the matter could ever be. Grady was me. Except that his father, his own blood, was still alive. He still had Martin.

I stepped out into the snow, and pulled the door closed behind me.

I stood before the barn. I was looking up at it, my hands in front of me, snow collecting on my shoulders and arms and hair, and I looked down. On the ground before me were two sets of footprints leading into the barn, one set crisp, new, the other dull with snow, only soft indentations.

I paused a moment, and I went in.

It was dark inside, near pitch black, the holes in the roof giving the only small light. I looked up to the rafters a moment, to the light up there, and I wondered which beam Martin had found her hanging from, his mother given up to the hate of a brother. I wondered, too, what Martin could have thought, could have known, a retarded child finding his dead mother, and then I realized I already knew: like any child, he would have felt love, and loss.

"There," I heard Martin whisper, and I turned. My eyes had almost adjusted to the dark, and there, there in the corner of the barn, huddled up next to each other and against the cold, sat Martin and Grady: Grady silent, eyes closed, arms around his father's shoulders, Martin looking up at the rafters, pointing to one of them, his body shivering in the cold.

I walked over to them, and I knelt before them, put Martin's coat across his chest and over his shoulders.

I said, "Come. Come on. Let's go back inside."

By the time we got to the Friendly's parking lot, the snow had stopped.

I had made the two of them share with me the coffee once inside the house, the front room now warmed by the fire I had made, and I told them we were going back home. Neither one fought me; they only nodded, took last sips of the coffee, and then we put out the fire, tamped it down and out.

They both sat in the back seat on the way out, the two of them nestled next to each other. I could see them in my rearview mirror, could see them watching first Chesterfield pass us, then Williamsburg and the General Store, the store as always choked with customers, a place where one day next week I knew I would be, buying the wreath I wanted, the one that would be placed on the front door, on that gray and weatherbeaten wood, a wreath that would signal the place as being our home.

And a Christmas tree. Tom and I would buy a Christmas tree for the house, I knew then, place it in the front room and decorate it, no matter what the walls looked like, no matter what condition the floors were in. We would put up a Christmas tree, and some time after New Year's we would cut it up, burn it in the stove to help warm our house, our home. We would burn it, *use* it, instead of leaning it against the foundation and forgetting it.

We passed the white fairways in Leeds, and came into Florence, the two strips of black pavement in the snow growing wider until

here, at the Friendly's, the road had been plowed already, the blacktop merely wet, snow already melting.

I moved to climb out of the car, but Grady reached up from behind
me and touched my shoulder.

He said, "That's okay. We'll ride back. We'll be okay."

"But we can put them in the trunk," I said. "The bikes."

His hand still rested on my shoulder. I had my door open an inch
or so already. Cold air wrapped around my ankles, my calves. He
said, "Tell you what. Tomorrow, when we go back up there, you
just pick us up at the apartment. You know where we live. But just
let us ride home today." He smiled.

Martin leaned forward, put his hand on my shoulder, too, right
next to Grady's. He said, "You already know where we live."

I smiled, and reached up and touched both their hands. "Tomorrow." I paused. "I'll be there."

"Fine," Grady said. "Tomorrow is fine." He brought his hand down
and popped open his door. "We'll be looking for you."

"We will," Martin said, scooting across the seat. He got out, closed
the door, and then stood at my window. I looked up at him, smiling,
and he motioned with his hand for me to roll down my window.

I pulled the door to, rolled the window down all the way. Grady
was already back behind the dumpster.

Martin leaned toward the window, his hands on his thighs. He
had his wool cap down over his ears.

He said, "You'll take good care of your house."

I said, "I will."

He smiled.

I waited until they had pedaled out of the parking lot and headed
off toward their home, Grady still leading, Martin close behind, and
then I pulled onto Route 9, headed back toward town. A minute
later Cooley-Dickinson Hospital was on my right, red brick, the roof
covered with quickly melting snow, and as I neared it I wasn't
certain what to do anymore, whether to look at the building, stare
and remember back to when Paige's child had been born there,
and, of course, back to when I'd hoped for children of our own; or
if I should do as I'd resolved, and force myself *not* to look, *not* to

remember, try and forget that I'd held her baby only days after birth.

But I found myself driving more slowly as I approached the hospital, my foot easing up on the gas without my thinking of it. To the left, across the street, was a small strip mall: video shop, dry cleaners, package store. I saw a phone booth out on the sidewalk between two of the shops, and I turned left across the double yellow lines, pulled into the parking lot. Without thinking, without knowing precisely what I might do, I parked the car and took a quarter from my wallet. I climbed out onto the wet asphalt of the parking lot, went to the pay phone, picked up the cold plastic receiver, and dropped in the quarter. Then I punched in the phone number I'd known by heart for what seemed my whole life.

I heard it ring, and I turned around, leaned against the wall, the hospital across the street from me. Tires of passing cars hissed away water, melted snow.

"Neuroscience and Behavior," I heard. It was Paige.

"Paige," I said. I paused, and I could not help but remember holding her baby, feeling the warmth of that small life. Though I would have no children of my own, I understood, finally, that I could not deny the joy I'd felt holding that child. There was nothing wrong with hoping for life, or with taking joy in the life given someone else. And, I saw, there was nothing wrong with taking sorrow in a life lost by someone else.

"Hello?" Paige said, and then I closed my eyes, the sound of passing cars and the cold air filling me up, and I realized why I'd called. It wasn't to talk to Paige, though I would. I would ask her sometime soon how Phillip was, how big he'd gotten in the month or so I'd been gone, how many new teeth were in.

But I'd called to talk with Sandra.

"Paige," I said again, "is Sandra there? This is Claire."

Later—I don't know how much later, the day passing in its own time, the sky never changing its slate-gray color—I went to the newspaper, walked past rows and rows of cluttered desks and computer terminals, all those shiny green symbols flashing, all that clicking, all that noise. Faces turned up to me as I passed, some smiling the smile of faint recognition, others only glancing up and back to the green.

I made it to Tom's desk against the far wall, a desk pushed back into a recessed cubicle. He, too, was clicking away. He glanced up at me, then back to his terminal before it seemed he recognized who I was. He stood. He looked at his watch, surprised, as though he had perhaps lost an entire day.

"It's only eleven fifteen," he said. "I thought you were at the house."

"I was," I said. "But I came back. Because I need you to help me." I took a small step toward his desk, put one hand to the edge. "To go somewhere with me."

"To the house?" he said.

I took my hand away, and held my pocketbook with both hands. I looked at his desk, littered with work.

"Yes," I said. I did not know how to tell him, did not know which words I needed to explain to him the shapes on the wall. I wanted to take him there, show him those figures, those outlines. I wanted him out there with me.

"Are you okay?" he said, and started around the edge of his desk.

I could feel eyes on me, eyes of men and women around me who would imagine me insane. Tom was next to me now, his hand at my elbow.

I looked up at him, and I swallowed at the hard truth I knew I was about to speak.

I said, "I'm not. I'm not okay. You know that."

He put his arms around me. He held me, and I could feel his arms encircling me. I could feel his face next to mine, warm and dry.

He eased up, and pulled away. He looked at me. He had his hand next to my face, and brushed back a tear with his thumb, a tear I hadn't even known was there.

He was still a moment, and I looked at his face, unable to tell what he would do, his mouth straight, his eyes merely looking into mine, and I was terrified at living with a man this long, at loving him, giving up the hope for children of our own with him, trying to make a home with him, and still not knowing him, still being unable to see in his eyes what he would do.

He held me for a moment longer, but let go of me, moved back to his desk, looked at things there. For an instant I thought I had lost him, that he'd run from a house falling down around me, but then he gathered up his coat and gloves and muffler and hat from the chair beside his desk, and we were gone, headed for a half-finished house in Chesterfield. Headed for home.

About the Author

BRETT LOTT has received several awards for his fiction,
which has appeared in a variety of publications. His first
novel, *The Man Who Owned Vermont,* is also available from
Washington Square Press; his collection of stories, *A Dream
of Old Leaves,* will be available in paperback in 1991. Lott is
writer-in-residence and assistant professor of English at the
College of Charleston, South Carolina. He lives nearby with
his wife, Melanie, and their two sons, Zebulun and Jacob.